ON A FAULT LINE

FORBIDDEN CONTRACT
BOOK 2

VICTORIA DAWSON

PAPER HEART PUBLISHING LLC

Publisher: Paper Heart Publishing LLC

Cover Designer: K. B. Barrett Designs

Editing: Happily Editing Anns

ISBN (Paperback): 978-1-959364-13-9

ISBN (e-book): 978-1-959364-12-2

AUTHOR NOTE

On a Fault Line is the second book in the *Forbidden Contract Series* that follows the same two main characters throughout both books. It is advised to read the two books in order.

The *Forbidden Contract Series* is intended for mature audiences. Sensitive topics discussed could be triggering and not meant for anyone under the age of eighteen.

To the lovers of love...

I hope this story makes you fall heart over heels.

1

PENNY

My hand reaches over the silky sheets in search of Collins. They lack the warmth of where he once lay but still bear the indentation of where he was. My inner thighs clench at the reminder of where he has been—multiple times—and where I hope he stays.

I roll to my side, curling my legs and bringing my knees toward my chest. Collins may not think he's romantic, but he's nothing short of amazing in my eyes. My body aches with a delicious soreness from his worshipping. Maybe it's a honeymoon phase or maybe this is just how he commits all-in to a task. Regardless, I'm expecting this arrangement that we are about to make to be beneficial to my goal list—at the very least.

I trust Collins.

I have confidence in him to fulfill my needs but do so without causing me harm.

Despite feeling like I coerced him to even consider this

type of relationship, I hope that I too can please him and give him the satisfaction that he would otherwise get from some hookup at the club.

Clutching the sheet under my neck, I revel in the comfort of having no place I need to go and no schedule I am forced to follow, at least for today. Funny thing is—apparently neither does Collins.

If I'm being boring, then so is he.

I am his responsibility.

And keeping him sexually satisfied will soon be mine.

Of course, I also plan to be working more regularly at Plus None. Nothing has really picked up yet with the modeling shoots, so I've been immersing myself in the marketing side of the business and loving it so far.

While Angie and Claire swore that my brothers had nothing to do with my hiring, I still wonder if guilt on their part played an important role in the process.

I want to work.

I want to be less bored.

I want to contribute my own earned money to my bank account and not have it magically appear into it—most likely courtesy of Graham and Nic. If anyone lacks discretion when it comes to oversupplying bank accounts, it's those two.

Money doesn't grow from trees, but it does grow from a pair of overprotective brothers.

And Collins is made of the same overprotective material, so he's not any better. He already threatened to add money into my account in the past if I insisted on paying.

That man…

Rolling over in bed, my stomach growls to remind me I haven't eaten in a while.

I have a box of sugary cereal calling my name back at my place.

Will it still be my place for the duration of our arrangement, or will it just be Luke's for that time?

Questions of how this all is going to work pop into my head. Yesterday it seemed like such an easy, no-brainer decision, when I was desperate to act on my sexual revolution that Collins repeatedly wanted to block.

Maybe Collins is having regrets?

I glance over at where he should be lying, thinking about the amount of awkwardness that would ensue if he were to back out now—especially after the level of intimacy we had last night.

I definitely know my heart and my self-esteem wouldn't be able to handle the huge disappointment.

But I wonder... Could things ever go back to how they were before, and he just be my bodyguard?

Rolling off the mattress, I make my way over to the blackout curtains. With just a little push, the sun comes spilling into the room, casting a warm glow on everything it touches.

Collins's space is immaculately clean. I expect nothing less from someone with obsessive-compulsive tendencies. I won't be surprised if the contract doesn't have a clause stating something along the lines of "don't mess up my shit."

Why be subtle when you can be direct—I guess? And if Collins is anything—he is direct.

He might not be a man of many words, but at least you know from his scowls and how he rubs at the back of his neck whether he's grumpy or not.

I meander into the bathroom, enjoying the scent of strawberries that lingers in the air from the freshener. My stomach rumbles again, reminding me that I need to eat. Not seeing my clothes, I exit the room and enter the closet.

Last night is a bit of a blur when it comes to wardrobe, but I vaguely remember wearing Collins's T-shirt. I doubt he will mind me doing it again.

Plucking a perfectly folded one from the shelf, I slip it over my naked body, enjoying the soft cotton feel against my bare flesh.

I could get used to wearing his clothes. It's the already worn ones I prefer because they smell of him.

Hair bands rest on top of his dresser, making my lips curl up. I swear these things multiply when they are left unchaperoned. Twisting my hair into a messy bun, I secure it with a band. I pull out some hair from the bun to make it looser and less tight at the top of my head.

I already have a headache starting, but it's isolated to the back of my brain, which signifies I just need water—and of course, breakfast.

Collins's place is quiet. I don't even hear signs of him moving about. Did he leave?

My feet carry me down the hallway, past the living room, and into the kitchen. Standing on my tippy-toes, I stretch up to see if he has any cereal in the cupboard.

I giggle at the lineup of microwave popcorn that definitely wasn't there a week ago.

Who is this man? I can't see him being a fan of this type

On a Fault Line

of food but also don't want to be too presumptuous to think
he purchased it with my eclectic appetite in mind.

I shift the perfect row of boxes one by one to see behind
them.

And then I feel it…the instinct that I'm not alone.

Whipping my body around, I come face-to-face with
Collins who looks…

Angry?

Shocked?

Disappointed?

"You scared me," I gasp, clutching my chest. "I thought
you skipped out or something." Why is he wearing a suit? A
bit formal for a casual breakfast, but what do I know about
Collins Stone? Apparently not much. "You left me all alone.
I missed—"

"Get dressed." His words come out in a two-syllable
direct order, causing me to take a physical step backward.

I think he's in need of some cereal as well. Collins
already has a naturally stern disposition, so when you add
hangry into the mix—look out.

As much as I want to test my boundaries and see just
how far they stretch, I'm not willing to do so if his stomach
is empty.

"Let me make you some cereal. I'm really good at it."

Sheesh. I don't even get a smirk.

It's a tough crowd this morning.

Collins's eyes glide over me, settling on my bare thighs.
He takes a few steps forward, shielding my body in his
shadowy presence. With purpose, his fingers tug the hem
down, trying to conceal more of my exposed legs, I assume.

"Okay, you aren't a leg man. Got it."

I turn my head, catching an image of black and white in my vision.

Oh. Shit.

When my eyes register the man dressed in a similar professional looking suit as Collins, I stumble back into the counter.

"Good morning."

My eyes dart to Collins, who seems to be extra mute today. "I didn't know we had company." My words come out as a high-pitched squeak.

"Now you do."

No wonder he's so bent out of shape over my lack of a real outfit.

"Who's the suit?"

"My lawyer handling our contract."

"Wow, you just have a lawyer on retainer to do your bidding?"

"I…" He seems caught off guard by my bold question. "No…"

"Just how many contracts have you had in your lifetime, Collins?" Then I turn to the strange man standing on the sidelines. "How many contracts has Collins called in your services for?"

The man holds up his hand as a way of providing a nonanswer.

Of course, he wouldn't throw the man who supplies his salary under the figurative bus.

Guiding my attention back to him, Collins asks, "Are you second-guessing what you have put into motion?"

My lips flatten into a hard line. I have no right to punish

Collins for his secretive past when it's me who suggested becoming another name on his list of conquests.

But why do we need to do this in front of an audience?

"No," I finally supply after a long pause.

I stand taller, trying to portray confidence, but with Collins's towering frame shadowing me like an impenetrable building, I start to wonder just how confining this contract will be.

Without another warning, Collins guides me into the guest room where the clothes he already has purchased for me are stored in a closet.

"Please make yourself decent."

I look down at the shirt I'm currently wearing, feeling a bit sad over his disapproval. "Okay..."

"Penelope?"

I turn my attention to him, feeling the sting of tears hit my eyes. We've been here before, and I'm mentally kicking myself for being too damn sensitive. "Hmm?" I look away. I don't need him to see me cry again.

I feel stupid.

Collins stalks toward me, closing the distance in three long strides. Cupping my chin, he tilts it up so I'm looking directly at him. "You never look more delectable than when you are wearing my clothes, Princess."

"Oh," I say breathily.

And then he kisses me—like he already owns me.

"But I don't want to share even that knowledge with anyone else."

A smile forms on my lips. "Well, then stop inviting people over without giving me a heads-up."

"Fair enough. We can put it in the contract."

"About house guests?"

"No. About you wearing my clothes on a regular basis."

I laugh. "You really are funnier than…" I don't know where I'm going with this statement.

"The world sees me?" he provides.

"Yeah."

Collins grabs an elegant pink wrap dress off a hanger, and I sift through the panty and bra drawer until I find something cute to go underneath it. He's bought more things for me since the last time, and I can't help but smile over this little revelation.

"I'll be moving your items into the master bedroom as soon as you sign the contract. And you'll also be given an open credit line at all the boutiques in town to shop from at your leisure and without worry over cost."

"Why the formality?"

Collins stares at me while I get dressed. "Because I function best when I'm in control." He walks backward to the door leading to the hallway. "I'll meet you in my office when you are ready to get started."

"Okay."

I quickly dress, and then go through my typical morning hygiene routine. I'm careful not to apply too much makeup and upset the beast. The last thing I need is to waste time exfoliating my skin when I accidentally overdo it.

When I feel presentable, I make my way to Collins's office.

If I didn't want this so badly, I would be too intimidated by the process alone to continue. It feels like I have been naughty and am getting sent to the principal's office. Now that there can be a fun fantasy. Surely Angie has a smut book recommendation for that topic.

But who I really want is Collins Stone.

I give a series of knocks to his door, and when I hear the invite, I push it open and enter.

"Good morning, Miss Hoffman," the lawyer greets again, holding out his hand for shaking. "I'm Leonard Copnisky. I'll be handling your contract today."

"Thank you, Mr. Copnisky. I assume you are well experienced in handling all of Collins's contracts with the ladies."

He clears his throat just as Collins seems to be choking on his tongue.

"This is my first."

"Oh?" My eyes look to Collins, confused.

"I never cared about all the details as much as I care about them with you. Now, please take a seat, Penelope," Collins instructs, pulling out a chair for me from in front of his desk.

Leonard sits beside me in another armchair, clearly amused.

I take a look around the office, as if really seeing it for the first time. It's pristine, polished, and impersonal—just as I first pegged Collins to be—so it's fitting.

"Here is the contract that Mr. Stone has proposed." Leonard hands me the folder that contains a thick packet. "Please look over the clauses, and if in agreement, sign the last page's dotted line."

I flip through the stapled document, looking at the numbers on the bottom. "This is twenty-six pages long."

Collins clears his throat. "It is."

"That seems excessive."

"I assure you, it's not."

"Well, I'm not sure a glance at these documents would happen in the next five minutes. I need time to make sure I'm not getting ripped off."

Collins gives me *the look*. "I would never cheat you, Penelope."

I make a face. "I just want to make sure my needs are going to be taken care of over the next"—I skim through the pages until I find the location of the time frame—"one hundred days."

"What do you need in order to move forward with the contract?" Leonard asks.

"I need time to read it. Surely you can give me that —yes?"

"Yes," the lawyer complies. "Of course. How about I return in an hour? Is that sufficient time?"

I nod. "Thank you."

Leonard exits the office space.

"You have an awful lot of monitors in here for someone whose main job is to be a bodyguard."

Collins eyes me suspiciously. "I never thought I'd see the day where my bulldog of a lawyer gets intimidated by my soon-to-be"—a sparkle hits his eyes—"cum slut."

"Eww"—I playfully stick out my tongue—"don't call me that."

Clearly he is joking, which I'm still getting used to. "I am just using the title you once told me."

"Maybe I was horned up and hungry…"

"Maybe…"

"Or was I under the influence of fun and fruity drinks from Limit-X?"

"Probably. Those two things definitely help you lose all inhibition."

I shrug. "Being your little cum slut does have a nice ring to it though."

Collins's eyes darken. "Keep it up with the innocent flirting, and you won't need a contract to protect you from me."

I wave the document into the air. "I'm going to need space from you to read this monstrosity of a contract. Why you need twenty-six pages to tell me to obey and me to tell you to fuck me will always be a great mystery."

"I'd rather you be fully prepared for my expectations."

"You said you had three rules."

"I do."

"How about I exchange your three rules for my three holes?"

Ignoring my question, Collins sighs. "There are some things that need to be described in detail."

"Sounds boring."

He narrows his eyes at me and then when he realizes I'm joking, he shakes his head.

"I'm going to give you time alone to read at your pace. Feel free to make notes of anywhere you have questions, and we can discuss it."

"Okay," I say, watching as Collins leaves his office, gently shutting the door.

As soon as I'm alone, I take up shop on the leather sofa that rests along the side of his office, propping up my feet onto the cushions and getting myself comfortable.

I can already tell by the size of this contract that this is going to be intense, and it's best I understand every detail.

This document holds more than just rules. It is basically a window into Collins's psyche.

And understanding that man more is an amazing perk to this entire operation.

So I absorb myself into reading—every written word.

If there is a singular moment in time where I'm faced with a choice that can change my entire life, it is now. I thought it was when I had put my trust in my abuser, Mark Tanner, but I was wrong.

Choosing between what my brothers would want and what I want is the real turning point.

It's a line I know will have devastating consequences if crossed and caught, and yet I can't help myself from taking that leap.

I am fucking tired of doing what others expect of me. I am tired of denying my heart what it truly wants.

So for once, I am choosing me.

I am choosing my happiness over anyone else's.

And I am choosing my horniness.

Grabbing the pen, I sign away the next one hundred days to Collins Stone.

And as soon as the final curve of my signature presses onto the document, a sense of relief floods me.

I did it.

I made the choice.

And it feels fucking good.

To celebrate, I do what anyone in my position would do —I snoop.

Rushing behind Collins's desk, I try every drawer. Seriously, why must he lock up everything fun?

I jiggle a couple of cabinet doors, finding them all secure.

"You really couldn't help yourself, could you?"

"Shit." My heart is in my throat.

Turning back, I see Collins taking up the entire doorframe. Just a glance at him, and I'm busting out laughing. "I was just—"

"Taking advantage of an opportunity to snoop?"

"Never," I lie.

"Penelope, I would never allow you to have access to a space that could potentially cause you harm. I'm not that careless."

"Harm?"

"Yes, harm."

What is he talking about? "How so?"

"Let's just say that I do a lot more at my job than just bodyguard."

I make an O shape with my lips. "You kill people."

"I relocate bodies when necessary. It doesn't happen often. However, it is part of my job, but I think deep down you already knew this about me."

I nod slowly. I know how much danger my brothers have been in the last couple of years. And it all started when Mark Tanner decided to drug me for his own sick purposes while I was looking at modeling in college.

"I know we don't talk about that part of your life. But I wanted to thank you for taking care of my brothers and

Angie and Claire. Those people are my world, and you have protected them countless times. And I never really showed —" I choke on the tears I'm trying to hold back, and Collins is on me, scooping me up and cradling me to his chest.

"It is an honor to provide that protection. And no matter what happens with this contract, I will always want what is best for you."

2

COLLINS

There is no worse pain for me than seeing Penny crying her eyes out.

This girl has shed too many tears this last year, and I never need her to waste any on me.

She doesn't realize that guarding her family is what has breathed life into me from a cycle of self-hatred and self-loathing.

Graham and Nic Hoffman provided me with a new life. And I will forever be grateful to them for making me want to stay in it.

After getting discharged from the military, I was destroyed. I thought I would stay in it for decades and retire at a high rank.

But then I was betrayed by the people I trusted.

And the irony is not lost on me...

Fuck.

This could easily be the biggest mistake of my life, yet I

am out of willpower to keep stopping the inevitable from happening.

I carry Penny out of my office and into the living room. Helping her get comfortable on the couch, I prop up pillows behind her back and a couple under her ankles.

"I'll make you some coffee and get you some break-fast." I can't believe I didn't feed her. I was more concerned over another man seeing Penny half-dressed than tending to her basic needs.

She nods. "I just need some low-nutrition cereal."

"So sugar in a bowl?"

"Sounds delicious."

I move into the kitchen to get to work. I will concede and feed her this garbage that I have no idea why I bought other than the fact she loves it, but I plan to provide her with better quality food for the two meals that follow.

And if she signs this contract, then she'll have to comply as well. There are few things I negotiate on, and my ability to care for her will not be one of them.

If Penny thinks her brothers coddle their women too much, she has yet to experience the lengths I will go to make sure she is happy and well. Plus, I've had a lot of practice already looking out for her. This contract is just an extension to what I've already been trying to do.

It's just that now once she signs it, she has to accept all of my services.

It would be a genius plan, if I wasn't guarding the little sister of my bosses.

Grabbing the box of Sweet Puff Paradise—who the hell markets this shit?—from the cupboard, I laugh over the three-dimensional googly eyes Penny must have glued to the bird mascot that is on the front of the packaging.

She is so freaking funny with her little pranks.

Reaching for a bowl, I'm careful to check for anything out of the norm in the cupboard. I know Penny is prone to adding fake critters to unsuspecting glasses.

When I have her cereal prepared the way she likes it, I walk it over to her on the couch.

"Do you want some coffee?"

"Yes, please."

I give her a smile and then move back into the kitchen.

After a few minutes, the aroma of espresso fills the air, and the sound of Penny moaning with each spoonful of cereal causes my cock to stir. If enabling her brings her this much joy, then so be it.

Plus, I'm pretty sure she would die on the sugary cereal mountain to prove a point if needed.

She can win that battle. I preemptively forfeit.

"I'm going to give you more time to relax and think over the contract. Come find me whenever you are ready for the next steps. No rush. Take your time."

Penny nods and offers me a smile. It feels weird leaving her on my couch looking so cozy, but I also have more responsibility in my job description than just taking care of her. And this other component just got more complicated.

Moving back into my office, I find my place behind my desk and enter the password on the keyboard for my computer to start up.

Using multiple screens, I open up several emails and text chains from workers who were hired to provide intel on Mark

Tanner at the prison. The Hoffmans are privileged enough to supply supplemental income for several of the guards and a few delivery workers who periodically visit the prison.

Their job is to provide information about the layout of the prison, the routines of the inmates, and the staff schedule.

Unfortunately, with a high profile and very public case, the chance of getting to Mark Tanner in prison is next to impossible.

The Hoffmans and I have been watching Tanner since he arrived there to await trial. While I regret not ending his life when I had the chance, I have zero regret about putting my life in danger to protect the ones I love.

And everyone I cared for survived his evil plan, so I'm thankful for that.

But now we are scrambling to figure out how to end Mark Tanner and make it look like an accident before the initial trial date occurs.

Penny will crumble on the stand, and I am determined to intervene now so she doesn't have to suffer later.

Unlike what the movies show, most state prisons don't have secret tunnels under the facility that allow product and people to be moved in and out of the prison unnoticed. So to get access to Tanner, it has to be through staff members who've already been hired and vetted.

It's very easy to play both sides of the line between right and wrong, and I would be naive to think Tanner doesn't have any influence from his prison cell.

To counterbalance that fear, I check financial and cell records and make sure no one is double-dipping from the money bank and being a traitor.

I don't even realize an hour has passed until I'm pulled from my thoughts by the soft knocking at the door.

I exit out of all of the windows I have opened on my screen and log out.

"Come in."

It opens.

Peering around the door, Penny gives me a smirk. "I think I'm ready to sign away my rights."

"You make it sound so dramatic."

"I do have some modifications and amendments."

"I'd be surprised if you didn't."

Picking up my cell, I send out a text to Leonard to summon him. He's probably hanging out in the foyer or in the lobby. Regardless, he arrives in my office in under three minutes.

"Let's get started..." Leonard says, getting into lawyer mode and less of a friend mode.

We've known each other for years. He's handled most of the legal issues that come with being *more* than a bodyguard for the Hoffmans.

While handling contracts with the women I go into "relationships" with is trivial work in comparison to what he's qualified to do, he does this for me as a courtesy.

It's just that Penny is the first woman to be part of the negotiation process. In recent years, I guess I've chosen women who have less of a spitfire opinion—on basically everything.

That's Penny for you.

She sure has a mind of her own.

Before her, the contract would be written up and signed without ever meeting with a lawyer.

Penny is different. I actually want her to push back on certain things and challenge me. It's when she's being her fiery self that I get the biggest look into her heart and her mind.

"Miss Hoffman, did you sign the nondisclosure agreement?" Leonard asks, his tone direct but kind.

"Yes."

She hands over the document that contains her signature.

I glance at it and shake my head over the hearts she used for letters anytime she needed to write an *o*.

Cute.

I reach for a pen, and my eyes catch on the little rubber topper of a fire-breathing dragon. My finger flicks the thin plastic flame coming out of its mouth.

Where the hell did this come from?

I glance across the room to Penny who can't stop biting her fist, most likely to keep from breaking down in giggles. Her eyes try to avoid me, as mine narrow on hers.

Pressing the tip into the paper, I start to sign my name as the pen lights up in an orange glow.

I refuse to look at Penny. She's working way too hard at keeping it together. I'm sure one look from me will have her rolling on the floor in stitches.

Leonard clears his throat, oblivious to anything that is transpiring between me and this feisty girl. "I figure it would be best to go through each page. If you don't have a question about the expectation or clause, then skip it. Understood?"

"Yes."

I watch as Penny moves through the packet until she

stops at a certain page. She appears to have a section high-lighted in pink.

At least she is back to taking this all seriously again.

"What page is that?" I ask, wanting to use my own copy for reference.

She flips her contract around for added emphasis. "Page seven."

Why does her highlighted section look like a penis?

For fuck's sake…

"There," Leonard says quietly.

How does he not notice her drawing?

"It states here"—Penny points to the middle of the page —"that tracking devices will be worn at all times."

"That is correct," I agree.

"Cross that shit out."

"No," I say boldly. "This is one of my three rules."

"No. Your three rules are: I will not lie. I will be safe. And I will not fuck anyone else."

Leonard clears his throat, trying to mask a laugh with his hand rubbing over his mouth.

I shake my head at my little princess. She's got quite the mouth these days. Looking at my lawyer who can't wipe the fucking smirk off his face, I clarify with, "It says 'I will be monogamous.'"

"That's what I said," Penny defends. "But with less flowery terms. Let's not sugarcoat things, please."

And then she lets out a giggle.

I know instantly it won't be her last.

So I just sit back in my chair and allow her the three minutes she needs to recover.

The worst part is, she has managed to charm my rigid and cutthroat lawyer into joining her giggle fest.

"Whose side are you on?" I whisper to him.

"Clearly hers," he deadpans. "She's way more fun than you."

"Traitor."

Every time I look at Penny, she does an exaggerated deep breathing inhale and exhale, probably as a calming technique—who knows. "Are you done yet?" I ask, trying to get this meeting back on track.

She holds up her hand. "Yes."

"Okay, back to the trackers. I won't budge on this. You can either wear one as jewelry or I can embed one under your skin." I am joking on the last part—well, kind of. It would definitely save me a lot of worry.

"Oh my gawd! Fine!"

"There. That was easy," I say smoothly.

"Can you at least tell me where they will be located?"

"Not all of them, but sure. You will have one placed inside all of your shoes, as well as on a bracelet you are instructed to wear."

"And other places…"

"Yes, and other places."

"And this is nonnegotiable?"

"Yes, Penelope. And you will be punished if you refuse to follow the order."

"Will I like it?" she asks.

My eyes narrow in on hers. "Like what?"

"The punishment?"

"What? No. Then it wouldn't be punishment, Princess."

Her eyes smolder, and I try to look away from her before I concede on something I clearly shouldn't.

"Okay...I wasn't sure if it would be kinky or not."

"What the actual fuck?"

Leonard makes a noise, and I shoot my eyes to him to silence whatever comment he is on the verge of spewing.

I don't have time for him.

"Let's move on," she says with the clap of her hands. "Page sixteen..."

"Found it," Leonard says with jubilation.

"Congrats," I mumble under my breath.

I'm starting to wonder why I even need him here. He's more entertained than helpful right now. I think he's enjoying little Miss Penelope Hoffman.

Too bad she's mine.

"On the topic of monogamy, ha, that's a silly word..."

"Focus, Penelope."

"Top of the page, it says that I won't flirt with other men."

"And you won't if you want them to keep breathing."

"Whoa, whoa, whoa," Leonard calls out, his hands waving in exaggeration.

Clearly his ass should have stayed home. I watch as he blocks his ears. "Quit being so dramatic."

Penny crosses her legs and plasters on her sweetest smile. "What happens if women flirt with you? Does that give me permission to rip them into pieces?"

"No."

"And why not? Isn't this a classic case of double standards?"

"It breaks rule number two, where it clearly states that you will be safe."

She folds her arms over her chest. "I very well might still be when I cut a bitch."

"I won't let you engage in physical combat for any reason." I can feel my blood pressure rising.

"Then it would be in your best interest to send out a signal to all your side pieces that you are off their booty call list."

What? Never mind. I refuse to engage with that nonsense. "Do you have any more questions?"

Penny holds up the document and rips it in half, handing me the two sections. "I quit. It's going to be too much work."

When she goes to stand up, I meet her where she is. "Are you serious? What the hell just happened? Can I at least have a chance to counter whatever stipulation you want to add or delete?"

I can feel my blood pressure reaching dangerous levels over Penny not wanting to engage in a relationship with me the only way I know how.

Then the corner of her mouth lifts. "Just teasing. I already signed the document an hour ago. Leonard has everything notarized or whatever lawyer lingo he used. No clauses were added, but I did have the section where you promise to sexually satisfy me bolded and underlined just for dramatic effect and so you don't forget your end of the bargain."

I turn to Leonard. I can't believe they played this joke on me. "You're a bastard."

"An efficient one," he says, shaking my hand while

exiting the office. "At least I sealed the deal for you and didn't allow you to jack this up."

I flip off Leonard and then, looking at Penny, I let out a sigh. "That stunt just earned you your first real punishment."

"This is my cue to leave." Leonard snickers.

"Yes, leave," I snap.

Penny claps her hands. "I'm so excited! I can't wait."

Yup. I'm fucked.

3

COLLINS

I already knew going into this that Penny was going to love every second, so I can't be upset with her. Her enthusiasm and willingness to try out new things is freaking adorable.

"Where are we going?" Penny asks.

"To my bedroom."

"Now that sounds ominous." But she follows behind me anyway as I lead her. "But why?"

"To fulfill your punishment." Which at this point is a joke...

A year ago, Penny was a shell of who she is, fighting her everyday demons to swim up to the surface and come back to us. In moments like this, where she is carefree and excited for the unknown, I can't help but think back to that time of seeing her broken.

And use that as a reminder that having Penny laughing —often at my expense—is *always* worth it in comparison to her catatonic state at Soulful Mind.

"What happens if I like it?"

"If history is any indicator, then you probably will."

She waves her hands into the air, pumping them a few times. "Oh, good."

Yup—she's way too enthusiastic. This girl is going to make me brainstorm and improvise more than I've ever had to do in the past to come up with more creative punishments.

Moving over to the wall of windows, I pull back the curtains to allow in more light. Then I sit down in my armchair in the corner of the room and relax into the cushions.

"Dance for me."

"You're kidding."

"We both know I don't joke."

She looks at me through narrowed eyes. "Good point."

"And let the removal of your clothes, one article at a time, be your goal."

This wasn't part of my particular plan walking into the bedroom, but seeing Penny in this cotton candy-pink wrap dress is inspiring me to dirty her up some.

She's so fucking sweet and yet is the sexiest thing I've ever seen.

It's the contrast that gets me.

She's like a filthy-talking angel.

She looks nervous, and I have no clue why. She is every man's fantasy.

Who doesn't want someone with a lot less experience who they can help sculpt?

"Get on with it, Penelope. I'm not a man with a lot of

patience right now." My words come out authoritative and a bit harsh.

But she stops overthinking and starts swaying her hips.

"You're a fucking dream."

Penny closes her eyes, probably trying to shield herself from my prying gaze. I allow her this one moment of privacy, despite not being able to take my eyes off her.

She just needs some time to adjust to my demands.

"Untie that dress. Slowly."

With shaky hands, she fidgets with the knot. I can tell she's getting frustrated. But after a few tries, she has the panels loosened.

"You are being such a good girl following my orders."

If I wasn't staring at her face for any subtle reactions, I would have missed the corner of her mouth lifting into a little half-smile.

"You like following directions, don't you? Does it turn you on to be told what to do and to have no choice but to do it? You love it when I tell you how to move that delectable body of yours—don't you? You enjoy not having to think about anything but what I tell you. Is that right, Princess?"

Her words are a whisper, and I'm not even sure if they made any sound at all.

"Speak up."

"Yes."

"Good. Because I love to pull the puppet strings on my little fuck doll."

Color blooms on Penny's face as her eyes open to stare into mine.

That's my good girl.

"You thrive on all the dirty talk, don't you?"

Her nod is subtle, but it holds so much truth in that little gesture.

Penny might have a lot to learn when it comes to sexual experiences, but I also have a lot to learn about just how to get this flower of a girl to bloom.

And right now, she is melting as things get heated and edgier.

"Keep dancing. And get that dress off and onto the floor where it belongs. Only sweet and innocent girls get to wear pink. And we both know that you are far from those two things."

It's all an act... Part of the fun...

Penelope Hoffman is the sweetest girl who has ever existed. But she loves it when I treat her like my bad girl— one who needs a punishment to remember her place.

Sitting back in my chair, I adjust my dress pants to make some accommodations for my growing cock.

I have been going through the better half of the last two weeks with a semi hard-on most of the day.

That's what the Penny Effect is on my self-control.

When her dress is lying like melted pink ice cream on the floor, I allow my eyes to inspect her flawless beauty.

I feel like the villain who got the girl.

And I don't think I'll be able to let her go...

There once was a time when I thought Penny needed to be treated like a fragile porcelain doll that I could set up on a shelf to look pretty. But then she quickly proved to me that she didn't want to be treated as such.

No, Penny Hoffman may be pretty, but she wants to be played with—not just displayed.

And I'm going to enjoy playing with my little toy.

"Do a turn," I say, admiring her pretty pink panty and bra set. "Yes, Princess, you're being a good little slut, aren't you?"

Again her face flushes. Dirty little thing…

"Face away and bend over." I watch with awe as she complies. "Yes, just like that. You're being such a good girl. Now, reach behind you and peel back those panties with your fingers."

This girl is going to make me come in my damn pants like a fucking teenager.

"Like this?"

"Yes, Princess. Just like that. I have the best view of your pretty pussy and asshole from behind."

It takes everything in me not to rush to her and roam my hands over every square inch of her body. But I need to slow myself down. I need to savor this experience, not speed through it.

While Penny doesn't want gentle, I have to pace myself and keep her emotional state in mind. This girl wants to be roughed up—but with the right person.

And I only have one hundred days to get my fill and quench my thirst.

While I'm not suggesting I am the right person, I will definitely keep Penny's physical and mental health in balance.

Penny's eyes connect with mine from the framing of her toned legs. A glistening sheer liquid coats her pussy lips and soaks into the bunched-up fabric of her panties. I want to lick that wet spot and taste her sweet nectar. Her gushing all over herself is a reminder that she is in this with me and not a one-sided attraction.

30

"Crawl to me."

She finally lets out a whimper and breaks hold to look at me upright. "What?"

"Get on all fours and crawl to me." I stare at her as she hesitates. "Now."

"Okay," she whispers, lowering herself to the floor.

I nearly come in my pants at the sight of this enchanting princess making her way toward me, eyes cast down to the floor, with her ass and hips swaying with each push forward.

Despite them being contained by a bra, I have ample view of her tits. I could bury myself for days in those lush mounds.

"Fuck, you're beautiful."

I can tell she wants to squeeze her eyes shut but makes them stay open, probably to see my reaction.

"Little Miss People Pleaser is a fucking sex goddess."

When she gets within arm's reach, I beckon her closer. Reaching behind me, I grab the pillow that I once was leaning against and place it on the floor between my legs. I coax her forward.

"Up on both knees, face against my knee. Relax your ass against your heels." I watch as she follows every directive, as if she's done this a million times before. Fuck. She better not have. "Yes. Like that."

I never want to see Penny on her knees unless it's for my pleasure—and no one else's.

Feeling a rage building in me at the mere thought of someone else witnessing this beauty, I quickly try to get back on track before I need to punch something to make the anger pulsating through me stop.

"You're being such a good girl for me, Princess."

Her skin ripens to a beautiful shade of pink at my words, flourishing in the praise I will freely give to her if it makes her react like this.

Penny settles into the position, resting her cheek against my leg.

Gliding my hand over her face, I pet her.

And she purrs.

Taking the same hand, I slide it down her neck and then outline the strap of her bra.

Penny lets out a whimper from the pleasure of just my touch.

Moving to her hair, I caress the place behind her ear, eliciting a moan from her pretty pink lips.

She's a divine, sugar-coated princess.

"I'm going to ruin you for any man after me, so that when the one hundred days are up, you won't be able to think of another cock breaking in that tight pussy of yours but mine. And it will become this lucid fantasy that you'll never be able to achieve again. Because no matter what time period we place on this, I will live in that mind of yours forever."

I trail my fingertips down her arm and then up to wrap around her neck.

"Are you my little kitten?"

She nods with her head still against my thigh, only able to move a few inches with the hold I have on her.

Her body feels good in my hands. Just witnessing her in this vulnerable position sends jolts of lustful pleasure through the lower half of me.

What a sight…

"We have to do a few things before you get your cream. Okay, kitten?"

She is an obedient pet. I'll give her that.

The typically spunky Penny definitely can settle into her role of being cooperative if she allows her mind to stop overthinking all the ways she can be defiant instead.

Reaching below my chair, I retrieve the box that I was going to share with her tonight. But some things can't wait.

Penny does this to me. She makes me get impatient and moving off-plan.

And while I like to keep my hand close to my chest, she possesses a hold on me that has me showing all my cards.

I nudge her head to be upright, presenting her with the small box.

She looks at me expectantly.

"It's a gift. Go ahead and open."

Taking the box from my hands, Penny's delicate fingers pull off the lid to reveal the choker necklace inside that is made of the softest leather and a pendant that is sparkly with diamonds. Etched in the center is the word—*princess*.

"It's your collar and can be worn for my pleasure when the atmosphere allows."

Removing the jewelry from the box, Penny rotates it in her hand. "Thank you."

"You are so welcome. Can I put it on you?"

Shocked that I'm even asking, she nods her head. "I would love that."

I unhook the clasp in back and wrap it around her delicate neck.

Placing two fingers under the strap, I examine the tightness, making sure it won't cut off her circulation regardless of how she moves.

"There."

It fits perfectly.

Penny's fingers reach up to touch her custom accessory, giving me a beaming smile when she catches me staring at her.

"And just when I thought there was no way you could look any more delectable, you prove me wrong. I could stare at you for an eternity and be convinced it isn't enough time."

This girl wearing my jewelry with pride instantly has me growing even more attached.

We are just a few hours into the one hundred days, and I can already tell I'm not going to be able to let her go.

Tugging on the pendant, I get Penny to rise to her feet as I follow her up. I lead her to the four-poster bed that needs her body as its centerpiece.

"Crawl to the middle."

I watch her from behind as she follows her order.

There's something about seeing her on all fours...

It's like watching someone submit and reign at the same time.

"Lie on your back. It's time for me to check if you are as turned on as I am."

Now it's my turn to crawl, and I do, to meet her in the middle.

I help her spread her creamy thighs, already smelling her heat and seeing the telltale sign of her arousal in the form of a wet spot on her pink silk panties.

Bending forward, I smother myself between her legs—diving in headfirst.

I lick and bite at her damp spot, making her squirm and writhe on the mattress, trying to get away from what I assume can only be the intense pleasure racing through her.

Nibbling, I make a feast out of her.

And just when I don't think she can take anymore, I rip through her panties with my teeth, framing her body with the lacy pieces.

"Fuck," she growls.

I dive in again, this time on her naked flesh.

Her little tuft of hair tickles me as I thrust my tongue into her warmth, trying to quench my thirst with her warm honey alone.

Penny's thighs clench together, holding my head in place as I eat and eat, like a starved man.

She makes me hungry...

It's as if I'll never get full enough to stop the craving to binge.

Taking two fingers, I slide them into her pussy and then stretch her open to allow my tongue deeper access.

"Let me in, Princess," I say when I come up for air. "This is my pussy now."

I want to have her pierced and marked with my ownership. I want to do all the depraved things to her—with her.

There isn't a part of her that I don't want to explore and make mine.

She's every dark fantasy of mine come to life, and I will cherish every moment I have with her.

Stretching my thumb up, I rub it against Penny's clit,

while thrusting both my tongue and fingers inside and curling them upward toward my thumb on the outside.

Her orgasm arrives so fast and so intensely that I feel it happening before Penny can even get her lips to form the words.

Like lighting a match to kindling, Penny goes off with a spark.

4

COLLINS

"What are you doing?" Penny asks me frantically, watching as I grab supplies from the bathroom closet and drop them onto the bed.

She hasn't moved since I rocked her world with an intense orgasm, skyrocketing her straight into a post-pleasure nap.

That's how I like her—sated and compliant.

All of her clothes are discarded, and the only thing on her besides contentment displayed through her smile is her collar.

While I was limited on what could be engraved in less than twenty-four hours, I'm pleased with how the pendant turned out.

Penny looks exquisite.

I never purchased jewelry of this caliber for anyone before, and while I have a standing invite to use Graham Hoffman's jewelry company, Jealousy, for any of my needs —I can't for something like this.

It would just feel wrong.

"Collins?"

"Yes?"

"What are you doing?" she repeats.

Daydreaming about fucking you with just your collar on...

I shrug. "Having fun."

"Okay. Now I'm nervous."

"Why?"

"I get scared over the unknown. Plus, fun isn't in your repertoire of emotions."

I start to laugh and then find the sudden need to know more about what she's thinking. "What emotions do you think I am capable of possessing?"

"Grumpy and grumpier—but mostly grumpier."

"Well, then I better live up to my true potential," I deadpan, making her eyes turn even bigger when I start twirling the razor that was resting on top of a pile of fresh towels in my hand.

"You want me to shave your ball sack?" she asks, with a huge smile. "Fine, I'll do it."

Taking a towel, I lift Penny's hips, splaying her out for my viewing pleasure. "Oh, Penelope, what am I going to do with you?"

"I promise to be gentle."

I stop smoothing out the towel to look at her. "Funny. But no. I'd prefer not to go to the emergency room for some stitches to my genital area."

"Same!" she says, bolting upright.

"I know what I'm doing."

"Oh, really? How many bushes have you landscaped

before? Huh? Actually, no. Don't answer that." She takes a few huffy breaths, clearly getting herself worked up. "No, yeah. Tell me. Tell me now."

"None, Penelope."

"Oh, great." She then throws her hands up in the air. "I'm the guinea pussy for you to experiment on?"

Confusion hits me. "Would you rather me have a ton of experience making pussies bald?"

"Yes. I mean, no. Of course not! But how do you know if you're qualified for the task?"

"Because I'm certain that I won't ever approve of anyone else, professional or not"—I rub my palm over her core while giving it a firm squeeze—"touching this sweet pussy."

"That doesn't speak of your skill."

I turn the razor over in my hand, examining the blade. "I am a man who values precision and attention to detail. You're going to have to trust me on this one."

"Okay, fine. But I'm going to want to show off my new haircut at the beach. So let's plan a trip."

"We can go to the beach, but this"—I slap it—"is for my eyes only."

She scissors her legs together, trapping my hand from exiting her hold. "That hurt!"

I smile, mainly because I can't help it with her. "I'll kiss it and make it feel all better."

She shakes her head adamantly. "No. Then you'll make me forget I'm mad at you."

"Mad? You can't be mad at me if you are dripping from that little bite of pain."

"What? No, I'm not." Her face changes, letting me in on the little secret.

Taking my finger, I trail it along her slit. "Tsk-tsk. Someone's a liar."

I press the tip into her entrance, reveling in how her wall of muscles clenches at my intrusion. Her responsiveness is what lures me in, but it's her innocence that forces me to take my time.

I push enough to cover my first knuckle.

Arching her back, Penny lets out a moan.

Thrusting in the rest of the way, I get my finger saturated with her juices before pulling out completely.

Holding my glistening finger up to her, I show it off.

"How does it feel to have spent the last twenty-two years with your body, but I just needed two minutes to completely own it?"

"Quit being so smug," she bites out.

"Now, now, sweet Penny. No need to get an attitude. It's not like you aren't reaping the benefits of being wrapped around my finger." I hold it at her mouth, hovering over her lips. "Open that defiant mouth of yours and suck off your arousal." My tone is gravelly. "Now."

I watch as a blush hits her porcelain white cheeks. But she complies, opening that sassy mouth of hers to let me in.

Her tongue works its magic, and it's me who moans this time, which seems to only give her more confidence.

Playing with the tip of my finger with her teeth, Penny lets me know that she has some tricks up her sleeves after all.

What a surprise she is…

For a man who values predictability and my impeccable

instincts, I never would have predicted the turn of events over the last forty-eight hours.

"Don't miss a drop," I warn, sliding my finger in deeper to test her gag reflex.

When she starts to cough and her eyes water, I give her a second to breathe through the discomfort before sliding out.

"Soon, you'll have a lot more than my finger pounding into the back of your throat."

Penny hums, and I can't quite figure out if it's from nerves or excitement.

I can't wait to see how hot she looks with my dick sliding down her throat. I wonder how much she can take before she starts to choke and plead with her eyes for air.

Adjusting my hard-on in my boxers, I smile as Penny's eyes are drawn to the outline.

Soon.

I have business to conduct first.

"You okay?" I check in.

"Just distracted by your naked torso and your pretty ink."

"There could be worse things to pull your attention."

Sliding off the bed, I go into the bathroom to get a bowl of hot water and some shaving cream meant for an occasion as special as this one. If I'm going to do this, I better not cut any corners.

"I need you to bend your knees and push your heels back to your ass cheeks. Relax your thighs so you look like a mounted butterfly." I fold up a towel into layers. "Now lift your hips." I then smooth out the cloth to not have wrinkles underneath her. "There. You can lower."

Dampening a fresh washcloth, I glide it over Penny's core, careful not to squeeze out any water.

I then apply some moisturizing gel cream that foams up when applied, wiping the excess off onto one of the towels.

When I knew there was a chance Penny was going to be having overnights at my place weeks ago, I invested in a lot of strawberry-scented products.

I will never regret it.

Grabbing the remote control from the nightstand, I turn on the speakers and adjust the volume for some instrumental music to play softly.

"You are to breathe and relax. Do not move."

"Just go slow and gentle."

I smile at her, despite her eyes being tightly sewed shut from her fear that I will mess up.

I'm sure there's a chance for anything. But I'm not one to mess up.

"I promise."

She squeaks, thinking I'm about to start, and tenses up. "Is it over with?"

I look down at her. "I haven't even started yet. Now get out of your head and just listen to the music. You will be punished if you don't comply. And it won't be the type of punishment that will make that pussy of yours drip."

Out of all the things we've done thus far, this is what makes her nervous? I honestly wouldn't have guessed it.

Wetting the razor, I glide it over her mound, enjoying the feel of the friction between my fingertips. Hair slices off as I shovel the foam toward the cheek of her ass. I rinse off the residue and start again with my meticulous shaving process.

When I get toward her center and the delicate skin of her inner labia, I place two fingers from my left hand over those sensitive parts as a shield and continue sliding the razor through the thin layer of shaving cream.

Then I do the other side, stopping periodically to wipe and wash Penny to check my progress.

"Stop holding your breath, Penny."

I wait until she releases the air from her lungs before continuing.

"How do you feel?"

"Like a baldy. I really hope this doesn't itch."

"I have some lotion to apply as soon as I'm done. I'll reapply it a few times a day to make sure you are as comfortable as possible."

Penny lets out a strained laugh. "I hope this magical lotion wasn't bought from an infomercial. Those things are all scams."

I let out a laugh. "Time will tell. If you experience a rash of red elevated bumps, we can go to a doctor."

"Ugh! Collins!"

"Just joking… You're going to be fine, Princess."

Taking the dirty bowl of sudsy water, I dump it into the sink, rinse it out, and refill it with fresh hot water.

Returning to the bedroom, I kneel on the bed and then help clean Penny up from any residue lingering from the shaving gel.

I bend and kiss each of the lips of her shaven pussy, one by one, making her quiver on the bed.

"All done. Let's look in the mirror."

Trying to sit up, she reaches out a hand. "Mirror, please."

When I realize our miscommunication, I scoop her up and walk her into the bathroom. She squirms in my arms, squeezing her eyes tightly shut.

"There's no room in this space for self-doubt, Penny. So start getting your mind used to the idea of seeing yourself as the sexual goddess you are."

I've literally just shaved her pussy bare and now she's being shy?

I set her on the countertop facing the huge vanity mirror with her knees bent and pushed back by my arms.

"Look at yourself. See how fucking incredible you look while I watch as well."

Forcing her own eyes to open, Penny takes a peek. And then shuts them.

And then opens them again.

I don't think I've ever seen her eyes grow as much as they are right now.

"I'm stunned," she mutters and then lets out an awkward laugh. "I don't think I've ever seen myself this close up. And definitely not with someone else enjoying the view as well."

"You look so fuckable. I love being able to see all parts of you. I like you wild, but I also like you tame."

"Variety is the spice of life," Penny says, clicking her tongue.

I unclasp her bra and then reach around to hold both globes in my palms. It's the perfect amount. More than a handful but not overwhelming to her smaller frame.

Giving them a squeeze, I watch as her head falls back onto my shoulder.

"That feels so good."

"Too hard?" I challenge.

She shakes her head. "I like it a little rough, Collins."

"Oh yeah, you do. But I want to dirty you up, Penny, and come all over those freshly shaven pussy lips."

"I want that too," Penny says, her voice full of desire.

Spinning Penny around, I push her ass back against the cold glass and help her to bend her knees onto the counter.

I strip out of my boxers, gripping my cock in my fist.

Pumping it a few times, I feel the skin pulling to an achy level.

Holding my palm out and under her mouth, I provide her a one-word directive—"Spit." And she does.

My hand finds my cock again, and I use Penny's saliva as lubricant.

"I need you to be a good girl and play with yourself. I want to see what you enjoy, Princess."

There is nothing more mesmerizing than watching Penny get lost in pleasure. She makes me want to fuck her into submission.

Penny glides her fingers along her bare slit, rubbing her moisture all over her clit, before dipping a finger inside her pussy.

"Look at my porcelain doll playing with herself. What a good little toy you are."

"Yes," she says breathily, stroking herself and causing her juices to leak out.

"I want your body to crave what only I can give to you."

She is breathtaking. "Hmm…"

"Tell me a dark fantasy of yours, Princess. I want your words to get us both off."

"I, ah…"

"Don't be shy now. I want to know what you think about when you're being super naughty."

"I sometimes fantasize about you taking me to Limit-X, but this time as your…"

I imagine she wanted to say *girlfriend* but stopped herself. "Keep going," I encourage, ignoring her inability to label us. I never care about labels anyway.

"I have this kink about other people watching us find pleasure with each other. I think it's having eyes on me that makes it extra hot."

Well, that's not going to happen because I'm pretty sure Yuri would look down on it if I were to start ripping out the eyes from anyone witnessing Penny hitting her climax—something only I'm privileged to experience.

I continue sliding my cock between my fingers, finding a rhythm that starts to warm me from the inside.

Sure, the physical touch—albeit my own—feels good. However, it's Penny's awed expression that spurs me on to continue.

"When I discovered you there, did you enjoy watching other members in the viewing booths?"

"Yes—absolutely. It was all just a pleasure playground. I was so turned on."

Clearly, Penny's on board with frequenting Limit-X again.

It's me who is the reluctant one.

But just thinking about how she described her fantasy, I wonder if I could pull it off.

"Are you ever going to allow me to stick your cock deep down my throat?"

And that's the moment I lose my control.

"Use your hands to spread your pussy apart. I'm going to come," I announce, as ribbons of white cum release from my cock and splatter all over Penny's shaved lips. "Fuck!"

Her thighs, knees, stomach, and pussy are suddenly splashed with hot cum, as wave upon wave of pleasure circulates through my entire body.

Looking down at the product from my release, Penny admires the artwork.

"You look like the most priceless masterpiece."

"Well, you make a fabulous artist."

Scooping up some cum, I massage it into the skin of her bare pussy lips. Then I work her back up to a panting state, until she is screaming my name from an orgasm so strong that it rattles the mirror behind her.

With reluctance, I remove my fingers from her clenching pussy and offer her a taste of both of us mixed together.

"Taste our pleasure. Clean these fingers, my dirty girl."

"Hmm," she hums, trailing her tongue along my entire hand.

"You are exquisite. I hope this memory of you sitting here, perched on my vanity, stays in my brain forever."

And just like that, the first day passes.

5

COLLINS

"There's no better way to enjoy dessert than fresh from the source," I declare, licking my finger of Penny's juices from her first orgasm of the day.

We are five contractual days in and have yet to venture out of the actual apartment building. We've been ordering in food, utilizing the private gym for self-defense lessons, and enjoying the hermit life. Our only dose of Vitamin D thus far has been hanging out on the semi-private terrace in the midafternoon.

Penny is my responsibility, so if she's content with seeing how many times I can get her off in a day, then who am I to complain?

While I want nothing more than to sink myself into her heat, out here we must be discreet. I doubt Penny cares based on her last visit to Limit-X and her inability to keep her clothes on while there, but I must draw the line somewhere.

Her curves are for my eyes only. But it's her smart mouth that stimulates my brain the best.

We have a certain level of privacy, but not enough for me to risk anyone else seeing Penny's delectable body. But under her flowered sundress—the possibilities are endless.

"When can I enjoy my dessert?" Her bottom lip pops out as she eyes my crotch. "I feel deprived."

My eyes darken as I suck my finger back into my mouth to make sure I didn't miss a drop.

She tastes divine.

"After my fill."

"*You* are the greedy one."

"Guilty."

Penny gives me an amused look, as I allow my hand to snake back up her sundress once again. I'm having fun sneaking around when we are up here. Pushing her panties aside, I dip my finger back into her furnace, making her thrash around on her lounge chair.

"Aghhh…"

"That feel good, Princess? You like it when I touch you under your cute dress while we are out here in the open—don't you?"

"Yesss…"

I guess I need to add sunshine to the list of the things that make Penny horny. It's becoming a very long list. Just the other day she tried to jump my bones in the kitchen because I was making coffee in just a pair of well-worn jeans.

Who would have thought denim got the girl going?

Penny tries to shift in her seat to give me better access, but I just remove my hand to remind her who is in control.

"Tsk, tsk."

"More. I need more."

"You need patience."

"It's overrated."

Taking her own hand, she reactively slides it between her thighs and leans back to get comfortable.

And I watch.

This completely violates a clause in the contract, but I don't care.

Penny's eyes close as she gets into a rhythm. "Hmmm…"

"You're such a naughty girl."

"I am," she agrees, her voice breathy. "And it feels so good to be bad."

She builds up speed, lifting her hips off the lounger to mimic the actual act.

What a fucking dream…

But when I think she's going to tip herself over the edge, I reach for her and pull her on top of me and my lounger, causing her hand to be released.

Penny squeals in frustration but is silenced when I suck her juices right off her finger and use my hands to model how she should get herself off by rubbing against me.

As much as we've already done the deed, there's some-thing so forbidden about humping against one another in the open air to get off, and that is exactly what I plan for Penny to do.

My hands control her hips, grinding her panty-covered pussy all over the fabric on my shorts.

Penny throws her head back, and her hair goes flying in the gentle breeze. She's close.

"Oh, fuck," she says, her voice deep and lust filled. "I'm…"

"Yes, Princess, come all over my thigh like a slut in heat. Grind that pussy all over me. Good girl. You're doing great."

And it's those dirty words of praise that send her over the edge, plummeting into that dark space of ecstasy.

"Ahhh!"

Her thighs clench and her breathing stays ragged, as she bends forward looking for stability.

"I got you. You did great, Princess."

Once she rests her head enough against my shoulder, she comes up for air. "I think you are secretly an exhibitionist."

"Maybe so," I tease, "but you are my inspiration."

I lift Penny to take a look at the beautiful damp spot she left on my khaki shorts. "If only I could save it as a souvenir."

"If only I could hump something more than just your thigh. I feel cheated."

Smoothing out her dress, I pick her up with a squeeze to her ass cheeks and carry her into the elevator. I press the button for my floor with my sandal, not wanting to remove my hands from her highly-charged body.

"Someone's going to see," she finally says when we arrive on our floor.

"Eight tenants are at work, each with a commute averaging about twenty minutes away. Two tenants go to Canada for the summer months to fish at their lake cabins. Five tenants are on vacation this week. And the remaining ones are vacant."

Penny gives me a look, her brows knitting together. "You know everyone's schedule who lives on this floor?"

"Yes. Well, unless they decide to be impulsive or tend to an emergency."

She playfully smacks my shoulder. "That's creepy."

"It's beneficial."

Shaking her head at me, she looks down the quiet hallway. "To whom?"

"To you and your modesty."

"Psst. I'm not even showing much skin."

"You don't need to be naked to let everyone know your intentions. I can smell your arousal all over you."

Penny takes a long inhale through her nose. Her cheeks turn red at confirmation that I'm correct. She can tell too.

We are almost in my apartment when a timid voice sounds behind us.

"I have a delivery for this residence," a girl says, making me go rigid.

I place Penny on her feet and turn my attention to the delivery girl.

Penny tries to look over my shoulder, but I shield the view of her the best I can with my body.

She transfers a huge box into my hands and glances at us with a knowing smile.

Shit.

I hope she can keep her mouth shut.

"I feel like such a hussy," Penny whispers, more to herself than to me.

I open the door with one hand, type in the security code to shut off the sensors, and toe off my sandals.

"What's in the box?"

I look at the bakery label on the top. "Umm, sweets?"

"I'm definitely hungry for my dessert," she says with a laugh.

Penny flings her flip-flops across the room until they hit the wall.

I chuckle at my hot mess of a girl. "Nailed it."

I place the huge box on the counter and go back to handling business.

Scooping Penny up into my arms, I hear her squeak.

"Are you going to allow me to walk at all?"

"No."

I carry her into the kitchen to grab two bottled waters from the fridge, then to my bedroom and into the bathroom where I set her on the edge of the tub.

Without being told, she puts her arms up and allows me to gracefully remove her sundress from her body. Then I unhook her bra and give her breasts some attention while I admire her beauty.

During the last five days, we've managed not to be needed in the outside world.

And it's been glorious.

I thought I would be bored, as normally I'm a fill-every-part-of-my-day type of man. But Penny elevates the ordinary to extraordinary.

"That feels so good," she moans, allowing me to have full access to her body.

I love that she feels safe enough to give me this and doesn't try to shield herself from what I obsessively desire from her.

My hands move to her back and shoulders, massaging and sending shivers up her body. This is for my pleasure as much as it's for hers. I'm addicted to making her respond like she is right now.

She is not sassy or defiant. And while I love all of those wild sides to her, I also enjoy this calm and quiet version.

A relaxed Penny is a pliable Penny, and I plan to continue to stretch her boundaries.

Penny isn't hiding herself from me. She's just melting to my touch, as I knead and caress the creamy and sensitive skin.

Beautiful.

I soak in her submission and her peace, as I peel off her panties that are damp from all the terrace foreplay.

The smell of her is intoxicating. And every soft mewl whispering in exhalation out of her mouth is like a signal straight to the beast living inside me—the one that wants to hunt, to mark, and to claim all parts of Penelope Hoffman.

That's what this temptress does to me.

In just a short amount of time, Penny has completely infiltrated my once very lonely apartment and has caused me to want to make plans.

I'm not a romantic man and yet I want this girl to experience all the things that a new relationship brings.

It's impossible to look at Penny and not want to give her the world.

And no matter how many times I remind myself that this arrangement is only temporary, I know that I won't be able to completely eradicate her out of this apartment when our time is up. Her memory and the little trinkets she'll leave behind will be permanent reminders of something that I had possessed and then lost.

Between Penny's hair bands showing up on nearly every

doorknob and the place always smelling like a movie theater with her need to serve popcorn as if it belongs in its own food group, I don't think I realized just how much I needed her in my life to shake things up. And now I can't imagine her not being in it at all.

But long-term isn't realistic, and the false safety of forever isn't in the cards.

Every day Penny wakes up in my arms, I imagine the day when the only version of her I have will be a ghost of the memory.

Bending down, I turn on the water for the bath and secure the stopper into place. I add some bath products that smell like strawberries and help Penny slide into the bubbly water.

"Ahhh, this feels so good."

I smile at my sweet girl, as she closes her eyes and rests her head back along the edge of the tub.

She makes me wild with desire, and deep down, I worry that my possessive nature will scare her beyond repair. It's not in my DNA to do things halfheartedly.

I want all of her. I won't leave any part of her unexplored. I am that greedy.

But it's Penny that holds the power to destroy me.

And that feeling of being out of control is what drives me to want to put up those emotional barriers.

"I am lonely," she whimpers, as her hand slides between her legs under the water. "And…"

"And?"

She wiggles, making the bubbles dance along the surface and causing a few to float up before popping from the pressure. Her brows knit together, and it's that pained expression that has my own emotions on overdrive. "It's just that…"

I sit along the edge of the tub, reaching over to gently move Penny's chin so she is looking me in the eyes. "You can tell me anything, Pen. And you will tell me what has you so distraught."

"I think when I was"—a blush blooms on her cheeks—"getting railed early this morning and then coupled with the angle that I was grinding you on the terrace caused a bit of a brush burn inside of me. I *think*. I honestly don't know. But it feels funny now that I'm in the water."

I knew we were being too rough, but I didn't weigh the consequence of her getting hurt.

Fuck.

"I am sorry I hurt you."

"No." She shakes her head adamantly. "No, no. It actually doesn't feel funny *bad*. It feels"—she twists her legs under the water—"like I can't stop thinking about my…" Her throat clears. "Pussy. It's making my mind hyperaware of the sensitivity."

I inwardly groan at her sweet innocence. It's that part of her that I've been tainting and stealing every chance I get.

But how does someone not react when this little princess is struggling to say dirty words and trying to explain the sensations she is feeling?

Drunk Penny is sassy and stubborn, but Sober Penny is sweet and shy.

I am a fan of both sides.

Reaching down between her thighs, I gently touch her under the surface of the water, watching her squirm as my fingers come close to slipping inside. She clenches her thighs together as tight as she can, forcing me out.

My eyes darken at her blatant refusal of my touch. "I just want to check you and make sure everything is okay."

I probably created little tears inside of her that need some time to heal.

She shakes her head no. "I can't. It's too intense."

The gentlemanly thing to do would be to give her that needed space to get better.

But I'm no gentleman. I may appear to be one in public. However, behind closed doors, I'm the monster that is secretly relishing Penny's mild discomfort because now when she sits or walks or takes a bath, she's going to know that I own her sweet pussy.

She's going to have that tangible reminder of where I've been and that I'm the one who will kiss it and make it feel better.

Me. No one else but me.

Before Penny filled all hours of my life, this bathtub was simply a decoration. I was content taking showers. But now, seeing her lush body underneath the canopy of strawberry-scented bubbles, I don't think I can look at it again and not see Penny.

With her eyes solely on me, I remove my hand from the water and stand up. I undress and fold each article, placing them neatly into the hamper in the closet.

I'm not one to think of myself as a vain person. Sure, I work out and work out hard. But by the way Penny is tracking my every movement and can't hide the smirk dancing on her lips—oh, and the playful whistling—I would assume that my dedication to personal health and well-being is appreciated on her end.

"Do a dance," she chants.

I chuckle. "Not a chance."

"C'mon. Bend over and spread those cheeks."

I shake my head at her. "Nope."

I hand her a bottle of water and watch as she drinks half of it. "Good girl. Stay hydrated because I need you nourished and replenished for all the fun things I have in mind…"

When the bathtub is filled, I shut off the water. Penny moves to the other side, allowing me room to join her.

I settle in and then motion with my hand for her to come over to my lap. "Get over here, Princess," I demand when she hesitates.

Reluctantly she slides over. "Fine, but don't touch."

I can see the uncomfortable expression on her face, and under the water, her legs are quivering. "I'm going to do more than just touch."

"Go gentle."

I help her rest her bottom in my lap against my hard cock with her back pressing against my chest. It frightens me just how perfectly we fit together. "Spread those legs. Show me what's mine."

Her ass cheeks wiggle against me, while her legs naturally part and drape over mine. My fingers trail along her inner thighs, teasing and toying with the edge of her sanity.

I can hear the shift in her breathing as she anticipates my next move.

I want her, but I need to make sure I didn't hurt her too

badly. Because Penny is way more to me than a conquest. She's my responsibility.

I'm her protector—her bodyguard.

Smoothing one hand out on her leg to keep her still, I take my other one and cup her pussy.

Penny remains relaxed in my arms, so I know I can move forward. With one finger, I walk it along her slit under the water, up to her clit, and back down again.

"Hmmm…that feels good."

I kiss her still-dry hair, along her ear and jawbone.

Taking my finger, I slide it slowly into her, twisting it.

It's then I feel her thigh muscles contract, signaling to me that she is feeling tense.

"Does that hurt?" When she doesn't answer me, I grow anxious. "You will use your words, Princess. I need to know just how far I pushed you so I don't make the same mistake again."

"But it wasn't a mistake," she blurts out, trying to turn to look at me.

I kiss along the side of her neck. "Pen, my job is to keep you safe and well taken care of. All of your needs will be my responsibility to fulfill. So please be honest with me. Did I hurt you?"

Penny shakes her head. "It doesn't hurt necessarily. It just feels really sensitive inside. And when the hot water hits me a certain way or your finger, it causes a sensation that is slightly uncomfortable—but mostly it just makes me want to make the friction more profound."

I slowly remove my finger and smile as I feel Penny attempt to hold it inside her, moaning as she gets the friction she claims to want.

Spinning her around to look at me, I capture her lips in an open-mouth kiss. And then we feast. Hands and legs intertwine, and I revel in the feeling of trying to mold our bodies together to become one.

My mouth devours hers, tasting all parts of her and exploring just how far my tongue can slide into her mouth.

She's perfection.

When we finally part, Penny is panting into my shoulder.

"I think we need to take a couple of days off so you can—"

Sitting up in a hurry, she looks at me with pleading eyes. "No. Please don't do that."

"But you are in pain."

"It's still worth it. And we are down five days already."

"It doesn't mean we can't connect in other ways, Pen. It will just allow for some creativity."

Before she has time to ask more questions, I place both hands on her hips and lift her so my cock is pressed snugly under her pussy but not inside. Taking the hint, Penny gets up on her knees, using my shoulders to anchor her movements, and then slides back and forth.

And it feels divine.

Too good.

We did this on the terrace but the clothing got in the way.

Now is different.

"Take from me, Princess."

"Why does this feel so good? Like it shouldn't feel this good, right?"

"Everything with you feels better."

And then she finds her rhythm, riding me and grinding against me with the pressure she needs but never having me go inside. "Mmm…"

"Yes, Princess. Get yourself off."

And she does.

"Get in this kitchen right now."

I steady my breathing as I wait for Penelope Hoffman to make her way to me.

"What? What's wrong?"

I gesture toward the huge box that was delivered here when we were coming back from our escapade on the terrace.

Her hands fly to her mouth. "Oh, my. That's way better than I was expecting for cartoon cocks."

"Better?"

"Yup."

"This is from you?"

She props her hands onto her hips. "Who the fuck else would send you a cock cake, Collins? Hmm?"

"Good point."

Penny trails her finger along the skin-colored icing at the base of the box, gathering chocolate sprinkles. "Look how realistic the hair stubble looks with these chocolate shavings."

"Genius," I deadpan.

"It really is." She pops her finger into her mouth and sucks off the icing. "It's so good. Let's cut some slices."

"Are we going to continue to ignore the question of why this was sent to me?"

"Oh, I sent it."

"Yes, I know that. We've already established that part. But why, Penelope?"

She shrugs. "Oh, because you were being a giant dick."

"Was I now?"

She nods. "Pretty much."

"And this is your way of drawing attention to that one moment in time?"

Pulling out her phone from her bag, she snaps of picture of me with my cartoon penis cake before I can protest.

"Oh, I'm sure it was multiple times. You are excessive like that."

"Am I now?"

She clicks her tongue. "Yup. And this was the most mature of all my options for telling you so. So count yourself blessed. It would have arrived sooner, but the bakery was having supply chain issues. At least I got to see your authentic reaction in person."

I look at the enlarged eyes made of fondant that are staring at me. And then I do the unthinkable…

I castrate my cartoon replica for the sake of having dessert.

6

PENNY

If there ever was a moment where time sped up, it would be at this point in my life.

Every time the sun sets and rises, I mourn the loss of another day spent with Collins.

He brings a joy to my life that I didn't know was lacking.

He's beyond anything my mind could conjure up with words. There's just no explaining it, and my body certainly can't deny its magnetic pull toward him. It's so strong that I sincerely doubt I'll ever again be able to enjoy a healthy sex life like I have with him thus far.

Bending down, Collins kisses me on the forehead, hovering over me with his rock-solid body.

It's moments like this, when his clothes are completely discarded, that I'm able to fully comprehend the magnitude of this man. He is gorgeous. Sculpted. Tattooed. And a towering force above me, who I never dreamed would be able to prove to me that not all men are assholes.

Last night he proved that to me, and right now I know he'll do it again—and continue to do it until I learn the differences between a boy and a man.

Collins is one of the good ones.

I trust him implicitly to not hurt me—even during discipline.

He might think we need a contract to keep the lines from being blurred, but that's too late. They are blurred. From the moment we both realized just how much we are attracted to one another, the line was crossed, and that was long before our signatures were pressed into a piece of paper.

Now there's no looking back. I can't go back to my life before Collins Stone forced his way into it, because I'm irrevocably changed because of him. He doesn't even realize the impact he has had thus far on my life, but it's only because I don't want to mess up the good thing we have going on here.

Collins has sparked a joy inside me that I haven't experienced since before Mark Tanner destroyed my life. And even then, I'm not quite sure I was ever really happy.

Sure, I've always had a good life, with the luxury of a family who loves me unconditionally and the financial resources that sustain me, but it was always missing something—*someone*—to fill the void.

"You are glowing," he says softly, almost reverently.

My lips curl into a smile. "I'd call it postorgasmic bliss. You wore me out last night."

His hand slides down to between my legs, and I revel at the feel of his attentive fingers on my bare pussy. "Good. Then I'll wear you out again."

"Promise?"

"Yes. And I'm a man of my word."

"That you are."

Bending my knee up, I angle my hips to grant him better access. Pressing my head back into the pillow, my eyes squeeze shut as Collins lazily explores my body, which is ironic because he is learning it better than I have in the twenty-two years I've had with it.

Collins slides a finger into me, pressing it against my inner walls. "Are you sore?"

"Mm-hmm," I moan my affirmation. "But not more than usual."

Hovering over me, he bends down to nibble at my neck.

Reaching down, I wrap my fingers around most of his cock, enjoying the groan vibrating out of Collins's throat at my touch.

"Are you too sore"—he clears his throat—"to come all over my cock?"

My eyes pop open. "No."

Collins chuckles, pulling out his finger to pinch at my clit. The contrast in sensations causes me to buck upward and lose hold of him.

"That's because you are so greedy for something to fill you up, even if it hurts a little. Aren't you?"

I pause, which only earns another pinch. "Yes..." The word comes out as a hiss.

Taking his cock, Collins grinds against me where his hand once was, coating himself in the natural lubrication that has leaked out of me just from anticipation alone. Then with a thrust forward, he enters me without any prelude, stretching me to what feels like max capacity.

And I know without a doubt that in just a few hours, I'll be deliciously sore again and not have a single regret.

My lips open in a gasp that gets swallowed by his mouth clamping onto me in a possessive kiss. I silently wonder if I'll ever get used to his size or if it will take me all of the one hundred days to not react like it's our first time together.

Rocking forward, Collins hits *the* spot, and I let out a string of curse words. Grabbing onto the back of him, I hold on tight while he pounds into me until we both explode.

Panting, I wiggle underneath him so he can move a little to give me easier access to air. "I need to breathe."

Rolling over, Collins takes me with him so I'm splayed on top of him like a weighted blanket. "I guess I'll allow that."

"Gee. Thanks," I joke. "I'm never going to want to leave this bed when you make it so worth the stay."

He flips me over to my side so we are both facing each other. "Staying buried in your pussy does sound like a great way to spend the rest of the day."

"We've spent more than just a day like this. We're going to have to stop being hermits sometime. And I need to check in at the office later this morning."

Kissing along the side of my neck, Collins makes a trail down to my breasts, and instantly I stop worrying about the outside world.

They can all fuck off.

Collins rubs his hands over my back and shoulders, causing goose bumps to form on my skin. It feels so good to be in his arms, sated and cared for—just like I've always imagined a healthy sex life would be.

He is spoiling me with all his attention, and I'm soaking it up like a thirsty sponge.

With his mouth at my ear, he growls, "Ready for round two?"

And just like that, I revel in his ability to fulfill his contractual vow to keep me utterly and undoubtedly satisfied.

Between these walls I find contentment.

But it's not about the place. It's about the person.

"Remind me why we are doing this again," Collins states, putting on real clothes for the first time in days.

We've really been rocking the lounge clothes lately, and I almost forget what it feels like to wear undergarments that are meant to be functional and not meant to tease.

Maybe he won't rip these from my pussy, and I can enjoy them for more than twenty minutes.

Time will tell…

I turn to look at him, as if he should already understand that I don't have much of a choice. "It's called work, Collins. I need to check in at work."

"That's what texting is for."

I roll my eyes. "If you don't want to come out into the world with me, then just stay here. I can get there myself."

"Not a chance."

"Then stop being a sourpuss and enjoy the change in scenery."

"Fine. But I would like warning prior to you doing photoshoots so I can mentally prepare."

I finish putting on my pink pencil skirt and off-the-shoulder white top. "I'm not modeling today. That actually hasn't even started yet."

When his brows furrow, I realize that he isn't aware that my duties have shifted.

"I'm actually working with the marketing branch of the company."

"Are you enjoying it?"

My smile can't be contained. "Very much so."

"That's awesome, Princess. I'm very happy for you."

"I mean, I still want to try modeling again if just to rewrite my narrative and heal some of that"—I pause—"trauma."

"And you will. You just need to give yourself time."

But time keeps running out. It feels like a ticking time bomb ready to go off, and each day that passes brings us closer to that deadline.

I slip on my white sandals with the light-pink flower embellishment and attach a fun heart bracelet around my ankle to complete my look.

Glancing at Collins who is in a charcoal grey button-down and designer jeans, I admire my view. "You look really good."

His smile is genuine. "We can stay here and fuck each other out of these clothes, you know."

I tap a finger along my jawline. "Or we could send each other naughty texts all morning and make each other super horny."

"And wait to act on it?" Collins shakes his head. "No. That sounds horrible."

I giggle. "C'mon. Let's go."

We exit the apartment, take the elevator to the parking garage, and enter Collins's SUV. During our ride to Hoffman Headquarters, I sing obnoxiously to every Grace and Jace song that plays on the shuffle list and enjoy every second of it.

"Are you getting excited for the concert coming up?"

But I just bounce in my seat, hitting some pretty off-key notes as my answer.

Collins keeps the SUV idling in front of the Hoffman Headquarters main entrance, claiming that he's doing my feet a favor since I wore stupid shoes—according to him. And these are my most sensible.

Sheesh.

"I need you to message or call me as soon as you are ready to come back. I have a few things I need to do."

"Isn't it amazing what you can accomplish in a day when you choose to start your day wearing pants?"

Collins grins and places a hand over the crotch of my fitted pencil skirt. "I accomplished a lot more without them."

"True story."

He gets out of the car and makes it over to my side while I struggle to get out of my seat, since the fabric is so snug. It earns me a warning look.

"Be good today."

I make a face. "I'm always good."

With intense eyes, Collins watches me walk into the building and make my way through security.

While in the elevator to Plus None, I shoot out a text to Collins just for fun.

Penny: At least my skirt is tight enough to keep my thighs from spreading and dripping out all your cum throughout the day

And he bites—immediately.

Collins: Isn't that what panties are for?

This is fun.

Penny: Umm…in theory

Collins: Or in practicality

Penny: Then I'm not practical because I'm not wearing any.

Penny: Oops!

Collins: Dammit, Penny. I'm coming inside.

Penny: I love it when you come inside.

I exit the elevator and walk along the corridor toward the Plus None office, unable to hide the grin on my face.
Well, that was way too much fun.
Glancing at my phone, I see Collins's text pop up.

Collins: At least your ass will be ready for my hand-print later.

Penny: I look forward to wearing any mark you want to give to me, Mr. Stone.

And then I put my game face on and walk into work, ready to get some things done.

———

I feel the whirl of wind and hear the cracking sound before the stinging pain registers to the rest of my senses.

"That's for being a tease all day and making me think you weren't wearing any panties when in fact you were. You make me wild. I had to walk around with a hard-on," Collins says, making me bite my bottom lip to keep from laughing.

"That sounds uncomfortable."

"Oh, it was."

"Does this give me the right to spank you then?"

"For what?"

I look over my shoulder at him. "For looking so fuck-able in your jeans and shirt. This is all your fault but yet I'm the one paying the price because you have the sex drive of a teenage boy."

Shaking his head at me, he wields his palm through the air again and pays attention to my other ass cheek. "That's for your smart mouth."

I click my tongue. "It matches my smart ass."

Collins smooths his hand out onto my burning cheeks.

Ouch, that hurt.

But it was so worth it.

"Your turn."

He digs his fingers into my fleshy globes, and I wince from the change in pressure. "Oh, no. There's no way I'd trust you even with just a little bit of the power."

I laugh maniacally. "Oh, c'mon. I'll be gentle."

Flipping me over, Collins pins me with his body. I pretend to struggle, but only because I love the feeling of him grinding against me. It's probably my favorite type of foreplay, because it feels primal.

Snaking his hands underneath me, he lifts my butt off the mattress, then rubs his length down my entire slit to lubricate it for my taking.

"Bend your knees, Princess."

And I do, giving him easier access to my pussy.

As he slides in, I arch my back and let out a moan. "You make me feel so good."

Leaning forward, Collins captures my lips. "The feeling's mutual."

7

PENNY

"Remind me why you're so adamant to do this," Collins says, pacing the bedroom.

"Because Angie and Claire are begging me to come hang out."

"Didn't you just see them yesterday at work?"

"It's not the same thing. I think Graham and Nic are driving them both crazy, and they could use me as a buffer. And it's not like we have plans today anyway."

"Maybe they are using *me* as a buffer."

I let out a one-syllable laugh. "Doubtful. You are way too biased toward my brothers. You will always pick them."

As soon as the words leave my mouth, I realize yet again the weight of the decision on his shoulders to go against all his instincts and code of honor to enter into a contract with me.

Because he didn't pick my brothers.

He picked *me*.

While he's said it before in the moment, I very well

could be the worst mistake of his life. And it's the weight of that guilt that I find the most debilitating.

Dammit.

Why does he have to work for my brothers? Life can be so unfair.

While the girls don't act like I owe them, deep down I feel like I do. They've given me so much already by trusting in me that hanging out when I clearly have no other plans is the least I can do.

"And you're going to behave once we get out of here?"

I sigh. "Yes. I always behave."

Collins's eyes crinkle at the corners as he glares at me. "There's no way you actually believe that."

I shrug. "We just have different definitions of *behave,* I suppose."

"And yours is wrong."

"Only in your eyes, Master Collins."

Oh great, now he looks even more displeased.

Oops.

"Besides, I have already proven that I can leave your sex shack without any incidents. So just trust me to do it again."

I swear the man is sulking. Every time we leave this safe place—inside the confines of his apartment—we have to put up a fake front and pretend that he is just my bodyguard, and I am just his client. Yet up until now, we haven't had a ton of days where we actually left the building.

Sometimes trying to be sneaky can be sexy. We just haven't experienced it yet to the extent we will today.

Today I'm breaking out of my pampered palace no matter how grumpy Collins is about it.

"It'll be fun. And besides, I don't have much choice

where Angie and Claire are involved. Those two make it very difficult to say no to."

I text back a confirmation on the group chain and get the details that we are all meeting up at Graham and Angie's place for some girl time first before we decide on the real plan.

"You know I don't do well with the unknown."

I prop my hands on my hips. "You don't do well with anything that isn't your idea."

Collins shrugs. "It's difficult to go through life always being the bearer of the better ideas."

I laugh. "Oh yes, you have it sooo hard."

"I'm going to be so freaking hard not being able to touch you all day while being in close proximity."

"Well, I'm sure you'll make up for it later," I call out over my shoulder while moving into the closet. "I don't call you Boy Scout for no reason. I'm sure you'll be resourceful."

His smile is one of mirth. "Absolutely."

Despite this arrangement being temporary, Collins decided to move all my clothes to his master closet to be adjacent to his. He also thought that I needed an abundance of options—despite not really leaving his bedroom—and provided for every type of weather and every type of color trend.

So when I put on a flowing sea-glass-green skirt and a white tank top, it feels special, like he had some say in the selection.

My fingers smooth out the soft fabric, enjoying how it stretches to look flattering on every curve of my body.

It's shocking how well this outfit fits me. Just knowing

that Collins was the one who chose it for me makes me feel pretty empowered as I walk past him sitting on the bed just for him to stand up at my presence and rake his eyes down every inch of my body in slow motion.

"You can't wear that."

My eyes narrow. "Why not? Did you buy it for someone else?"

"No, Penelope."

"Then why?"

"Because I'm not walking around with another hard-on most of the day while visiting with your brothers."

Turning my back, I walk away. "Sounds like a boy problem and not a man prob—"

Suddenly I am upside down with my ass high in the air on Collins's shoulder. He is so fast that my legs catch the breeze.

"Hey! Put me down!"

He stalks into the closet, using his hand to push through items on hangers. "I'm serious."

"So am I. I love this outfit. I'm not changing."

Growing unsatisfied by the available options, which are probably all too sexy for his own liking, he growls. "I'm buying you a bulky jumpsuit."

"Oh, that will look great on me for summer," I bite out sarcastically. "Make sure it is five layers of fleece sewn together just for added measure, you brute. Better also ensure it has one of those flaps so I can pee easily."

Collins places me on my feet and takes a step back to examine what I chose. "Pull the hem of your shirt down more."

"No. This is all your fault, and I refuse to take responsibility for your inability to plan ahead. Also, this is not in our contract and has nothing to do with my safety."

"It most definitely has to do with your safety when I'm street fighting men who look at you like they want you."

"Just as long as I can street fight some bitches that want to have their eyes linger on you a tad bit too long." I gesture toward his body. "That real estate is all mine."

Staring at each other, we finally agree with a silent truce that I will wear my outfit and Collins will accept this one concession on my independence.

Before walking out, I blow a kiss to my other outfits in the closet.

"What was that for?" he demands.

"Oh, it was just in case you go on a rampage and burn all items in a massive *Burn the Bra* campaign."

"Humph," he grunts. "I'm not that dramatic."

"Yeah, you kinda are."

We exit into the hallway, careful not to touch or show any interest in each other, which just causes me to smirk. Well, until I realize how rigid and serious Collins is taking this all.

Sheesh.

Is he mad at me?

I've definitely not seen him this stern since unofficially moving into his place.

We get into the elevator where it's just us. My hand reaches down to try to touch his, and he dodges by placing it in his pocket.

"Why are you so tense?"

"I just have a lot on my mind."

"Like what?"

"Stuff, Penelope."

"Stuff," I repeat. "Care to enlighten me?"

"No."

"Does this *stuff* involve me?"

"Please, Penny, let's not do this right now."

"What am I doing?"

Silence.

It's then that I realize I am being shut out—emotionally and physically—and I can't decide which is worse.

Removing the safety net of his apartment reinforces the reality that outside of those walls, we don't exist.

I go back to just being Penny, and Collins goes back to closing me out of his life.

He might have a lot of things on his mind, but my feelings aren't any of them.

I feel demoted from my princess status.

The quiet between us festers as we go through the motions of making our way to the parking garage.

Once we are inside the confines of his car, the awkwardness continues and I start thinking that the short drive will feel like it has tripled in distance.

Maybe I'm in a mood too or perhaps just hungry.

He starts the engine and navigates us out of the garage with ease.

"Collins?"

"Hmm?"

"Can we go to the Rose City Cafe first?" Maybe I'll actually be able to try out the food there, as the last time we left in such a hurry before we could order.

"Why?" he snaps.

I roll my eyes—and not in the cute way. He's being straight-up cold. "Never mind."

Forcing my attention to look out the window, I try to drown out the toxic energy seeping onto my side of the vehicle. This is going to be the longest ride in the history of rides to get to my sister-in-law's place.

But then Collins swings into a street parking spot, cuts the engine, and is already at my side of the vehicle before I realize that we are in front of the little cafe.

I take his offered hand, but it doesn't feel like any of the other times he's presented it to me. This time it feels cold.

I'm the job.

And in this moment, nothing more.

Collins scans the street around us, as if he's looking for some monster to jump out of the huge flowerpots decorating the store front. We walk inside together, and instantly I feel his body tense beside me.

"What's wrong?" I ask, genuinely concerned when I look up into his eyes.

"Grab something fast and let's go."

He's serious.

What the hell is going on? It's like déjà vu all over again. "Do you not like this cafe?"

"Get some fucking food, and we are leaving, Penelope. *Now.*"

I swallow hard, feeling my own temper stirring deep in my belly.

Glancing at the already made sandwiches, I grab one and drop it onto the counter. When I reach for my purse, Collins already has it covered.

He grabs my hand and pulls me from the shop, causing

me to accidentally bump into another patron on the way out. I don't even have a chance to apologize, as he ushers me into the passenger seat and locks me inside.

He hovers outside the vehicle, and I watch as he snatches his cell from his pocket and animatedly talks to the recipient on the other end.

Something is wrong, and the more I try to figure out what is going on in Collins's head, the easier it is for me to be confused.

When he enters the driver's seat, he glances my way. "Put on your belt."

"Oh," I mutter. Looking down, I see that I forgot to secure it.

Collins snaps his on and then pulls out onto the street, resuming his premeditated vow of silence.

I just wish that he cared as much about my mental health as he does my physical health. All of the hot and cold mood swings are messing with my head.

Taking my sandwich from the brown paper bag, I peel back the wrapper and am bombarded by the smell of mustard and the sight of sprouts.

Yuck.

Double whammy.

I take a nibble at the corner that doesn't seem to have any of the nasties on it, but the scent is so intense that I can't stomach eating it, especially with it being my first food of the day. Wrapping it back up, I shove the sandwich back into the bag and inwardly grumble over the waste of a trip there.

This isn't my day…

Weaving through the city, Collins gets us to Graham and

Angie's with relative ease, parking us in the garage in one of my brother's reserved spots.

"Thanks for the ride," I mumble, as I exit the car despite Collins's look of disapproval.

Oh, he's really in a mood.

I follow him over to the elevators like an obedient servant and toss my uneaten sandwich right into the trash can that is nearby.

An uneasy feeling creeps up my throat, and I just pray it's not foreshadowing of how the rest of the day will go.

Everything just seems off. And the trip to the cafe is only making everything worse.

"What happened back at the cafe, Collins?"

"Nothing."

I turn to face him. "You are lying to me, dammit." I swallow down the lump in my throat. "The same thing happened before when we tried to eat there, and you are giving me the same silent treatment as you did then."

He shrugs.

He fucking shrugs!

"Get inside the elevator, Penelope."

"Get out of your head and face the reality that is standing right in front of you."

Taking his hands, he places them on my waist and then lifts me forward so that I'm inside the car. He then proceeds to use his key to access the penthouse floor.

Fuck him. Fuck him and his stupid mouth that refuses to share anything of worth today.

Within a minute, I'm walking into my eldest brother's foyer, feeling a bit drunk on the brooding silence flittering around Collins and me, ready to separate from the awkwardness.

"Thanks for coming over," Angie says, giving me a much-needed hug.

I want to cry. Suddenly it feels like my fairy tale is over, and we haven't even lasted but a few days into the contract.

Something is very off, and it has been since I decided to come here.

But it's not like I can talk to the girls about anything that is bothering me, so I just plaster on my best attempt at a natural smile.

"Yeah, let the festivities begin," Claire chants.

Collins and Graham shake hands, while Nic greets him with a nod of his chin.

He's a way better actor than I am. It's as if nothing is even wrong based on his interactions, and jealousy strikes my heart at how he's able to tune me out like I don't exist way faster than I can do the same to him.

"So, you've been holding out info on us," Claire says, trying to turn serious.

I take a step back. "Huh? And what is that?"

"She's referring to your roommate's profession. Rumor has it, he's a *dancer*."

I laugh. "Yeah, well, that's one way of saying it."

"Oh my gosh. He's a stripper!" Claire wiggles her eyebrows. "I have a *thing* for strippers."

"You don't have a thing for strippers, Claire," Angie says with a laugh. "You have a thing for naked men."

She looks down at her feet, rocking on them. "This is actually true, but I don't like to discriminate at all when it comes to the male physique. I love them all."

"You also have a *thing* for defying me." Nic takes a step closer to his woman, pulling her into him. His eyes trail down her body. "Seems like you have a lot of *things* these days."

"I like your *thing* just fine. So don't get jealous. It's ranked in my top three."

A low groan escapes Nic's lips as he presses a very possessive kiss to the base of her neck. It's Claire's yelp that lets me know it was more than just a peck. She rubs at her now reddening flesh, glaring daggers at her man. "You better be counting inanimate objects for the other two in the rank."

"Oh, no. My objects very much are *animated*. I don't invest in the cheap kind without a horsepower motor."

I cover my eyes with both my hands like I'm five years old watching a scary movie. "You two seriously teeter on the edge of mass destruction on the daily." Smirking at Claire, I give her a bump with my elbow. "So what if my new roomie is basically a thirst trap. You aren't hurting in the relationship department like I seem to be."

From across the room, Collins shifts his weight. It's subtle, but I can tell he feels off-balance with my comments.

Good.

I feel off-balance with his lack of them.

Claire nods thoughtfully. "Yeah, I agree. I basically have my own personal fuck toy whenever I—"

"For fuck's sake, woman," Nic hisses. "Keep it up with your filthy mouth and see what happens…"

She smiles like a Cheshire cat but turns to me. "Can your roomie get us VIP tickets?"

Nic lets out a snort.

Graham laughs. "You all are going to start a war in my foyer."

"I just don't understand the big deal," Claire whines. "It's not like I plan on going home with anyone."

I almost feel bad for Nic. He is about to lose it, and Claire is oblivious to it all.

My eyes slide to Collins. And sheesh…

He looks murderous as well.

Too. Fucking. Bad.

"There is no way I'm allowing you to step foot in another strip club. Wasn't Vegas enough?"

"Penny wasn't with us. And besides, now we know someone—well, kind of—in the show. That makes it special."

"Oh yeah, *super* special," Nic deadpans.

Claire shrugs. "If you're worried about people flirting" —she points down to her stomach—"well, then don't. There's no hiding this belly bumpity-bump, even if I tried. Nobody would even give me a second glance."

"You look freaking gorgeous," Nic says boldly. "And if I need to fuck another baby into you just to—"

"Ahhh!" I scream out, holding my hands over my ears.

Collins can't keep his smirk from his face this time as he watches my every movement.

Picking nail polish off her fingernail, Claire frowns. "Exaggeration just makes me feel even more insecure, ya know?"

"Punk is speaking the truth," I chime in. I know Claire is having some self-esteem issues as her belly grows, but she really has no clue just how attractive she is. I think her whole pregnancy glow is just making her even more beautiful. "You are the cutest pregnant person in existence, Claire. And any man with vision capabilities can see that."

Nic drapes an arm over my shoulder, giving me a squeeze. "Thanks," he says in a whispered voice.

Squeezing him back, I mouth, "You're welcome," when Claire's not looking.

Graham ushers us into the main part of his and Angie's residence. When Collins turns to leave, Nic gestures for him to stay. As I walk into the main living space, I hear their muffled voices, feeling the pangs of jealousy that he can be social with them but not me.

Yeah, I'm butt-hurt.

And borderline about to be petty with my emotions...

"So, do you ladies want to order in food and watch movies?" Angie asks. "We can flip through some of the summer fashion catalogs and talk about boys?"

"I'm up for anything," I say quietly.

I still have so many emotions running through me. I'm feeling lonely at the moment, and sometimes hanging out with Angie and Claire reminds me how badly I still need a best friend.

They always have each other. And while I'm being included in today's festivities, I very much feel like an outsider and an obligation.

"Hey," Claire says, getting my attention. "Penny, you seem like you have a lot on your mind."

I look into her concerned eyes, and then out of nowhere, the tears flood out in a rush before I can trap them.

Dammit.

"Well, that wasn't part of the plan," I say with an obscene amount of sniffles.

Angie wraps her arm around me and pulls me down the hallway with Claire. We move into one of the spare bedrooms that is so luxurious that it could easily be a second master.

My brother must have upgraded some of the rooms, splurging on a designer and some upscale items since the last time I was here.

Once the door shuts, I feel a little better and less exposed from the open floor plan of the living room.

Claire passes me some tissues and takes some for herself, settling in on the bed.

"You are crying too?" Angie asks, joining her, and then chokes on her own tears. "Oh, dear. Every time I see someone cry, I join in."

Claire blows her nose loudly. "It's contagious."

"I'm sorry," I mumble, reaching for another tissue before plopping down onto the bed. "I didn't mean to cry."

"It's okay." Angie rubs a hand over my back. "Apparently we all needed to let it out."

"It does feel good to actually cry," Claire agrees. "I'm sad to see you so upset though, Penny. What's going on?"

"I am lonely today."

Angie sits up straighter to make eye contact. "You have us."

"I know, but I know you both are busy. And sometimes I just need a friend to chat with."

Claire levels her eyes with mine. "We are never too busy for you."

"I just know that for over a year I was a burden to my family, and the last thing I want now that I'm released from the facility is to be needy."

Angie wraps me in a full-on hug. "Being needy and having needs are not the same thing. You have *needs*, Penny, just as we all do. You were never a burden. We love you."

I want to open up more. I want to tell them that the emotional distance I'm feeling today with Collins is deflating my happiness balloon at the first hint of sharpness. I want to tell them that I have a haunting feeling in the back of my mind that something—or someone—is going to snatch away everything good in my life that I'm trying to build.

It sure doesn't help that I can't even eat at a freaking cafe in the city without becoming paranoid. Something for sure happened today, and I'll be damned if I allow Collins to keep me in the dark about whatever perceived danger is lurking.

We all rest on the king-sized bed, melting into the huge fluffy pillows. I dry my eyes using tissues from the box resting on the nightstand, trying to get my breathing back to normal.

"You need to tell us what's going on," Claire prompts. "What changed from the last time you and I talked?"

I trust the girls. I do. However, putting them in a position where it's best to lie to my brothers is not something I'm willing to do. If I'm going to open up to them, then I need to do it on generic terms.

"There's a guy…"

Claire smacks her hands together and lets out a squee, earning a look of disapproval from Angie—who calmly pats my leg for me to continue.

I shrug. "He is cute…" But in the dirty, rugged kind of

way. There's so much I want to share, if just to get advice, but I know I shouldn't. Anyone associated with my brothers is strictly off-limits, and I'm basically trying to confide in the two women who are the closest to them.

Why is life so unfair?

Claire tries to roll to her side to better look at me but struggles. "Throw me a life preserver. I'm drowning in this bed," she whines. "And to think that I've studied, mastered, and performed every single Kama Sutra position in the handbook, and now am unable to roll my beached whale body over on a bed. I have officially reached a new low."

Angie giggles and slides off the mattress to give her a gentle push, while I pull her arm to get her to rotate. "Well, that tidbit of information is—"

"Impressive?" Claire asks.

"Entirely too much information. Besides, you are barely at the halfway point. I can't imagine how the next few months will go," Angie teases.

"Poor Nic," I chime in, clearly joking.

Claire makes a face at me. "Don't give that man any sympathy. He made me this way."

"Now, Penny, tell us more about this guy of yours," Angie insists.

"It's complicated," I supply.

Angie lets out a huff, bouncing back onto the bed toward the bottom. "Always is."

Claire clears her throat, coughing into her elbow. "Is he the same guy that got delivered the cock cake?"

I nod. "Yup."

Claire taps her jaw, looking deep in thought. "Okay.

Then there's only one other way to get him to see what he's missing out on."

Angie folds her hands in prayer in front of her, looking up to the ceiling and muttering quietly, "Please give this girl sound advice."

"It's all about making him jealous."

"Oh, no," Angie blurts out, breaking out of her pose.

"Oh, yes!"

Angie cringes. "Please tell me you don't have a plan." I imagine she's the voice of reason for about ninety-five percent of Claire's ideas.

Claire pumps her fist into the air. "Oh yes! Nothing revs up the libido on a man more than thinking another dick is in a few yards' radius. And it's a twofer plan. Not only will it test this guy's attraction toward you, but it will also serve as a way of getting you noticed with another potential match."

"And how does this plan work?" I ask, intrigued but also scared.

"It's simple."

"It never is," Angie adds, making Claire fake scoff.

"Keep in mind, Angie, it was little ol' me who got you back together with Graham during your breakup with a similar plan."

"That plan was a hot mess! You secretly forced me into a double date."

I suck in my bottom lip and then pop it out. "I bet my brother lost his mind."

Claire nods eagerly. "Yup. And it worked, thank you very much."

I shrug to Angie. "She has a point."

"I do," Claire interjects, snapping her fingers for attention. "You just need to start living your best life."

I let out an awkward laugh. "I feel like that will need its own separate mission. How do I even do that?"

Claire thinks about it thoughtfully for a moment, obviously winging this as she goes. "Ask Angie for details. She's the expert."

My eyes move to my sister-in-law's. She shrugs.

"Tell her, Angie," Claire encourages.

"Tell her what?"

"Tell her how when you first met Graham, you decided to defy him at every chance you got."

"She still defies me," Graham chimes in from the doorway.

"Stop eavesdropping!" I scold, making Angie giggle.

His tall body fills the frame. If he wasn't my brother, I would definitely be intimidated. But deep down, he is one giant softie for those he loves.

"It's not eavesdropping if it is my own place. Anyway, can I interest any of you in a drink?" When none of us take him up on his offer, he sighs. "Nic is on a call at the moment but he insists on you having some water, Claire."

She rolls her eyes. "Of course he does."

"I figured if everyone around you has a beverage, you'd be more inclined to follow suit. Otherwise I'll have to deal with"—he points behind him—"that madman."

Claire lets out an exaggerated exhale. "Fine."

Graham walks down the hallway and after a couple of minutes returns holding a glass of ice water, which he hands politely to Claire. "Drink."

"Sweetheart?" He leans down to press a kiss to Angie's temple. "You sure you don't want anything?"

She smiles up at him. "I'm good."

"That you are."

I shake my head at the deliriously happy couple. Will I ever find someone that adores me like Graham does Angie? What about how Nic and Claire fit perfectly together as if they were created with the other in mind?

What I have with Collins is temporary...

And he's proven it today with how easily he can shut me out if he's determined.

I should heed this little warning and protect my heart.

8

PENNY

When Graham exits the spare room, Claire jumps right back into what we were talking about prior to the interruption. "Here's how you live your best life. You do what makes you happy and screw the rest of the world. Well, not literally screwing the world. I mean, unless that's your thing, then no judgment."

"Okay, I rarely say this," Angie chimes in, "but Claire is right."

"Hold up," Claire interrupts. "Let me savor this moment."

Ignoring her best friend, Angie continues. "You need to show this guy what he's missing out on. Just be yourself and start having fun. Life is just one big trial-and-error experiment. You'll find your stride and then he'll either step up to the plate or you'll just attract someone even better. Either way, you will have won."

I nod, allowing their ideas to marinate in my head. "My brothers are hella lucky to have you both."

Their faces break into smiles. "One hundred percent," they say in unison, causing each other to laugh.

"You know what we need to do?" Claire says, trying to roll off the bed.

I get up and help her. The last thing she needs is to fall down. "And what is that?"

"Let's go shopping in the Pearl District and then grab lunch. We all could use some sexy clothes to add to our wardrobe, am I right? And there's this new naughty shop that just opened."

"The controversial one that caused people to protest out in front of it?" Angie asks.

"That's the one!" Claire chants.

"Oh boy," I mutter. I'm not even familiar with this shop, but it sounds edgy enough to possibly do the trick.

"And we can shop for something to wear to the stripper show thing that your roommate does."

"Lovely," I say with a laugh. "I'm sure this will go over well with my brothers."

Claire thinks about my comment for a few seconds. "We won't tell them."

"Oh, yeah," Angie says sarcastically. "They'll never figure out we are there."

We head out into the main living area and find the men gathered around the island, deep in conversation. They catch our movement and stop talking, but I make out enough words to know that they were talking about the cafe incident from this morning. If only I could have eavesdropped sooner. Spying might be my only way of getting any information from these men.

Graham and Nic narrow their eyes as Angie and Claire make a beeline for the exit.

"What has you all in a hurry?" Graham asks, catching up with Angie.

"Are you ready to go back home, baby?" Nic asks Claire.

She struggles to slip on her shoes. "I'm not going anywhere if I can't get my shoes on. Pretty soon I'll need to wear pontoon boats on my feet because of the swelling."

We all laugh. She really is the funniest pregnant person I've ever met.

Nic kneels down on the ground and assists her in her time of need. "Where are you really going, Baby Girl?"

"We are going out. Girls shopping trip," she informs him.

"Now?" Graham asks. He looks blindsided, and I imagine this can't be the first time. These girls are so impulsive—and fun.

I stay back and silent, not wanting to get involved in this intensity.

"Yes, now," Claire presses. "We are on a mission and want to be spontaneous and all that jazz. It's time you let your exotic birds out of our gilded cages to go see the world."

Ironically, I got let out of my cage today and it only brought me heartache. I want to go back inside the safety of the bars.

"We will stay together, and nothing will happen to us in broad daylight," Angie says with a pout. "If it makes you feel better, I can bring some mace."

"No, that won't fucking make me feel better," Graham snaps.

"I have an important meeting in about thirty minutes, and there's no way in hell I'm allowing my pregnant fiancée to be wandering the streets without protection. Can't you ladies go shopping from your phones? Buy whatever you want, and I'll pay for it."

Claire gives her man a look. "That sounds as boring as you've become."

Graham leans down and whispers something into Angie's ear, making her smack his arm. "I have that meeting to attend as well. Collins, can you escort them around on their adventure?"

"No offense, Collins, but we don't need a babysitter," Claire says, glaring up at Nic.

I think my brother is going to hit the wall or toss Claire over his shoulder and lock her away from the world for the day. I know Claire and Nic play with fire on the daily, but watching this as a front-row witness is causing me anxiety —especially when I can see both perspectives.

"I'll accompany them," Collins says smoothly.

Of course he will. Because if I'm going, then it makes sense that my secret bodyguard—the one I'm not supposed to know is actually guarding me—tags along as well.

Do my brothers really think I couldn't put the pieces of this three-piece puzzle together?

"You ladies behave yourself," Graham says with a directness to his tone.

"Always," Angie says.

Claire smirks. "Never."

I bite my bottom lip to keep from losing it. Something

tells me that today's shopping trip will be anything but ordinary.

We enter the elevator, and I notice that Claire can't remove the smirk from her face, not that she appears to be trying.

"What has you so happy?" Angie asks, nudging her with her elbow.

"I love driving that man of mine crazy. Later, he'll give me the best sex of my—"

"Sheesh, Claire," I yelp, covering my ears. "You know I'm related to him, right?"

She manages to look sheepish. "Sorry. But for reals though, anytime I venture out without him for a few hours, it makes him extra frisky. And with all these pregnancy hormones, I need to entice him before he starts to worry about my '*condition.*' His word, not mine. I mean, if he's labeling my"—she adds air quotes—"*condition* as being horny, sign me up."

I glance to Collins who has the decency to pretend he's temporarily deaf. He's good at being situationally blind too —when it suits him.

When we get to the getaway vehicle, the girls take up the back seat, leaving me riding shotgun in front. I'm not sure I want to be this close to the man who continues to drive me wild. I'm already nervous in his presence while in public, and after all the intimate moments we've shared thus far, my body and mind can't help but want to find that same comfort from him, despite who is watching.

My hands twist in my lap as Collins expertly pulls out of his parking spot, up the ramp, and exits onto the busy street. He drives north toward the Pearl District, not offering up any type of conversation other than a grunt here and there as Claire dictates directions from the back seat.

I really don't know what to expect from today's shopping trip, but I know that it'll be interesting at the very least.

"Stop there," Claire shouts, nearly jumping into the front seat with us. "The little boutique on the left."

"Got it," he says, parallel parking with ease.

I have yet to give driving a go but doubt I'll ever be as smooth as Collins behind the wheel. Does the man do anything half-assed?

Angie is out of the car first, getting scolded by Collins. At least I'm not the only one he overreacts with in regard to that. He ushers her to the sidewalk, helps pull Claire out, and then glares at me when I'm already joining the girls without his stamp of approval.

Too bad.

"You need to dial back the testosterone," I grumble, staying back a few paces while Angie and Claire choose the first store.

"Or what?" he challenges. His facial expression gives nothing away.

Why is he looking so hangry? Maybe we should stop for lunch first before he sinks his teeth into our impulsive plans.

"Or you'll have an aneurysm from whatever passive-aggressive shit you have going on inside your head. I don't even understand why you're in a bad mood right now. If you didn't want to babysit us, then why volunteer?"

Collins's eyes darken, causing my heart to pause in rhythm. "Is this what you think I'm doing? Babysitting?"

I shrug, while still trying to keep pace with the girls.

"There's no part of this job that even remotely looks enjoyable to you right now, so yeah."

"Being of service to your brothers is honorable in my eyes. So, while I wouldn't call this *fun* being out in public trying to act normal around you, I would call it part of the job—that I would like to keep."

I direct my attention in front of me, as Claire enters into what appears to be a custom lingerie shop. Welp, this should be fun.

"You can't possibly think this is a normal way to interact with me. If you act any colder toward me, they will know something is off."

Claire holds the door for me to enter, followed by a rigid-looking Collins. He looks about as comfortable as a cow visiting a slaughterhouse.

The girls flank me, as we meander through the store.

Glancing around the space, it's easy to tell that there is something here for every taste. There are items with sparkles, lace, silk, cotton, and leather.

"Can I help you ladies find anything?" a tall middle-aged worker asks. She is stunning in a pencil skirt and lace-up tank that I'm sure are both sold here. There's no better way to show off the merchandise than to have the employees wear it during their work shift.

"We are just trying to find outfits for our next Girls' Night Out," Angie shares.

Claire leans toward the worker and lowers her voice to a whisper, "Which happens to be at a strip club."

"Oh, fun."

"So, the spicier the better." Claire nudges the worker. "If ya know what I mean."

"Well, you ladies have come to the right place. We actually have our new naughty collection upstairs that hasn't even hit the main floor yet. Would you be interested in—"

"Yes!" we chant, making Collins close his eyes for a few seconds before opening them again.

I think he has a migraine forming.

We all follow along up the stairs, as Collins takes up the rear. I can feel his eyes on me as I ascend. My breath catches in my lungs remembering the way his lips felt on my flesh just hours ago. I miss the way he tasted and how his hands roamed over my curves with reverence, yet desire.

When I get to the top, I'm already flushed and a bit out of breath. Maybe spending most of the last week in Collins's bed has made my muscles experience some atrophy. Granted, what we were partaking in was *very* physical.

"Oh, this would look amazing on you," Angie says, pointing to a black sheer dress. "Here, let's start a pile. There's a dressing room up here, and we can all have fun trying some things on."

I find my size and hand the garment to the worker, who is being very helpful and accommodating. I know we are being a little loud, but she doesn't seem to mind at all. If anything, she's encouraging it.

After we've gone through the entire collection, we make our way back to the dressing room area. Champagne bottles are popped and chocolate-covered strawberries are served.

"Drink mine," Claire says with an adorable pout. She rubs her hands over her belly. "This baby doesn't need any encouragement to be bubbly, so drink mine for me."

"Aww, you can feel movement?"

"All the time now."

We go into our assigned dressing rooms and start the long process of narrowing down the keepers. The nice thing about this shop is that many of the items can be worn as an actual outfit, and not just lingerie. The quality seems top-notch while still maintaining some of the comfort.

I honestly don't know why anyone protested outside the doors. There's nothing here that is so out of place that it isn't socially acceptable.

After each round, we meet at the sofa and give each other an opinion of the ensemble.

"Oh, wow, Penny. That outfit will sure get some attention," Claire says, admiring my sleek, silver sheath dress.

I turn in the mirror, feeling Collins's attentive eyes on me. I catch his reflection, watching how fast he averts his gaze. Maybe this whole experience can turn out to be a little fun.

The worker puts some upbeat songs on the sound system, refills our flutes of bubbly, and helps haul away any outfits we do not want. I feel lightweight and a bit dizzy— yet good.

Too good.

I stumble into my dressing room, switching outfits to something more risqué. I slip the sheer babydoll style shirt over my head, followed by a pair of lace booty shorts. The color is sea-glass green just like the skirt I arrived in today.

There's something about this color that is making me feel confident.

Pulling my hair up, I twist it into a messy high bun using the band that I had wrapped around my wrist. A few blonde strands fall out around the sides of my face. I spin in my personal mirror, not knowing whether or not to head out into the viewing area.

"Pen? You done yet?" Angie asks.

I open my door, peeking out to find the girls eagerly waiting.

"Let's see," Claire says with a whine. "C'mon."

Opening the door more, I step out.

"Holy cannoli," Angie says with wide eyes. "Well, that's the outfit. The color is great."

I turn again in the mirror, catching Collins's livid expression. What's his problem? Why does he care?

There are no men around to witness me. It's literally just us girls.

The dude just needs a snack.

I quietly move back into my dressing room.

"We are going to hit up the restroom," Angie says quietly from the other side of the door. "I'm going to go with Claire to see if she needs any help."

"Okay, sounds good."

This time I try on the black dress that we first picked out when we arrived on the floor. My hands shake as I down my champagne, feeling my vision go a bit cloudy. Bracing myself on the frame of the door, I push it open and then—

THUMP.

9

PENNY

An ache surges in my elbows as I crash onto the floor in a heap of black lace.

Well, that hurt.

"Penny! What the hell?"

I look up into Collins's concerned eyes as mine fill with tears. My bottom lip quivers. "Ouch."

His strong arms scoop me up as if I'm the weight of a feather. "Shh...I got you."

And he does.

Gone is the frustration over most of the day with him not paying attention to me.

Gone is the look of indifference and silence.

And gone is the boundary he so carefully maintains when we are outside his apartment.

"I'm sorry," I whimper.

Collins soothes me, his voice hushed, as he cradles my body like I'm the most precious thing to him.

His heat radiates through the thin fabric of my dress, and

suddenly I feel very exposed. It's one thing for him to be looking from afar while in public, but it's a whole other thing for him to be this close and me looking so scandalous.

I try to wiggle from his hold. "Someone will see."

"I need to take care of you."

"I'm fine."

"You are *not* fine. What hurts?"

"My ego."

His face is so gentle and full of concern. It isn't the sourpuss expression he plastered on all day thus far. "Nothing else?"

"I'm not hurt-hurt, I don't think. I'm just so embarrassed. I think I just drank too much. I'm not used to consuming alcohol, especially this early."

"What's the last thing you ate?" he snaps. "The Rose City Cafe sandwich?"

I shake my head no. Is he really this clueless about what went down this morning? "I tossed it in the trash."

"What? Why?" Then realization appears to hit him, as he's been with me all day and hasn't been the most pleasant person.

I shrug. "It was really yucky."

"Fuck. You should have had something to eat at my place before we left."

Wonderful—his bad mood is back in full swing.

"Oh, no." I hold my hands up in front of me in protest. "Don't blame this all on me. We were a little distracted this morning to remember breakfast, hence why I suggested stopping at the cafe." It's the truth. "Then things got weird, and you rushed me out of there. Yet you still refuse to inform me of what actually happened."

Setting me on the sofa, Collins stands in the entranceway of the dressing room and waves over the worker.

"Sir, is there a problem?"

Even strangers bow down to his calm authority, as if he is the owner of this boutique and everyone inside answers to him.

"I need some crackers and a bottle of water and orange juice. Oh, and maybe some cheese or something with protein?"

"Certainly," the worker says before rushing off.

"This isn't a grocery store," I grumble. He most definitely has been hanging around my brothers long enough to know that money and power will get you anything.

Picking up a strawberry from the champagne garnish tray on the table, he places it at my mouth, silently urging me to bite.

I try to sit up, but my head feels like a bowling ball. "It's no big deal."

"Eat. Your health and well-being are a big deal to me."

"Really, I'm fine."

"Let me take care of you, Princess."

I don't dare blink as my eyes brim with another layer of tears that I can barely hold back.

It's that one-word endearment that makes me believe that maybe we are okay. Maybe he is just stressed that we are in public.

And maybe he isn't actually having regret over our little arrangement.

"But I *am* okay. I think the floor stopped moving, and your face is back to being just one and not three."

His eyes narrow on me. "You still look like you're going to faint again, and you haven't eaten anything all day except for a couple of strawberries just now. So I don't trust your assessment on the size of this problem, because your health is nonnegotiable."

I look at the strawberry Collins is holding and concede by opening my mouth to accept his offering and give in to his demands. I chew carefully, as to not humiliate myself even more by choking. "You have quite the presence, Mr. Stone."

I can tell my formality catches him off guard. Good.

One minute he is acting like my boyfriend and the next he is pushing me away. The back-and-forth is giving me whiplash.

The worker returns with some crackers and beverages, informing us that Angie and Claire got distracted with a shoe display of new arrivals on the main floor. She then exits to leave the two of us alone.

I want to make a joke about this almost being a date, but I don't want to rock this sinking boat any more than I have somehow today.

Collins cracks open the seals and alternates between giving me sips of water and sips of orange juice. I feel very stupid for not snacking on something at Angie and Graham's house prior to coming here. My mind just feels so cloudy today.

But Collins really knows how to handle situations. He always knows what to do—like a Boy Scout.

"What was your nickname growing up?" I ask, trying to use our alone time together to gain more insight into his life.

"Boy Scout."

My jaw drops. "You're joking."

"I never joke."

I tap a finger along my jaw. "This is true."

"Keep eating, Penelope."

Sliding a cracker into my mouth, I bite down.

Collins is still sporting a scowl so I add cheese to the next mouthful.

Why is he so upset? Nothing bad happened.

Collins's eyes scan down my outfit, making a tingle run up my spine. "You should change."

My confidence wilts. Does he not like it? I go to stand up, finding my trusty shadow right beside me. I move into the dressing room, but before I can shut the door, I feel the looming presence of Collins at my back. "A little privacy would be nice."

"Privacy is earned by good girls. Are you a good girl, Penny?"

I nibble at my bottom lip, resisting the urge to crane my neck backward to check out his facial expression. "You only want me to be when it suits your needs."

"That can't be further from the truth. We are in a public place and surrounded by those you love who would be able to sniff out anything between us if we step out of line just one time."

"Well, then I guess I'm not a good girl. Because I refuse to act like nothing is wrong between us when your coldness is making me want to withdraw."

Suddenly I'm pressed forward so I'm flat against the full-length mirror.

Taking his palm, he presses my face against the glass surface so my cheek is getting the brunt of the coldness.

It feels good to have the contrast between that and my heated flesh.

"Is this what you want?" He bends at the waist to gain access to my dress with the slide of his hand up my naked thigh. "You want to be felt up in dressing rooms while your sister-in-law and future sister-in-law are shopping in the other room?"

Clearly he doesn't understand that since walking out of the safety net of his apartment, it isn't the lack of physical attention that I've been upset with. The fact he thinks that's what I want makes me feel like some whore.

I want more from him than just to be fucked. If he can't see that then he doesn't know me at all.

Regardless of being good or bad, I fear I won't be the type of girl Collins wants anyway. And while his caress feels amazing now, I'm not sure I can pretend I don't have anxiety over the heartbreak I will surely endure when our contract comes to an end.

The more strings I tie to him, the more I'll have to untangle when the false hope of forever blows up in my heart.

"Maybe I'm just not good enough," I finally say, unable to eradicate the sound of defeat completely from my tone, in fear of sounding pathetic.

Collins releases me, trying to make eye contact—but I refuse. Quickly I strip down in front of him and replace the clothes for purchase with the ones I arrived in.

We aren't on the same page today. We aren't even reading from the same book.

"You're mad at me?" he asks.

I shake my head. "No. I'm just sad this lightbulb moment didn't come sooner."

Cornering me against the wall and mirror, he blocks me in with his arms at the sides of my head. "You are enough, Penny."

"You say that, but I don't even think you believe it yourself."

I dip under his arm, making my way out of the dressing room first and checking to be sure the girls aren't out there to witness us being together.

Collins takes up the dutiful bodyguard position against the wall, while I plop down onto the comfy sofa.

"Drink more juice, Penelope."

I glare daggers at him.

Collins may be good for my body, but he can cause major damage to my heart. Maybe it's just destined for breaking.

Time to start erecting those walls to protect myself.

"Penny? Is something wrong?" Angie asks, rushing to my side when she enters the room with Claire.

"I must look really bad," I grumble.

"You look pale and weak," Claire says. "Did you pass out?"

"Yes, but—"

"Oh my, here...have something to eat," Angie says, making me a cracker with cheese from the platter that the worker brought to the table.

Claire uses a long skewer to add fruit to it, arranged in the colors of the rainbow. "Here, eat. You probably have low blood sugar."

Angie opens up a bottle of water. "Drink."

I accept all the offerings for another round of unnecessary coddling, but only because I don't like disappointing them. Feeling like a deflated balloon, I probably do need the hydration, so I comply with everyone's bossiness.

Feeling good enough to move on with the day, I start to stand up, but quickly remain seated when I catch Collins's reaction to my movement. "I just got a little dizzy. Nothing to worry about."

"We're going to go eat lunch," he says, his tone unwavering.

Claire claps her hands together. "Where are we going to eat? This baby"—she rubs her belly like a genie lamp—"has gotten way less picky. So the world is our oyster." She makes a face. "Ew, but no, and I repeat—*no*—seafood. We both have our limits."

"I don't have a preference," Angie says softly. "Let's let Penny pick."

Oh. Shit. I hate making decisions. "Umm, maybe the taco shack down the block?"

"Yum," Claire hums.

I tap a finger along my jaw. "And you know what goes well with tacos…"

"Orgasms!"

"Claire, no," Angie says with a giggle. "Those go well with anything."

"True," her best friend agrees. "This is the problem with being horned up and sober. It's never a good combination."

I get my own laughter under control. "I was going to say margaritas."

"Always down for tacos and margies," Claire says with excitement, causing us all to frown. "Sheesh. Obviously minus the tequila… You can drink one for me though, and I can live vicariously watching each sip. It'll almost be the same thing."

I accept Collins's hand that he offers to me, lifting me up from the couch. We make our way downstairs and to the cash register. Apparently Graham insisted on buying whatever we wanted to get today, so checkout is fast and efficient.

When we get to the taco shack, which is as basic as it sounds, we order a variety platter. The girls walk ahead to find outdoor seating, while Collins stares at me with his judgy eyes.

"No more alcohol."

I narrow my eyes at him. "I don't have a drinking problem. I barely drink."

"I was not implying you did."

"Then why the fuss?"

"You need to stay hydrated so you don't have a dizzy spell again."

"So bossy."

He growls. "So defiant."

I stick out my tongue.

"I'm keeping score," he says smoothly.

"How am I doing then?"

"You're doing fine. It's your mouth and your ass that are going to pay the debt."

I give him another smirk and then saunter to the table that the girls chose, overlooking the river. I can feel Collins's gaze burning into the back of my head. Good. He needs to know what it feels like to not get his way all the time.

He might own me in the confines of his home, but he doesn't own me when I'm out in the wild. He just thinks he does.

I have free will and don't need to determine at the moment if his threats are empty or not. That can be figured out later.

When the bell rings at the counter where we placed our order, Collins gets up and retrieves the prepared items, also grabbing us some napkins and silverware. Placing the pitcher of margaritas down in the center of the table and Claire's virgin one down in front of her, I can already hear the mental groan he must be doing over our "bad choices."

Whatevs.

He can deal with it.

I am tired of following some arbitrary rules that were never officially laid out in black and white in the contract.

So none of this is my fault if that man takes issue with how I'm handling today.

This is my life. I might as well start living it.

10

COLLINS

If Penny is trying to rile me up, it sure as hell is working. She has been hell-bent on proving some sort of point that I have yet to figure out. Ever since we walked out of my apartment today, she's been different.

But so have I.

When we got to the Rose City Cafe earlier today, I got that same eerie feeling as I had the last time we attempted to dine there, and it's only added to my shitty mood. It's clear I'm being a jerk. Even I know that. But no matter how many times I try to convince myself that I can protect Penny from the evilness of this world, I'm starting to grow paranoid that maybe I can't.

And that fucking terrifies me.

She's getting to me, and it'll be my emotions toward her that will get us all into trouble.

I need to keep a clear head. I need to remember my job. And I need to not allow lust to cloud my judgment.

Except wishful thinking is useless.

No matter how hard I try, Penny melts a layer off my heart that has been encased in ice for so many years. She's different—special.

And being in public and around those we both care for has made it all become very real.

I'm falling for Penelope Josephine Hoffman, and there isn't a damn thing I can do about it.

Except be fucking angry with the universe for giving me the most beautiful girl in existence and then making her be the one girl off-limits to me.

Even when Penny is irritated with what she probably thinks is a sudden mood swing on my part, she is still radiant and confident when she speaks to me.

I love her passion.

But it's her innocence that makes me want to be the villain. And no matter how many times I can fuck her into exploding on my cock, she will always be the sweet girl that I can never corrupt.

She's too pure of heart. And it's that sweetness that causes me to go crazy at the thought of losing her.

As soon as we walked out of my apartment today, I felt the clock start ticking for the first time since we signed the contract.

We are finite. And finite things always have an end.

So I silently vow to savor each day I have with Penny like it's my last.

Reaching for my phone, I send her a text.

Collins: I'm sorry for being in a mood today. It isn't you. It's me.

Grabbing her phone, Penny drops it on the ground and then nearly falls out of her chair to retrieve it. I watch as she struggles to type in her unlock screen password, and when she finally gets it entered, she appears to forget what she was doing and just shuts off her phone entirely.

By the way she's throwing back margaritas after already having a dizzy spell, Penny's making it clear I should show her she needs discipline and boundaries.

Is she trying to make me go crazy? It's not like I can make a scene right here at the table and cut her off without drawing suspicion. Surely she understands the effect her defiance has on my self-control.

Sliding out her tongue, Penny rims the glass, gathering salt onto it.

"You've had enough," I whisper into her ear, causing her to shiver.

She picks up her cactus glass higher, sloshing liquid out of the top. "Here, here, here," she slurs proudly. "I've got a cheers so perk up those ears."

The girls raise their glasses, looking at Penny for her to continue, while I silently brace myself for the next set of words that will pour from those fuckable lips.

"Did you forget the lyrics?" Angie giggles, only causing Claire to laugh.

At least I know one of them isn't drunk.

Dammit.

How does this even happen on my watch? Today has been a complete shit show, and it's barely halfway over.

Was I so distracted by Penny's presence alone to not cut off this source of fun? This is sloppy work on my part. In the past, I'd just slip the bartender or waiter money and they made everything weaker.

Penny clears her throat, takes another sip, and then raises her glass above her head, shaking a few crystals of salt into her hair. How can someone acting so tipsy be so fucking adorable? She makes me want to spank her raw but then cuddle her at the same time.

While this is all fun in the safety net of my bodyguard services, I worry about what trouble Penny would get into without me at her side. She has completely infiltrated my life. If only she knew just how much control she has over me.

"To friendship, tacos, orgasms, saying what you mean, and doing whatever the fuck you want!"

"Here, here!" Claire chants, while dipping a chip into the guacamole and gnawing on it. "I'm always down for orgasms."

"Are you now?" a masculine voice booms behind us.

"Nic?" she squeaks, almost knocking the table over as she spins around. "You come to check up on me?"

"I came to get my woman."

Her eyes light up with mischief. "You know I'm always down for some role-playing and exploring this caveman kink."

Penny covers her ears. "Ew. Seriously, you two!"

A few seconds later, Graham appears, making Angie pout her bottom lip out.

"Game over."

"Or it's just starting," he says with an edge to his voice.

"Say goodbye to the margaritas. They were fun while they lasted."

Graham bends to give her a kiss and whisper something into her ear, making her laugh. "I'm taking you home, Sweetheart. Let's go. You can test-drive some of those outfits for me." When she looks at him with confusion, he smiles and shrugs. "The credit card statement popped up on my phone, and I assume it wasn't just Penny and Claire spending a few grand on only themselves."

Angie snorts. "Of course it did, stalker. Besides, you aren't seeing any of them. You have a habit of just tearing them off me anyway. And I like these outfits!"

"Seriously," Penny hisses, each *s* sounding more like a *shh* sound. "I'm right here soaking up all your weirdness. Please stop."

Nic and Graham give me a look and I nod, confirming I'll see to it that Penny gets back home safely. When they texted earlier, I was relieved that they planned to meet us here, and especially now that I know how strong the margaritas are. Penny's either a lightweight or they have a heavy-handed bartender. Regardless, she needs to be cut off and given a chance to sober up.

The brothers shake hands with me and thank me for taking care of their women, and I can't help but feel that raw feeling of betrayal sneak up my throat as I think about how I'll be taking care of Penny in the bedroom as soon as I can get her home.

That girl has driven me nearly to implosion over her antics today.

Taking my last bite of a taco, I wipe my mouth and push back my chair. "Ready to go?"

"Yesh," Penny says, but then whines and starts looking underneath napkins and behind drink glasses.

"What's wrong?"

"I can't find my phone."

"The one in your hand?" I point out.

Tossing her head back, Penny lets out a laugh. Yup. Spanking sounds pretty good right now. This drunken princess needs a lesson in overindulging.

Regaining her focus, Penny tries to unlock her phone using weird faces. What the hell is so funny? She won't stop laughing as her screen rejects her. "My phone doesn't recognize my tipsy face."

"That's probably true," I say, resisting a laugh. At least she recognizes her state of mind. That's semi reassuring.

"Bingo! Now I can call a ride thingy," she says with purpose.

"The hell you will."

"You not the boss of me, Mr. Boss Man."

"Why would you call a ride when I'm right here willing to drive you back to my bedroom?"

"Because I'm not even sure you like me after today."

I growl. "I like you, Penny. But when we get home, I'm going to fuck you like I hate you. You pulled way too many stunts today."

This girl is going to cause me to lose it in public. I've been on the verge all day.

I toss some bills onto the table to cover the tab and tip. "Let's go."

Her arms cross in defiance. "Fine."

I can't help but smirk at her distaste for giving in to my wishes. I'm all about testing boundaries, but drinking like she did today is irresponsible. What would have happened if I wasn't here to watch over her?

I watch as Penny struggles to stand up, yet refuses the hand I'm offering to her. "Take my hand, woman."

"No."

"Yes."

"Oh shit," she snaps, as her handbag contents spill out onto the concrete slab underneath the table. "I made a boo-boo."

I help her pick up her items and then haphazardly toss the entire handbag into one of the shopping bags. "C'mon," I say, taking her hand.

Penny doesn't resist this time as we walk back to my car with her two left feet. It's a sheer miracle I keep her from face-planting multiple times.

I get her settled into the front passenger seat and then round the back of the car where I have a case of water in the trunk. I grab one, put the shopping bags inside, and then enter the driver's seat.

"I'm not thirsty," she says, but takes the bottle anyway when I insist.

"Drink it all."

"No."

"Telling me no is only adding kindling to a flame. Drink it all, Penny."

She pouts out her bottom lip, and instantly I want to bite it. But she starts to comply, downing a large sip and flicking the lid at me—which I easily catch. I think my reflexes surprise her, and I resist chuckling.

"What if I have to pee?" she blurts out, a bit panicked.

It's such a simple question and yet so human. My eyes soften. "Then I will find you a place to relieve yourself."

Leaning over the center console, her expression turns

serious. "What happens if I need to *relieve* myself in other ways?" And she has the nerve to spread those little thighs a few inches to punctuate her desire.

Fuck.

I should have known this is how the drive back to our apartment building would go with a tipsy Penny riding shotgun. Every time she drinks too much, her mouth loses its filter and her body craves to be worshipped.

At least the apartment is closer to us than the past two times at the club where the drive was over thirty minutes long.

I'm not sure how much I can take before losing all control.

After a long pause, I sigh and then ask, "Are you ready to go?"

"Back to the convent? I guess so." Then she proceeds to mess with the seat adjustments. Busting out in laughter, she sits up so straight that there's no way possible it could be comfortable. I just watch. And she just grunts and keeps playing with the buttons, making herself into a human accordion.

She's a beautiful disaster.

"Are you okay?"

"I can't get comfortable." Her slurred words come out as a whine. Her bottom lip pops out again, and I doubt there can be anything more adorable in the world than this image. "Quit enjoying my struggle and help me."

"Slide the button on the right toward the back seat and then tilt the back portion of that button down so that you can recline some. Just go slow."

I start the engine when she seems to have found her

sweet spot with the settings and pull out of the parking spot to merge onto the street.

Penny takes it upon herself to reset all my radio stations to some with static and classical music.

And I let her.

Even in her drunken state, she is angelic, with the sunlight causing her blonde tresses to shine gold. A fiery enchantress with the sweetness of a strawberry.

We drive in silence, listening to a choppy Mozart song.

In my periphery, I notice Penny doing some stretches.

Why she finds the need to perform chair yoga is beyond me.

But it's her moaning that causes me to sneak a real glance.
Fuck.

"You're just going to touch yourself while I drive you back?"

"I'm a passenger princess after all, right? I don't know how to drive, and I don't know how to go out without an entourage. So I might as well enjoy the benefits of self-care while having my ass toted about the city."

I watch as her hand disappears between her thighs and under her skirt. "Penny…"

"Don't worry. I won't come all over your precious seats. I'm wearing panties today."

Dammit. "Penelope…"

"Panties that you bought me. These panties were touched by your hands. And now my slutty pussy is reaping the benefits of using them to protect your seats from my cum." She shrugs. "It's all about the simple things in life."

"Is it now?" I half groan.

She continues to stroke, and a high-pitched squeal escapes her lips.

Dammit to hell.

"I'm going to have so much fun fucking you raw when we get back."

My fingers grip the steering wheel, about to rip it off the column. Is she trying to get me to pull her onto my lap so she can grind and dry hump herself to release?

Because I'm on the verge of finding us a shadowed alleyway for her to do just that.

"Let's take a detour. Can you see if the strip club Luke dances at is open?"

My eyes dart to the clock and then back to her in disbelief. "At one o'clock in the afternoon?"

"It's five o'clock somewhere."

"Pretty sure that expression doesn't apply here."

"It's one size fits all. Now take me there."

"You are not going to a strip club."

Penny runs a hand up her leg. "Why not? I love supporting small businesses."

"It's not happening."

Shit. I swear she murmurs *yet* under her breath. This girl really has no idea what lengths I'll go through to keep her from looking at other men's dicks—especially her fucking roommate's. I'm still irritated as hell over the fact she scored herself a male cohabitant. It really sucks to be this unlucky.

"Oh no," she yells.

"What? What's wrong?"

My fingers grip the steering wheel, as I glance over at

Penny. Well, now her entire outfit appears to be soaked from that water bottle she should have been consuming.

"Oops."

"It's okay. It'll dry."

Her clothes are drenched, and the pout of her lips will literally get her anything in life—at least as far as I'm concerned. It's my weakness. The way her soft bottom lip curls outward, nearly begging me to pull the car over and show her just how badly I want her and have wanted her for the entire day.

"I messed up."

"It's okay," I soothe. "It's not a big deal. It's just water. You will dry."

"But I promised I wouldn't come on your seat."

"You did not c—"

"I basically did one worse. Uh, I'm sowwy."

How she can make sweet look sexy has me mystified.

Then she starts trying to lift up her shirt.

Oh, hell no. Does she want me to wreck?

I take a deep breath and then hold it for a few seconds, while counting to ten before releasing.

Penny downs the remainder of whatever water is left in the bottle, sputtering from probably drinking it too fast.

When I get to our building, I park the car and then help Penny out. It is now that I can see the full water damage to her outfit. She must have dumped the majority of the bottle on herself, as there's not much on the seat or floor. Her hands cross over her chest, where the tank top is completely see-through from the fabric being thin and white.

Penny must be sobering up for her to all of a sudden

care about her modesty, when just minutes ago she was trying to remove her clothes entirely.

Her skirt sticks to her thighs, and every movement causes the fabric to ride up higher, toward her squeezable ass cheeks.

I grab her bags from the trunk and usher her toward the elevator, feeling the relief that I have her back on my turf again.

Time seems to pass in slow motion as we make our way to my floor.

I unlock my apartment door, deactivate the alarm system, and go through my routine of removing my shoes and placing them perfectly under the storage bench. Then I feel it. A shoe hitting into my leg, as Penny toes it off and flings it at me.

"Catch."

I look at her and wait for her to do it with the other one, and she stumbles backward into the door as she extends her foot.

"You're going to hurt yourself. You know that?" Maybe she isn't sobering up as fast as I thought.

She shrugs. "I don't care. I'm having fun living danger-ously. Today I was let off the leash, and I lived it up."

"Is that so?"

Clicking her tongue, she gives me the biggest smile. "Yup. I'm gonna make you work for your money a bit and have a hella lot of fun tempting the beast within you if just to see how hungry he can get." I watch as she pulls the hem of her soaked white tank over her head.

And then she—

"Penelope!" I yell, pulling the sopping shirt from my face.

I stalk toward her, and she takes off in a mad dash through my apartment, squeaking like a mouse as she tries to get away.

A thrill runs through me as doors slam.

"Three," I say loudly.

"Two!"

My hand rests at the back of my neck.

"One!"

I rub my hands together.

"Ready or not, you better hide! When I find you, I'm taking you for a ride!"

11

COLLINS

A nervous energy runs through me as I hunt for Penny.

I know she's somewhere in the bedroom, and the excitement over finding her and fucking her is making the chase worth the effort.

"I *will* find you, Princess," I say, loud enough for her to hear.

Walking into the closet, I move the hanging clothes around and check behind the chest of drawers.

"Not in here," I say confidently. "Now where should I look?"

I meander back into the bedroom and make a show of checking behind the pillows on the bed. Moving over to the curtains, I look behind them.

"Nope. Not behind there," I comment. "Oh where, oh where can you be?"

Kneeling on the floor, I take a look under the bed. I discover the damp sea-green skirt in a rolled-up ball, but no Penny.

Enjoying this game of hide-and-seek, I move into the master bathroom and check the linen closet, the storage under the vanity, and the bathtub.

"Tick, tock, tick. I better find you quick!"

Giving up in the master suite, I walk out into the hall and hear a rattle coming from the kitchen, concluding she was clever enough to change hiding spots.

The adrenaline running through me mimics the levels I've had during military combat missions.

That's what this girl does to me.

She gets me excited and dangles me off my own cliff of self-control.

It's her actions that control mine.

I stalk very slowly into the kitchen and round the island. It's the back of her little toes I spot first. Reaching down to grab her foot, I am blinded by the feel of something cold and creamy all over my face and the sound of Penny giggling.

Wiping the sweet taste from my eyes and mouth, I realize she sprayed me with a can of whipped cream.

It's a blur of naked limbs as she takes off running down the hall again, with me hot on her trail.

Her feet slip, and I catch her before she falls, holding her to me as we both become sticky from the mess.

"Got you," I say in victory.

Reaching over her shoulder, she hits the spray nozzle on the can I forgot she was holding, and an eruption of white fills my vision before I have time to react.

Moving my head down to hers, I smear the whipped topping onto the side of her face.

"You're going to pay for this," I say with an amused tone, taking her can and setting it on a stand.

"Thank the sex gods!"

Scooping her up, I carry a naked Penny to the bathroom, laughing the entire way there. I turn the water on for the shower and use my wrist to test the temperature before placing her inside. Then I go to work removing my own clothes.

The cascading water cleanses us of all the whipped cream residue.

Once our hair is washed and the soap is all rinsed from our bodies, I shut off the water and wrap us in an oversized towel.

Leaning her weight against me, Penny pulls me down with her to the floor, where we lie in a fluffy heap.

Our eyes connect, causing something to stir deep within my heart.

"Let's cuddle," she proposes.

"Right here?"

She nods, burrowing herself into my warmth. "There's no time like the present."

How can I argue with that?

Looking down at the blissful angel resting in my arms, I can't help but smile as she takes a little nap.

Penelope Hoffman is one of a kind. Reckless. And resilient.

So I just hold her, petting her damp hair with my fingertips and enjoying this calmness that I'm not often granted where this girl is concerned.

Minutes go by, turning into an hour.

My legs have fallen asleep and my elbow is starting to go numb. And yet I have never been this comfortable in the silence with a girl. Our breathing matches and when my princess starts to stir, a beastly force also moves within me. I want to claim her. I want every part of her to know that I'm the one she answers to, and I'm the one who is the deliverer of her pleasure.

"Collins?" she asks, looking up at me in confusion. "Did I fall asleep?"

I nod. "You did. Feel better?"

Her eyes look around the bathroom. "Yes. I definitely can think better and see better."

I chuckle. "Good. No more overindulging on margaritas like you did back at the taco place. You need to know your limits."

"But I was safe because I had you."

"Don't run away from me again."

"Or what?"

"You'll unleash the man within me who you might find scary."

"You'd never hurt me, even if I couldn't think clearly. Don't you get it? If I didn't have you and the contract, just imagine what stupid shit I'd be doing without your protection?"

"That's true."

The towel slips and I'm able to get a front-row view to Penny's delectable body. She's exquisite. Perfectly innocent.

She wiggles in my lap. "Collins?"

"Yes, Princess?"

"You caught me, so what are you going to do with me?"

Fuck you into next week... "Do you trust me?"

Penny's eyes find mine. "Yes." She looks confused but compliant.

I'll take it.

I kiss her on the forehead. "I'm not going to be gentle at times. You tell me if it becomes too intense or if something is scary. We can talk about it and adjust the pressure to make sure you have a fulfilling experience."

Her nerves are present in how she is biting at her bottom lip and rubbing her ankles against one another.

"Okay..."

"I'm going to fuck you with *my* pleasure in mind, but that doesn't mean you won't enjoy it too."

Before Penny has time to overthink, I lift her up with my arm under her knees and an arm at her back, cradling her to me.

Walking into the bedroom, I voice command some soft piano music to broadcast through the sound system.

Laying her on the bed, I adjust her location to be in the center.

I then crawl over her to hit a button on the headboard that releases two cords from a secret compartment, as well as two leather cuffs.

This catches her attention, and her apprehensive eyes find mine.

"Let me be your anchor, Penny. Keep your eyes on me and not on everything I'm about to do to you. You drove me crazy today. Now it's my turn to return that favor."

I busy myself with getting the cords and cuffs ready for use.

The one thing that sold me on this bed was the ability for it to be discreet. It was wishful thinking buying it at the time, because it wasn't like I ever planned to have anyone join me at my own residence. And I haven't up until now.

I'm just a man who likes to have options.

And my options are going to look so sexy on my princess.

"Do you trust me?" I ask again, staring at her in the eyes.

She looks timid yet excited. "Yes. But I'm a bit scared."

"I know you are, Penelope. But that is not my intention. We can stop at any time."

"Okay…"

"I want you to empty your mind and think only about following my directions."

I kiss her left wrist and then secure her into the leather cuff with the belt loop adjustments. I kiss and do the same with her right.

Penny tests out the hold by trying to tug on them.

Kneeling back on my heels, I soak in her beauty.

She's exquisite.

The custom nature of the restraints are what sold them for me. They aren't bulky, yet they can withstand the force of anyone writhing around on the mattress—in torment or in ecstasy.

I slide off the bed and move toward my nightstand.

Opening the top drawer, I pull out a black scarf.

"Do you remember your little goal sheet?"

"Yes…"

"Well, we are about to cross off restraints and blindfold from the list."

Penny cocks her head to the side. "But I thought you hated my ideas."

"Only when I thought of you fulfilling your goals with someone else."

A knowing smile forms on her face but then is quickly masked by apprehension. "Collins?"

I hate seeing her so unsure. "Tell me what you're most afraid of."

"Freaking out and having flashbacks."

"Have you had one with me yet?"

She thinks about it for a minute. "No. Not really. I was scared by the self-defense lesson with the blindfold but didn't have a real flashback."

"Then trust yourself to not have one today. Let me eradicate your mind of all the trauma you experienced. We aren't reliving old, fragmented memories. We are making new vivid ones together."

Once I think she accepts that, I take hold of her ankles and pull them apart to restrain them to the two bottom posts of my bed.

"You look like the sexiest thing I've ever seen."

Then taking the scarf, I move it up to her eyes and place it over them for her to get used to the opaqueness before I secure it to her.

"I'm going to check in with you often—okay, Princess? And to do that, I'm going to place a little object into the palms of your hands. If you are content and wanting to progress forward, then hold on to the item. If you need time to adjust or take a break, let it fall to the mattress. Understood?"

"Yes."

"This will free up your mind from having to construct

VICTORIA DAWSON

sentences together, but if that's your preference, by all means do that and I'll comply."

Reaching over into the nightstand, I grab two little polished stones that are carved into heart shapes.

"Open up your hands."

When she does, I place one stone into each of Penny's palms.

We do a few practice checks and once I think she understands the concept, I get up from the bed and make my way back over to the nightstand. Reaching inside, I take out the gag, a container of lube, and the remote control for the bed and place the items on the pillow beside Penny. I do this only to have my options handy, but not to rush into things too fast before she has a reasonable amount of time to adjust to all of the changes.

Kneeling between Penny's spread thighs, I roam my hands from her ankles up to her knees, and settle them at the underside of her thighs, where I massage and caress.

With Penny's moans guiding me forward, I continue my upward ascent and coast along her hip bones and her abdomen.

"Ahhh…"

Her back arches, as I find refuge between her breasts. But it's when my hands slide around her throat, just loosely resting at the apex of her neck, that she melts into the mattress.

This princess has a dirty side to her, and I'd be a stupid man not to explore all avenues of her desires.

Leaning forward, I allow my cock to slide against her heat, grinding into her and capturing her gasp with a territorial kiss.

132

Mine.

But it's the lazy smirk of contentment on her face—before I even do anything profound—that ties yet another invisible string from her heart to mine.

This girl trusts me.

And I'd be a fucking idiot to do anything to break it.

Resting my weight on my elbow, I use one hand to grope and squeeze her breasts, tugging at each nipple to test her responsiveness.

Sliding the same hand down between us, I tease at her opening and use two fingers to give her a little stretch just an inch inside.

Glancing at her hands, I find her fingers curled around her stones, signaling for me to keep going.

Lining my cock up at her pussy, I coat the head in her juices that have been leaking out of her ever since my hand was on her throat.

There's nothing better than sliding into Penny without any protective barriers and with our own arousal as lubricant.

Rocking my hips, I get two inches inside before I'm met with Penny's tightness.

Why does every time feel like the first?

Sliding a hand to her throat, I massage the muscles along the side that seem to be holding some of her tension. I continue working my thumb along the band of muscle, until I feel her entire body relax enough for me to push my hips forward and gain more access into her.

"That's a good girl. Let me inside," I whisper into her ear, thankful I didn't decide to impair that sense of hers.

Penny's arousal starts in her head anyway. Once I can

take over her thoughts, I know she'll be pliable and compliant.

I push all of the way in, and now it's my turn to be vocal about it, as my throat erupts in a growl.

"Fuck."

It takes a few seconds to adjust myself, not wanting to blow my load too soon. She makes me feral with an indescribable need to mark my territory like an animal.

Looking at her hands, I find that she is still signaling that she is okay to progress, so I slide my way out reluctantly just to slam back in.

My hand around her throat becomes more secure, impairing her breathing just enough to cause that euphoric feeling probably buzzing through her system.

Snaking my free hand underneath her ass, I use her body as leverage to thrust in and out of her pussy, until she can't prevent the orgasm from spiraling her out of control.

"I'm going to come!"

But I slow down. I need her on edge but not over it yet.

Reaching for the remote, I hit the switch to raise up her ankles and legs to hit a different angle.

"Oh, fuck," she chokes out, causing my fingers to vibrate against her words fluttering out from deep in her throat.

Removing that hand, I kneel up long enough to grab the lube and remove the lid. Dipping two fingers inside, I reach between us to get access to her back hole—the one I promised I wouldn't ignore—and apply lubricant to the outside rim.

With the sight of a stone falling from Penny's fingers, I give her a kiss to her forehead.

"Trust me, Princess. I'm going to make you hit a high, but you have to grant me permission."

"It's going to hurt."

"It might."

She shakes her head. "I'm scared."

"How about if I just put in one finger? Can you take one finger?"

I watch as Penny's forehead wrinkles underneath part of the scarf. Her hair is all matted from our previous shower, and I can't tell if the dampness is from the water or from her sweat.

"Okay," she says.

And that's all I need to go back to teasing her back entrance.

"You promised me all of your holes, Princess. And I'm going to have the best time breaking in this one."

My glistening finger circles around her back rim and then pushes in just an inch, just to circle around inside to spread the lube.

"You okay?"

"Mm-hmm…"

I smile at my princess trying something new, despite being scared. It's this allowance that bonds me to her more. Her trust for me outweighs her fear, and that's something I'll never take advantage of, as it's a rare gift.

Removing my finger, I slip the free one in and move it around.

When I think she's all slicked up, I slide my other hand back to her throat, thrust my hips forward to send my cock balls deep inside her pussy, and slide a finger into her delectable ass.

Capturing her lips with my mouth, I go to work at building Penny back up to dangle along the edge of no return.

And she gets there, with me close behind.

"Ahhh," I call out, throwing my head back and tightening my hold on her throat.

"Yessss," she hisses between closed teeth.

I pump my finger in her rear and do the same with my strong-as-steel cock. When Penny's about ready to take the leap, her inner walls clench and we both go over the edge.

Our mixed expressions of pleasure overwhelm the piano music playing throughout the sound system, until we both come down from that high.

I've never reached this level of intimacy before, yet I know it's what Penny needs to feel grounded.

She isn't the fuck-and-forget type of girl.

No.

Instead, she has me lowering her restraints and undoing her cuffs. She has me wrapping her in a blanket and running to get her juice I have now stocked in my fridge.

And she hasn't even given a verbal command.

Yet I'd do anything for this girl.

Anything.

12

COLLINS

I'm relaxing on the sofa when Penny joins me after a post-sex nap, flopping down onto the cushions. Even I am shocked I was able to pull myself away from the girl who has my heart tied up in knots and let her actually sleep without initiating another round in the sheets.

I wanted to though. And it's that broken moral compass inside me that would find some way to justify it too. And get off on the control.

Penny makes me feral with need. When she darted through the apartment to get away from me, I wanted nothing more than to track her like a hunter hungry for his prey and then fuck her into the floorboards.

But it's her delicate nature that made me stop.

She is the sweetest thing to ever enter my apartment, and I want to cherish her just as much as I want to defile her.

Giving me the side-eye, Penny lets out a little cough. "Hi."

"Hi."

Twisting her fingers into her lap, she releases a breath. It confuses me how she can be shy now when just an hour ago I was making her insides twist from the intensity of some strong orgasms and probing her ass with my finger, something I'd be honored if she let me do again.

It's that feeling of being able to teach her and train her that I never expected to enjoy so much.

But I do.

And every time she stretches her boundaries, I claim another part of her that no other man will ever touch.

Even when the contract ends, I want to live in her mind.

"Sorry I crashed afterward. I was so tired."

"It's no problem at all—really. I just hope you feel rested?"

She nods. "Very much so." She toys with her still damp locks that I managed to braid and secure. "When did I shower the second time?"

"Wow, you really were out of it," I say with a chuckle. "We showered right after you came down from your high. I think you were just too exhausted to notice much else."

I get up from the couch, pat her on the leg, and go into the kitchen to grab us both some iced water.

Before the contract, I found work to fill up my time in my day, never actually having a shortage of it. Then Penny crashed into my orbit, and suddenly I'm valuing and seeking out ways of enjoying leisure time.

That's what this girl does to me.

She has shifted my focus—but in the best way possible.

When I return from the kitchen, I hand her the glass and then put my own down onto a coaster on the end table.

"Thanks," she mutters. "I guess I should continue to hydrate after all of the alcohol I consumed over lunch. I think I went wrong at the third margarita. It was the turning point for sure. That tequila is a crazy bitch."

"She can be," I say with a smile. "Keep sipping that water."

And she does, without her normal fight.

Penny is definitely more agreeable after orgasms. I've gathered enough anecdotal data to draw that conclusion. And as a man who loves science, I'll be running more trials just to further test my theories.

"Thanks for always getting me the nicest things," she says as she strokes her hand down the leg of her pajamas.

Her compliment warms me from the inside out. She is wearing a matching set of charcoal-gray pajamas that I forgot I even purchased until I was digging in the closet for something comfortable for her after shower number two.

"You are welcome. I enjoy spoiling you."

Who would think that simple cotton pants and a shirt could look so good on someone?

But that's the Penny Effect.

She has an understated beauty about her and makes even the most ordinary things sparkle.

It's her softness that I'm attracted to, yet her fiery personality keeps me yearning for more. I know I shouldn't want her to the extent I do, but I can't help myself. The more days we spend together out of the one hundred allotted, the more I wish for time to slow down.

I am her bodyguard.

I am sixteen years older than she is.

And I'm going to end up in a hole in the ground if her brothers find out what I've done with their sister.

More time won't fix this. The only thing it'll do is cause our bond to become even stronger.

It is taking every ounce of willpower not to toss Penny on the couch and kiss the hell out of her. I want to be rough. I want to be all-consuming. Yet, she deserves better. Penny needs time for her body to heal from our last session.

I need to find a way to curb my appetite for wanting to be inside her all the time, and it's selfish of me to justify and say that she can handle every fantasy my depraved mind conjures up.

Just the thought of tarnishing her sparkle in any way makes me nauseated inside. Yet, the way she is scowling over every channel she turns to, making a silly face before changing it again, is so cute.

She has already filled my apartment with more joy than it has ever experienced, and the thought of having her leave at the end of the one hundred days and go back to her place in the world sans me causes an unbearable pain at my core.

Pulling out of my self-loathing trance, Penny awakens me by wiggling her toes into my hands, beckoning me to rub them.

"Remind me to never wear stupid shoes again. I forever want to walk around the world barefoot."

I laugh as my fingers rub circles into the bottoms of her soles. She doesn't have socks on and her feet are on the cooler side. I watch her tremble as shivers run up her body.

"Feel good?"

Penny leans her head back onto a throw pillow. "You

have no idea. It feels like my whole body is being rejuvenated."

It seems like the alcohol finally has left her system too.

I typically wouldn't have sex with any woman with anything impairing coursing through her system. Yet I can admit that the margaritas Penny inhaled during lunch had a positive impact on her ability to stop overthinking.

I'm definitely going to exercise better self-control in the future.

Well...I can at least try.

"What are your plans for this weekend?"

She sits up and laughs. Hard. Like really, really laughs.

"What's so funny?" I ask, amused by her humor.

"My uber intrusive bodyguard is asking me—I repeat, *me*—what my plans are? Ha! Like he doesn't already know. Don't you have access to my email and probably texts and such? You probably know even when I go to the bathroom and which part of my cycle I am on."

She is obviously joking, but must be clueless as to what hurdles I would jump over if necessary to get the information I need. My moral compass broke the day I was forced to leave the military. While I was devastated at the time, my skill set made me a valuable asset to anyone in need of protection. Because I stopped caring.

Settling down became less of a priority.

And my happiness took a back seat to my survival skills.

It wasn't until I was hired to help the Hoffmans stay secure that I found my passion again and my reason for wanting to live.

The Hoffmans were my turning point.

I try to keep a straight face. "Your brothers said not to pry too hard."

Penny eyes me with suspicion. "Oh, did they now?" She gives it more thought. "Like that would ever stop you. You love knowing all of the information."

I shrug. The corners of my lips move up into what I know is a smirk. "I can be intrusive if that makes the image of my job more vivid in your mind. Clearly, you need my services."

Her mouth gapes. "I'm a good girl, you know? I probably would have done fine without you."

"You may think you're a good girl, but it's the bad girl inside that has the most fun. And fun translates to trouble for you."

"True. I much prefer my bad-girl persona."

A warmth washes over me, with the image of Penny on her knees swallowing my cock down her throat, while my fingers tangle in her hair and the words "good girl" roll off my tongue as her mouth works its magic.

Penny may be a good girl, but not in the conventional way she thinks. She would need to learn to pace herself. She would be instructed on how to relax her throat and breathe through her nose. And I would encourage her each step of the way.

"It's my job to cherish the good girl inside of you and train your bad-girl tendencies."

Training Penny's throat to accept all of me would be a great source of joy. I know she would gain a burst of self-esteem the moment she masters how to cope with her gag reflex.

Penny would be my good girl.

I shake my head in hopes to clear it of the filthy thoughts so I don't fuck her into the sofa cushions when her body needs to relax and adjust to my needy-as-fuck sex drive.

It's entirely her fault for being so alluring and making me want her at all times of the day.

I never needed sex as much as I do now with her in the protection of my home, where she belongs.

This place may not have been a fuck pad prior to Penny, but she sure is making it into one. I can't see a surface and not visualize how her body would look pressed against it with me pumping my cum inside of her.

"Can we do that?" she asks, making me snap out of my fantasy reel.

"Do what?"

Gesturing to the screen, I see an advertisement for popcorn.

"Make our own popcorn."

Grabbing my cell phone, I call Chris.

"Hey, Redeye, what's up?"

"Can you run to the store and pick up supplies to make homemade popcorn?"

"Like the microwave bags?"

"No, the…" I glance back at the screen before the commercial disappears. "It's a maker thing, and you buy kernels."

"Dude, you're having a midlife crisis, aren't you?"

"What? No."

"It's okay to tell me."

"Shut up. I knew I shouldn't have called you."

"You always think of everything," Penny says breathily, after she sees me end the call with Chris.

"I enjoy taking care of you, Princess."

"Then why not tell me the truth?"

My eyes narrow in on hers, clueless as to the direction she seems to be taking this conversation. "What truth are you referring to?"

She shrugs. "Something happened at the Rose City Cafe, and I need to know."

I feel a lump forming in my throat. "I honestly don't know."

"You mean that?"

"Yes." I pull Penny into my arms, cradling her as the television buzzes on in the background. "I am a man who uses my instincts to keep me out of danger. And there's something about that cafe that rubs me the wrong way. I can't put my finger on it, and I have a team of men looking into the possible cause for my paranoia. But until we understand why I feel the hair stand up on the back of my neck every time I enter that building, it's best that we just avoid it entirely."

"Mark," she whispers, "promised me he would get to me."

"That fucker is in prison. That much I know."

"But there's other ways to infiltrate my brain."

I kiss her on the forehead. "Which is precisely why I hesitate to share any of this information with you at all."

"But I need to know."

"No, you don't, Penny. Let me handle this. It's probably nothing and just me being overly cautious."

She nods reluctantly. "Yeah. You've been known to overreact."

I tickle her sides, enjoying the way she squirms in my lap. And when she tries to reciprocate, I rotate us so she is pinned to the cushions with me on top of her. Snaking a hand between us, I give her pussy a squeeze, feeling her body twitch with pleasure.

"It's almost as if you enjoy being my little fuck doll."

"Oh, I do. Just don't forget the purpose is to play with me."

"You are insatiable."

13

PENNY

If living my best life means being snuggled up in Collins's arms while his warmth surrounds me at all angles, then I want to stay in this bubble that we've created forever.

He's easily the best thing that has ever happened to me. It should be no surprise that I want to relish in his protective embrace and his expert touch.

I pull up the comforter that has slid down during sleep and sandwich myself inside, luxuriating over the simple pleasure that clean linens can bring.

Rolling over, I feel the little rush of liquid seeping from between my legs and panic at the thought of it being pee.

Oh, please no, please.

Looking down, I see the crimson stain.

No!

This is way worse.

"Penny, what's wrong?" Collins asks, not understanding yet what I've done.

"I'm sorry."

Well, that wakes him up fully.

His body is upright, as his hands search my body. I roll into a ball over the stain, shielding myself from the embarrassment that I'll never live down, all while crossing my legs so no more leaks out.

If only this was a dream…

But life is rarely kind like that.

All this time I've been counting down days of our contract, hoping that I can somehow slow down time, but being careless with another important type of calendar.

Peeling me off the mattress in ball formation, Collins spots *the spot*.

"I will pay for dry cleaning or new sheets—whatever you want," I mumble.

"Penelope, are you hurt?"

I peek up at him between my lashes, while I stay curled up on his lap. "Emotionally damaged? Yeah."

Collins looks at me with such kindness that I can't help but look away. "Sweet girl, did you start your period?"

"Yes." My one-word affirmation can barely be heard even by my own ears.

"Look at me."

"No."

Gently prying my chin to face him, he coaxes me to give in to his wishes. "Look at me, Princess."

Finally I do. Tears sting my eyes. "I am mortified."

"I'm not sure what assholes you've surrounded yourself with in the past, but make no mistake… I am not some *boy* that gets all bent out of shape over something as natural as a woman bleeding during her cycle. So, Princess, my concern is not for some damn sheets but for how your body is coping with this time when you could be in physical pain."

I wipe at the tears in my eyes that have morphed into ones of gratitude for a man I never saw as ever being mine. But I can't stand the thought of him being anyone else's. "I don't deserve you."

Bending down, he kisses me on the forehead, and it holds just as much intimacy in that one sweet gesture as a mouth kiss would during some of our passionate moments. "You deserve the world, Penelope Hoffman. And this world is a better place with you in it."

I shake my head. "I've done nothing to contribute to society, Collins. I don't have a college degree. I don't put forth any volunteer efforts. I'm not running any charities. I've literally done nothing but find some way to force people to take care of me. It's pathetic."

"No, sweet girl. One day you will see what you do for others. And it isn't as insignificant as you think. What you provide is plain magic."

Collins scoops me up, just like he always has, and walks with me into the bathroom. There isn't a squeamish bone in his body as I probably bleed onto his arm, as I've already done his leg.

I still can't believe I let this happen.

That's the thing with injectable birth control—some women get sporadic periods, albeit lesser in intensity. If I was responsible enough to manage taking the pill, at least then I would know exactly when I would start my period.

Regardless, I've never met someone of the opposite sex that didn't shy away from all things pads and tampons—

ever. He is definitely breaking down some stereotypes that memes are made from.

He sets me gently onto the side of the bathtub and busies himself getting it ready for me. I watch with awe as he adds some essential oils to the water before helping me settle in.

Collins steps out of the room and returns with hot tea, a glass of water, some crackers, and a container of ibuprofen.

"You think of everything."

"You make me want to be the best version of myself, Penny. And caring for you is the easy part. *You* make it easy."

"I'm really sorry about the bed. I'll wash the sheets."

"Stop worrying about something so insignificant."

I take a few sips from the mug that Collins hands me. "Hmmm...chocolate-covered strawberry tea. Delicious."

"Glad you like. Are you in a lot of pain?"

I shake my head. "Not a ton, but the cramping seems to be picking up. I usually get pre-period cramps to warn me that it will be arriving soon. But this time I didn't get much foreshadowing. I should have been watching the calendar. I am one of those unfortunate ones who still get a period on the injectable birth control. I'm forever unlucky."

Collins shakes out a couple of pills and hands them to me. "Here. Make sure you eat some crackers with them and drink a lot of water. Staying on top of the pain will be best."

I relax into his version of pampering, allowing him to take care of my basic needs.

Sitting on the edge of the tub, Collins massages my neck and shoulders.

"You keep rolling out the red carpet for me, and I'll never want to leave."

It doesn't take long for the massages to move lower, over my heavy and sore breasts that get so sensitive around this time. Collins adjusts his pressure based on the tightening and loosening of my body, using my reaction as feedback on what I like and don't like.

My head tips back, resting against the side of the tub and between Collins's legs that are soaking in the water. He's still wearing his boxers.

"Is there room for me in the tub?"

It's a silly question because we've spent time in the water together, so I take it as if he wants to ensure my comfort level is okay—which is weird. If anyone should be uncomfortable, it should be him with sharing the same water with me.

I nod, craning my neck to give him a smile. "There's always room for you."

If Collins is fine with it, then maybe I should be too.

I revel in the front-row view of Collins undressing, enjoying every ripple and flex of his muscles.

The man is built like a statue made of steel.

"There's no part of you, Princess, that I am not enchanted by," Collins says, adjusting himself behind me so I can sit on his lap.

My legs splay open, allowing my knees to be on the outside of his. His fingers play with my inner thighs, walking along the path upward to my core.

"You always make me feel so desired."

"You are," he agrees. "And I know that there are ways to ease some of the tension from your cramps."

His fingers massage northward, getting dangerously close to my pussy.

Will he really want to sink his fingers into me when I'm on my cycle? Surely not.

Even being in the water, it has to be mentally weird.

Some guys can't even walk past the feminine hygiene aisle at the grocery store without getting squeamish.

Yet here is Collins, possessively sliding two fingers into me—claiming me during a time in my life that I didn't think he would find desirable.

"That feels so good," I moan, leaning into him.

"I want to get to know all parts of you, in every season." He swirls his fingers around, causing me to gasp. "I want to know even the parts that make you slightly uncomfortable. I crave that vulnerability, because it gives me the chance to convince your mind and body to align." He pulls out his fingers just to push them back inside. "Your pleasure is my pleasure."

"Hmmm…"

"We may not have everything figured out but just know that I am addicted to you. You are my greatest weakness and my greatest triumph. And I plan to savor our days together. Because I know that no matter how badly it will hurt me to let you go, it will hurt more to force you to stay."

"But what if I wasn't being forced? What if I want what we have created in the one hundred days?"

"It would be irresponsible for me not to allow you to fly, Princess. I have lived longer and had a chance to make mistakes and learn from them. You need that space to spread out and live as well."

I don't argue with him. Maybe he just needs time to realize that I'm willing to handle the fallout of us being together if it means that we get to choose one another after the embers turn to ash.

Shifting on his lap, I just try to live in the moment of Collins lazily finger fucking me, luring the pleasure I didn't think I could feel at this moment from my body.

Resting his other hand over my lower abdomen, he massages it in a circular motion, applying just the right amount of pressure.

I moan at the loss of fingers when Collins slips his hand down toward my ass, sinking between my cheeks.

"I'll have all of you, Penny."

I know what he's referring to, and I'm just not sure I'll ever be able to get more than his one finger up in there. "I've never…"

"I'll make you beg for it one day."

I highly doubt that, but I also didn't think having his finger there the other day would do anything either. And, well, I was driven crazy over that feeling of being full.

I allow Collins to continue to massage my most private area, toying and teasing with my backside entrance.

My body turns to mush as he caresses and plays with every erogenous zone, and I give him full access to do with me as he pleases.

When a hum escapes, it takes me a second to register it was from me. I never thought these types of touches would be able to harvest any pleasure from my already overstimulated body, but I was wrong.

Clearly, I don't know my body as well as he does.

Collins has my mind playing tricks on me, making me enjoy things I didn't think I'd ever consider. That's the effect he has on my self-control.

My face twists with some cramps, feeling like the medicine has yet to kick in. Reaching for my mug, I sip my tea and then offer some to Collins.

I need a distraction, something that will help me to forget that my insides are shredding and shedding.

Detaching myself from Collins, I back up and give him space.

I can feel a wicked grin forming on my lips over his curiosity. "Up and out," I instruct, slipping into my authoritative voice.

It's all fake. I don't have a dominant bone in my body in comparison to him. But this is too good of an opportunity to pass up.

I wait until Collins stands, his smirk in full-on display. Phew, he's enjoying this as much as I am. That's a relief.

"Now what?" he encourages.

"Butt on the edge of the tub. Legs slightly apart." I give him a moment to adjust. "More." I lower my voice. "You can do more."

Collins looks at me as if I'm someone else. It's kind of fun to keep him on his toes. "So bossy."

But at least he does what he's told.

I can't help but giggle. "I am, but too bad for you, you signed the contract. Now you are stuck with me."

"It's okay. I kind of like it."

"Kind of? Hmmm…we'll see how you feel after you're shooting your hot, thick cum down my throat."

I watch as Collins's eyes darken, and he reaches for the back of my head, guiding me forward gently but with clear intent—and it instantly changes the dynamic.

I had a few seconds of control getting him into this position, with me on my knees between his strong legs, but there's no part of me that has that power now.

It's as if I'm completely under the influence of Collins Stone.

Possessed by his possession...

And I'm not complaining.

"Open that sweet but sassy mouth of yours, Princess. Time to live up to the promise you just proposed."

I comply.

"I can't wait for you to fulfill the promises that you so freely offered."

When Collins leans forward, my natural reaction is to lean back, but the hand on the back of my head holds me still.

"You're being such a good girl."

His thumb pets the skin of my cheek, while the other holds firm in my hair.

One touch is soft.

The other touch is possessive—urgent.

"Loosen your lips and just give me a kiss. You can give me one kiss, right?"

I allow my lips to relax and feel the pressure at the back of my head coaxing me forward. With gentleness, I place the tip into my mouth and hum around it.

"Get accustomed to breathing through your nose, sweet girl. You're about to do a lot of it."

The tension I've been holding in my shoulders relaxes as Collins takes his time and walks me through every step along the way.

"I'm going to feed you another inch."

My hands use the backs of his knees for support as I

sink my butt farther into the water to get into a more natural position.

"Eyes on me."

I do as I'm told. And it feels fucking powerful to obey him.

"I don't want you to think of anything other than swallowing my cock." His hand that was once grazing against my cheek now curls around my throat, and I instantly feel my pulse quicken. "Relax your neck." He gives it a little squeeze. "More."

I nod and accept another inch.

"Keep breathing through your nose and press your thumbs into the palms of your hands to have less of a chance of triggering your gag reflex. Understood?"

"Yesh," I sputter, instantly regretting trying to talk. Spit dribbles from the corner of my lips, traveling down my chin.

Another inch.

My nose starts to flare as I try to maintain the eye contact.

"I'm going to love the feel of my cock deep in your throat. You can take another inch for me—right, Princess?"

Collins waits until I take a few breaths through my nose before he decides to push me forward to go a little deeper. I clumsily adjust.

"Look at you." His fingers tangle into my hair, gripping a fistful at the root.

I moan and tremble at the tight pain.

"Easy. I won't do anything your body doesn't crave."

Steadying myself, I allow all the saliva pooling in my

mouth to escape around Collins's cock and then rock on my knees.

In and out.

Collins's hand at my throat massages me, while playing around with the pressure of his hold.

I feel stuck…bound to him.

And I revel in it.

I want to be his good little girl.

And it's that praise and the way his eyes darken when I push myself beyond what I think I'm capable of that motivates me to keep trying.

To keep swallowing…

And I do to the point where I'm choking and tears are running down my face.

But I keep going.

In and out.

More and more.

With my nose pressing against the skin of his lower abdomen, I keep sucking.

"Look at you, swallowing your first cock. Just like a good girl…"

I feel his eyes on me without being able to make that contact with him. And I feel like a freaking warrior.

The water around me has since cooled, but the heat running through my face and upper body is at scorching levels.

And for a second I forget to breathe and struggle to maintain focus.

My eyes cloud.

I groan around his cock and then return to steady nose inhales and exhales.

"Yes, Princess, choke on me. Give me those beautiful tears. Swallow me down like a good girl."

And when he removes both hands from me and uses them to rest his body weight on, I know I'm too far gone to stop now.

"Now I need you to slide your mouth and tongue along the length, pulling back and then swallowing in. Can you do that, Princess?"

"Mm-hmm…"

Mimicking the motion with his hips and with the help of one hand on the base of my neck, I get into a rhythm.

Saliva drips down my chin, but I ignore it and am silently thankful for the lubrication. My jaw tenses as I work Collins in and out of my mouth, loving the low growly sounds vibrating from his diaphragm.

"Fuck, I'm close."

I suck him in and pull myself off of him. Over and over.

But it's his roar and the feeling of his length going as rigid as steel that prepares me for the eruption of hot and thick cum hitting the back of my throat. Some pools inside my mouth and some shoots completely down into my stomach, as I drain him of every last drop until he has no more to give.

Still thrusting his hips, Collins maintains the rhythm, lifting up off the tiled tub.

I slump forward, feeling the exhaustion from the full-blown workout.

Collins slips out of my mouth.

Reaching his hands for me, he tilts my face to him and squeezes my cheeks inward.

"Swallow," he commands.

And I do, drinking the last bit of him.

"That's a good girl. You did so well."

I offer a lazy smile. Feeling the side effect of coming down from the high, my body is overcome with exhaustion.

My cheeks are the best kind of sore, and I am thankful that I could give Collins this one experience, when he has already given me so many more.

Within seconds, I'm picked up and cradled.

Taking his thumb, Collins wipes some of his release from the side of my mouth that I didn't even realize escaped.

I laugh.

"What's so funny?" He looks amused.

"It's like you make my brain go to mush."

"I feel the same way."

He then takes his thumb and slides it between my lips for cleaning. I suck on it, enjoying the taste that is only Collins Stone.

Grabbing a washcloth, Collins wets it under some warm water from the faucet. Then he proceeds to clean off my face.

I must look like a mess. I basically feel like one.

But I just don't care.

Closing my eyes, I allow Collins to take care of my basic needs, laughing as he places the water bottle back up at my lips and orders me to drink.

I am feeling so relaxed that I just comply.

"It's as if you face fucked all the sass out of me," I mumble.

"And I'll do it again if you use that filthy mouth of yours as a weapon against my willpower."

"Challenge accepted."

We stay like this, in the moment, laughing and enjoying each other's silliness.

I never thought Collins would have a non-serious side to him, so when it comes out from hiding, I pay extra attention.

"Collins?"

"Yes, Princess?"

"Do you have, um, feminine products for me? Or should I just go grab something from my place?"

Moving to his linen closet, he pulls down a bin that appears to have everything I need—and even a few things I've never tried before like six types of menstrual cups and hypoallergenic wipes. "If there is anything missing, I will get it promptly delivered. Just name it. I also have a heating pad for you in the middle drawer of the nightstand."

I dig through the pile of supplies, trying to think of anything I may need. "This is great. Thank you."

Collins gives me some privacy, and I tend to my personal needs and get dressed in a lounge set while he meanders into the bedroom.

When I join him, he's standing at his window, looking out over the city.

So many contractual days have passed, and it feels like it was a day ago when we signed the papers. It's hard not to draw a comparison between this experience and my time at Soulful Mind when I thought of it as wasted time.

This experience doesn't seem wasted.

This seems relevant. Essential.

Opening his arms, he gestures to me to walk into them.

I hum and close my eyes, enjoying the euphoric feeling

of contentment, while leaning my weight against the man who I never thought would want me.

He smells my hair, burying his nose in my layers. "You smell divine."

"Do you have a strawberry-scent fetish?" I tease, wiggling my body against his to find the perfect place.

"Only when your body is the host."

Turning serious, I lean back to try to find his eyes in the shadowy darkness. "Thank you for taking care of me, Collins."

Sweeping back some damp hair from my neck, I feel his lips at my ear.

Kissing.

Nibbling.

Collins is making all the pleasure sensations pulsate through me on a current that I never want broken.

"I take great care of my possessions, Princess. And you are the greatest one of all."

I should see this as a raging red flag.

This should be my reason to run.

I should demand for him not to consider me as an object —his property.

But with Collins, his need for control goes beyond the normal range.

And I am okay with it. I actually really like it.

Because if treating me like a princess on the streets and a slut under the sheets is how he takes that control...

So be it.

If collaring me and demanding me to crawl to him is how he gets his thrills...

So be it.

On a Fault Line

I'm in way too deep to back down now.

And why mess with a good thing when the universe basically delivered me the best sex of my life via a fancy contract that was signed in front of a real lawyer?

I wouldn't dare.

I can't mess with fate and live in peace.

And if staying months at Soulful Mind taught me anything, it was to preserve my peace.

I snuggle into his warmth and feel like I'm being lifted and carried to rest in a warm cloud.

Time passes in a funnel, and it isn't until a fuzzy comforter is pulled up over me that I realize I must be drifting off.

"You changed the sheets," I state the obvious. My words slur from drowsiness.

"I did."

"They smell so good."

Collins takes his place behind me in his bed, as I grip the blanket up to my neck in fistfuls.

In the safety of his arms, I dream of the future, when the one hundred days lapse but our relationship still continues.

As I shift, I feel Collins's strong arm slide over my hip, up to my stomach, and then attach itself with a light squeeze of my breast. His other hand settles right into my shorts and against my bare pussy.

It is so possessive.

So intimate.

Not even the string of a tampon will keep this man away.

And I can't remember a time that I've been this comfortable in front of someone.

Collins accepts me for me, mess and all.

And that is a beautiful realization.

When my mind starts to take stock of my surroundings, I hear Collins chuckle. "Hmm?"

"You're talking in your sleep."

I am? "What am I saying?"

"That you wish I was born with three cocks so I could please all your holes at once."

My eyes pop open, but then I realize quickly that he is teasing. "And the man has jokes."

Collins laughs, shaking my body slightly. "It's true."

"What did I really say?"

"That you want to go ice skating. Do you?"

I dart up in bed. "Hell yes, I do!"

14

PENNY

"Ooff!" I call out, as my knees and palms hit the ice. It's the fourth time I've fallen, and the dampness is soaking into my jeans. "It's these new skates." I examine the birthday gift that the girls got me, wondering if my laces aren't tight enough. "Maybe I just need to get used to them."

"Or it's your coordination," Collins counters with a laugh, basically doing donuts around me.

"I'm not a tree. Move along," I say.

"There's nothing wrong with marking my territory."

I glare at him. He's not even trying to help me up. I mean, I'm sure he would if I asked, but I'm not asking that smug man for a thing right now. And he better not pee on me. I am already so bitter that he's basically good at everything. Sure, he gave me the whole, "I've only ice skated once or twice," garbage, but he basically hit the ice doing twirly things and has the grace of a swan.

So annoying!

It's when I'm struggling to get upright that I feel myself

being tossed airborne. With a smirk that seems to be permanently etched onto his face, Collins places me back onto the ice and tugs me along with his hand, as we skate to some boy band throwback song.

We stay connected like this as the song fades into another.

And another.

And another.

A coating of sweat lines my face as my lungs pant for air. I didn't realize how fast we were skating until we stop and move off the ice for a bench break.

"Yes, my comfort zone."

Collins looks at me and shakes his head. "You might need those little kid walkers on wheels."

"I'd still manage to fall with one."

He thinks about it for a few seconds. "Yeah, most definitely."

"Hey! I'm just in awe that I didn't manage to knock us both down." I nudge him with my elbow. "I'm talented like that."

Collins smiles, looking like he barely broke a sweat. His body fills out a gray-and-black striped sweater, and I can't help but notice how buff it makes him look. "Do you want something to eat?"

"Cotton candy!"

"Any—"

"And caramel apples!"

"Do you—"

"Maybe nachos?" I shake my head. "No, I want popcorn. I love popcorn with the fake butter sauce that still tastes sort of like butter. Yeah, that. I want that."

Collins looks like he wants to say more but resists. He knows when I get this excited and passionate that he's at the mercy of my munchies.

"Junk food is my jam," I say softly. "We can share."

His eyes darken, sending a shiver down my spine.

Now that my body has had a chance to cool down, I watch as Collins stands up and walks toward the concession stand.

After several minutes, Collins returns with an empty calorie buffet tray of goodies. We both dig in.

I dunk a tortilla chip in the processed cheese dip, savoring the synthetic taste. "These are so good."

"I'm glad."

His eyes follow my every movement, making the butterflies in my stomach grow anxious. I never really cared if a man watched me eat before, and now I suddenly am conscious of how unladylike I must look as I shovel in chips oozing with cheese dip one at a time.

I switch over to the cotton candy—fully committing to stress eating—ripping off a piece from the pink sugar cloud and popping it into my mouth. Closing my eyes, I savor the taste. "There's something magical about this fairy goodness. I swear they put drugs in this stuff to make it so addicting."

When I decide to come back down from my high, Collins is still staring at me. I keep catching him watching me, and every look coats my insides with warmth.

If he continues to analyze everything I'm doing, I might scream. He looks hangry but refuses to dig in to the pit of carbs with me, at least not to the extent I'm blowing through a day's worth of calories. I wipe at my face with a napkin, worried I have something smeared on my cheeks.

VICTORIA DAWSON

"Here, let me," Collins says, grabbing my napkin and moving it along the side of my mouth. "There."

We have to maintain a platonic relationship when out in public, but he's the one who keeps initiating all of the seemingly innocent touches.

I look down at my new skates, rocking the blades along the rubber floor. "Thanks."

His eyes stare at my lips. "Anytime."

"I'm not just referring to you saving me from the food stuck on my face but for today. I have so much fun with you."

Collins's smile is genuine. "I haven't ice skated in a long time. I'm surprised I remembered how to do it."

I turn my body on the bench, propping up a knee. "Is there anything you're not good at?"

He thinks about it for a couple of seconds. "Hmm, no."

I smack his arm, causing him to fake wince. "You can be so cocky, Mr. Stone."

"And you can be so sassy, Miss Hoffman."

"You like it."

His smile is wicked. "I more than like it."

We pack up our belongings and put on our normal shoes, exiting the facility into the parking lot.

The drive back to Sky View is pleasant. I watch the sun set and think about how I got to this stage in my life.

A couple of months ago, I'd have laughed in anyone's face if they told me that I'd be signing a sex contract with this ultra private man.

But here I am, riding shotgun, being his passenger princess.

"I know you aren't going to like this…"

"Oh boy," Collins says, shooting his gaze my way. "Go on..."

"I'm going to need to at least show my face in my own apartment for a couple of hours."

"Why?"

"Because I haven't checked in with Luke in weeks. He has my cell number and we text on occasion, but I'm not really being a good roommate by deserting him."

"Fine. But I'll walk you to your door. And you're coming back to my bed tonight."

I nod and allow Collins to help me out of my side of the vehicle, which he always seems to enjoy. He grabs our skates from the trunk and carries them for us.

We walk to the elevator and exit onto my floor.

Digging through my handbag, I search for my key. After several seconds, I feel his warm breath on my cheek, as he leans over to put his key into the lock.

"Really?" I ask, turning and propping my hands on my hips.

"Yes, really."

"Don't you think that's a bit overkill?"

"What? Me opening your door or your reaction to me doing it?"

I feel a growl from deep in my belly, as I swipe the key from his hand and dump it into my handbag. "Thanks for the spare."

"You know I have more."

I grumble something unintelligible and wave goodbye without inviting him in. We've had this same repeat experience, and I doubt I will ever get used to him having his own set.

"Honey, you're home!" Luke calls out from the sofa. "Perfect timing."

He has on some sports game that I know nothing about nor care to learn. As a kid, I was dragged to my brothers' wrestling matches, and while I enjoyed screaming from the stands and eating buttered popcorn from the concessions, the extent of my enthusiasm ended there.

"For what?"

"For you to tell me all your secrets."

"What if there aren't any?"

Luke tosses a hand into the air. "Just make some up. The juicier the better. I need drama in my life."

"So there's this guy…"

Luke sits up straighter and plasters a serious expression on his face. "Tall, Dark, and Overcompensated?"

"What?" I shake my head. "What does that even mean?"

"Like he's using money or social status to overcompen-sate for inadequacy"—he points to his groin—"in the tool department."

I stare at him blankly and then flop down on the couch beside him. "I, um, I don't even know how to answer that. I mean, he has money."

"Is he older?"

"Yeah."

Luke plasters on a knowing smile. "Like a sugar daddy." When I don't answer, he lets out a huff. "Come on, you have to give more details. It's a rule."

"There's no rules, Luke."

He shrugs. "It's listed in the handbook."

I make a face. "What handbook?"

"How to Survive Being Roommates."

"Sounds boring."

"Sounds practical. And with you I need all the help I can get. Your species is so complex," he says with a whine.

"Luke, we really aren't."

"See, then it must just be you."

"Gee, thanks."

The doorbell rings, and Luke nudges me with his toes. "Go get it."

I glare at him. "Why me?"

He gestures to the screen. "I don't want to miss the game."

"It's a commercial."

"Shhh...you're being too loud."

Pushing myself off the couch, I make my way over to the door, half expecting to see Collins through the peephole. He would do something like that...drop me off for a minute and come get me again because he can.

Instead, I see Rex standing out in the hallway, holding a pizza box. I haven't seen him since the dating event that was such a disaster. Granted, that's not that surprising since I haven't seen much outside of the walls of Collins's bedroom.

I unlock the door and allow him in.

"Hey, Penny," he greets, giving me a one-handed hug.

"Hi. Are you coming to watch the game?"

"Yup. It's going to be a good one too."

I laugh. "Of course, you can predict the future."

He shrugs. "It's part of my charm."

Walking inside, Rex places the box down onto the coffee table, and the boys dig right in for a greasy slice.

"Is there even cheese on those things?"

Talking with a mouth full, Luke mumbles, "It's under all the meat."

I make a face. "Sounds manly."

"Oh, it is," Rex says with a laugh.

Luke pats the space between him and Rex. "Come join the threesome."

I walk down the hall to my room, calling back, "I would have if you didn't just make it weird."

"Dammit," I hear both of them hiss.

15

PENNY

"You're the only person I know who wakes up and immediately needs to take a nap."

Stretching my arms above my head, my fingers play along the headboard, as a yawn escapes my lips. "I feel like ever since I've been invited into your bed, you have made it impossible to think about sleep much."

"That's because your pussy is a greedy little thing."

Rolling on top of Collins, I giggle as his fingers tease along my sides. "I don't remember you complaining."

"Never. That was a compliment."

I laugh even harder. "When has calling anything greedy been a good thing?"

We spend the next few minutes laughing over absolutely nothing in particular. And it feels good.

It feels *too* good.

Yesterday, we spent a couple of hours apart, and I missed him—a lot. Despite having my own apartment separate from Collins, it's his enigmatic personality that makes me gravitate toward him.

We are friends and lovers, rather than bodyguard and client.

"What's the plan for today?"

Rolling onto my back, I look up at the ceiling. "Today, you teach me how to drive."

"Is that so?"

"It very much is, and I won't accept anything but 'yes, Princess' as an answer."

Collins lets out a boisterous laugh. "Get ready for the day and meet me downstairs. I'll get your car."

"It's here?"

"Yeah, why? Where else would it be?"

"Oh, I don't know. I just wasn't expecting you to actually be on board with teaching me today."

Collins gives me a confused look. "I'm trying to help you soar, Penny, not clip your wings."

I mouth a *thank you*, and then hurry myself through my morning routine.

When I'm done in the bathroom, Collins has already left the apartment to grab my car, which I assume is being stored in the parking garage down below.

It wouldn't be weird for Graham and Nic to deliver it here. I live in this building after all.

I lock up and walk toward the elevator and hit the call button.

I'm used to Collins being within a few inches of me but definitely appreciate the space to be independent. He must know I've been itching for a little space.

As promised, I'm wearing known but hidden trackers.

Some, I know their location while with others, I'm not privy to that information.

To be with Collins, this is something that I just have to accept.

Entering into a contractual relationship with him meant more to me than the annoyance of him knowing where I am all the time.

Plus, I wouldn't be able to trust that he wasn't putting trackers on me whether I agreed to them or not.

It's just easier this way.

Angie and Claire have accepted this—so maybe I can as well.

Men that have been surrounded by the evilness of this world need to make sure their loved ones are safe and accounted for at all times.

But I'm not Collins's loved one.

I'm just a client with benefits.

When I get to the lobby, I'm greeted by the friendly staff. Several ask me if I need anything, probably not used to seeing me without a chaperone.

I can't even open my own door without someone rushing to assist.

It's endearing... At least that's what I tell myself to normalize the abnormal.

Standing on the curb of the street, I wait until Collins parks my shiny new birthday present from my brothers in front of me.

When he gets out, I let out a whistle. "If I knew how hot my driving instructor was, I would have worn something super skimpy."

I'll never be able to prove it, but I swear he blushes.

I mean, he looks freaking hot with his casual clothes, so it's not like I'm exaggerating. He must have forgone shaving today, and I most definitely approve.

Dayum.

Mighty fine and all mine...

Collins eyes my exposed legs. "If your skirt gets any shorter, it will turn into a belt."

He helps me into the front seat, behind the wheel. I feel his attention on how much skin I'm showing. I didn't think this outfit through for actually sitting down.

"I probably should have worn panties."

"Fuck."

"No, thank you. I want to learn how to drive today, Sir. Come be my passenger prince."

"You're already driving me wild."

"That's the plan. Maybe if I distract you, I'll pass my first lesson."

Collins gives me the side-eye.

In all seriousness, I do want to learn the basics today and try to move past the guilt of missing out on a portion of my life. I was too afraid to even attempt to drive when I was originally old enough to try. I didn't see much of a purpose for it.

But now I do.

I take a few deep breaths, shaking off the nerves.

"How hard can this be?" I say it more to myself than to Collins. "I'm pretty good at those racing video games."

"This is a lot more serious than some video game, Penelope."

I bite the inside of my cheek to stop the onslaught of a giggle fest. I'm going to give him an aneurysm. "Sure, yeah," I agree, earning yet another look of disapproval. Sheesh.

Getting myself comfortable, I click my belt into place, which isn't much different than the miniskirt's width. He's right. I do look like I'm wearing a belt.

Then I get to work on the preparation.

Collins isn't in the passenger seat but a few seconds, and he's already huffing and puffing out his exasperated air. "What in the hell are you doing with the mirrors, Penny?"

I try to keep a straight face, but it's hard. Collins is just so...

Proper.

I rotate it clockwise and then switch and do it counter-clockwise. "I feel like the angles are all wrong." Settling on the mirror directed right on my face, I wait for his reaction.

"They aren't for doing your makeup, that's for sure."

"Well, I've been getting pointers from Claire on driving." Okay...that's what is going to set him over the edge. Clearly. But it's too fun to stop. "She says 'mirrors are for mascara.'"

Collins lets out a huge groan, and I can almost hear him counting to ten.

Aim higher, buddy.

This is way too much fun.

"Have you ever seen her drive? She's terrifying. So detox your brain from any advice she has given you."

"If it wasn't for Nic forbidding her from being behind the wheel, maybe she would stop sending me unsolicited driving lessons via text. I swear getting the car for my birthday has inspired her."

"She's unpredictable."

"Yeah, I agree. But she did predict you would overreact over this. And as I can see, you totally are."

"This is the normal reaction, Penny."

I shrug and take off my lightweight jacket to reveal my new T-shirt that Angie made for me for this very occasion. I can already tell he hates it. So, yay!

I look down at my custom shirt that says, *Stop Signs Are Suggestions.*

"Look at me."

"Hmm?"

"You are to follow all of my instructions, Penelope. Understand?"

I pout out my bottom lip but nod. "Fun time is over."

"That's correct. You goof around during this first lesson and there won't be a second. You can continue to be my"—he seems to search for the right word—"passenger princess for the unforeseeable future."

Except it is foreseeable...

Our entire relationship is built on a fault line, destined to fail at the first rumble of trauma or end after the one hundred days are up.

Regardless, the future is finite for us.

"Press the brakes, start the ignition, and put the car in drive."

We already had several pre-lessons, so the terminology is fresh in my head. I do as I'm told.

"Use your side mirror and check your blind spot, and when and only when it is clear, pull out onto the road."

We continue like this, where Collins bosses me around and I comply without hesitation. It is oddly comforting allowing him to take the reins, and I don't have to overthink anything.

There's no music.

There's no small talk to fill the quiet.

I just drive and drive, while Collins provides praise and feedback when necessary.

But when we start getting out of the city and into the more rural parts of the suburbs, I can't help but look over and admire my view. It literally stabs at my heart to think that the contract whose purpose is to give us the freedom to be together might be the kiss of death for us when it ends.

Can we go back to just being bodyguard and client?

Can we move on with our lives and act like we didn't just spend one hundred days exploring all parts of our bodies intermingled together?

I don't think I'll be able to maintain a professional relationship with him when we've been so *intimate*.

What happens if we can't stand to be around one another because it's too painful—traumatic?

"Watch the road, Penny."

"Hmm?"

"You are moving awfully close to the shoulder."

"Oh."

"What has you so distracted?"

"Your ball cap, worn jeans, and face stubble."

"You like me unkempt?" Collins's tone is of genuine curiosity.

I can't help but smile. He cares what I think. "I like you a little rough around the edges. It makes you look badass and less bodyguard-ish."

"Good to know. Now focus on the damn road before I force you to switch places with me."

"Sheesh, it's as if you were an army sergeant in your last life."

From the corner of my eye, I see a sadness wash over Collins, and I suddenly remember that he did mention he was in the military.

I want to look at him and dissect his reaction, but I also want to continue being in the driver's seat with Collins bossing me around. I kind of like it.

"I'm being insensitive," I say softly. "And I'm sorry. I completely forgot that you shared that sliver about your past with me, albeit with no details."

Collins clears his throat. When a minute has passed, I assume he is just ignoring me. "You know why I do contracts with the women I decide to have"—out of the corner of my eye, I see him make air quotes with his fingers —"relationships with?"

"Because you are a control freak who loves to have his pussy and boss it too?"

He lets out a hearty laugh. "I haven't laughed as much in my entire life as when I'm around you."

"You're welcome." I change my grip on the steering wheel and rest my back against the seat, finding my rhythm. "Seriously, though...I would love to hear your explanation." And I mean it.

"When I was in my twenties, I was moving up in rank in the military—a lot faster than the average soldier. I was quick, had reliable instincts, and thought fast on my feet. I was gaining respect and staying out of trouble, which was my reason for joining to begin with after high school."

I nod and offer a smile to let him know I'm listening, while steering the car straight.

"My best friend at the time was harboring a lot of jealousy, most likely stemming from insecurities in his past and feelings of inadequacy. It also didn't help that we liked the same woman, which was unbeknownst to me until I was too involved to let go of my own feelings."

I focus on the road, even though it feels as if Collins is about to drop a truth bomb on me. "And he blamed you for making a move on her?"

"Yeah, apparently. But he was very passive-aggressive about it. I didn't think he cared. My relationship with him changed as soon as she and I started to secretly see each other."

"Why in secret?"

"She happened to be our officer."

"That sounds very dramatic."

"It was. She was in a position of power over me, but she knew we both had a thing for her."

"Okay...women seem to pick up on those signals, so I'm not surprised. Then what happened?"

"We had a secret relationship for months. And we both had similar tastes in"—he pauses as he looks out the window and then back at me—"kinks."

"The spanking stuff?"

"Yes. And some more activities in that same lane."

It's starting to make more sense as to why I found Collins at Limit-X. I keep the steering wheel steady as I continue driving, while he keeps on talking.

"Our secret relationship progressed, until my best friend went behind my back to poison her mind with lies about me.

Saying I'm abusive to women. Trying to convince her that I'm the bad guy—despite most activities being her idea."

"That's really sad. Then what happened?"

"One night at a group gathering on base, someone slipped something in my drink."

My fingers clench the steering wheel. "You were drugged?"

"Yes."

He does understand. "I'm so sorry."

"I didn't remember anything from the night before, but photos surfaced that allowed me to believe that she was in on the entire thing as well."

"As one big setup?"

"Yes. They were both in on it and knew that the only way to fully be together and get him to move up in rank faster was to eliminate me."

"But how?" I pry.

"A drug test that should have been completely random followed the next day. And I knew then that my best friend set me up over the officer we both liked. I got kicked out for drugs in my system, coupled with relations with my superior."

"From the photos?"

"Yes."

"Did she get kicked out too?"

He shakes his head. "It doesn't always work that way and it doesn't always make sense. But being drugged and not remembering destroyed me. Building my life around the military and then that falling through was a hard pill to swallow. And getting discharged after years of service to my country was devastating."

It all makes sense. "This is why you sign contracts with your partners and are selective in who you allow into your life."

"Yes. I'd rather have consent be in writing and not used against me later on."

"I'm really sorry that happened to you. I can see why it would be very difficult to trust anyone after something as horrendous as that."

"I never made a best friend since. The closest thing to friends I have are your brothers."

"Thank you for sharing all of this with me."

"I'm simply telling you so you can understand that we all have things in our pasts. Things we wish we could change... But it's those things that sculpt our futures and help us to grow. Graham hired me long before you were drugged, but once my responsibilities shifted to finding your predator, it was clear that we were more connected from our pasts than I could have ever imagined. And that ability to find justice for you was what saved my life from the depressing downward spiral."

A solo tear falls from my eye, and I quickly wipe it in hopes it doesn't produce more. I wish Mark never kidnapped me, drugged me, and made me believe I was raped. I wish that I didn't spend time in a mental institution fighting to come back to the family that loves me without a single condition. I wish that every stranger I pass on the street wasn't tainted by the figurative dark glasses I can't stop wearing.

But here I sit, in my car, with my bodyguard talking about life.

And slowly, this enchanting man beside me becomes a

little more human, and I've become less bitter. Collins Stone sees me where I am and where I've been, because he has endured that pain of someone taking advantage of him for their own selfish gain.

And that is what suffering does for the human race. It bonds us together.

Ignoring Collins's directive to go straight, I take a sharp left.

"Where are you going?"

"Just a little detour."

"Pen..."

"Coll..."

Between Hillsboro and Portland, there are many scenic paths that I've taken on rides with my family growing up. Lazy Sunday road trips with Graham and Nic bickering nonstop from the back seat shaped my childhood. It's no wonder why Momma and Dad needed to have me to balance out that testosterone rage.

It was probably a blessing as well that my brothers took up wrestling as their sport of choice—if just to blow off some steam. It might have kept them from massacring each other as well.

But even at a young age, I didn't have a clear path. It wasn't like I excelled in any particular type of sport or hobby. I tried out dancing and gymnastics, but nothing really interested me long enough to pursue it past just something to do to keep busy.

It was as if I just coasted through life, doing relatively well academically and staying under the radar socially. Well...until Mark Tanner took me under his wing and then violated my trust in all men thereafter.

I was an easy victim, by coming alive with just a little attention.

Being naive is a curse…

And that's a curse I'm willing to try to break.

Taking another side road, I enjoy the feel of control at my fingertips.

Collins has only grabbed the steering wheel twice during the entire lesson, so I don't think I'm doing too badly.

He has a calming aura about him. And it's his gentleness that makes me want to keep driving with him, never wanting it to end.

Then I see a butterfly. So naturally, I slam on my brakes like any good human would do.

"Hell, Pen. Easy!" He looks over at me with concern, his fingertips digging into the passenger seat's leather. "What was that for?"

I point out the window. "I saw a butterfly. Obviously."

"Nobody brakes for butterflies, Penelope."

"I do."

I think about the silliness for a few seconds and then burst out laughing.

He's right.

"Maybe Angie can make you a custom shirt with the phrase 'I brake for butterflies' on it."

"I would love one," he deadpans.

And I just can't stop the giggles. "I can't see."

"That's a problem, Penelope. Pull over."

"Where?"

"Over th—" Collins grabs the steering wheel and then

slides his foot over to hit the brakes. "You almost got us stuck in a ditch."

He cuts the engine, holding out his hand for the keys.

"Uh-oh, I did it now."

And then the giggles return.

"Collins?"

"Yes, Princess?"

"I've never laughed this much either."

16

PENNY

It's only taken a few weeks to conclude that Collins and I are basically boring—but in a good way. A really good way...

I just never met someone who is content just being with me.

He makes me believe that my company is enough.

That I am enough...

We've been eating all meals together. Our outfits often consist of the same color schemes—which is only comical because some days we don't even bother with clothes at all. And we now have inside jokes on the stupidest things.

When I wake up first, I like to pull pranks on Collins by replacing his toothpaste with garlic paste. I unalphabetize his cupboard shelves and add mustaches to any pantry items that have faces on the labels. Or googly eyes... Those are basically the best ever, especially the really large ones that are in the craft aisle in any department store.

When I'm feeling super ballsy, I tie his shoelaces together or hide my panties around for him to maybe find. Another good prank was when I put a pair in the dry cereal box, and I timed how long it took him to notice.

Tied as my favorite with tricking him over the contract is the time I switched out one of his pens with one that says in a little voice, "I love penis," every time the tip contacted a surface. It cost me over forty dollars from one of those online boutique shops, but it was worth it. Collins is worth it.

But most importantly, I'll never get tired of seeing his reaction to my lame attempts at humor.

Almost always, I end up over his knee with the shape of his hand imprinted on my bare ass cheeks, loving every second of his version of revenge.

As much as it stings and as much as I try to wiggle away, it's that roughness from someone that won't truly hurt me that I crave.

My therapist at Soulful Mind told me it's my way of gaining back control from a situation that went tragically wrong. I bet Margo would agree too, although I haven't been to a session in a while.

Everything Collins and I do is consensual. I allow it. I have a choice.

But when Collins wakes up first, I'm often roused from my sleep by his mouth finding its home between my legs. And that is by far the only thing that will trump my need for a prank any day of the week.

Because when he's sliding his tongue between my folds, he savors it.

It's as if time stops and he has no better place to be than living in the moment.

And it's then that I also center myself and truly remember that I am worthy of that level of pleasure.

"I can't wait to find out what flavor of toothpaste you chose for me today," he says with a chuckle, as he grabs ahold of my waist and tickles.

"Don't worry, I didn't wake up much before you. I think part of me was hoping to be eaten out, but I could only fake sleep for so long before I gave up."

Collins's hands take a leisurely stroll down my body, and I melt into his touch. "You never need to fake anything with me, Princess. If you want something from me, ask. I enjoy taking care of your needs."

I shift my legs to allow him better access. "Yes, right there, right there."

He laughs, which in turn makes me laugh.

It's this lazy comfort that I find so addictive.

"What's the plan for today?"

I try to think but just can't, because Collins can't stop making me feel good.

His skills are better than caffeine when it comes to waking up my senses.

Arching my back, I allow him to massage me to the stirrings of an orgasm.

He squeezes and rubs my breasts, while his other hand pinches and pulls my clit.

I can't tell whether it hurts or feels good.

The walls of my pussy contract with the anticipation of being penetrated again by Collins Stone. I want him to ruin me and make me crave only his body so that any other guy that comes along will pale in comparison. I know this is temporary, but I want the permanent memory etched into my head of being owned by my bodyguard.

His lips find my neck and—

Yup. That definitely hurt.

"You bit me?"

"You tempted me with your delectable neck."

"Oh, no. This isn't my fault."

But when he goes rough with his hand on my breast and soft with his hand on my pussy, it's my undoing.

"Let go, Princess."

And I do, with his name imprinted in my throat, as I scream out in ecstasy.

"Fuck, yeah. Scream for me."

And that is how fast an hour can pass.

It takes several minutes to come out of my pleasure fog and form a coherent thought.

"As much as I want to spend my day in your bed, I have to work."

"Why?"

"Because some of us have to do more than just be a fuck doll during the day."

"All I'm saying is if you need money, I will always have you covered."

"I don't need money, Collins. I need a purpose. Because…" When this is all over, I'll need something to bury myself in while I recover from the heartache.

"You have a purpose, Penny. You just think you need work to define you, when you don't."

"Well, what defines you, Collins?"

"Work."

I slap his arm. "See? This is my point."

He kisses me on the forehead, which is such a contradiction to how he rails me in the bedroom. "Listen. You *shouldn't* allow something as nonpermanent as a job define you. That's all I'm saying."

I prop my hands on my hips. "Then what is my purpose?"

"You bring joy to everyone you encounter."

"Yeah, right." Tell that to Jill at the office. I swear she doesn't like me and tolerates me at best.

"And you are so humble about it that you don't even see the effect you have on others."

A sadness washes over me. "I appreciate you saying all of that. I just think that for someone to be more than a ghostly memory after their time on earth is up, they need to do something more profound and meaningful."

"Sometimes it's the smallest, seemingly insignificant things in life that can make the biggest impact."

"Huh," I say thoughtfully. "I never thought of you as being so philosophical. But I like it."

Collins smiles. "Glad you approve. Now, tell me about the agenda today. How can I be of service?"

Then his phone rings.

And it rarely rings. So I predict it is important.

"Take the call. I'll go get dressed for my first photoshoot with Plus None."

As much as I enjoy the marketing side of the business, I was first hired to do the modeling. It's a big day for me, and I just want to do a good job to show how versatile I can be.

I meander into the closet where my wardrobe is hanging. Because hair and makeup are done on-site, I don't need to do much to prepare other than show up in some clothes of my choosing. The email with the details said that a dressing room will be set up in a portable tent and that the shoot will start in a studio and then move to the river.

I throw on a pair of cute shorts and a tank, pairing them with some bejeweled sandals. I then mosey into the bathroom to wash my face and brush my teeth.

It feels like so long ago that I was here at Collins's place just to sleep. Even then, he was protecting me and looking out for my best interests.

I find Collins sitting on the end of the couch when I make my way into his living room.

"Everything okay?" I ask.

"I'm going to need Chris to drop you off at your shoot. I have something that needs my attention that cannot wait."

I rock on my heels. "Okay."

"He might not be able to stay the whole time. But Plus None has their own security, as per Graham and Nic's demands. So you should be safe."

"Of course I'll be safe. Why wouldn't I be?"

"I don't like being away from you," Collins states simply, as if that's enough explanation for his now hyper-paranoia. "Keep your phone on, even if it's in your bag. And keep your ankle bracelet on."

I look down at the dainty platinum chain that I often forget I'm wearing because it's that comfortable. "Got it. You seem really stressed."

Collins fakes a smile. "I just want to make sure you are safe. You really have to go to this photoshoot?"

I nod, growing concerned that he'll forbid me from

going, knowing that there's probably a clause I skimmed over that will make this even more challenging. "I need to go."

"Okay. I'll take you to the lobby. Chris should be here soon."

Grabbing my stuff, I make my way to the front door.

As soon as my feet step out into the hallway, I remember to detach myself from Collins—just in case. It's not that I expect my brothers to pop around the corner and surprise me, but the paranoia of getting caught is still very fresh in my mind.

When I'm in public, I have to constantly remember that we aren't together. I can't just put my arm around him or fix his tie or prank him.

"Did you tell Chris about us?" I ask, as we enter the elevator.

"No. But that's only because he figured it all out on his own."

"Oh... Is it that obvious?"

"Chris and I go way back. We used to train together and go on missions together."

"I'm assuming not for a church youth group."

He looks at me with mirth. "No, Penelope. Missions for the United States military—ones that were a bit more complex."

"I'm sorry you had to leave on bad terms."

"Me too."

I silently hope Collins tells me more. He's already opened up so much more than I ever expected during my first driving lesson, but I want to know about his youth.

"How do you cope without having a family network?"

He shrugs. "I just got very used to having no one to count on."

"You are a self-made man, Collins Stone."

He lets out a chuckle. "I guess I am."

It does make sense, in a way, that he always has time to do whatever my brothers hire him to do. It's not like the man really has a day off. He is always working.

I may be Collins's current responsibility, but the dedication to my entire family is what really bonds us all together.

With so many thoughts lingering in my mind, they are quickly forgotten when the doors open and Chris is hovering like a hot air balloon waiting for us.

The man is tall and bulky with huge muscles. He looks more like a bouncer than a bodyguard. I doubt I'll ever get used to his presence.

He tilts his head to me. "Miss Hoffman." And then shakes hands with Collins. "Good to see you again, Redeye."

"Why do you call him that?" I ask, finding my voice again.

"Because—"

Collins shoots him a look. "Because I used to handle a lot of the night missions and red-eye flights."

"And he could do crazy stuff with little sleep. Best there was."

"What constitutes crazy?" I ask, genuinely curious.

"Oh, that's all top secret. But Collins Stone is legendary."

"Was," he corrects.

I frown. There's a sadness to his voice over his discharge. He seemed to excel at that type of work, which is not surprising. When Collins has a job, he goes all-in with the challenge.

Dammit to the assholes who screwed him over.

Leaving the only thing you think you're good at had to have been traumatic for Collins. He opened up to me during the driving lesson, but it's now that I see his interaction with his friend that makes what he left behind all very real.

The more I get to know this man, the bigger the picture I can paint in my mind of what makes him who he is.

Collins's gaze turns to Chris. "Keep her safe. The photoshoot should have security on-site. Touch base with them before leaving the premises for any reason."

"Easy, man, I got this."

Collins directs his attention to me. "Miss Hoffman?"

Oh, we're doing the formalities now? I straighten my posture, but resist saluting. "Yes, sir?"

A smirk plays on his lips. "Please don't advocate for a detour."

"Not even to Twisted Shake?"

"Correct."

"How about Scalawag's for the dinner special?"

He shakes his head at me. "No one goes to a Gentleman's Club for the food."

I pout. "No fun."

"But the food is great," Chris points out. "Been there twice already. I found it on Google."

Collins whips his body around to glare at him. "Shut up."

Then I stick my tongue out at both of these men. I do it because I know my ass cheeks are safe here in the lobby of our apartment complex. I also do it because I know Collins will punish me for my sass later.

And it's that sparkle in his eyes that tells me it will all be worth it.

When I accepted the job at Plus None, I knew that the overall work environment was going to be fantastic based on my bosses, and every time I do anything affiliated with the company, my initial instincts are proven to be true. I just never expected to be having this much fun, while splashing in the Willamette River.

The last four hours was spent in the studio doing indoor shots for upcoming boxes. However, being outside and in nature is my jam. All of my senses are awakened, and I feel like I'm in my element, so much so that it will never feel right accepting the salary and benefits the girls are offering to me. This is way too much fun to be considered work.

But deep down, I know that to stand out, I need to put forth a little extra effort to make this special.

Despite Angie and Claire not wanting to pressure me, I feel like this is my one moment to prove myself.

"Give me flirty, with a side of sophistication," the photographer directs, snapping pictures of me, while I scrunch up the hem of my white sundress. "Yes, that. That there makes Gino happy. Do more of that. Bring it up to your face. Now look off in the distance and smile." His friendliness allows me to relax into the task, making my mind float off into another place while my movements become as fluid as the river. "Beautiful. That. Keep doing that dreamy thing. You look like an angel."

Swaying my hips, I find my groove, allowing my movements to match the energy.

"Is this newfound inspiration about a boyfriend or someone you have a crush on?" Gino asks.

"I, um, don't…" Have a boyfriend. I mean, Collins isn't a crush either.

But what is he?

My bodyguard with benefits… That's what he is. But I sure as hell am not revealing this information to Gino.

"Oh, I see…"

"Hmm?"

"This is a secret relationship?" he asks, but it comes out more as a statement, as he continues to snap shots of me that I can only assume aren't that flattering. "Nothing says 'fuck me now' like a forbidden romance."

And I lose my composure, bursting out into laughter.

"Yes, girl! These candid shots are going to be gold. I just hope that this secret man of yours is the kind of guy who will suck you at a sex club and then vacuum out your car the next day."

My giggling can be heard probably a mile away. Not only is Gino's description of Collins spot-on, but every time I think of him, I can't help but feel joy radiating through me.

Pictures get snapped as I recover from laughing so hard my cheeks hurt.

But when I tilt my head to the side, I catch the sight of a crowd of onlookers, hanging out on the beach watching me *perform*. A shyness rushes over my skin, and I can feel the heat from the golden hour's sun reach my ears.

"Hey, I lost you," Gino says, snapping his fingers. He turns and looks back at the shoreline. "Wow, you already have a fan club starting."

I hide my head into my hands, peeking out between my fingers. I'm trying to sell the clothes that Angie has made with her own hands, and yet, the audience gathered makes it seem like I'm selling myself instead.

Gino keeps snapping away, but my eyes keep shifting to those gathered around watching me. "Why are you in your head now?"

"Because I feel like my job is to sell the clothes, and I'm not sure I'm doing that great of a job at that."

Allowing his camera to fall around his neck on the strap, Gino makes his way toward me, sloshing through the water. "Girl. It's rarely ever about the clothes in this modeling world. If we just wanted to sell clothes, then we would put them in a light box and skip having anyone wear them. But you are a brand. You are a vibe. You are the *it* girl for the company. When potential customers see the photos of you having fun, they will want to buy in to that experience too."

I offer him back a weak smile. "I just don't believe in myself the way I think Angie and Claire believe in me."

Gino clasps his hands over his heart dramatically. "Oh, my heart. When you doubt yourself, you also doubt everyone else working on this team. But when you believe in yourself, it shows that you trust us all to make this adventure work."

Well, when he puts it that way… "Thank you."

Leaning in to each other, we hug. I needed this.

Moving back into position, I roll my shoulders and

shake off the self-doubt that seems to plague me every time something good is happening in my life.

And I try not to think about the expectations of getting the perfect picture. I try not to obsess over moving in flattering positions.

I just allow the experience to take over me.

Time passes, and the golden rays of the sun move forward into the horizon, casting a warm glow to everything it touches.

There's something special about this time of the day.

When the adrenaline surrounding the photoshoot wears off, the water sloshing around my calves feels a little bit cooler. The air a little less balmy.

I scan the crowd and then—

No.

I blink.

But he's still there…

Mark Tanner.

Snippets of memories flash across my vision, like marbles rolling around in a box.

Mark Tanner is here.

I squeeze my eyes shut, trying to eradicate my mind from the ghost of him.

He's in prison. I confirmed he was there. And he's still rotting away behind bars.

He was the promise keeper for me becoming something in the modeling world.

And I was the catalyst that eventually brought him to his knees.

His face darkens in the recesses of my mind, and a

sinister laugh escapes. I feel a chill running up my legs, working its way to my arms.

"Penny?"

Hands grab me, and I crumble into the water's current, allowing the coldness to soak entirely into the clothes I'm here to model.

"I need help," I whisper.

I will always need help.

The memory of the monster is a disease waiting for the most inappropriate time to declare war on me.

"How can I help?" Gino asks, hesitant to touch me, probably worried to set me off even more.

My shoulders curl forward, trying to wrap myself into a cocoon of safety.

I dare not look back at the crowd.

Chills run up my arms.

"Let's get you dried off."

I don't blame Gino for being afraid. I'm even afraid of myself sometimes. The guilt is extreme, knowing that my bad judgment of character in Mark Tanner has had my brothers risking their lives to exact revenge on the whole drug ring. What I thought I had healed from is really just an illusion.

"Don't tell Angie or Claire," I whisper. First freaking day on the job, and I already have made a fool of myself. Maybe I'm not ready to be back in front of a camera. Maybe I am just as broken as I was the night that Mark shattered the belief I had inside that some men can be decent humans. "Please." My voice cracks with my plea. This is so embarrassing.

"Miss Hoffman, are you okay?"

It's Chris. He's here.

"Please don't tell Collins that I freaked out."

He'll never allow me at another photoshoot again if he learns how upset I got at this one. Maybe it's too soon to be here. Maybe I'm not as healed as I pretend to be.

If Collins sees me now, he'll know right away something is wrong with me.

Gino watches as I pick myself up out of the water and wring out my outfit. "I'm sorry I ruined the photoshoot." Then I notice Chris is soaked from the knees down. "I'm sorry."

I can't stop apologizing.

I literally ruined everything.

"Sweet girl," Gino soothes, "you didn't ruin a single thing. I got so many amazing shots."

"Ones of me crying?"

"You'd be surprised how gorgeous someone can look when they are a slave to their true emotions. It's not just pretty posed pictures that sell merchandise. Real women sell it." He gives me a warm smile. "And as far as I can tell, you are beautifully real."

I wipe at a tear running down my cheek. "Thank you," I whisper, feeling vulnerable again. I'm long overdue for a therapy session. If I'm going to stay out of the facility, I need to start taking better care of myself.

When we make it back onto dry land, Gino's assistant hands me a towel. I wrap it around my upper body, twisting the ends between my fingertips. He eyes Gino, who brushes him off with the sweep of a hand.

Chris is back to his hovercraft ways.

Taking out his cell, he appears to send out a text.

Dammit.

"Please tell me you aren't betraying me."

He sighs. "I don't think you quite understand my self-preservation skills or Collins's need to make sure you are safe at all times. If I choose to lie, I choose to die."

"I'm safe," I grumble.

"You need to be mentally safe as well," he chides.

I shrug. "I cried. People cry. Let's move on."

A chill hits my body again, as I remember seeing Mark Tanner's face in the audience of onlookers. He's haunting me, and he isn't even dead.

And I don't think there are enough therapy sessions that can negate the impact he made on my entire future.

He tainted me.

And his memory is a stain that can't be eliminated.

I hate him.

I fucking hate him.

And as long as he is on this earth, I feel like he'll always have a choke hold on me.

I am wrapped in a blanket that I don't even remember being placed around me when Collins arrives.

There's no point being mad at Chris. He was just doing his job—just as Collins is doing his.

I am the assignment.

The assignment…

The assignment…

I am the assignment.

I am the pathetic assignment.

Pathetic…

I am the dramatic, pathetic assignment.

I am the whiny and dramatic, pathetic assignment.

I am...

"Pen?"

I am...

"Penny?"

I am...

"Penelope?"

I am...

"Princess?"

I...

17

COLLINS

"Penny? I need you to come back to me."

I'm kneeling on the rocky ground of the river's shore, rubbing soothing circles along her cheekbones.

C'mon, dammit.

Penny rocks back and forth, hugging her knees to her chest. Her eyes are blank, like she is looking right through me.

Snap out of this!

"She's in shock. What happened here?" I demand. "Did something spook her? Did someone say something wrong to her? How did this happen?"

Not many things cause me to panic, but seeing Penny in this state again—after all the months of progress made at the facility—is causing me a high level of unease.

"Nothing that I saw," the man with the camera says. "One second I'm getting beautiful shots of her at peace. The next, I'm getting beautiful shots but with tears rolling down her cheeks."

Something had to set her off. "Penny, what scared you?"

I glance around the space. Nothing seems off, except for all the eyes watching us, and the mild feeling of unrest I have itching at my spine.

"Get rid of the audience," I yell at the security guards who are surrounding us. "I'm moving her."

"Should we contact Mr. Hoffman?" one of them asks, obviously talking about the one who supplements his paychecks with what are most likely weekly bonuses.

"I'll fill him in."

"Penny? I'm going to lift you up and carry you to the SUV, okay?"

Gently, I place an arm under her knees and one around her back. It's like lifting a feather. A fragile feather…that can fall at the first sign of wind.

It's as if the life in her no longer is there, and the weight from that vibrancy is hollowed out.

Turn on the light, Princess.

Within minutes, I have her—in ball form—in the passenger side of my SUV.

Rounding the front of the vehicle, I keep my eyes trained on Penny.

I've seen her like this before, but it was when she was first brought to Soulful Mind. She wasn't talking to anyone. It terrified and destroyed the Hoffman family, and it will destroy them again if she slips back into that state of mind.

I open the driver's side door and slide inside, rolling my shoulders back.

I'm tense.

But nothing compares to the emotional torment Penny must be feeling.

She is paralyzed by fear. But what got her this shook?

Reaching for my phone, I find the number for Dr. Saber.

"Hey Mitch, it's Collins."

"Hey, is everything okay? I mean, probably not if you are calling."

"It's Penny. She's slipped into an unresponsive state."

"Where are you?"

"I am down at the waterfront"—I scan the area for a landmark—"just two blocks from High River Cafe. North."

"I'll be right there. But in the meantime, just keep talking to her and try to lure her back to the present. She's likely stuck in the past and just needs a reason to be in the present."

"Okay. I'll try."

"I just hopped in my car. I'm ten minutes away."

"See you soon."

I disconnect the call and find Chris's name in my contact list and shoot him a text.

Collins: I need you to investigate everyone present at the photoshoot. See if they have a head count or list of those present. Check if anything seems off. I need to know what happened with Penny.

Chris: On it - going to request video footage from any of the parking lots and area businesses

Collins: I also need you to alert Graham Hoffman that I have his sister and that I'm getting her help

It's the unknown of what has caused her to freak out that is bothering me the most.

I don't do well with the unknown.

Because I am a fixer. And I can't fix things when I don't know what caused the breakage.

Using my phone, I pull up the Grace and Jace soundtrack that Penny insists on me storing on my phone, and play it lightly through the car's sound system.

Penny can't stop shaking.

My windows are tinted, so I move my seat backward and pull her into my arms.

Selfishly, I need to hold her and feel her warmth.

"Come back to me, Princess."

My hands rub at her back, slow and deliberate circles, while I whisper in her ear.

"Do you remember when I told you I was adopted? Yup. I always yearned for a family like yours. The people who adopted me after my grandparents passed were older, and they too left this life before guardians really should. I'm not jealous or anything. I'm thankful that you have the parents and brothers that you have. They love you, Penny. And I do too."

I shift her in my arms, playing with her hair. And I continue to try to just be with her.

"Your brothers love you so much they hired me to come check in on you in Seattle. I visited a few times a month. Sometimes I would even get a hotel for a long weekend and stay and monitor your progress. I was there, Penny. Like an invisible string, just trying to be the tie that held the Hoffmans together, just as I am now."

The song changes over to a different one, and Penny leans her head against my neck.

"Come on, sweet girl. I know you are in there, probably screaming to come out of the fog. You can get there. Focus on my voice. I need you back with me, changing out my iced tea in the fridge with water and chocolate syrup. You know I almost choked that day you did that? How about that time you changed all my shoelaces to neon pink ones? Or the time you plastic wrapped the door? You didn't even get to see my reaction when I tried to walk th—"

Penny's little giggle is barely a whisper.

"Princess?" She doesn't say anything, so I keep talking to try to coax her out of her hiding place. "I think the smell of popcorn is permanently engrained in the wall paint of my apartment. I catch whiffs of it when I walk past certain areas."

Penny's fragile body stirs, as if she's fighting some mental demons. She just needs to allow me to fight them with her. It's not realistic to do this alone.

"I need you to come back to me, Princess."

And then her eyes open. "Where are we?" she whispers, her throat seeming dry.

Holding her face in my hands, I kiss her cheeks, squeezing her warming body to me.

"Oh, thank goodness you are back."

"Where did I go? I'm really confused."

Tears roll down her cheeks, and I try to catch as many as I can with my thumbs.

"Don't cry. Please, don't cry. You're going to be okay."

"Are you listening to Grace and Jace without me?"

I let out a laugh. "No. We were listening to it together," I defend.

"I don't remember."

"I know. But you might once your brain has a chance to sort through the pieces."

I'm just not sure I want her to remember. If remembering causes her to enter a semicatatonic state, then I'm not sure it's worth it. I need Mitch here to guide us through the next steps.

While he's not a psychologist, he'll know what to do. Dr. Saber has been a positive influence on so many people, it's no wonder he's the doctor on retainer for most of the Hoffman family.

Penny looks down at her damp dress. I didn't even consider she's still soaking wet, and now I am too.

"I was at a photoshoot, wasn't I?"

"You were."

"And you had something to tend to beforehand, so Chris brought me."

"That's correct."

She shakes her head, as if trying to get all the fog to fade so she can understand what got her to sitting on my lap in my SUV.

Confusion mars her features, wrinkles forming on her forehead. "I saw something…"

Penny hasn't had a major setback like this in a while, and now she is confirming my suspicion. "I think so too."

I'm hesitant to pry for details, and don't have to make that decision because I see Mitch walking down the sidewalk toward us.

Penny slithers back onto her seat, and I instantly feel the void.

I want her in my arms.

I want to listen to her breathing and feel the warmth of her soft skin.

I also want to continue on with the rest of our one hundred days without drawing any conspicuous attention to us.

Enough information will get relayed back to Graham. The last thing we need is to deal with that fallout.

Going to Penny's side of the vehicle, Mitch opens the door.

"Hi, Penny. It's Dr. Saber…Mitch. How are you doing?"

A sob breaks out of her throat. "I need help."

He gives her a hug while she cries into his shoulder.

They share a special bond, and I bite back the jealousy trying to claw its way to the surface.

Releasing the hold, Mitch examines Penny by shining a light in her eyes and asking her a series of questions involving the year, the president, and her birthday.

"Have you been attending your local sessions here in Portland?"

"Yes. I saw Margo. But I'm not doing it regularly."

My head jerks over to them. I thought she was going consistently.

Dammit. I should have pushed her in that direction or at the very least paid closer attention to her schedule.

So much has happened since she got released from the facility.

With Penny now spending all of her free time with me, I should have realized she wasn't following through on her end of the deal that was the stipulation to being released in the first place.

"Well, we need to change that," Mitch states. "There's a reason the therapists were diligent about making sure you understood the importance of the protocol once you got released. If you neglect the essential components of recovery—and, Penny, you will probably always be in some stage of recovery—then your equilibrium will be off-balance. This is why holistic medicine is being studied more now. We finally realized that fixing things from only one point of view doesn't actually fix anything. We aren't looking for a Band-Aid approach for this. Instead we are looking for fluid healing through multiple channels."

"Okay," Penny agrees. "You're right. I'm going to take my therapy regimen more seriously."

"Great. You seem like you are back to a good state, so I'm going to go. Be sure to let me know if you need my assistance in any way."

"Thanks, Dr. Saber," Penny says, looking a little shy now that the excitement has worn off.

Mitch closes the door gently.

"Leave it to me to cause all the drama."

"Penny..." My tone is of warning. I don't want her to ever think like that.

"Maybe I can go back to the photoshoot and continue shooting. I'm certain Gino got nothing out of today that is worth salvaging."

Turning to her, I snap on her seat belt and tuck the fleece blanket around her legs. "There's nothing I am concerned with right now, other than taking care of you." My fingers tilt her chin up so I am looking into her eyes.

"There is not one thing you should feel ashamed of or shy about."

Penny sighs, probably too emotionally drained to argue. "Okay."

"I'm glad I was able to get here for you."

"But you had something important to do…"

"Nothing is more important than you, Princess. Everything else can wait."

"Collins?"

"Yeah?"

"Thank you."

18

COLLINS

A week has passed since Penny's episode at the waterfront which shook me more than I ever let on. Every day since, I've had this clawing feeling in the back of my mind that something evil is lurking on the horizon. I felt it both days we visited the café but left before eating, and I felt it down at the waterfront.

But nothing unusual is popping up no matter how many more people I hire to keep a lookout.

In the days since that incident, Penny has been working in the Plus None offices and trying to cope with the possibility of not doing more modeling for the company—at least not for a while. She has been enjoying the marketing work, so that has taken up her focus until we can navigate her ongoing healing process. The last thing she needs is to be triggered again.

Rolling my shoulders, I enter through the back entrance of the gym and am face-to-face with both Hoffmans.

"How's Penny?" Nic asks in greeting. His shoulders are drawn back and his posture a bit more rigid than usual.

"Same as she's been each day you've asked. There's literally no change. She seems to have put the incident behind her. It's me who's having a difficult time shaking this."

Graham's eyes study me. "Where is Penny now?"

"She's at her session with Margo."

"Good. She needs to not skip those anymore."

"I agree, and I'll stay on top of it more."

"We have no doubt," Nic chimes in.

"I'll also make a point to connect with Mitch and keep him in the loop. He's always a valuable resource."

Graham straightens his posture, giving his back a little stretch. "Our legal team is breathing down our necks about getting Penny to prep for trial. I'm about ready for this all to be over."

"Soon," I promise. "I'm working on it."

"Have you seen anything unusual during your prison visits?" Graham asks.

"No. Nothing."

"Any more calls to her phone from Tanner?"

"No, just that one that I intercepted."

"We appreciate you watching out for her," Nic says quietly.

"I should never have left Penny during her photoshoot. I just never thought she would have a setback then. Perhaps she had a flashback? Until we can be clear on what happened at the waterfront, all we are doing is making assumptions."

"So you arrived back after she was already slipping away?" Nic asks.

I nod. "Yes. I missed Penny's initial reaction and was on location after she was already in a bad state of mind."

Graham nods. "None of us expected it. I just hope Penny understands why Nic and I didn't hover after it happened. We didn't want to upset her or cause her any more stress."

"I almost guarantee she understands."

"Who's with Penny now?" Nic asks, glancing at his watch.

"I have someone shadowing her. And then another person shadowing him. Everyone's already on the payroll. I just shifted responsibilities where I saw fit."

The men nod. They understand that my instincts are rarely wrong, and when it comes to Penny, I don't want to make any casual mistakes.

"And she's cooperating with all of that?" Graham asks.

I nod. "Yes. She's been very agreeable."

Nic lets out a huff of air. "How did you manage that?"

Well, I threaten to redden her ass cheeks if she dares to try to lose her guard.

I bite back a smirk and settle for a half-truth. "I explained in loose terms the consequence of not accepting her security detail."

Graham bumps fists with me. "Threats must be best coming from you versus us."

"It's true. You must have a magical way of getting her to comply," Nic says with a laugh, "because she basically exerted all of her energy to disobey her guards prior to you."

"I try my best."

"Any updates on the visitation?" Graham asks, changing the subject back to the real problem—eliminating Mark Tanner from the face of this earth.

"All my eyes on the prison and sources inside have reported that Tanner is quiet. He does not step out of line," I provide.

"He is a rule follower," Graham says with contempt.

Nic snarls, "Yeah, a real model citizen."

"He'll be a dead one very soon," I say under my breath.

I'm not sure why I even bother lowering my voice. The entire gym is empty but for us, and Nic has already made sure that it's a safe place for us to conduct business when we need to have a meeting place away from our homes.

The last thing we need is to have anything get in the way of our ultimate goal or worse—get caught.

While I'm sure the Hoffmans have some safeguards in check, it's always best not to utilize anything that may disrupt the lives of those they care about most.

Fleeing the country and getting a new identification doesn't sound like something any of us really want to do to avoid prison time if caught, but that's the risk we are willing to take to fulfill the revenge plot.

Tanner deserves to rot in prison, but the longer he is kept alive, the more of a chance that something goes wrong.

"So where does everything stand?" Graham asks, pushing hair off his forehead.

I hate seeing him in so much turmoil.

Penny's latest episode has shaken us all up.

"All plans have been finalized, and the payment cycle has been set, with the final installment given upon receipt."

"As long as everything looks like an accident," Graham

says, rubbing his hand along the back of his neck while pacing. "And nothing leads back to us."

"It won't," I reassure.

"Let's just hope that Tanner gets roughed up enough during the little brawl and has to take a trip to the hospital—the sooner, the better," Nic says. "Then maybe trying to figure out what we think spooked Penny at the photoshoot will be unnecessary."

"We just need to be patient," Graham interjects, "and be on guard for the signal."

Moving over to the tables lining the wall, Nic opens a sealed orange envelope and pulls out a series of photos. "I think it would be negligent to ignore what happened at the waterfront."

Clearing my throat, I sift through the images. "I agree."

Graham gives me a look. "You seem uptight."

I shrug. "I am. I hated seeing Penny the way I found her. And between that and how I felt at the cafe the last two visits, I can't shake this feeling clawing at my back. Tanner has phone privileges once a month and yet chose to call her to what—torment her further? Why? Why would he waste his time on that?"

My anxiety could very well just be guilt.

But there've been few times in my life where that feeling has occurred where it hasn't been monumental.

I pass a few of the photos down the line so the brothers can also take a look.

Nic points to one in particular. "Here's one that was captured the day you were at the cafe the first time. I was able to get surveillance footage from an hour prior to your arrival as well. It was grainy at best and nothing seemed unusual." He passes me another stack of images. "Here are ones that were taken from the security footage at the waterfront."

Graham leans over. "Fuck, I feel like donating a few million to the city to upgrade their damn cameras. How are they supposed to arrest any criminals doing damage to the waterfront when the quality is so bad?"

"Here, these are clearer," Nic says. "But, yeah, I agree."

I scan through the dozens of images, hoping to see something—anything.

A few photos have a decent view of bystanders from the photoshoot that were gathered watching Penny work. My eyes move along every face, searching for what—I do not know.

Perhaps something will stand out. Maybe I'll look into the eyes and find a clue.

If Penny's reaction to someone in the crowd sent her spiraling a few steps back on her progress, then I can't even fathom to think what kind of damage actually being in the same room as Mark Tanner would do.

It's one thing seeing him behind bars, thinking she is safe.

It's a whole other thing watching him stride into court, just looking for some loophole.

And I don't trust the United States justice system to deliver to Mark Tanner what he truly deserves.

When I arrive at the building where Penny was meeting with Margo, I am shocked to find her in the lobby with her mother, enjoying a fancy pink drink with the little balls at the bottom.

It looks like she's drinking watered-down body wash.

"Hey, Collins," Donna says, standing up.

She gives me a hug, and it's her warm greeting that coats my insides with a sense of belonging.

"Hi, ma'am."

She glares at me but says nothing.

I shrug. "Old habits die hard."

"Well, I will accept that over Mrs. Hoffman."

"Progress."

"I was in the city doing some shopping and decided to see what Penny was doing. I was only a block away. Did you know that this building has the cutest little tea shop?"

"I had no idea."

Penny stands, handing me a drink. I look at the artificial orange color with the chunky stuff floating around.

"I got you a mango bubble tea with the juicy popping boba pearls."

I stare at the bottom of the drink, trying to decipher all the things she said about the drink. "Thank you."

She bounces on her feet with excitement, which only makes me nervous. "Try it."

I take a hesitant sip.

"Does it taste as good as it looks?" Donna asks, also a bit eager.

"Better."

Penny looks at her mom. "I told you he would like it."

"Now I know what hand soap tastes like. Yum."

Penny slaps me on the arm, causing her mom to laugh and look from me to her daughter and back again.

Taking a step back, I try to detach myself, as I do best. But Penny makes it hard when she is being playful.

"Cheers," Donna says, raising her bright purple drink.

Now that doesn't even look drinkable. It looks like grape cough syrup blended with milk.

We bump cups together, and I take a slurp through the straw.

Coughing into my arm, water fills my eyes.

Penny smacks my back. "Did you choke on a boba?"

"I think so," I say with staggered syllables. "It was slimy."

She giggles. "You are supposed to chew them and make the juice squirt out."

Donna examines her cup. "Yeah, these need a warning label for first-timers. It definitely takes a mental adjustment to consume something that looks like a paint cup."

Penny nudges her mom with her elbow. "Don't forget to ask him, Momma," she says, drawing my attention to Donna.

"I'm throwing a Labor Day party, and you must come to it."

I resist laughing over Donna's invitation that never turned out to be an actual question. "Of course, I will be there. Thank you for the invite, ma'am."

Turning to her daughter, she smiles. "Can you bring a dessert?"

"Yeah, sure. I'll make something fun and festive."

Carrying our drinks, we make our way out of the building and onto the street. With a glance around, I see all the members of Penny's hired entourage blending in with the people on the sidewalk.

At least they are being discreet.

Just knowing that Penny has some extra protection when I'm not with her is getting me through these moments where I am biding my time before I can make the ultimate move.

We can't have a repeat incident of the waterfront fiasco.

But I also can't be with her twenty-four seven like I have been.

Protecting Penny means snuffing out Mark Tanner.

Because there can't be light in her world with the pollution of his darkness.

19

PENNY

"Don't you dare!" I say, smacking Collins's hand away from sneaking another blueberry from the pile. "You keep eating the cake decor, and we'll be down to only forty stars."

He chuckles, holding his hands up in defense. "Okay, okay."

"And we can't celebrate Labor Day without a flag cake. It would be un-American."

"If you say so…"

"I say so. It's tradition."

"What about actual Flag Day? Do you make a cake for that holiday? And what about Fourth of July?"

"Oh, no." I turn to glare at him. "This is not the time to interrogate me."

Collins lets out a laugh. "If you call logical questions an interrogation, then I guess that's what I'm doing."

I go back to my work while he starts nibbling at my neck. Then he places his hands around me onto the counter, essentially caging me in while I dice up strawberries.

Resting his chin on my shoulder, he opens his mouth to be fed.

"Now you're after my stripes?"

I pop a piece onto his tongue and one onto mine.

When I am finished decorating the cake, Collins spins me around, takes the knife out of my hand, and places it onto the island. Gripping my ass cheeks, he lifts me up and plops me down onto a bare section of the counter. My legs spread to accommodate him.

And unexpectedly, we make out.

Like one would expect teenagers to do...

But not someone who is sixteen years older than I am.

This is not something men like Collins would want to do, right?

But he does it. And he is damn fucking good at it.

Suddenly I am airborne and being transported to the couch, missionary style.

I try to wiggle out of my shorts, but my effort is futile. They are just too tight. I really should invest in easier-access clothes so my needs can be met without so much work.

Then Collins's thigh is against my core. And he—

"Oh, fuck!"

"I'm obsessed with your filthy mouth," he growls into my ear, while continuing to grind his leg against my fully clothed pussy.

"Why does this feel so naughty?"

We've done this several times, and each time gets me hotter and hotter. How can not having actual sex be hotter than actual sex?

"Because you are a bad girl who is sneaking behind everyone's backs to be with the hired bodyguard. And innocent girls like you shouldn't like grinding against men like me. But you do. Don't you, Penny? It turns you on to rub that sweet pussy against my leg like a depraved little girl that you are. You love getting that pussy nice and hot so that it leaks out all over the sofa and my thigh." Collins bites at my neck. "Maybe this time I'll make you lick it all off to clean it up."

"Yes," I breathe.

How something so wrong can feel so right will forever be a mystery to me...

Collins continues his onslaught, sending a cacophony of sensations through my body, with both his words and his intentional touches. The combination wreaks havoc on my nervous system and whatever mental capacity I have left.

I thrust my hips upward, wrapping my legs around his waist, trying to get closer to him.

The friction of my panties and my jean shorts coupled with the pressure from Collins's leg nearly tips me over the edge.

"More," I beg—for what in particular I'm not sure. "I need something..."

But he knows and has the audacity to chuckle at me. "Okay, time to go?"

"Where? To subspace?"

He shakes his head at me. "We're going to be late."

"I don't care."

He pulls me up reluctantly from the couch. "Come."

"That is exactly what I didn't get to do." My lips pout and my feet stomp. He's going to make me lose it. "Quit smirking at me."

I follow Collins into the kitchen, hot on his trail. Why is

On a Fault Line

he voluntarily leaving me in a state of need? I'm going to combust.

He puts the lid on my flag cake and then places it into the quilted carrier that is layered with ice packs for transport.

"Got everything?"

I give it a few seconds of thought. "No, I need to pack a bag with some swim gear, and I need to change."

Collins nods. "Well, get on with it."

"Can we have car sex? If so, I will dress inappropriately."

"No, Penelope."

"We really aren't having car sex, are we?"

Collins manages to keep a straight face and not wreck the vehicle. "No."

"I knew I should have driven."

His eyebrow lifts. "And where would you have taken us?"

"Oh, on the side of some dusty road so that I could take advantage of you in the bushes."

He chuckles. "Sounds very romantic."

I scrunch up my face like I just ate a rotten lemon. "Who needs romance?"

"Not me," he laughs. "Not when the joys of being uncomfortable are at the forefront of your mind. That for sure would take precedence."

"Well, you are making my current physical state uncomfortable! I knew I should have brought my toys for the long ride."

"We are thirteen minutes away."

"Quit gaslighting me!"

He lets out a sigh. "You know there is nothing I would want more than to fulfill all your dirty fantasies—most of them involving being fucked in tight spaces where we potentially could get caught—but we are already late because of your *needs*."

"Oh, no you don't. Don't blame this on me."

He looks over at me, probably trying to decipher if I'm being serious or not. "It's not my fault."

"Clearly, it is."

"How so?"

I think about it for a few seconds. "The more sex I have, the needier I get. And you made me needy."

"Noted."

"And you didn't even allow me to get off."

Collins taps his fingers along the steering wheel while humming. "You tempted me in the kitchen."

I scoff. "How so?"

"By looking so cute making a flag cake."

"I would like to make either an amendment or a revision to our mutually agreed upon contract, Mr. Stone."

"Now you want to negotiate terms? That seems counter-productive."

"It's necessary."

There's something about being in a car with Collins Stone that makes me super horny. Maybe it's the fact that neither of us can easily escape.

"Is that so?"

"It is most certainly so."

"State your terms, woman."

"Welp, I would like to add a clause that states that you either *service* me properly or I'll be allowed to seek assistance elsewhere for my deprived—no, *greedy*—pussy."

"You have such a filthy mouth."

"You like it."

"I most certainly do. However, it's best when it is silenced by my cock sliding down your throat. Would you like to continue with your ill-advised revision suggestions, or should I take care of your deprived and most undoubtedly greedy little pussy the first chance I get?"

I fake yawn. "I think I'm actually in the mood for a nap."

"The hell you are."

"I just don't see the problem. If we are going to be late anyway, why not be a little more late?"

"That's what you want—to be railed on the side of the road, in the small space of the car?"

Before I can answer, my phone vibrates. "It's Graham," I announce. I slide the bar over. "Hi, Graham."

"Hey, Penny. I was just making sure you had a ride to the barbecue. I can go back into the city and pick you up if you don't."

That's my big brother—always looking out for me. He was even looking out for me when he hired Collins.

"That's very kind of you. Collins is actually giving me a ride."

"Oh, great. Glad to hear that." I hear relief in Graham's tone.

He's probably thankful I stopped fighting the bodyguard

he hired for me. It's not like we sat down and had a real conversation about what I know and don't know in regard to what happens behind the scenes related to my welfare, but at this point, he probably realizes that I understand Collins's role.

I just don't think he expected Collins to turn into more than just a bodyguard, and for me to be bold enough to advocate for my own sexual needs.

"See you soon."

Hanging up with my brother, I try a different approach with this stubborn man beside me. So I do what anyone in my position would do—I spread my legs and start touching myself.

"What are you doing? Are you even wearing panties?"

"Hmm… I forget. Let me check." Bending forward, I make a huge production of looking between my legs. "Yup. I did remember."

"I can smell your pussy."

Now he has me curious. "And what does it smell like, Collins?"

A devilish smirk plays on his lips. "Mine."

Shimmying in my seat, I remove my patriotic panties and loop them around my finger. Circling them like a lasso, I—

"Hey! Give those back!"

"No."

My eyes narrow at Collins who brings the material up to his nose and breathes in my scent.

"Those are mine."

Taking his hand, he reaches over and places it possessively right over the top of my hairless pussy, underneath my sundress. "This is mine."

Lazily, he pets me, stroking the outside of my lips with his fingers.

Adjusting my seat, I recline back and spread my thighs to give him better access and an intentional invitation to have his way with me.

"Yesss..." I hiss.

I want more.

Sliding his finger along the inner lips of my pussy, he plays with my natural lubrication that has leaked out.

"I hope you drown the interior of my car in your juices, Princess."

My hips grind into the seat, silently coaxing him to continue—to keep touching me. "Hmm..."

"You have less than three minutes to get off."

My hands push at his. "Move aside and let me get the job done."

Gripping both of mine in his one, he pulls them off of me. "Tsk-tsk... You aren't allowed to touch yourself."

My jaw unhinges. "Then how?"

"Think of something. You better get creative."

My eyes dart to the scenery. We are on the main road to my parents' house.

Fuck.

I let out a growl and then grind my bottom into the passenger seat, trying to get the friction I desperately need that I have yet to receive all day.

Growing frustrated as the seconds slip away, I whimper. "This isn't going to work."

"At least you'll be ready to go later when I fuck you into next week."

"If I don't die from the wait."

Collins chuckles at my misery. "Here's your panties. Put them on."

"Yes, sir."

Feeling adventurous, I reach over and massage his cock through his shorts, feeling it come to life.

"Don't tease me, Penelope."

"Or what?" I challenge. "What are you going to do about it? Oh, I know. Nothing. And if you do end up spanking my ass red, then at least it will be festive as fuck to go with your blue balls."

Sliding the panties back up my legs, I spend some extra time stroking myself.

"You are playing with fire."

"Good thing for me, I love the burn."

20

COLLINS

I don't even have the car shut off before Penny is undoing her belt and opening her door.

"Easy, woman. I'll help you out."

I know she's irritated with me. But it's not my fault she is insatiable and couldn't work with the timeline of getting to the party at her parents' house.

"I'm a grown-ass woman, Collins. Quit acting like a time traveler from a different century in history."

Clearly, she's in the mood to exert her independence today. "It's a mighty fine ass," I point out, watching with appreciation as she gets out of the car. It takes everything in me not to coddle her and lay the imaginary red carpet down for her arrival.

Her body snaps around as she glares at me while shutting the door. "Maybe I'll let you touch it later."

I feel the blood drain from my face, as I kill the engine and rush to catch up to her. "There's no *maybe*, Penny." Clearly, she's choosing violence if she thinks she is going to have the upper hand in this fight. Nope. And if I need to drag her back to this car just to prove my point...so be it.

"Oh, there most definitely is—especially after you refused to pull over so we could have a quickie before arriving here."

"There's nothing remotely *quickie* about pleasuring you. Your body deserves more than a steering wheel pressed into your backside while I wring out our orgasms."

Leaning into her stance, she scoffs. "You make me sound like some needy bitch in heat."

"Not you," I say, gesturing to her pussy. "Her."

"Oh, that's cute. *Real* cute." She starts walking back to the car.

"What's wrong?"

"I forgot my flag dessert."

She walks around to the driver's side with me on her heels to get the covered dish she made from the back seat. I take the American berry flag cake from her hands.

"How does one get back in your good graces, Princess?"

Smirking, she reaches behind me to give my ass a squeeze.

Little minx.

"Hmm...be a good boy today and keep your paws to yourself in front of my family." Penny then moves to fix the collar of my button-down shirt, and I'm not even sure it needs her attention. "We both know how good of a Boy Scout you can be, so I doubt that will be a problem."

I bite the inside of my cheek to keep from smiling like a demented clown. That's the thing with Penny; she can make a silly childhood nickname be downright sexy. I can't stop smiling around her. I feel like I'm using facial muscles that I haven't exercised in decades.

And in what world would I ever allow someone to playfully mock me every chance she gets and not want to cut their throat and then watch them bleed out?

Yet, here she is…my little hellion.

I don't stand a chance.

I watch in awe as Penny runs up toward her childhood home—the one that helped raise her—and enters with the elegance of a category five hurricane.

Summer looks good on her, with her hair pulled up in a high ponytail and her sundress riding a little too high for my liking as she rushes the house. Granted, this is a family gathering. We aren't at a club where I'd be trying to resist the temptation of blinding any onlookers with my fists.

My eyes scan my surroundings, a habit that I doubt will ever die.

It feels good to be back in Hillsboro. However, I'd be lying if I said being here didn't give me mixed emotions.

I never grew up with a house to call home. Yet, every part of me realizes why Penny is eager to be here. It is nostalgic. Familiar. Despite not having the luxury of time to make memories here, it is by far the closest thing I have to a home, and it has everything to do with the people present.

Draw the line…

But all I do is keep moving it.

Sure, there's a contract in place that lays forth the details of our little arrangement, but it's my heart that is attaching strings in places that will only get me hurt in the end.

Every part of me knows that the closer I get to Penny, the harder it will be to let her go. We are bound together by a piece of paper that highlights a sexual relationship—not an emotional one. Yet, the experiences we've shared with each other go beyond the rules of a detailed outline. Our connection is not limited to some bullet points that were agreed upon with a legal witness.

I'm just not sure how things can go back to normal after our time is up. Can I really be around the Hoffmans and not have images of Penny's perfect body floating around in my head? Can I completely cut ties with a family that has given me so much to live for?

I glance to the front door of the house as Penny runs through it. So many things have happened in a short amount of time that I'm sure she is craving a sense of normalcy, and being here helps. It's hard to feel like I belong here when all the thoughts flittering through my head are laced with guilt that I'm currently pursuing a sexual relationship with the youngest Hoffman—the only daughter to Donna and Germain—and keeping it a secret.

And our little tryst must stay hidden. I can't afford the fallout if this ever gets out.

"Collins, come on in," Donna greets with a smile and open arms.

I shift the cake carrier to one hand and walk into her embrace, accepting the warm welcome. "Thank you for inviting me."

"Of course. You are always welcome here." Donna gives me a motherly look. "Penny already rushed out back. She sure has energy running through her today."

"She does," I agree, biting back a telling smirk. If anyone could figure out what is transpiring between Penny and me, it would be Donna Hoffman.

"It's good to see her so happy. Oh, what's in the carrier?"

"A berry flag cake."

She unzips the quilted fabric and takes a look inside. "When did you find time to Pinterest?"

"Oh, not me, ma'am. I don't even think I know what that is exactly." I gesture toward the pan. "This is all your daughter's idea. Although she made me…"—my words trail off, as I think of how to complete my thought without drawing any suspicion about just how much time we spend together—"drive extra slow to not mess it up in the back seat."

The real reason I was driving slow was to not cut off my hard-on with any sudden movements from the steering wheel…but I don't share that information.

Donna laughs. "Sounds about right. Let's not let Nic cut into it first. Then all the pieces will be wonky. Have you seen that boy of mine wrap a present before? No finesse. Like *none*."

I chuckle as I feel a presence behind me. Turning, I see Germain make his way toward me. "Quit monopolizing all of Collins's time, honey. Let him socialize."

"Oh, shush it. We were bonding."

I give her a smile. She's so freaking likable—just like her daughter.

"Beer is in back. Come join the rest of the guests outside," Germain persuades.

I follow the patriarch of the family through the house that he remodeled with his wife. It always shocks me at how a little attention to detail can transform a space. Donna has an eye for interior design, and it shows in everything she does.

The back deck overlooks the pool and patio, and it's set up with all things red, white, and blue—from garland to potted plants to flag decor. We make our way down the stairs, over the patio area that is being set up for a barbecue, and toward the garden that provides ample shade with some of the fuller willow trees.

Like with most big social settings, I do what I do best—stand back and observe.

I've seen Penny in her element many times in the past, but there's something different about today's event, even when compared to when I was here for her birthday. Donna is right. There's a lightness to her steps. She is bubbly and blossoming before my eyes, and I didn't even take note until now.

Greeting her brothers, Penny gives them both big hugs. However, it is when their women emerge from the walkout basement doorway that the chattiness electrifies.

Angie and especially Claire have a way of making those they care about feel comfortable in their own skin. They are accepting of others, and while I didn't appreciate their spontaneity while I was their acting bodyguard, they sure bring the fun.

"Wow, you look amazingly happy," Angie says softly, giving Penny a hug.

I inwardly smile, hoping that I somehow had some influence on her good mood today, although she did leave my vehicle grumpy and unsatisfied.

Overall, we've been vibing really well together, and I sometimes ask myself why I didn't create this arrangement sooner.

Oh, yeah…I almost forgot. It's the fear of getting my throat sliced by the two brooding brothers who can't help but keep a keen eye on their women—and their baby sister.

The brothers are busy chatting with their dad, so I'm able to eavesdrop without interruption from the drink table that I assume Donna had a hand in setting up.

I watch as the girls chat animatedly. I'm anxious that I can no longer hear what is being said. If it's anything of importance, I'll have to figure out a way to get that information later.

At least Penny seems to have a way of opening up to me after she's exhausted from multiple orgasms and her body is in a boneless state of submission. Maybe it's because I work the stubborn aggression out of her system, leaving me someone who is more pliable and agreeable.

She is neither of those things right now.

Just watching her move about the space, wearing clothes that were designed for her body, is making me tense and on edge. I will have a lot of my own aggression to work out of my system when we get back to Sky View. Every little glance and rise of her eyebrows is making me want to claim her—again and again and again.

Even then, I doubt I'll have my fill.

"Hey Collins," Graham greets, with a pat on my back.

"Good seeing you."

Nic joins us, offering his fist for a bump. "Up for some cornhole?"

I give a nod, watching as Angie, Claire, and Penny make their way back inside the house via the basement door. "Sounds good." I'm sure they will be fine without me hovering.

We make our way to the shed, where Germain is pulling out the wooden boards from the storage shelf. We each grab some supplies and set up the game in the shade.

"Who's up for a beer?" the patriarch asks, grabbing several bottles from the drinks table. He shakes off the excess water collecting along the sides from being stored in an ice bath and starts popping off caps. He hands them over to his sons. Turning to me, he offers one in my direction. "Want one?"

"I'll grab something later. Thank you."

I rarely drink on the job. Penny needs my clear mind to keep her out of trouble as it is. Hell, the woman is a danger magnet. If there was a fire, I question whether she would walk straight into it or not.

Even with my list of contacts and safeguards in place, my blood pressure rises every time she is not within arm's reach.

Am I overprotective? No, I'm being just the right amount, I am sure.

Would I lay down my life to protect her from harm? Absolutely—and without hesitation.

But apparently I'm also willing to die just to sink my cock into her in secrecy—with the fear of being caught at any time.

So there is that minor issue.

Maybe we both like playing with fire. But out of the two of us, it will be me who burns in hell. No matter how she thinks she seduced me into giving in to her, it is me who is at fault if this all blows up in our faces. I knew exactly what I was doing.

"Collins, you're on my team," Graham says quickly.

"That doesn't seem fair," Nic says with a chuckle. "I've seen his aim, and there's no way I'd bet against it."

"Quit being salty," his brother remarks.

"He refused my attempt to get him drunk prior to stealing the win too," Germain jokes, while organizing the beanbags into piles according to their color.

I laugh, taking my spot beside Nic, as we are on opposite teams. I watch as he throws the first bag—a red one—landing it on the board, just shy of the hole. My blue bag flies through the air, knocking his off but landing in the cutout hole.

An eruption of high-pitched cheering comes from the sidelines, and when I turn, I see Penny jumping up and down with the girls, who are equally enthusiastic.

Fuck.

How am I supposed to concentrate, while Penny is sporting daisy dukes and has managed to make an already tiny T-shirt look even smaller by tying the front into a knot, just south of her tits?

She cannot be serious.

I know she didn't arrive like this. What happened to that cute sundress? And she had to know I wouldn't have allowed her to leave my place looking like she currently does either.

There's no way in hell I'd purchase these clothes for anyone's eyes but mine, and I'm scolding myself for not adding her choice in wardrobe to the contract. If she continues to dress like this in public, I'm going to get into a bar fight with someone. I just know it.

Luckily we are only surrounded by family.

Plus, in my defense, Penny never used to dress like this

when I was keeping tabs on her in Seattle when she wasn't even aware I was there.

This whole freedom of expression is new...

"Whose team are you cheering for?" Nic calls out to his girl.

"It depends."

"On what?" he asks with a fake scoff.

"If cheering for the opposing team will upset you enough to act on it."

Nic hisses under his breath. I can't help but laugh at how these two drive each other wild. Graham and Angie are more discreet about their hidden messages, but they are the same as well.

It must run in the family, because if Penny flashes me her navel one more time when she lifts her arms into the sky, I won't be able to resist coming all over it later when I get her to myself.

"No jumping, Claire. You're still a few months away from fully baking the Bunzie."

She rolls her eyes, while shaking the skirt of her stars and stripes maternity dress. "I'm pregnant, Nic. Not disabled."

Graham looks at him in disbelief. "Bunzie? Oh my, you are so—"

"Shut your face," Nic snaps. Turning back to Claire, his eyes soften. "I mean it, Baby Girl. Tone down the sudden movements, or I'll stay firm on my previous threats."

She chants across the yard. "You'd have to catch me first!"

"And you know I would."

Claire slows down her jumping, but that doesn't stop Penny from making a scene.

Why am I being punished? I can't be walking around a family gathering with a fucking hard-on.

Nic shoots again, landing his bag straight into the hole. I wait until the cheering stops, and then toss my blue bag so hard, it skitters right over the hole and off the back side.

Dammit.

Nic's smirk lets me know that I've lost my focus. If he only knew which blonde bombshell has completely stolen it, I'd be losing more than just the game. No, instead, I'd be forfeiting trust and my ability to work for the Hoffmans ever again.

Oh, and the luxury of owning my own teeth...

It's moments like this—where we are all hanging out together—that remind me that I could be making the biggest mistake of my life.

I glance over at Penny as she bounces in her sandals. I'd like to hope that she's worth it, and this temporary sacrifice of my ethics and the code I live by will not be forever tarnished after the contract ends.

Telling myself that at least Penny is physically safe is not justification alone for all the wicked things I'm doing with her—to her.

I finish tossing my last bag, while Germain calls out the current score. I feel my phone vibrating in my pocket, while I watch Graham toss his first bag toward the board closest to me, landing it straight in the hole. Retrieving my phone, I see that Penny just texted me, despite being just a few yards away on the sidelines.

Penny: Quit making me want you

I can't help but smirk at her, when I think no one's watching. Shifting my focus back to the game, I discreetly type out a response.

Collins: Can't wait to fuck my memory back into your brain

Penny: Good. Because my pussy is deprived.

I swallow hard over her usage of the word "pussy." Just thinking about her sweet lips saying the word makes my cock twitch in my shorts. Penny looks innocent on the outside, but underneath the good girl facade is a badass woman, who is making me work hard at keeping her sexually satisfied.

Her taste in sexual gratification rivals my own. All these years since leaving the military, I've been able to go through life with less, but the only thing I desire now is *more*.

I want more time with Penny.

I want…

Thump.

"I called heads-up," Germain says with a laugh, as we all look down at my foot where the canvas-filled bag landed.

Kicking it up into the air, I catch it and roll it around in my hands.

Clearly, I'm distracted. If Germain only knew what choke hold his daughter has on me, then maybe he would understand that winning cornhole is the least of my worries.

For fuck's sake…

What is happening now?

"Water battle!" Angie announces, launching two water balloons at her husband who manages to catch one, causing it to break in his face.

"You have got to be kidding me," he says with a laugh, charging toward her before she can throw another from some hidden cooler that they must be stored in.

I turn to look for Penny, and—

Splat.

Shaking the water from the tips of my hair, I can't help but smile at her audacity.

Penny bends down to grab two more from the cooler, as I take long strides toward her.

"Stay back!" she yells, as if that's even an option.

"Oh, no. That's not how this game is played."

Grabbing a handful of balloons, she tosses them at me as I close the distance. Cool water cascades down my chest, absorbing into the fabric of my shirt.

"Are you starting a war?" I ask softly, as I reach into the cooler.

"No!" she says, running as fast as she can to hide behind a tree trunk.

Come out, come out.

She is lucky her family is around, because if it was anywhere else, I would have gone feral for her until she was squirming in my arms and paying the penalty she undoubtedly deserves.

And she knows it.

"Don't let my sister get away with that!" Graham yells to me.

"I don't plan on it!"

He throws a balloon, smacking Angie right in the ass.

"That stung!"

"Good."

As I wait for Penny to let down her guard, I glance around the space.

What a sight...

Nic has Claire cradled in his arms, as she balances a pile of water balloons on her belly. She looks like she got him pretty good before he captured her, if the huge wet patch on his shorts is any indication. She definitely was targeted in her aim for a certain part of his body.

Donna and Germain have exited the battlefield to tidy up the buffet area that will soon be stacked with food. I feign the loss of interest and make my way up to them, only to have Penny lured out of hiding just long enough for me to swing around and nail her right in the chest.

"Oops," I say proudly so only she can hear.

"That was on purpose," she grumbles.

"Absolutely."

"I'll get even with you."

"I hope you try."

"Why are you so cocky?" she asks, her tone playful.

"Because I have the receipts to back it up. Now, go grab a drink to stay hydrated. And stay in the shade. Otherwise, you need to put on some sunscreen so you don't burn."

"Yes, Daddy."

21

COLLINS

I growl. This fucking girl. I can't believe she called me Daddy. The sass coming out of her today is going to earn her a punishment. "Keep it up, Penny…"

"Or what?"

"You might just find out what happens to bad girls."

"I hope you try," she says, echoing my previous phrase.

She doesn't believe me, and that just makes me more impatient.

When we get up to the patio, Penny and I separate. I really don't need any suspicion drawn to me that I'm doing anything more than being the dutiful bodyguard.

It is taking all of my energy to contain my grin, already annoyed with my lack of self-control that exposed itself just moments ago when I openly gawked at Penny while she threw around the word "daddy" at her family's fucking barbecue. Her body was made for the sunshine, so I can't fault her for wanting the rays to kiss as much exposed skin as possible. Problem is, I want to kiss it as well.

Graham moves to stand beside me, cutting off my internal monologue. He sets Angie down, smacks her on her backside, and then smiles to her as she scurries away to be with the girls, who are huddled up together near the buffet.

It makes me so twitchy when they get together.

One of them is hard enough to handle.

But put together all three, and they form an impenetrable girl squad.

"Seriously, man, how did you manage that?" Graham asks.

When I look over at him with confusion, he clarifies.

"How did you get Penny to accept you toting her around like a little princess?"

I nearly choke on my own spit.

Penny *is* my little princess.

And I have my ways.

I pour some water into a cup from the dispenser and take a sip. "I don't give her much room to decide against me."

"Nic's right. You must have the magic touch."

I cough into my arm. Recovering as smoothly as I can, I try to act normal—whatever that is supposed to look like.

"I think she just accepted that I wasn't going anywhere." I mean, it's not like I can say we ran into each other at a sex club twice and she convinced me through bad decisions to sign a contract with her, while I maintain the one I still have with him. I can't tell him that now we are unable to be in the same room together without wanting to rip each other's clothes off.

Yeah… I can't say any of that.

Reaching his hand out, Graham waits for mine to shake.

After we connect, that all too familiar rush of guilt floods my system, making me question if this is all worth it.

But then when I look across the patio, on the other side of the pool, and can hear the faint sounds of Penny's laughter as she spins a tube inside the cotton candy maker— I know this is all worth it.

To spend any amount of time in Penny's presence would be worth anything compared to a life where she wasn't in it.

And that there is what will be my ruin.

I am in way too deep as it is, and there's no end in sight other than the confidence in knowing that it will destroy us both.

"Just keep her safe and out of trouble," Graham says, leaning in closer so there's no chance anyone but me can hear. "Any updates?"

We just met recently to discuss everything, but I can tell that he is anxious to ask again so soon.

I clear my throat and shove down the hatred for the fucker that nearly caused the entire Hoffman family's demise. "I'm working on getting more eyes inside." It's honestly what's been keeping me up late at night—besides Penny. "Tanner needs to stay out of solitary if we want stronger access points for delivering messages. The last little fight nearly got him protection for a week, and he plays such a good victim that he could be up for an Academy Award. The next hit on him needs to be impactful."

"Tanner better…" his words trail off as the girls get near, holding pink and blue cotton candy on sticks. "Let's meet up again soon to discuss."

I nod my understanding. Part of the reason I was hired

to watch over Penny was because she visited Mark Tanner at the prison. Even locked up, he is still tormenting her life.

Shifting my posture, I smile at the girls who seem so relaxed and are enjoying the holiday together.

"Want some cotton candy?" Angie asks us, handing over some for me.

"Oh, no thanks."

"No?"

When she pouts, I just accept the offering and rip off a piece to pop into my mouth. It's way too...

Potent.

I would much rather have one of the iced star cookies with the sprinkles, but I'm also trying to make sure I have room for real food and not just junk. Plus, there's the flag cake that Penny spent most of the morning on.

"What's wrong, Collins?" Penny snickers. "Too sweet?"

"Maybe."

She lowers her voice. "I thought you liked sweet little things."

I narrow my eyes at her. She's being extra bold. "Oh, I do."

"Then why not this?"

"Well, when the only ingredient is straight-up sugar, what do you expect?"

"Just live a little." She bumps her shoulder into me, but as she walks away, she turns back and stuffs some cotton candy into my mouth before I have a chance to stop her. Luckily no one sees. "It might be fun."

I chew it up and then whisper, "No. Fun will be having you draped over my knees later while I take out my frustration on that cute ass of yours."

Penny's eyes grow when she realizes I'm being serious.

"As long as you promise to kiss it and make it feel better. Then we have a deal."

Dammit. Why does she always seem to have the upper hand?

Little temptress.

"Mr. Hoffman," a masculine voice greets from behind me.

I turn my focus to find a tanned guy, about my height but probably a decade younger.

He's not family.

"Please call me Germain, now that we aren't in the office."

Donna has a hand resting on the small of his back and is all smiles as she guides him closer to us. "Everyone, this is my friend's son, Ivan Moreno, who also happens to be Germain's new apprentice."

"Nice to meet you," Angie and Claire say in unison, causing my arm hairs to stand on end, when Penny's attention shifts from me to tall-dark-and-tanned.

"My pleasure," Ivan says, scanning through all the members present.

And then his eyes catch fire when they settle right on Penny.

Mother fucking hell.

Ivan's eyes crawl all over her body like a rash. He's being blatant about his attraction to Penny, and I hate every fucking second of the show of possession.

Who does this fucker think he is?

Can he be any more obvious?

Jealousy bubbles inside me, as anger competes to become the dominant emotion.

"Hi, Penny," he says in a choked but rehearsed deep voice.

I can't wait to hear what his voice will sound like after I actually choke the air out of his lungs.

And then he creeps closer like a slithering snake to envelop her in an I'm-going-to-detach-his-arms-from-his-body hug. Fucker probably has a boner, the way he is eyeing the girl, who no one knows is mine.

He clears his throat, backs up, and mumbles something in a fake deep voice. Is he trying to prove he hit puberty? Prick better watch himself or I'll...

I'll what?

Murder someone at the Hoffman residence?

What has gotten into me?

Penny giggles and says something to him that I can't make out. Then she moves over to a lounger and wiggles until she seems to be perfectly comfortable.

I can't keep my eyes off of her either, so I can't blame others for appreciating her beauty.

But she's mine to protect.

Mine.

The kid better watch where he puts his eyes if he wants to keep them intact. I tap out a message on my cell to Penny and hit send before I have time to think.

Collins: The kid better not make a move on you.

It takes her a minute to look at her phone, but when she does, I see the corners of her lips curl up. Of course she would find my response to another man sniffing around her humorous.

Penny: Not every guy that I encounter wants something to do with me. Just chill. Quite frankly, it will be refreshing if anyone actually pursues me. Let me enjoy this one-off occurrence!

Collins: I don't like it.

Penny: You don't like a lot of things...so it's hard to take you seriously. You should be more selective so you can have a bigger dramatic effect.

I am trying to figure out what Penny is even talking about when my phone buzzes again. This time she sends me a picture of her damn Labor Day panties that she must have changed into when she went into the house with the girls during cornhole.

Where is she getting all of these spare clothes that I can't decide if I approve of or not?

I read the caption: "Your Benefits Package."

There's an arrow pointing to her entrance.

Penny: Behave today and I'll let you chew these off of me later.

Fuck.

Why is she trying to torment me?

I resist growling...

Our eyes meet from across the way.

Well, until Ivan steals Penny's attention back and takes a seat right on the end of her lounger, making her bend her knees up to allow him space.

Fuck.

I'll be damned if I become a third wheel to their little *moment.*

I'm going to burn those jean shorts when we get back home. If another inch of her thigh gets exposed, I'll see if I can order a pair of pants and get them delivered here in the next hour. Maybe even a pair that go up to her neck with those adjustable straps.

She could use the extra coverage.

I'm not so emotionally inept not to realize that I'm jealous right now. I know I am. But that's because I know how special Penny is. She's one of a kind. It would be weird if guys didn't notice her beauty that goes beyond her hair and eyes and lush body. At the core, Penny is sensitive and sweet. She's smart and sassy.

"Ivan just got back from a trip to Colombia and brought us some iced coffee to try," Donna announces, holding up a pitcher. "Make sure you all try some."

Who brings iced coffee to a holiday barbecue? That spud. That's who.

"Go easy on the caffeine, Claire," Nic warns, as she pours herself a half cup.

"Only if you lay off the mom blogs that are full of wannabe doctors and keyboard warriors." She turns to him with a big smile—albeit fake. "Plus, it makes the baby really dance."

Anyone other than Nic can tell that she's exaggerating and trying to make him get a little crazy. He brings it upon himself with his overprotectiveness. But that doesn't stop him from topping off her huge refillable water bottle that is already three-fourths full from the dispenser and then bending the straw to her lips.

"Sip."

I swear he says *good girl* under his breath after she complies.

Ironically, both Graham and Nic have found the most stubborn and independent women. Neither of these ladies are shy about going head-to-head with their possessive and overprotective men. It's a sight to see.

And Penny falls in the same lane as their women do.

What have I gotten myself into?

"It's good seeing you, Penny," Ivan says, shifting his body to get a better view of her from his end of the lounger. He gestures with his chin toward the pool. "When are we getting in?"

And she fucking smiles.

"Soon."

Taking out my phone, I shoot her another pointed text.

Collins: Quit flirting

Why sugarcoat my disapproval? Surely by now Penny knows how I feel about other men moving in where they don't belong.

Glancing at her phone, she makes a subtle face then tries to shove it into her jean shorts pocket, but instead drops it on the ground.

And in swoops the hawk, saving the day.

"Here you go, Penny," he says, nearly bumping heads with her when she leans forward to also try to get it.

"Thanks, Ivan." As she takes the phone out of his hand, his fingers brush hers. She doesn't react though, and that makes me happy—but he sure does.

Ivan looks like one of those Thanksgiving parade cartoon balloons that has the plastered-on smile.

He's a demented clown head.

"Your dad was telling me the other day that you moved into the city."

Does he have a mute button? I can see his game a mile away.

I should have fucking claimed her pussy today on the couch and in the car. Maybe the smell of another man's cum all over her would deter him from thinking he even had a chance.

He doesn't.

Penny is mine.

"Yeah, I think it was time to be on my own."

And then Ivan leans in and whispers something into her ear.

Don't you fucking smile, Princess.

22

COLLINS

"Dude, are you okay?" Nic asks, detaching himself from being Claire's water boy.

"Hmm?"

He gestures to my face. "You look a little pale."

My attention has been on Penny and Ivan so much that I forgot I'm supposed to be pretending to be unaffected.

"I think it's just the heat." It's not a lie. It is hot out here when not in the shade.

"Why don't you all get in the pool to cool off while Germain cooks up some burgers and kabobs?" Donna suggests, overhearing our conversation.

Instantly my stomach sinks. The last thing I need is for Penny to be prancing around in a bathing suit while I try to conceal a hard-on. From the creepy look on the Colombian's face, I doubt I'll be the only one with the struggle.

I feel volatile.

If Ivan makes a move on Penny, I'll detach his dick

253

from his body, and he can throat fuck himself with it to get off. I don't care. But he better stay away from what's mine.

"The pool sounds fun," Penny says sweetly.

Of course it does, with a capital F-U.

And let's face it—I'm fucked.

If her skimpy outfit is any indication of what she chose to bring for swimwear, then I know it's going to be some type of bikini.

Dammit.

I hope Penny knows who she's coming home with tonight, because it isn't going to be Mr. Iced Coffee. I made it clear I don't share, but if I need to do a refresher course, I will.

"Collins, can I get the keys to your car so I can get my swim bag out?" she asks, holding out her hand in expectation.

"I'll walk you there."

"No need."

"There's very much a need," I whisper, my voice gravelly, so only she can hear.

Turning on her heel, she walks across the patio toward the house.

"I'm gonna grab a bag from Collins's car," Penny says to Angie in passing, probably trying to draw suspicion away from our closeness.

I usher her up the deck stairs, allowing her to go first.

When we get to the top and out of view of the others, Penny spins around, her eyes alight with anger. "What has gotten into you?"

"I don't want that asshole flirting with you."

"Really? Now you're name-calling? With age doesn't always come maturity. You are the case in point."

I sigh, placing both hands on the back of my neck and rubbing them upward to try to ease the building tension. "Penny, make him stop, or I will."

"What does that mean, Collins?"

"It means that I will get rid of him."

She shakes her head. "Not that. And stop acting all hitman. You can't just eliminate every guy that looks at me. What I meant was, how can I make someone stop doing something that I'm not even aware he's doing? I don't think Ivan was flirting with me at all. He is being nice."

"Guys aren't nice without a purpose. We're basic like that."

Her eyes narrow. "And now you are the expert?"

I sigh. "He is fantasizing about taking what's mine."

"Now you're a mind reader?"

"He's making it obvious, Pen. Wake up."

"Cut him some slack."

The only thing I'm going to cut is him into pieces if he steps out of line. "Why?"

"Because he doesn't know we are bound together by a contract."

"Quit making accommodations for someone who doesn't deserve your kindness."

"He's my mom's friend's son, Collins. Chill. We aren't going to get naked on the first date."

"There will be no date," I snap. I take a few breaths, trying to decide which approach I should use on her to get her to see reason. "Listen. I am jealous of every man in your past and present who has ever seen how beautiful you look when the wind catches your hair. I am jealous of anyone who has smelled how the sunshine warms your strawberry scent from your skin. I am jealous of those who have tasted the sweetness of your lips. Childhood friend or not, I don't like it."

"So you'll scare him away like you did my boyfriend from Soulful Mind?"

Is she still not over that? "Well, I sure as hell won't stand back and watch someone move in on you. If you don't want a full-out war in your parents' backyard, then stop encouraging Ivan's flirting."

"In my defense, male attention makes me horny."

"What the fuck, Penny? Do you want me to lose all my control right here, right now? You do, don't you?"

"Why Mr. Stone, that's exactly what I want you to do."

"Do you want him?"

After a long pause, I look down into the patio area at the group that is still gathered and then back into Penny's crystal-blue eyes. I can feel the tic in my jaw starting at the mere thought of her pursuing another man while we are in a contractual relationship. There's no way in hell I am sharing.

Having enough of this conversation, Penny makes her way through the back door to the house, meandering through the living room and working her way through the kitchen.

"Answer me, dammit."

Watching as she pulls back her shoulders and grinds her teeth, I prepare for the fight it seems she's ready to start. "The only thing I want is to be chosen. And unfortunately for you, some other guy beat you to the opportunity. It's like I don't even exist to you when I'm not in your bed."

"Why do you provoke me and then expect me not to react?"

Her hands push at my chest, but I don't budge. "I'm not doing anything to you. Believe it or not, I'm simply enjoying spending some time with my family and friend."

"Why do you think I don't choose you?"

"Because I basically had to beg on multiple occasions for you to even consider the possibility of being an *us*. You didn't choose me. I chose you. I was simply stating that fact."

"You knew my reason for hesitating."

"I did. But sometimes I yearn for a different type of closeness."

"With Ivan?"

"No, Collins. Ivan works for my dad, and his mom and my momma are friends. Our paths crossed years ago but the timing was wrong. And it's still wrong."

My eyes glare down at hers. "But there was an attraction there?"

She shrugs. "He's tall, dark, and muscular. Of course I don't find him attractive. Ew. Gross." Then a giggle escapes. And now she can't stop them from multiplying.

Great.

Dammit.

But she's so freaking cute when she's having fun—even at my expense. I allow her to continue, but the more I think of that kid trying to stake his subtle but obvious claim on her, the angrier I get. "If you haven't noticed, I'm not laughing."

"Well, you never laugh, so this really isn't special."

"It's almost like your ass is begging to be spanked. Is that what you want, Penny? You want me to punish you for taunting me—right here, right now—at your parents' barbecue?" I glance at my watch. "Because for the past eighty-seven minutes, I've been dreaming up all sorts of ways I'm going to take out my aggressions on your most sensitive areas."

Her hands fly to her waist. "You already took out your aggressions when you decided to not give me ample time to get off in your car."

"You're still not over that too?"

"Nope. I hold grudges." But it's that corner of her lip that lifts and lets me know she is just a little salty.

"If you don't make it clear to your *friend* that you are not interested, I'll hire a tattooist to brand your skin with my damn name and the label 'property of.' Is that understood?"

She clicks her tongue. "I hope it's the wash-off kind, because you've made it very clear that this"—she motions with a hand back and forth between us—"is temporary." Her eyes hood over, and she sticks her tongue out at me.

I take a step closer to her, as she takes a step back. We do this slow dance until her back is pressed against the hallway wall and our bodies are molded to one another's, as if pieced together like the perfect puzzle.

"Stay away from him, Pen. At least until our contract ends." It'll give me time to figure out how to dispose of his body.

"Maybe, just maybe, my choices don't revolve around you."

"We have an arrangement."

"Yeah, one that is supposed to leave me sexually satisfied—not frustrated." She glances down between us. "And right now, no part of me is feeling the benefits of this—"

My lips are on her, sucking the next words out of her mouth, as hers vibrate against mine. She's been taunting me and tempting me since we got into the car to drive here. And when we did get here, I'm challenged with her sassy text messages and flirting. Oh, and let's not forget about her freaking panty pic.

Taking her hand, I move it to my crotch, allowing her to feel my growing erection.

Pulling away from my assaulting mouth, she lets out a growl. My mouth finds her neck, kissing my way up to her ear. But it's her eyes I need to see to know that my next message is getting across to her.

"Ever since you walked out of your parents' house wearing that scrap of an outfit, I've been fantasizing about all the ways I'm going to fuck you out of it. So, for the record, I see you. I see every fucking inch of you. I see you bending down to pick up a water balloon. I see how the muscles of your thighs contract when you walk past me for no reason other than to make me want to rail you right in the middle of a family barbecue. I see how your hair glistens in the sun, and how your smile becomes brighter when you're around your loved ones. I see it all, Penny. So, don't think I'm not affected by you prancing around in front of me, knowing full well that I'm unable to do to you what I would like. Because if it were up to me, I'd haul you over my shoulder and have you openly displayed and strapped to the first flat surface I can find—just so I know you won't move or defy me like you've done all day."

"I don't like him," she says confidently.

"Feeling's mutual."

Penny lets out a laugh. "You are just like my brothers."

"How so?"

"All three of you basically hate all men sniffing around your women."

"That's all men that have a bone in their body other than their dick, Penny. We aren't special."

"But the thing is, Collins, we both know this is just temporary. So maybe I'm just planning for the fut—"

Looping my fingers into the belt loops of her too-tight shorts, I tug her closer for added emphasis, cutting off her last word. "I'm not going to sit back and watch you secure a backup plan, while currently I'm your only plan." Penny's not planning a fucking future with that spud. She can do better. "So, let's enjoy this while we can."

"I fully intend to."

"I don't share."

"Neither do I."

"Good."

Penny pouts out her bottom lip. "I'm just trying to be nice. You need to not read into everything I do."

"My job is to evaluate situations and make judgments based on what I see and my impeccable instincts. And Ivan already sees you as his. And I don't like it."

"Sees me as his? That's a bit of a stretch, even for your wild and overactive imagination—don't you think? You're reading into some friendly conversational exchanges."

I shake my head. "I know the kid's intentions, and if he doesn't ask you out after today's barbecue, then I will admit I misread every cue he's giving off."

Pulling back, she places her hands on her hips. "You do realize that he and I are basically the same age."

"Moot point."

"Well, you better enjoy your time with me before it all runs out...or you die from natural causes due to your old age."

"Funny."

"Just think, you're only a year or two away from your whole life's worth being about how nice your lawn looks or how well you can cook a piece of meat on the grill."

Okay, now, she has a point there. But I can't give her any indication that I find her utterly hilarious. Based on the cheesy smile beaming across her face, she knows it too.

"Are you done deflecting?"

She shakes her head no. "Lucky for you, sugar daddies ripen with age."

I sigh. "This isn't helping your cause."

"I know, but it's fun as fuck teasing you about your age, since you have so eloquently been quick to point out Ivan's."

"Well, it's going to be equally as fun tormenting your sweet pussy by withholding your release until you beg. If anything, it might help teach you to stop teasing me by flirting with other men."

"Is this what jealousy looks like on you, Collins?"

"You're mine, Princess."

"Thought so."

"*Mine.*"

"Maybe you just need to fuck the memory of you back into my body, so the only man that ever crosses my mind is you."

"Oh, I plan to."

Her body slides against mine, as she stands on her tiptoes to whisper, "I can't wait to show you later the new swimwear I got. And by later, I mean now." Then she brushes past me, deliberately sliding her tits on my arm. Every touch causes an electric jolt through my system, as if her body is punishing me for not being able to adequately fulfill her needs at a freaking barbecue.

Fucking hell, Penelope Hoffman.

"I should tan your ass for the torment you're putting me through—in front of your family no less."

"Too bad you don't have it in you to make that level of scene."

"Your independence and resilience are commendable. But don't deliberately try to defy me, just to test my reaction. You won't like it. And if you think I wouldn't dare make a scene out in public—or in front of your entire family —you are wrong."

I can tell by her eyes that she believes me. "Bye, now." She wiggles her fingers into the air.

"You are going to be the death of me," I groan to myself, watching as her pert ass makes its way to the front door and out onto the covered porch. Then I remember why we left the group in the first place. Penny needed her swim bag.

Catching up to her, I unlock the trunk and help her retrieve her belongings. I'm already wearing a pair of navy blue swim trunks that also double as shorts when dry, so I don't need to change. Whatever Penny is carrying in that bag will most likely raise my blood pressure when she puts it on her body, and I'm dreading the lack of control I have over this entire situation.

"Go get dressed, woman."

Walking back to the house, she smirks over her shoulder. "Only because you insist."

Yup. And this is the moment I realize that...

I'm fucked.

23

PENNY

As soon as I glance in the mirror, I know I'm going to be in big trouble. When I ordered this suit online, it sounded good in theory. Now that I'm coming face-to-face with my impulsive purchase, I'm silently regretting the punishment I'm going to endure later when Collins takes it out on my ass.

This suit is going to sign, seal, and deliver that promise.

I can almost feel the sting already.

It'll be a mistake worth making—I'm sure. That man has a way of kissing and making things better.

I do feel good. Despite the weird tan lines that might develop if I don't apply enough sunscreen, the suit is very comfortable—more than it looks.

And it covers all the essential parts, so really he shouldn't be mad.

Consisting entirely of dark navy fabric, the one piece is a series of straps that wrap around my body. I look like I'm tied up in bondage, yet I am wearing more coverage than an average bikini.

But this thing is s-e-x-y. It's way sexier than anything I've ever worn in the pool.

I toss my scattered items on the vanity back into my bag and do one last check in the mirror. Taking a deep breath, I open the door to exit—coming face-to-face with Collins.

Even when I'm frustrated with him, I can still find a way to admire his tenacity.

He flinches over my revealing outfit, not valuing my choice to be spontaneous. Nope. He is the man who craves consistency and predictability—of which I am neither. I think I make him nervous.

Collins trails his eyes over every inch of my body. Yup, he definitely doesn't approve. It is written all over his face in a scowl.

I kind of like this.

It's as if I'm holding a bit of the power.

Collins might be a man of few words, but he sure as hell makes up for it in the looks his eyes give me. There is the "are you serious" look. The "get the fuck over here" one… My favorite is his smoldering eyes expression that makes me gush between my legs. But the one that stops my heart dead in my tracks is the one he is giving me now. And it means to brace myself for the fallout.

"Stop looking at me like that."

"Why?"

"Because you're invading my personal space." And he does it again. I sigh. "Seriously, stop doing that."

If his eyes alone could talk, they would tell me to get the fuck out of Dodge. He might be calm and collected, but I know his simmering temper will only mean a sore ass by morning. And while I normally enjoy the chase, I do not enjoy the friction of clothes. And tomorrow I must wear them.

"Doing what, Penny?"

He has the nerve to look genuinely confused. Must I spell everything out? For an intuitive man, he seems to be missing the mark today.

"The possessive caveman thing. It's creepy."

"Is it?"

I huff out a breath. "Yes. It feels like I'm on the verge of being kidnapped and have no way of preventing it."

"If I wanted to, I would. And I could make it look like an accident."

"See?" I point my finger at his face in accusation. "That right there."

"What?"

"The way your eyes darken, and it makes me actually believe what you are saying."

"You should believe me," he says matter-of-factly.

"Let's get you a cheeseburger. I refuse to be your next meal."

He takes a step forward. "You just might be." His breathy words tickle my lips, he's that close. "You *are* tasty."

"Am I now?"

"Yes. Like drinking the sweetest nectar from a life-giving source."

"Hmm…"

Collins's kiss is hard and needy, just like the growing erection in his shorts. "I want to get drunk off your taste."

After several seconds, I pull back. I can't allow his seduction to keep me from saying my piece. For a man of few words, he seems to know the exact ones to use on me. But I can't allow him to know that. He would use them against me any chance he got, and I would turn into a puddle. "And I want to get drunk off of actual tequila, because all of this"—I motion between us—"overprotective bullshit is making me anxious. I can't control what other people do, and I shouldn't pay a price for someone else's actions."

"If he touches you again, I won't care who witnesses me breaking his hands."

"No one is going to touch me. Not even you. This is why I need to buy batteries in bulk for my toys. Who needs a dick when you have a dildo?"

Taking my wrists, he pushes me back, pinning me effectively against the wall. Grinding his hips, he hits the right spot and I melt. My mouth opens as a moan escapes.

"Can your dildo do that?" he asks bluntly, releasing his hold.

He knows the answer. He knows the effect only he has over my entire body. Even my subconscious thoughts consist of him. He infiltrates every part of me.

When I'm awake, I think of Collins.

When I'm asleep, I still think of Collins.

But I can't give him this satisfaction. I can't allow him to think that he has won this battle—a battle that is still ongoing. I have approximately three more hours to be here, and if he thinks he can dictate every word out of my mouth that I speak to Ivan, then he has a big shock ahead. Because while we do have a contract in place, in no clause does it give him full authority over the people I associate with in my life.

"Penelope?"

"Hmm?"

"What did Ivan say to you when he whispered into your ear?"

Oh. That's what has him so haughty... He hates the unknown. I want to dangle this secret information around as bait but decide to just be up-front. It doesn't mean anything anyway. "He told me that when summer fades, hearts unite in the fallout. Hmm...it's kind of poetic."

"You've got to be joking me," Collins says, busting out in laughter.

He doubles over.

I've actually never seen him this far gone.

I prop my hands on my hips, waiting for him to find composure. What is wrong with him? "I'm not joking."

"He literally just fed you the lines from last summer's Grace and Jace album. Do you women really fall for that shit?"

"You're kidding?"

"We've already established that I don't joke."

This is true. But I'm more impressed that Collins was able to distinguish between song lyrics and bullshit. Impressive.

"On a scale of one to ten, with one being *mildly annoying* to ten being *on me like a leech*, what should I expect from you in the next thirty minutes?"

"Oh, that's tricky," he says, obviously humoring me.

"Well?"

"It's off the charts."

Damn. "Which side of the chart?"

He shrugs. "Hard to say."

"You need to get some food in your system before you get really scary," I say, pushing Collins toward the back door that leads out onto the deck. "I'll be out in a few minutes as to not cause too much suspicion."

"Fine." Looking at me with hesitation in his eyes, Collins does what he's told.

"Good boy."

Oops.

Now he's triggered again.

He points to his watch, tapping his finger along the face of it, to warn me that the time is coming for my punishment for all my sass.

I give him a couple of minutes and then head outside into the sunshine that warms my soul.

Collins's and Ivan's eyes are on me as I enter the party area again. This is my cue to get intoxicated. Only blurry vision will lessen the intensity of both of their stares.

So I make my way straight to the drink area and pour myself a mystery beverage from the dispenser labeled "Sex in the Driveway," and before I can even take a sip, I'm choking in laughter over the name.

"Dad, you missed this detail during your quality control check," I call out, making everyone look toward me. "Momma is calling her cocktail 'Sex in the Driveway.'"

Dad shakes his head at her. "I thought that was our little secret."

"Ew!" Graham, Nic, and I scream in unison.

"How does that name have anything to do with Labor Day?"

Momma's smile is bursting at the seams. "Sometimes sex in hard places is a *labor* of love."

I cover my ears dramatically, wishing I could erase my memory of this insight into my parents' love life.

"Gross," Nic hisses.

"Is the drink at least good?" I ask. If Momma made it, it will definitely be deceptively powerful.

"It's way better than Sex on the Beach," Momma says defensively. "And less painful. Sand is meant for the shore and not for the—"

"Mom!" Nic and Graham scold, making everyone laugh.

Except Dad isn't laughing. He's just staring at her with adoration.

I swear they love each other a little bit more each day.

I take a sip of the carbonated fruity drink.

And another.

And just one more.

And by the time the song switches over on the sound system, I am pouring myself another glass full.

I guess I'm a fan of Sex in the Driveway.

I grab a slice of my flag cake and start eating it like a cupcake with my fingers, using sweets to distract myself from Collins's eagle-eye solo staring contest he must be having with the side of my face.

I refuse to look his way.

Glancing over the icing and berries, I see Ivan perfecting the smoldering look.

Sheesh. He keeps doing that and I know Collins will bash in his face like a piñata.

My eyes flick back to Collins.

Seriously. He needs to take it down a notch.

The possessive thoughts are so obvious in how his eyes refuse to look away from me. It's as if he is amping himself up to go to battle with my invisible suitors. If he thinks Ivan is interested in me other than getting a deeper foot into the architecture business with my dad, then he simply is jealous. And with each sip of my beverage, I'm feeling ballsy enough to tell him just so.

To distract myself, I decide now is the perfect time to text my man-child.

Penny: You so jelly

Collins: Drink some water, Penelope

Penny: Ur cum tastes better I wants to be your lil CUM SLUT

I sneak a glance his way, while biting my lip like a seductive self-cannibal. At least I *feel* sexy.

I'm on a roll with my good ideas too, so I better ride this wave until I crash.

Penny: I just want a man to devour me like I dessert

Penny: Shit—deserve. Ducking auto correlate

Penny: duck

I growl. What is wrong with this thing?

Penny: FUCK

Great.

Even my phone is drunk.

I toss it onto a lounger.

Stupid thing.

Meandering, I shovel more flag cake into my mouth, doing anything I can to ignore this tense...awkwardness. Does anyone else feel it or is it just me?

But then I swallow my bite way too soon. Bending over and coughing into the crook of my arm, I am immediately surrounded by both Collins and Ivan.

One's a pit bull, and one's a poodle...

"You okay, Penny?" they both ask in unison.

I continue coughing and then once it turns into laughter, I nearly dump my cocktail onto both of their feet.

How am I going to get through the next several hours with two men circling me like rabid dogs?

"Penny."

I look up at Collins.

His features harden, moving from angry to livid, as if a switch was hit.

"I need to talk to you."

I look at my nails. Nobody has time to micromanage everyone's emotions right now. "Sounds serious."

"It is."

He gestures to a space in the corner away from Ivan, and with a predatory hand on my lower back, he ushers me there.

Is he freaking staking a claim at my family's barbecue?

"You can't tag me and bag me, you know?"

"Oh, I totally can."

My eyes narrow. "What's wrong? Why did you put baby in the corner?"

"You have icing on your lip."

My fingers reach up to wipe it off. "That's what you needed to separate me from the group to say?" I know he just wanted me away from Ivan. He's being so obvious. "Do you want a bite of flag cake?"

His attentive gaze drags over my body, exploring me unabashedly and without any intrusion. Nothing is standing in the way of us—except the fact we are at my family's barbecue.

"More than you know."

"Hey, Penny," Ivan says, joining us.

Jealousy erupts behind Collins's eyes, causing him to curse under his breath, as my body tingles with the realization that later he will be exerting his possessiveness over me, reminding me just who owns me.

"What's up?" Collins asks, before I can string together the words in greeting. "Ivan."

Why is he saying his name so weird? It sounds weird. At least I think it does?

With eyes still trained on me, his silent command to be a *good girl* transfers between us. The problem is...I don't want to be a good girl.

What I really want to do is smack him for his rudeness.

"I wanted to know if you wanted some cake with the berries."

Collins snaps his head toward him as if he was brainless. "You mean another slice of the one she made and brought? You just spent the last eight minutes watching her eat some, an—"

"Alrighty," I say, clapping my hands together.

Both men stare at me, as if I'm about to give a speech.

But what's the point? We are just potentially drawing more attention to this area of the patio than necessary.

Ignoring them both, I walk myself into the pool, while licking smeared icing from my lips and trying to avoid eye contact with anyone who wants to piss all over my Labor Day parade.

Just when I'm feeling comfortable on a pool float, I see Momma arrive with a huge cardboard scoreboard sign.

This is her favorite thing about family gatherings, so I can't help but smile over her enthusiasm.

"Who's ready for the most epic game extravaganza yet?" she half screams. Then she hits a switch on the back of the board, and red, white, and blue lights turn on around the border.

"Wow, Momma. You upgraded again."

"I'm glad you noticed, Penny," she says with a beaming smile. "Your father is still reminding me about the horrible trophies I purchased last year and the hate-crime medallions that arrived for your birthday. So this time, I opted for something better—classic."

"Oh, what's that?" Angie asks.

"Ribbons. Like no one can mess up ribbons—right?"

"You did check to make sure everything is good with the shipment, right?" Dad asks her.

"No. I live for a good surprise reveal. It's all the rage now with the young'uns on social media. So make sure you record me with a stellar filter. Make me look super fake."

Oh boy…

Grabbing the box from the chair, Momma carries it over to the table underneath the canopy.

We watch as she struggles to get through the packing tape.

"Here," Collins says, coming to her rescue. "I got it."

Pulling out his knife, he has the box open in just seconds.

"Always the Boy Scout," I mumble under my breath.

Sidling up beside me, he whispers, "I'm ready for every-thing—except for you."

"You ready to lose?"

"You ready to watch me soar to victory?" Collins challenges.

"I come from a dynasty of game fanatics and a strong female role model. So strap in for the ride, because as you know, I play to win." I glance around the area. "Where's Ivan?"

"Who?"

I smack his arm. "The kid."

"Oh." He manages to look sad, but I know it's fake. "Over there, playing cornhole by himself."

"I'll go get him."

"No, don't. He's quite enjoyable when he's being passive-aggressive."

I roll my eyes. "I can't be rude, Collins."

"Fine."

I run off toward Ivan. I hate that I feel stuck between my broody secret boyfriend and a boy who is a friend. It feels scandalous. The man I shouldn't want is the one who I can't stop obsessing over.

Ivan would be the easy choice.

But he's not the man I want.

"Hey, Penny," Ivan says, tossing a cornhole bag into the air and catching it. "Want to play?"

I shift my weight on my feet. "Well, actually, I think my parents are starting their famous round of group games. You're welcome to join us."

Ivan looks up at the patio area behind me and frowns. "Nah. I'm not much into party games."

"Oh, gotcha. Okay. Well, feel free to come watch if you get bored down here."

"Sure. Sounds good."

I rush back to the group, hoping I didn't miss out on any essential rules or stipulations.

Collins makes a face at me, and I swear he's gloating over Ivan not wanting to join us. This guy really can't help himself when he gets his way.

Making a drumroll on her upper thighs, Momma silences us and then pulls out of the box ribbons the size of leather belts.

"Wow. Those are intense," Graham says with a laugh.

"They are customized too."

"Why do they all say, 'Congratulations Red Dragon Soccer' on the front?" Claire asks, stifling her laughter.

"Oh, no. That was the default message. Mine probably didn't save."

"Did you click save?" Graham asks.

Momma looks at him pointedly. "Of course, son. I'm not silly. You aren't the only one who's good at the Internets."

"Anyway," Dad chimes in before Momma loses it on us all. "The first game is called Fill the Bucket, and it's a relay race between two teams."

Momma claps her hands and runs to the side of the patio to grab two stacks of buckets. One stack is red, and the other is blue. "Each team will line up in a row, and all members will hold a bucket. The starting bucket will be full of pool water."

"Everyone will face the same direction," Dad explains, "and then lift the bucket up and behind them to try to fill the next person's bucket without looking. We will do this twice, so once you are done pouring, move to the back of the line to wait your turn again."

"And the team at the end after both rounds with the most water in their buckets will win," Momma cheers.

Claire, Nic, Momma, and Dad make up one team. Graham, Angie, Collins, and I make up the other team.

I laugh as Nic runs to grab Claire a chair, and at her reaction to his overreaction.

"You better not get me wet," Collins says, as I stand in front of him with my bucket while Angie and Graham make up the front of our train.

Looking back over my shoulder, I bite my bottom lip and give him the look. "I'm already wet."

His nose flares, and I know I'm going to get into so much trouble later for teasing him.

Oh well, you only live once.

"Get ready," Momma announces, standing at the front of her team. "Get set."

We all lift our buckets into position.

"GO!" Dad finally says, sparking the start of the water challenge.

Angie lifts the bucket over her head and pours it blindly into Graham's empty one, only sloshing out a small amount.

She moves to the back of the line, while Graham dumps his into mine, splashing out just a few drops. But when it's my turn to pour next, my grip slips and the gasp of Collins lets me know that I at least hit a target.

Too bad it was the wrong one.

I can't stop giggling. "Oops."

"Yeah, right. *Oops*," he says with mirth.

It's on the third refill, courtesy of Claire who claims I am drinking one for her, that I start to feel like my stomach is a firework about to go off if I don't supplement its contents with some carbs.

Leaning over the side of the pool, I stretch with all my might until I can pull my swim bag closer to me without getting out.

Feeling brave, I type a message out to my gatekeeper.

Penny: I wanna be your little cum slut. Like one of those hottie girls from Limit-X. To do with as you pleasssse.

Hitting send, I scan the space to see where Collins is. Why can't I find him?

And then I hear the sound of coughing and...

There he is. Making eye contact from across the patio, I watch as he types out a response.

Collins: No more alcohol for you.

I send him an animated graphic of a cartoon liver throwing up.

Trying to pull myself up on the side of the pool, I fall back into the water and start giggling.

Oops.

This is harder than I thought.

Then I feel strong hands at my waist and the feeling of going airborne.

"Need a lift?"

It's Ivy.

Haaaa....

That's not her name.

Her name is Ivan.

Him.

His.

At least I think he's real. He did kind of materialize out of thin air. Where did he even come from?

But then I remember Collins's threats.

Oh, hell. "Get your hands off me if you want to keep them attached to your arms."

"What?" Ivan asks.

My head spins around trying to see where Collins is, and the sudden motion makes me queasy. "Gonna be sick."

24

PENNY

"Let her go," Collins demands.

He's here. But where?

I thought he was on the patio looking all bodyguardy.

"I see, no, I hear a ghost. Ghost of Collinzzz."

"Fuck, Penny, how much have you consumed?" He sounds so judgy.

"I just had a Threesome in the Driveway." As soon as I say it, I know I got it wrong. Bending forward, I grab my sippy cup. "Haaaa, haaa, I said sippy cup." Wait. No I didn't. "Did I? Oh, foo." I can hear Collins curse. "You gots a potty mouth, Mr. Stone."

"I got this. Back off, Moreno."

Oh, shit. Nothing good ever comes from men calling each other by their last name, in an angry tone like he just used.

I didn't even think he knew his last name.

"Easy, man. We go way back."

"Not way back as in bathtub pics way back. At least I don't think. That would be awkward," I mumble.

"I need you to remove your hands from Miss Hoffman's waist, or I will remove them and then break each finger one by one."

He did not just say that. But he did. Even in my tipsy state, I heard every word and all the other words that weren't said but implied.

Welp, that just sobered me up. I mean, kind of. I am still seeing everything with a fuzzy halo around it, and these men aren't angels.

Suddenly, I am transferred out of Ivan's arms and into Collins's stronger ones. I no longer feel nauseous. I feel confused. Why does his touch feel so different? *Wanted.*

I crave his attention.

We are the only three in the pool, which makes it extra awkward. It's as if I'm stuck in the middle of some show-down, while the rest of my family is probably playing yard games in back.

They definitely can't see this craziness. It will surely draw suspicion that Collins is doing more than just guarding my body. He is also corrupting it.

Reaching behind me, Collins grabs a huge disposable cup of water. "Drink this."

"Okay, Mr. Bodyguard."

"All of it."

I do as I'm told and watch as he grins approvingly at me when I smack my lips after the last drop is consumed. "Happy?"

"Ecstatic," he deadpans.

"Sheesh, you're in a mood."

"And eat this."

I stare at the cheeseburger he magically presents to me out of thin air. Like seriously, where did he get this from? "I'm not hungry."

"Eat it."

"She said no. No means no."

Ivan.

Ivan, you are going to get pummeled, and there won't be a damn thing I can do to stop it.

Collins twitches but doesn't pay Ivan any attention. Instead his entire focus is on me. "Eat the food, Penelope. *Now.*"

"I'm a vegetarian now."

"Bullshit,"—he lowers his voice—"I know you love swallowing my meat."

Well, at least I can't call him a liar.

One second I'm in the pool, and the next I'm sitting on the edge with a cheeseburger pressed into my palm.

I want to resist. Trust me, I do.

But Dad makes the juiciest burgers with a little bit of smoked gouda in the middle and white cheddar on top...

I need to soak up some of the alcohol I downed earlier. Collins is right—as usual—that I haven't eaten enough food today. And he would know. The man hasn't stopped staring at me since we arrived here. If anyone is going to cast suspicion onto us, it is him.

Moving the sandwich to my lips, I take a big bite, sinking my teeth down. With each chew, I think Collins gloats. He definitely won this battle. I just hope it doesn't turn into a war with the way Ivan keeps staring.

I'm definitely not used to having two possessive men vying for my attention.

"I had this handled, man."

Ivan, Ivan, Ivan…

He really doesn't give up. It's best though if he just shuts up. Collins is in no mood.

"No peeing in the pool from this pissing contest," I blurt out. And then I giggle. Like the uncontrollable kind where I'm worrying I might be the one to pee. I giggle myself back into the pool, and when I start to sink and sputter out bubbles to the surface, Collins rescues me. "I need to use the bathroom." I cross my legs under the water. "Hurry!"

With gentle precision, Collins has us both out of the pool, a dry towel wrapped around me, and his hand guiding me at my lower back to move toward the nearest bathroom.

Realizing I need my stuff, I whip around to try to look for my bag but find it dangling from Collins's wrist.

"Oh." I look up into Collins's eyes. "You always rescue me when I need it most."

"And I always will."

"What about when the contract ends?" I press. What will the dynamic be then?

"I will always put your interests ahead of my own." It's as if he wants to say more but holds back. And it's in that silence that I know I'll find the truth—the truth he is always resistant to share.

"But why?"

He continues to move me through the door to the basement and then into the bathroom. Shutting the door, he defaults to his natural reaction which is to ignore my question.

This man. He'll be the death of me.

Alone inside my parents' basement bathroom, I lean against the vanity to try to regain my composure. Why does Collins Stone continue to get under my skin without even trying? He does things to me. He gives me false hope.

So much has happened during this barbecue that I'm starting to get whiplash.

After a couple of minutes, I realize why I am here in the first place and start to undo my damp suit, but it's suctioned to my skin like another layer. It's basically bondage.

Cursing, I stumble into the shower door, creating a jarring sound.

"Penny, do you need help?"

Maybe if I just lie down, I can wiggle my way out of it.

Then I hear the click from the door opening, and the slow warmth from humiliation fills my body, hitting my cheeks which I know must be flaming red.

"Penny?"

"Yeah." I look up at Collins who is now hovering above me. "My swimsuit is attacking me."

"Is that so?"

"Quit looking like you're enjoying my struggle."

"It's hard not to enjoy a view with you tied up on the floor."

"Just help me get out of this straitjacket. This is a death trap."

"Gladly."

"Preferably before I pee all over this chastity belt."

Helping me up from the floor, he mumbles, "Got it," while stifling his laughter.

I want to smack him for finding this funny, but I can't

because I'm too grateful for him figuring out the maze which is my swimsuit. I definitely didn't think about practicality when I bought this thing.

My hands cover my breasts, while I bend a thigh to shield my pussy from his penetrating gaze.

I can't tell if he is amused or aroused. "Stop looking at me."

"It's impossible not to want to look at you, Pen." Taking a step closer, he pulls my wrapped arms down from my chest. And without warning, he gently kicks open my feet to expose all of me. "There. That's much better."

I rock up on my heels. "You can leave." I'm ready to burst.

"And miss the show?"

"Huh? I really do have to pee." Does he not understand the urgency I'm facing? What's he doing? "Like *now*."

"I'd rather stay. So sit. Do your thing. It would be silly of me to miss an opportunity to administer your punishment —yeah?"

"I can't with you watching."

Leaning against the vanity, Collins locks his eyes with mine. "We've done way more intimate things together, and I'll continue to push those boundaries. Because it's in your discomfort that you learn more about yourself. So get used to it. And never hide that beautifully delectable body from me again. Now, sit."

"Fine."

"And let this be a reminder that I see everything. I see how men look at you. I see how you get a dark thrill from driving me to my breaking point with desire to consume all parts of your mind."

Sitting down, I stare at him with my pouty lip pressed out in defiance. But I can't do it. Not with his eagle eyes watching me like his prey. So I find my loophole and close my own eyes.

There. Now I can't see him seeing me.

It's almost the same thing…

Relaxing my pelvic floor muscles, I try.

But there's no hiding from Collins. I can feel him even more when I am the one hiding out in the darkness.

Damn him.

"I don't want you drinking anymore tonight."

"Why? Drinking can be fun."

"Because you get super charged up and—"

My eyes pop open. "You mean *horny*."

"Yeah, that." He shakes his head at me while I giggle. "Then you'll be more prone to making bad decisions."

"Bad decisions can be fun." Okay, now I can't stop giggling.

"Only if you make them with me."

Faking seriousness, I straighten my posture. "Mr. Rule Follower can make a bad decision? Nah. I don't buy it."

"Many would say I'm making one with you." He watches me while I finish up and stand in front of him— fully exposed and vulnerable.

Silence hovers between us, like a ghostly third wheel, making me question if he is actually having regret.

I wouldn't blame him. I don't find pleasure in his constant state of turmoil over betraying my brothers, but he's not alone in his emotions.

I know I've betrayed them too.

My brothers saved my life by getting me the counseling

and therapy I needed to try to move past the trauma I endured from Mark Tanner.

And this is how I repay them? By sneaking behind their backs…

With their most trusted employee.

But Collins makes me feel alive.

He sees me when I am at my most vulnerable and doesn't want to run away.

Like the opposing poles of a magnet, we are drawn together like a force that is far bigger than either of us. And no matter how hard we resist, we can't help but find ourselves pressed up against one another when the opportunity presents itself—like now.

Collins's lips find my neck, and his fingers trail paths along the sides of my torso, coming to rest at my hips. Every self-conscious thought on whether I look good enough for him washes away, because I feel his attraction—every inch of it.

"Collins," my lips whisper. My head falls back, as he helps me stay upright. "I want…"

"Tell me, Princess."

My body melts a bit more. I love when he calls me that. I swallow the saliva pooling in my mouth as his fingers caress and squeeze the flesh of my ass.

It's a simple touch and yet it's all I crave. The closeness…

"I want you to"—I moan as he slides his hands down the backs of my upper thighs—"make me come."

"Oh, I plan to, but I'm not sure you've been a very good girl today."

Like a balloon deflating, my spirit sags. He won't deny me again, will he? "Please, Collins."

When I flop forward, he catches me, placing a gentle kiss on my nose.

Hoisting me up, he places my bare ass onto the cold surface of the vanity. His mouth finds the hollow of my neck and then trails kisses all the way down my breasts to my navel.

"I shouldn't want you, Penny."

His lips hover over my core, as if he's at the precipice of a big decision. And just when I think he's about to deny me what I so desperately need, he spreads my legs and kisses my clit.

"But I want you so fucking bad that I'm willing to travel the rings of hell if it means that I can have you at the center of it."

And then he licks me and nips, as I thrash on the countertop.

"Collins!"

Pulling himself off me, he spits on my pussy, and before I can recover from the shock of that surprisingly intimate act, he then slides two fingers inside. He knows just where to probe and press, but he seems to tragically—and I suspect, *purposely*—miss the spot.

"You are not to come. Do you understand?"

What kind of sick game of fuckery is this? "What? Are you just bitter I beat you at family games?"

Collins draws his eyebrows together. "We were on the same team."

"Well, we definitely are on different teams right now."

My inner walls clench, trying to suck his fingers in deeper. If I can just move this way, maybe I can...

Like a phantom, he's gone. And I am empty.

Deprived.

And trembling with unfulfilled need.

Then he—

"Ouch!"

Pain radiates through my pussy. Before I can slam my thighs together for protection, Collins is on me, eating me like I'm his last meal.

He's pressing his face into my core so determinedly that the back of my head hits the mirror, jostling it.

In the heat of the moment, I somehow slide down the vanity and manage to now scrape my spine against the rough edges.

Splayed out on the floor in my parents' bathroom, I surrender the only way I know how and submit to Collins as he feasts on me. The whole time, his hands hold my knees apart, giving me no other choice but to absorb every morsel of attention he wants to gift to me.

My whole body convulses as an orgasm so powerful pulses through me, gaining speed, and ultimately sending me over the edge of no return.

Tears flood out of my eyes, as I can't do anything but keep them tightly squeezed.

"What just happened?" I whisper-choke, genuinely confused if I actually lived that euphoria or if I'm stuck in some drunken fog.

Kneeling up, Collins towers over me. He keeps my legs spread, eyeing me with what, I'm not quite sure. But then, sticking out his tongue, he bends one leg and licks from knee to pussy, while tugging my entire body off the ground so he has access.

By the time he repeats the same process on the second leg, I'm melting even more.

"You were given one rule, Penelope."

"Hmm?" What is he even talking about?

"You were not to *come*."

I start to giggle, but then stop when I realize he isn't joking. "You can't be serious."

"Oh, I most definitely was clear with my expectations. You just decided that your desire for release trumped my desire for you to have a solid punishment."

"So now what?"

"Funny you should ask."

Helping us both up off the floor, he places me back onto the vanity. Then he slides a hand into the pocket of his swim shorts and pulls out a shimmery pink…

What is that?

Collins…

My mouth gapes.

A sex toy?

"Did you just happen to find that on accident?"

He spins it around in his hand. "Maybe."

"You are just walking around with a pocket full of tricks…"

I don't remember him having it while we were in the pool. I can't imagine him having it in the water where it could easily fall out—but what do I know? I'm either oblivious or he's a magician.

My eyes study the curved device while Collins does what he does best—keeps quiet.

I motion toward the toy. "Is that for you or for me?"

There. I got him to smirk.

Finally.

I hate when he's this serious. I think it just makes me nervous over his next move.

"Scoot back, bend your knees, and place your feet up on the counter."

I do as I'm told, mainly because I'm curious what Collins has planned.

He rotates the toy in his hands, and then brings it to my lips. I open and suck on the smooth device, lubricating it with my saliva and testing its weight on my tongue.

"You are such a sight. A feast for my eyes."

His words of praise help soften me, as I melt right onto the countertop.

Who needs spit when I have been charged and ready to go all day?

Collins removes the toy from my mouth and then presses it to my clit, making me jerk from the contrast. With a delicate touch, he inserts the device into me and then adjusts the external arm to align on top of my clit.

When he has it situated to his liking, Collins stands up and unzips my tote bag. He pulls out my panties and helps me into them while I'm still perched on the counter like some cupcake on display in the window at a bakery.

Just when I start to question what is so special about the toy embedded inside of me, Collins hits some button on a tiny remote, and suddenly I'm transported to another place in my head.

Staring up at the ceiling, I let out a moan. "I, ah, I…"

My bottom wiggles, trying to get away from the

vibrating sensations wreaking havoc on what I can only assume is my G-spot. But the piece that is sitting on my clit, with my panties holding it firmly into place, is my ultimate undoing. That thing needs to go away or I will…

"Don't come."

"Oh, shut up!"

"Tsk, tsk."

"Listening to you make these wonky demands is like listening to someone give directions on how to get to purgatory."

Collins narrows his eyes, locking them in with mine. "That's no way to speak to your deliverer of pleasure, is it?"

My eyes squeeze shut, and I instantly feel the moisture breaking out from the corners. I'm going to die. I'm going to die on this bathroom vanity from…I don't know what.

But I just know I'm a goner.

"Turn it off."

Collins presses a kiss to my forehead and then my nose. If he calls me adorable, I may attack him. He then pulls out my backup outfit from the bag, consisting of a red, white, and blue striped sundress.

I guess I did bring an obscene amount of outfits. I think I just bought too many festive ones, and with this being the last big holiday of summer, I am running out of time to wear them without it looking weird.

"Arms up."

So he's just going to ignore that I'm melting away right in front of his eyes. Is that what's going on right now?

"I can't."

"You *can*. And you will."

I shake my head no, which causes Collins to laugh.

Then I jump into his arms as he triggers the higher setting on the toy buzzing between my legs.

It's like he's electrocuting me.

Bastard.

I go boneless and struggle to get my legs to hold my weight, and just when I think I'll combust, all the sensations stop.

My body sags against Collins, as I try to catch my breath.

And somehow during all of this commotion, he managed to get my bra on and the dress over my head.

Wizard.

"Ready to go back out to the party?"

"I can't." I pout out my bottom lip. "That sounds like torture."

"It will be invigorating."

"I can't," I repeat, my tone a bit more urgent.

That has definitely been the theme of this little detour... Thinking I can't, when clearly Collins had other expectations.

"You are forbidden from orgasming, no matter what you feel while we are out there"—he gestures toward the window—"having fun."

"What happens if I can't resist?"

"Then you get punished."

I cross my arms over my chest. "That doesn't seem fair at all. I should at least get a prize for accomplishing the challenge."

"What do you have in mind?"

"If I do as I'm told and be your good girl, then"—I jolt as he hits the remote suddenly to send a shock to my core—

"stop that!" I hit him on the arm that is controlling the next hour of my life, and he relents. "You are having way too much fun with a little bit of control."

"I am," he agrees. "Now what were you saying, Princess?"

"If I win, we have date night at Limit-X."

"No."

I frown. "Oh, c'mon."

"No."

"Just don't lose."

"Oh, trust me. I don't plan on it."

"So we have a deal?"

"Yes, Penelope."

25

COLLINS

When I get out to the patio, I scan my eyes along the backyard, doing what I normally do when I walk into a space.

The girls and Ivan are huddled up around a table in the shade looking at photos of some sort. With the slow setting sun, the patio lights have kicked on, casting a warm glow to the entire area.

I want to go to Penny, but I also see her brothers making their way toward me so I resist.

The magnetic pull I feel when she is around is dangerous. Not only does it make me twitchy, it also makes me impulsive. And if douchebag Ivan doesn't watch where he places his attention, I can bust both his eyes up so that everything he sees is through a lens of blood.

Ivan's tone was pleasant earlier, yet the smug glimmer in his eye let me know he appreciates himself—and definitely a tad bit too much. He glances around the group, probably taking poll of everyone's reaction. My teeth grit together at his attention on my Penelope, and there isn't a damn thing I can do about it now without ruining the facade I have impeccably maintained.

I just hope she realizes that every grin she gives him is accounted for, and I will enjoy each lick I give her pussy to cleanse her mind of the fucker who wants to take what is mine.

But in the meantime, I slide my hand into my pocket and hit the button to send her a little pulse where it matters most.

And a reminder of just who she belongs to…

Her little gasp is muffled by a cough, and when she whips her body around to find me, I pretend I don't notice.

When Nic and Graham catch up to me, they both gesture toward the girls, plus Ivan. "And so it begins…" the older Hoffman says.

Not on my watch.

"Well, that didn't take long," Nic snickers, his attention on his younger sister.

"Thoughts?" I ask, trying to gauge if we are on the same page or not.

Graham shrugs. "If you sabotage things too fast, it just makes Penny bitter and volatile."

I nod. "This is true."

But what they don't know is that there is no way in hell I'm going to sit back and watch Ivan move in on Penny. We also have a contract in place that prohibits such during our time together.

"What are they looking at anyway?" Nic asks, moving closer to their table.

Graham and I follow, seeing that the photos are from the riverfront shoot—and they look amazing.

"Who would have thought the crying pictures would turn out like they did?" Penny mutters, holding one in her hand.

She's right. They are phenomenal.

But her eyes tell a different story now, as I imagine she is trying to relive those moments at the water where she lost sight of reality.

I want to pull her in my arms and coddle her and make her understand I will do anything to remove that sad look from her eyes.

Anything.

"What if we did a Breakup Box?" Claire asks. "How cool would it be to help empower other women to find their new stride with the help of some revenge clothes and makeup? We can keep it comfy but also keep it purposeful."

"I love that idea!" Angie says, her excitement building.

Jumping up from the table, she runs into the house through the basement door and returns with some printer paper and a pen.

"When inspiration hits," Claire says with a giggle, "we waste no time."

Nic bends forward to kiss her on her hairline. "I hope you know how proud I am of you ladies."

"Yes, I agree. You have really found your path," Graham says with pride.

Penny's eyes connect with mine, and I can only hope I portray my emotions appropriately. She wipes at her mouth, and tries to hide a smile.

Good.

I'm proud of you too, Princess.

But the moment is ruined when Ivan decides to put a hand around Penny's shoulders.

So I up the speed on her vibrator for a pulse, causing her to be visibly uncomfortable.

Good.

I count the seconds—nine in total—she leaves his hand there before she excuses herself from the table, most likely to be polite and make his unwanted attention less awkward.

"Good girl," I whisper to her as she passes by me.

She ignores me. So I give her extra attention with the remote control, making her have a different walking stride with the change in rhythms. As she looks over her shoulder, I pat my pocket and watch as the color in her cheeks changes.

Then I crank up the juice and watch her squirm.

Sliding from his seat, Ivan takes the similar path as Penny.

"Can I have a word with you?" I ask confidently, causing him to stop in his tracks.

"Yeah, sure."

Moving over to underneath the deck, I rotate my body so I can still see my surroundings.

The sun has basically set, and I'm counting down the minutes until I can take Penny back to my place and have my way with her wicked sex drive.

"Penny's been through a lot this past year. The last thing she needs is a speed bump in her progress."

"I can look out for Penny," he says simply. "We have a past."

"A fictional one you made up in your head. She won't be one of your disposable women. You have quite the dating history."

"Why do you care?"

"Because the Hoffmans are under my protection, and I don't take my job lightly."

Fireworks from a nearby holiday festival echo in the air, causing everyone to look up in the sky to see where they are being set off.

Ivan and I separate, and I go to find Penny.

"What did you say to him?" she asks.

"I told him to stay away from you, and that you won't be one of his numerous take-and-toss women he has dated in the past."

"When did you have time to look that up?"

"It's not difficult when the showboater loves to post his face and who he is with on social media."

"You are obsessed."

"Not obsessed."

She fixes a piece of flyaway hair. "You could have fooled me. How would you describe it?"

"Hmm...concentrated information gathering."

"You are giving me buyer's remorse."

I eye her. "Is that so?"

"Is it too late to alter the contract?"

"How so?" I humor her.

"I want to add my exit strategy for when your overprotective tendencies become unbearable. Like they are now."

"No deal."

"Why are you so upset?" I ask, as Penny stirs in silence in the passenger seat.

I'm used to her telling me everything on her mind. I usually have a running commentary of just what she thinks of me and my methods, but right now? Nothing.

Silence.

And I'm about to lose my mind.

Then she places a hand between her thighs, removes the vibrator, and tosses it into the back seat.

But still, nothing. Not even a grunt.

"Talk to me, Pen."

Rotating away from me in her seat, she stares out the window, clearly avoiding me at all costs. Even her knees are pointing away.

After several long minutes, I decide to pull off the road. I've had enough of her not telling me what's upset her.

I cut the engine and open the sunroof to allow in fresh air. The tinted windows allow for some privacy. Luckily, the night air has cooled down a considerable amount.

From the distance, the echoing sound of fireworks fills the space, coupled with Penny's sniffles. Does she have a cold? What's going on?

When I turn to fully look at her, I can see the tears rolling down her face.

Fuck.

I hit the button on the side of my seat to send it backward to allow me more space between the steering wheel and my body.

"Penny?"

"Leave me alone."

She angrily wipes at her eyes as if she's pissed she is crying in the first place.

I unlock myself and then her from our seat belts, and nudge her toward me.

"Come here, Princess."

"No."

My face relaxes, as I try to coax her to obey. "Penelope, come here and let me hold you."

Come on, baby, give in.

Without another word, she climbs into my arms, straddling me.

Good.

She's exactly where she belongs. Her touch, being this close, is proof of perfection.

I want to demand she tells me what's really bothering her. I want to wrestle the words out of her mouth and make her promise not to give me the silent treatment again in the future…

But instead, I just wrap my arms around her and hold her to me, with one hand rubbing little circles into her back and the other getting lost in her beautiful hair.

And finally, when her breathing slows and she is relaxed, I peel her off the front of me—ever so carefully—and look at her eyes in the moonlit darkness of the vehicle.

"Why are you so angry with me?"

"You really don't know?"

"I would rather hear your pure thoughts without my own assumptions muddling anything."

"You were a jerk to Ivan," Penny blurts out without any prelude.

"Was I?" I knew she was upset back at the barbecue, but I thought we had moved forward from it. Maybe I just secretly hoped we had. "I actually thought I was being reasonable."

Penny's jaw opens, dropping with gravity. "Reasonable?"

"Yes."

She makes some unintelligible grumble sound but then clears her throat and clarifies, "I'd hate to see what unreasonable looks like."

"It usually involves a body bag and an alibi."

"Sheesh! Ivan is a friend. No need to put a hit out on him. Seriously."

"Guys can't be friends with girls."

Her eyes narrow on mine. "Says who?"

"Says science."

"Well, science can be wrong."

"We are genetically conditioned to want to mate. So keeping things friendly will be the last thing on his mind. Trust me. He wants you. And I refuse to give you up, Princess."

"Ivan isn't like—"

"Three times you've said another man's name while you are on my lap. Three times, Penelope." My fingers grip her waist. "When you are straddling me like you are"—I rock her back and forth for added emphasis—"you are never to have another man's name fall from those lips."

"Collins?"

"Yes, Princess?"

"I'm really horny. Can you make it all better?"

My eyes darken. I've been on edge for the last twelve

hours, counting down the time I can toss her onto my bed and bend her to my will.

And here she sits, perched on my lap like a freaking goddess, telling me she wants me to take care of her.

How can I ever deny either of us what our bodies are conditioned to crave?

"Lift up those gorgeous hips."

When she does, I unbutton and unzip the fly to my shorts. It takes me a few seconds to free my straining cock, and when I do, I can feel the pre-cum leaking from the tip.

"Hurry."

Oh, no, you don't. I'm in control of this despite how utterly out of control this girl makes me.

"I want you to slide those fucking tease of a panties aside and show me what's mine. That's it. You're being such a good girl, Princess."

Taking a finger, I trail it along her wet slit, spreading her juices all over the lips at her opening. Her scent fills the car, and I hope it never fades.

I want every memory with Penny embedded into my space.

And tonight, we surely are making some lasting ones.

When I've teased her enough, I slip my middle finger into her, pumping inside a few times. She's ready. All the foreplay at the barbecue prepared her for my claiming.

Removing my finger, I add a second.

And then a third.

"I need you," she moans.

Taking out all three fingers, I bring two up to her mouth in offering. "Open wide."

And she does—like the good girl she is.

So, I slide them in and out of her mouth while I lean forward to clean off the third at the same time.

It's moments like these where I fantasize about whisking her away and creating as many ties as possible between us that can never be undone.

I desire a *forever*, when the reality is just a *for now*.

Men like me play for keeps but always expect to lose. Because with Penny, I will perpetually suffer a loss. Every. Single. Time.

And while the odds are always stacked against me, it's a gamble I freely take.

So it's best I soak up every single, fleeting moment while they last, just as I am now.

"Collins..." she says breathily, slurring her words around my fingers pressed against her tongue. "I need more."

I remove my fingers and groan when she grinds her pussy against my cock.

My lips find refuge against her dampened ones, and the taste of her consumes me.

Just when I think I'll explode from Penny pressing herself against my hard cock, I decide to take us both out of our misery.

With two firm hands, I lift Penny off my hip, just to lower her slowly onto my desperate cock.

"Slide down, Princess. You control the tempo."

"You feel so good... I want to stay here forever."

As do I, sweet girl. As do I.

Biting back my feelings, I give Penny the freedom to set the pace. "Ride me, Princess. Take from me what your body desires."

And she does.

And tonight I saw fireworks more than just in the sky.

I saw them reflected back in her eyes.

"What you doin'?" Penny asks, before her eyes close from the brightness hitting them from the overhead lights in the parking garage.

"Putting a jacket on you and carrying you into our building."

"I can walk."

"Clearly, you can't."

"Someone will see."

I cover her head with the hood. "Now they won't."

Even in her grogginess, Penny still manages to pout out that bottom lip of hers. I want to bite and kiss it, but I also want her inside my safe haven as fast as I can get her there.

It's the safety net of having her in my space that helps me to be calm.

Pulling over on the side of the road to fuck each other's brains out wasn't what I would refer to as my norm.

In fact, I've never done something so impulsive before at night, along a low-traffic side road.

But that's what Penny does to me. She makes me move past my comfort zone.

What was I supposed to do when she was whimpering about being horny? It's not like I could really drive safely with a hard-on poking at the steering wheel either. Pair that with her tears, and I was a goner long before she slid her delectable pussy down on my cock and rode me to completion.

I should have known that leaving the party in our heightened states of arousal would only end one way. I still can't believe she won. I blame it on me being so committed to making her lose control that I was distracted. Deep down, I didn't want her to lose and risk the chance of that asshole noticing how she gets flushed when she's fully immersed in pleasure.

Now I'm going to have to cope with how to get us into Limit-X as a couple without losing my ever-loving mind over other men—and women—looking at what I have deemed as *mine*.

I know why people go there. They go for a kinky release. Or to find easy, malleable prey.

There are rules set in place, and Yuri works very hard at maintaining a safe environment for exploration, but things can happen…and nefarious people can slip through even the strictest protocols.

So I need to be prepared mentally prior to going.

Because I'll go fucking feral if someone thinks they can make a move on her.

There won't be a security guard or dungeon monitor there who will pull me off anyone who even thinks about messing with Penelope Hoffman—especially when we are under contract.

She is mine to protect.

Mine to serve.

I look down at Penny as she shifts in my arms and rubs her hand all over my chest.

I smirk down at her, and she catches me watching her exploration.

"Hi."

She manages to look innocent, and in the scheme of things, she really is that way.

I'm the one who is corrupting her.

I'm the wolf that is salivating over the little lamb.

My smile can't be contained around this girl. "Hi." She doesn't seem sick, yet I can't help but ask, "Are you feeling okay?"

Penny swallows. "I think I just need some water. My throat is dry."

I nod in understanding. The later part of the evening consisted of more alcohol consumption, so it's no surprise that she is slowly feeling the negative effects of those choices now.

I get us into the elevator and up to my floor. As soon as the door clicks into place and the security system is set with just the push of a button, I feel like I can finally relax.

This entire day was one big stressful event. Between the fear of casting suspicion on our arrangement and the desire to bury Ivan in the field behind the Hoffman house, I'm ready for some downtime.

All of the things I will need to handle can wait until tomorrow.

Right now, focusing my attention on taking care of my princess is just what I need to distract me from the life that is lived outside of these walls.

I toe off my shoes. Penny follows suit with hers, flinging them across the room in opposite directions.

Why do I find her chaotic behavior that is so opposite of my rigid routines charming?

Before Penny, any amount of mess would have sent me on a mental tailspin. Yet now I find the clutter comforting.

That's what Penny does to my space—my life.

She shakes it all up.

26

PENNY

Collins and I are a bundle of intertwining limbs when I start to come out of my sleep coma. I love these lazy mornings with him, where we have no place to be but in bed together.

I breathe in his clean, masculine scent. He smells like a beautiful rainstorm in the middle of an evergreen forest.

He makes it easy to lose track of time—and often days.

We have fallen into a peaceful rhythm of enjoying each other's company, while fucking each other into oblivion.

Every activity spent at home turns into me getting railed and impaled.

I've gotten very comfortable walking around naked in his space. It honestly makes it easier to enjoy a movie or chores together, when we both know how the task will end.

Collins makes me forget that just weeks ago, I was slipping into a bad state again at the photoshoot. It's as if he is consuming all of my waking thoughts, and if I just take that plunge, maybe he'll be the center of my life—and not the looming sense of doom that is surrounding the upcoming Mark Tanner trial.

"Your mind is elsewhere, Pen," he warns.

I know. And I feel guilt over it. It's not like I enjoy my negative thinking. It just seeps through sometimes—and especially in the morning when I'm lying in bed and it's quiet.

"Do you think I have to testify? I don't want to. What happens if I freak out on the stand? I don't want to see his face anymore. It freaks me out to think about him staring at me in court. I just don't want to do it. But I'll have to. Right?"

Collins tucks me tighter into his side. "I want you to listen to me, okay? Trust me that I will protect you, and your brothers will protect you at all cost. Do not worry about a trial."

Turning to look at him, I try to seek out the reason. "But what if?"

"I don't want you worrying over this. I will handle it."

"But maybe I should talk to the lawyers to see if they will delay the trial. I just don't think I can emotionally handle anything right now."

Collins's hands massage the tension out of me, kneading my muscles and sending ripples of pleasure through all of my limbs.

"I don't want you worrying another second over the bastard."

He may not be worried over the trial, but I sure am.

Yet, I have other reasons to worry over my own mental health. At this point in our contract, I've already tied those invisible strings from each of our hearts, and with each memory made by spending time together, I am making the knots get stronger.

We are living on the same wavelength, hoping that time slows down.

Saying goodbye is going to destroy me.

Rolling over, I nuzzle my nose into Collins's neck. "You smell so good."

His arms and legs wrap around me, locking me to him like a vise.

"I never want to let you go."

Same.

But that's the thing… We are living life on a fault line.

Our phones both start vibrating simultaneously from the nightstand.

"Unbelievable," I groan. "Can't anyone respect the need for sleep?"

"It's almost noon, Pen."

I thrust myself out of bed, running through my mental list of plans for the day, and then realize that my days consist of two things…pleasing Collins and being pleased by Collins.

"I really need to get a job. I mean, I have one but something more consistent." Maybe then I wouldn't find my only purpose for the day to be sneaking my way between Collins and the mattress.

And the man finds it comical when I try to veer from the plan—to change things up—when I always end up defaulting back to being his little slut for the day anyway.

Granted, I'm not complaining. I also know that I'm never going to find a job with as good of a benefits package as his. But Plus None is pretty perfect.

Collins leans over my boneless body to grab our phones, passing mine to me.

"It's Graham," he says with a nervous edge to his tone.

I can already tell that a little bit of guilt is slithering into our day—and it hasn't even officially begun.

"Days can't start until I am out of pajamas." I wiggle under the sheets and realize I don't even have those on. "Ha. I'm not wearing any. Oh well, clothes are overrated anyway."

I glance over at Collins whose focus is on the screen of his phone.

"Get dressed."

"What does Graham want?"

"He's in the lobby."

"No."

But Collins doesn't joke.

Oh, hell.

"He wants to check out your new place," he continues.

Quickly, I look at my messages. "Angie's with him."

I throw myself off the bed and rush into the master closet to find something appropriate to wear.

Grabbing my phone, I dial Luke's number.

"Answer, dammit."

I pluck whatever outfit I can from the shelves and put it on, all while my phone continues to try to connect with my semi-useless roommate.

And he answers. "And you do exist…"

"I need you to tell my brother and sister-in-law that I'm running errands and will be right back. They are on their way to our place now."

Luke chuckles. "You're with Mr. Broody Booty, aren't you?"

I shake my head although he can't see, and without dropping the phone, I twist my hair into a bun using a tie I find on the bathroom doorknob. "Please. I will owe you. And don't breathe a word of Mr. Broody Booty"—*Why did I just say that?*—"to my brother. *Please.*"

"I want double IOUs."

"Okay, fine."

"Yes!"

I can almost see Luke's fist pounding into the air, like he just won something magical.

Slipping on sandals, I rush out of the room and down the hallway. "Just distract them or give them a tour or something. I'll be right there."

Collins meets me at the main door, smoothing out some flyaway hairs coming from my bun.

"Wish me luck."

"If anything bad ever happens, I will take full responsibility for our actions. This won't fall on you."

My heart breaks a little with his need to always protect me. "That doesn't seem fair."

"We both know that I am old enough to know better."

"I'm not a child, Collins."

He closes his eyes, his fingers playing on my hips. "No. No, you're not. But no one will believe that I didn't take advantage of you. So I will accept any repercussions if that means protecting you."

"Whatever. We can discuss that later."

I grab my purse and rush out of the door and decide to

take the stairs down to the lobby. I need to run a fake errand, so I use this opportunity to check my mailbox.

"Hey, Penny."

I turn toward the voice coming from behind me, seeing Rex about to exit the building. "Oh, hi. What are you up to?"

"I'm going back to my place now, but Luke and I were just playing some video games together."

"Oh, gotcha," I say in a hurry, probably coming off a little rude. "Maybe we can all hang out soon."

"That sounds fun. Let's do it," he says, giving me a wave goodbye.

Fishing out my key, I insert it into my box and pull out a bunch of junk mail and then a bubble envelope. Turning it over, I see the return address is listed as the prison.

What the hell?

Why is Mark sending me mail?

With trembling hands, I place the envelope into the stack of mail I have contained under my arm and walk to the elevator.

I don't even need to open it to know what's inside. Mark's threatening me and taunting me. He promised me during my visit with him that he had ways of getting to me.

And he's proving it to me now.

I thought that my brothers finding out about me and Collins was the greatest threat to my happiness, but what if Mark Tanner polluting my head so badly that I get sent back to Soulful Mind is the real predator? What happens if the only way to get Mark convicted with a concrete sentence is to testify against him?

Feeling the pangs of panic rising in my throat, I get on the elevator and hit the button for my floor.

When the doors open, I walk in silence to my place and enter.

With their backs turned, I see Graham and Angie chatting with Luke, who seems to be soaking up the attention.

Oh, please don't make a snarky comment about me never being here.

I kick my shoes off and walk deeper into the room, making everyone turn toward me.

Angie greets me with a hug. "Hey, Penny." She takes a step back and looks at me with concern while mouthing, "Are you okay?"

I bite at my bottom lip and shake my head no.

"Hey," she says, leveling her eyes with mine. "Whatever it is, it will be okay."

Probably hearing the conversation, Graham makes his way over to me. "Penny, what has you so upset?"

I wipe at the tears forming in my eyes and hand over the unopened envelope.

"What's this?" my brother asks, staring at the return label. "Tanner? Fucking *Tanner*?"

"Yes. But I didn't see what he sent. I never opened it."

Graham curses under his breath and tears open the package. He takes a look inside and then shakes out a keychain into the palm of his hand. "Well, that's weird."

"A keychain?" I ask.

Angie clears her throat. "What kind of mind games is that evil man playing?"

Taking the ring from Graham's hand, I turn it over and

see the number three engraved into the flat piece of metal. What the hell?

"Penny?" Graham asks. His eyes bore into mine. "What do you know?"

I shake my head. "I don't know anything. But twice now, I've received these weird deliveries." I move into the kitchen and search for the postcard that I got weeks ago when I first moved in.

"What kind of deliveries? Were there return addresses?" he pries.

"No return addresses. But just"—I hold the card up that has the number one—"these types of mysterious deliveries."

"One," Graham says. "Is there a two?"

I nod. "Yeah. Well, I think. Hold on."

I rush into my bedroom, a room I have slept in cumulatively less than I have Collins's place, and grab the teddy bear that now has a limp number two balloon attached.

Walking back into the living room, I give Luke a weak smile. He appears to be confused but invested. I honestly haven't seen him this quiet ever.

"I missed you," he whispers to me.

"Same," I mouth. "I saw Rex in the lobby."

He nods. "Yeah, we've been hanging out more, since you're never here."

Guilt circulates through me. It must suck to have high hopes of being close to your roommate and then being disappointed when the image you created in your head doesn't exactly match reality.

I'm nearly positive Rex would make a better roommate for Luke than I am right now. We weren't even supposed to technically be roommates. I was supposed to be sharing space with another female.

Turning to my brother and sister-in-law, I show them the gift. Graham fixates on the two.

"One, two, three," he says softly. "And these only started appearing when you moved into this apartment?"

"Yes."

"And no name attached or note?"

I shake my head. "No. And today was the only sign of who was sending me things."

"And he obviously wanted you to know he was the sender."

"It appears that way," I say, my voice quivering. "What does he want from me?"

Graham hugs me to his side. "Do not worry, Penny. That man can't hurt you. I would never allow that."

Angie hugs me as tears cascade down my cheeks. Graham pulls out his phone from his pocket and sends a text to Nic, I assume. But no matter how hard my brothers try to protect me from physical danger, there is no one capable of shielding my mind from Mark's influence.

He is a poison that needs to be eradicated out of my psyche.

"You are safe, Penny," Angie says soothingly.

"No, I'm not," I say a bit too harshly and feel guilty for it. "Mark's haunting me from behind bars just like he promised me he would when I went to visit him. He's playing a sick game. I felt it at the waterfront during the photoshoot, and I feel it now. He's watching me. He's going to win."

Graham sighs. "Only if you let him get to you. He's

grasping at straws. He knows that his life is over and he's desperate."

Moving from Angie's embrace, I walk into the kitchen and find Luke loitering near the side. I'd kind of forgotten he was here. He's being quiet and not trying to lighten the situation, which is just odd for him.

"You okay?" he asks, his tone deep.

I shake my head, afraid to talk and allow my voice to quiver. I open the fridge and discover that I don't even have anything to drink. This makes sense since I haven't been here in days.

Settling for a cup of water, I force it down my throat, nearly choking on it.

Graham joins me in the kitchen. "You need a distraction."

Turning to him, I look him in the eyes. "Am I going to have to testify?"

"Fuck, no."

"Then why can't I shake this feeling that Mark Tanner is going to be released on some technicality?"

"He won't, Penny. I won't ever allow him to get to you."

Leaning into my brother, I rest my head on his chest. "I trust you. I do. But I also know that on the margins of my brain lurks the evil ghost that is Mark. It's like he's waiting for me."

After a minute, Graham and I separate.

"So, I originally came here to see your place and to offer to take you to go see Claire and Nic's new home."

"It's finished?" Wow. That was fast. I guess when you are loaded with money and connections, things can get sped along.

"Yes, and I can't wait to see it."

Excitement rushes through me. "I definitely want to see it."

"Claire even has an elevator so Nic can stop worrying over her missing a step," Angie volunteers with a laugh.

"Of course he does. Punk is probably driving her to the guest room with his overprotectiveness."

Angie leans against the counter. "Ha, I think she has four of those rooms, so at least she has options."

There's a light knock at the door, making us all turn.

"That's Collins," Graham says. "I am going to have him drive you, Penny. That way you can leave whenever you want."

It's more than that though. I think these men are strategically keeping information from me and are using this time at Nic's as a way to hold a meeting where I'm conveniently not invited. With the delivery today, I'm sure they have a lot more to discuss.

I walk to the door and let him in. "Hi, Collins."

He tilts his head toward me. "Miss Hoffman."

I step back and allow him to walk past. He takes the direct path to the keychain and examines it between his fingers. Having spent so much time with Collins, I know the subtle mannerisms that hint at his mood.

And right now he is livid.

His spine is rigid. And his eyes are focused on the envelope. He is holding it so tightly, I worry he's going to break a bone in his fingers.

I want to comfort him. I know he's upset that I'm being threatened. But I can't.

"You'll make sure Penny gets to Nic's safely?" Graham asks him.

Collins gives him a look and a slight nod.

I always find it fascinating that these strong-willed men in my life can have conversations without ever speaking a word. So much can be said in a look or with a gesture.

"Ready to go?" Collins asks.

His hand moves to where my lower back is, but doesn't connect. Quickly, he retracts it, and I mourn the loss.

My brother might think that going to Nic and Claire's new house will be a calm distraction, but getting there with my broody bodyguard will be nothing but tension-filled.

"Can I drive?" I ask, already knowing the answer.

"Sure."

My body snaps to Collins. "What?"

"Yes, you may drive, Princess."

My body relaxes. "It's going to be the ride of your life."

"I have no doubt."

27

PENNY

"You're doing really well, Penny."

My face warms from the positive praise. I spare a glance at Collins. Why does he always look at me like he's in need of some carbs?

Give the dude a snack.

"Thank you," I say softly. I pull into the driveway. "Maybe I should have taken a detour and got you some takeout to eat."

"Why?"

"You just look hungry."

"I am. But for you."

"I'm pretty sure having sex in my brother's new house would be wrong. So please don't flirt with me."

Collins chuckles. "Fair enough."

I cut the engine, hand over the keys, and wait like an obedient princess to be escorted out of my seat like I am part of a dynasty of incapable women.

"You know I can get my own door, right?"

"You know I don't care to entertain your opinion about it at the moment, right?"

I stick my tongue out at him, mainly because I can and also because I'm safe here from any repercussions.

Collins gets out of the vehicle, walks over to my side, and helps me out like the dutiful bodyguard who has to protect me from accidentally breaking a nail or stubbing a toe.

"Good girl," he says in a deep tone, sending shivers running up my spine. But it's his smirk of satisfaction over my submission that makes me melt even more.

"Behave," I warn.

"Or what?"

My eyes snap to his. He's not usually this bold, which only adds to my fear that some unspoken danger is lurking, and he's using every resource to keep me from noticing it. But I play along anyway. "I'll just have to seduce you at my brother's house."

"I won't complain."

I shake my head at him and his game he seems to be playing and distract myself by soaking in the scenery.

Located on the river and just north of town, Nic and Claire purchased a piece of land that is perfect for them.

And the house that sits on it is stunning.

Breathtaking.

Seeing Nic exit his house and make his way toward us, I take off running.

"Easy, Penny," he says with a laugh, catching me midair and spinning me around.

"This is so perfect. I love every detail."

"You haven't even seen inside it yet."

"But I know it will be spectacular because Momma assisted in the execution of your and Claire's ideas, and Dad helped with the architectural design."

Setting me on my feet, Nic shakes hands with Collins who has caught up to us.

"We are very fortunate to have two parents who enjoy that type of detailed work, because it isn't for me," he explains with a laugh.

"It's phenomenal. I just can't get over how pretty it is!"

Nic beams with pride. "Thank you. My girl deserved a forever home to raise our babies in, and giving her this is really a gift for myself just to see her happiness."

My heart feels like it is melting from the joy that my once-jaded brother has found his person.

"How is Claire?" Angie asks, joining us in the driveway.

I look behind him. "Yeah… Where is she?"

Nic shrugs, guiding me to the porch. "She *seems* to be doing well. I'm on the verge of bribing the doctor to order her to home confinement, just so she can slow down and take a rest."

I let out a little laugh. "You and I both know that she will hate that, resent you for it, and—"

"She won't find out."

"Ha," Angie chokes out. "You can't honestly believe that?"

Looking sheepish, Nic gives us a grin. "She'll know I had something to do with it the moment the doctor tells her."

I nod. "Exactly. Then you'll have to deal with her wrath." I fake shudder.

Angie giggles. "And there's not enough armor in the world that can protect you in that battle."

"This is true," Nic grumbles. "She would schedule removal surgery for my balls. And I need them if I want more kids."

I smirk. No one in the family ever thought Nic would find someone to put up with his overbearing ways. Yet Claire seems like she was created specifically for him.

Gah. I want to feel that way. Adored. Cherished. And then beastly ravished.

I yearn for that all-consuming and passionate love.

If it wasn't for my brothers finding it with their women, then I would think that it doesn't really exist. But I know it does. They are living proof.

Looking behind me, I see Collins and Graham chatting quietly.

And of course, the one man I'm truly connecting with is the one who I can't have long-term.

Why is life so unfair?

Nic leans his weight against the pillar, just as the front door behind him opens and out pops Claire.

"Oh, good. You all arrived and just in time. I made cocktails!"

She is by far the best thing that has ever happened to my otherwise boring brother. No wonder he is always trying to make her happy. He's afraid of her. I smile to myself at the irony of the controlling man being dished his own medicine. Serves him right.

"She's been prepping this event all morning," Nic explains with a forced smile.

"Oh, fun," I say, clapping my hands together.

"Well, come on in," Claire insists. "I'm going to use the bathroom and will join you ladies in the kitchen."

Once she's out of earshot, Nic leans into Angie and me. "I need a big favor."

"What is it?" Angie asks.

"I need you to pretend you like the drink she's planning on serving you."

My face scrunches up with confusion. I look to Angie and then to Nic. "Why would we not like it?"

Angie taps her foot, looking to be deep in thought. "Oh no... Not one of those healthy things she tries to endure."

"Ew," I agree. "Do we have to consume it?"

I turn back and see my oldest brother laughing.

"Keep it up," Angie threatens, "and I'll tell Claire to pour you some of her mystery juice. You've never had to endure any of her health fads like I had to during our college days. This will be a surprise for your taste buds for sure."

Graham holds his hands up in defense, but he can't wipe the silly smirk off his damn face.

"When Claire gets overwhelmed," Nic explains, "she goes full throttle on the nutrition stuff. And now that she can't consume the actual beverages herself, she is really playing up your part in her happiness."

I exhale loudly. "Ugh." No one wants to make that woman sad, so we are stuck with this one task. Surely, I can consume whatever she gives to me without christening her new kitchen with my vomit.

Surely.

"She says the concoction is a miracle cure for wrinkles, if that makes any difference in your mood..."

"Nic, I'm twenty-two. If I have wrinkles now, then there's no cure for the inevitable."

"Okay, fine, Penny. But when she cries, this is on you."

I smack his arm. "Wow. Way to guilt me, Punk."

"Yeah, really," Angie grumbles. "This drink just better not have carrots in it. I will boycott anything Claire makes with carrots."

I can't stop giggling. "That's where you draw the line?"

"Yup."

I remember Angie sharing the Carrot Diet story with us, and just thinking about it makes me shudder for real.

No, thank you.

When I walk through the front door, I am immediately overcome with awe.

The two-story entryway has a huge, modern chandelier hanging from the ceiling, polished wooden floors, and a grand staircase that looks like it belongs to a queen. Of course, if Nic had his way, Claire wouldn't be using it for the next few months.

"What do you think?" Claire says, joining us.

"It's exquisite," Angie says with wonder.

I nod. "It's truly magical. And just think, every holiday, you can decorate this entryway and make it your own."

Tears fill her eyes, and I can't help but join her in the emotion. "I've always wanted a forever home, and my Nic has given it to me."

I lean into my brother and wrap my arm around his waist. "You are a good man, Nic." My eyes meet his. "Are you crying?"

He sniffles. "No."

"Yes, you are."

"It's the onions Claire is chopping up in the kitchen," he defends.

"Onions?" Angie says in disgust. "Oh, please no. Bring back the carrots."

Claire waves her fingers at us, her eyes squinted. "No spying on my surprise."

Angie sighs. "Fine."

"Let me show you all around."

And she does. Room by room, she guides us through, telling us what she plans in terms of decorating.

"And this room can be yours when you visit, Penny," Nic announces.

I look around the space. "I love it."

"You did well, bro," Graham says, patting Nic on the back.

"Yes, well done," Collins agrees.

It is easy to be genuinely happy for Claire and Nic. They are so giving to everyone else that I'm proud of them for following a dream of owning their own home.

"Okay," she says robustly. "It's cocktail time, bitches!"

Nic moves to his girl to plant a full kiss on her lips. "I'll be in my office with Graham and Collins if any of you need us."

Claire pouts, putting her hands on her hips. "Don't you want to try my special mixed drinks?"

I bite my bottom lip, as Nic fakes his disappointment. *Oh, he's good.*

"Maybe later. I have some business to take care of and some emails to answer."

Claire tosses her head back and cackles. "He is a

horrible liar, am I right? No need to answer. I'm always right."

We all laugh. Well, everyone but Nic.

"I am standing right here, Claire."

She ignores him. "Anyhoo, let me run ahead and do one last thing to prep. You ladies just wait for the grand reveal."

"No running, Claire," he scolds, watching her skip down the hall.

Angie and I look at each other, and there's apprehension written all over her face.

"This is going to be bad, isn't it?" I ask her.

She's had way more experience with Claire's "bright" ideas than I have, yet something tells me neither of us could have prepared for what we will soon be experiencing.

"Ready!"

Angie and I both give each other solidarity pats on the backs and walk with trepidation to the screeching noise.

Claire meets us halfway and drapes her arms around our backs, guiding us into her massive kitchen. "Are you ready for your destiny?"

We all laugh. Well, until we see the containers of supplements resting on the countertop.

Oh, please no.

My posture straightens as I silently read the labels. I hate the taste of cough syrup, so I'm not sure I can actually consume anything that she will be offering.

"I need you both to do a taste test on my concoctions."

"Claire…" Angie says hesitantly, probably feeling the stirring of panic that I'm starting to feel.

"Yes?"

"You said cocktails…"

"Umm, well, that was a euphemism to lure you inside my home. I need you to do this—for science."

I laugh over her ability to make any situation fun. "So, what are you serving up?" I ask, looking at all of the little glasses lined up behind number tags, labeled one through six.

"There's a lot." Angie says what I'm thinking.

A whole hell of a lot...

Claire grabs the big pitcher of a brownish liquid. "Oh, just some special tea. I'm experimenting with the recipe."

And we're the guinea pigs. Yay, us.

I nudge Angie. She isn't saying anything. "Are you in shock?" I whisper.

"What's that?" Claire jumps in.

"Oh, nothing," I cover. "I was just saying that I love tea. But what makes it special?"

Claire reaches behind her and grabs a pink and white canister that has a cow printed on the front. "Collagen," she answers enthusiastically.

I can't contain my hesitation. "Umm..."

"It's found in your connective tissues under your skin. All natural." She takes a capful and adds it to the first glass, along with some of the tea from the pitcher.

I stare at the cloudy mixture. "What's the point of this again?"

"To collect our life insurance money," Angie finally chimes in, making me almost laugh, which then makes Claire glare at us.

"To keep your youth intact," she snaps. She stirs the cocktail, creating a murky tornado within the glass. "Once

I'm no longer pregnant, I'll be back on this regimen. It will do wonders for your body."

"And you promise it won't taste bad?" I pry.

She grabs the canister, rotating it until she can find the section on the label she seems to want. "See?" She taps the side. "Package says odorless and tasteless."

"Yum."

"Just try it," she coos, smiling so excitedly that I don't think I can resist. No wonder she has my brother wrapped around her finger. He probably can never say no to her. I know I'm afraid to disappoint her.

Claire hands Angie and me our individual portions.

I slowly bring the glass up to my lips, peering inside at the cloudy contents swirling about. Shit. This looks fifty percent congealed and one hundred percent nasty. I close my eyes, tipping back the chilled mixture. The bitterness of the tea hits my taste buds first, followed by the texture of gelatinized slime slipping past. My eyes pop open in shock, as I feel my stomach lurch. Did I just eat a mussel? Or a slug?

I just ate a slug.

I'm so grossed out that I quickly put the glass back down onto the counter and close my eyes again.

"I can't believe we survived this," Angie says, her voice barely a whisper.

"Good, huh? Everyone swears by it." Claire pats me on my back.

I'm going to throw up. I can just feel it. "Hmm," I hum, trying so hard not to yack all over the kitchen.

"It's going to make your already amazing skin look kissed by a baby angel."

What does that even mean? I think I just consumed chalk-flavored Jell-O.

"How about we take our baby angel skin to a real girls' night out?" Angie asks. "I feel like we are wasting our youth away."

Claire pops out her hip, placing her hand on it for emphasis. "Wow."

Angie looks at her with confusion. "What?"

"I'm not used to you being the one with the good ideas."

I laugh so hard some of my stomach acid rises in my throat. I look around for something to drown out the bitter taste and only see more collagen shots all over the countertop.

Ugh. I need an escape plan.

"I have yet to experience a night out with you ladies," I say, trying to distract myself from the burning in my throat.

"Well, you are in luck, Penny," Claire says, practically hopping on her feet. "I made you a survival kit for this momentous occasion."

I watch as she steps up on her tiptoes to pull down a bin in her cupboard labeled "How To Survive Girls' Night."

"So the goal is to live to tell about it the next day?" I ask, just looking for clarification.

Angie laughs. "I may need that kit too since I'll be drinking for all of your personalities," Angie says, earning herself a friendly slap on the arm from Claire.

"Angry Claire likes tequila. Sad Claire likes vodka. And Bitchy Claire loves Prosecco."

Taking the lid off the box, I explore the contents. Bottled water, headache medicine, Band-Aids, mini purse with cash, ear plugs, mints, and a granola bar take up the majority of the space inside. Holding up the pair of high heels, I dangle them from my fingers. "Why these?"

"For catching a ride home at the end of the night. It makes the process so much faster if you have those on."

"Yeah, but we have one major problem with all of this," Angie chimes in.

"What?" Claire asks.

"You know those men having a mysterious meeting in Nic's office? Well, they will never allow any of us to take a random ride home with anyone but one of them."

"That's for sure," I confirm. "I'll be surprised if they even allow us to go out."

"Oh, they better," Claire says. "We just need to convince them that it was their idea."

28

COLLINS

"He's threatening her from the inside out," Nic says, slamming his fist down on his desk. He scans through the mail that Graham confiscated from Penny's place. Holding the bubble envelope in his hand, he reads aloud the prison address.

"And he's been sending her shit like this for weeks?" I ask for clarification.

Graham nods. "Yes, apparently. One, two, three…"

How were we all not made privy to these mysterious deliveries?

Nic stands up and tosses the envelope onto the surface of his desk, nearly jostling the framed picture of one of Claire's ultrasounds. "We need to get this handwriting analyzed."

"On it," I say, scrolling through my phone contacts until I find the one I'm looking for. I take a picture of the prison address and send it off.

Graham clears his throat. "There is zero reason to even

write on the envelope. And yet the sender chose to print it by hand."

I rub at the back of my neck. "To make this threat more personal."

"Exactly," Nic responds. "He's tormenting her, and I want to rip out his heart and feed it to him."

"His death is going to happen with the same emotion and effort as he has put forth haunting our baby sister. This has always been personal," Graham says with a growl. "And I'm fucking over these games."

Nic paces his new home office space. "Penny's terrified. I could tell as soon as she arrived here."

He's right. I sense it too, despite her valiant effort at trying to keep calm and distracted. I'm sure my overprotectiveness isn't easing her mind either. If anything, it's making her more vulnerable.

"I've increased security on her," I offer. "And now knowing this development, I'm glad I preemptively upped it."

"Do what you need to do," Graham says, "but don't let Penny know too much about the process or she'll have ample reason to try to divert the watch. That's the last thing we need."

I nod in agreement. I'm all too familiar with Penny's view on a security detail. It was her reckless behavior that made it easier to get into this contract predicament in the first place.

The only way to keep that girl safe is to make sure she's within reach.

Unfortunately, I can't always be there to watch her every move and must find trust in the backup guard.

Chris may have seen a lot during his military days, but I doubt anything could fully prepare him for Penelope Hoffman. He saw a glimpse of her in action at Limit-X, but even then, he had me to orchestrate getting her safely back home.

"Is everything set for today?" Nic asks, changing the subject.

"Yes. I'm going to drop off a payment installment near the prison and get this ball rolling. The faster we can get Tanner into an altercation, the better. I'm getting impatient as fuck."

"Tanner's life clock is ticking," Nic says with a snarl.

I crack my knuckles. "And his death couldn't come soon enough."

It takes me a solid four seconds to look at the trio of giggling women in the kitchen and know what they are plotting—and it's not a Crock-Pot meal.

"No girls gone wild nights," I say firmly, speaking for Graham and Nic. There's no way they would approve of their women going out, especially with everything going on right now, so I feel confident being the spokesperson.

Yet, I am worried. These ladies look so determined, and if there's anything I shouldn't do, it is to underestimate them. I wouldn't put it past them to use sexual favors to get their way.

Penny, for sure, would resort to anything to defy me—that's a given.

"We will keep it tame," Claire insists.

Lies.

When Angie and Claire aren't paying attention, I pull Penny aside near the refrigerator. "You are not accepting an invite for a girls' night. So start practicing how you will let them down, because you are not dirty dancing in a club while I sit back and watch."

"No one is saying you *just* have to watch, Collins. You can join in too. There's always room on the dance floor."

My eyes penetrate into hers, hoping to see what she is really thinking.

I can tell she wants to run, and I hope she understands that I'm always calculating how fast I could get to her if she were to decide to be that ballsy.

A headache is already starting from the pressure to keep this girl safe and the revelation that someone is managing to send her mail from the prison. I feel on edge and in a volatile state with my emotions. The last thing I need is to chaperone a wild night out.

Nope.

This is where I draw the line.

"You're not going."

I glance over and see Angie and Claire move into the other room, probably to find their men, leaving Penny and me alone.

"I always heard amazing things about make-up sex," she whispers.

"Have you now?"

Where is she going with this...

"Do you think we could use girls' night as a little edging experiment, and then afterward fuck like horned-up bunnies to make up for all of the tension we had to endure? I like the idea of you going all feral and treating me like your slutty piece of real estate."

My eyes darken. "I don't think I'm physically able to guard you and keep our little secret when I'm certain other men will be wanting to shoot their shot with you."

"As long as they don't shoot their loads…"

"Penny," I hiss.

"Just kidding."

"I'm being serious."

"Maybe you won't have to guard me."

I know I make a face. Is she for real? But I humor her anyway. "And why not?"

"You've taught me a dozen or more self-defense lessons over the course of the past few weeks."

"I have. But I don't leave things precious to me in vulnerable positions to be taken away from me, Princess."

Her expression tightens, marring her once calm expression. "Don't you get it? There was an entire year where I didn't get to experience life. I was trapped in a mental prison, where the only key that would open the lock was the truth." Choking back tears, she straightens her posture, and instantly, I want to hug her to me. "I need to live my life to the fullest and not constantly fear my own shadow."

"Let me think about it."

We walk into the living room, joining the girls with the Hoffman men.

"We will keep it Disney," Claire promises Nic. "Rated G."

Nic stands beside me, and I'm silently relieved that I'll have support on this cause. We think a lot alike when it comes to privacy and security.

"No," he says flatly.

"Just let it marinate at least," Penny pleads.

Nic looks at his little sister like she is on his last nerve. I can so relate. "I need you to keep a low profile, Penny. There's going to be a lot of things happening over the next few weeks, and I need you safe."

"Like what type of things?" she challenges.

If it wasn't for my own concerns over her safety, I'd feel refreshed that someone else is on the receiving end of her attitude. But I'm not. Instead, I'm stressed and ready to lock this princess up.

Penny props her hands on her hips, poking out her bottom lip. "You aren't even giving us a chance to prove you wrong."

"We are never wrong," Graham says, making Nic and me chuckle. He's not usually the one to lighten the mood, so it catches us off guard. "You ladies are predictably a disaster out in public where music and margaritas are active catalysts in your often impulsive plan."

It's true. And none of us need this added anxiety to tack on to the day.

I just spent the better part of an hour going over prison layouts, looking at surveillance video, and cross-referencing employee schedules. The last thing I want to do tonight is have a migraine from worrying over Penny being out in public, making inevitably bad choices.

And unfortunately, I need to drop off a bag of cash as discreetly as possible to a prison contact who will be doing us all a huge favor.

Mark Tanner is going to be taking a little trip to the hospital for an unfortunate injury. It's going to be tragic when he doesn't make it back to good health in time for his trial.

Poor guy...

But at least he'll be attending his own funeral.

I just need the driver of the prison transportation to understand his responsibilities prior to getting to Portland General Hospital. And I need a solid alibi for every member of the Hoffman family.

"You guys look stressed," Angie responds. "Maybe if you all had a fun poker night, we could relax at a club."

"The last time I hosted a big poker game," Graham says, pulling his wife into his side, "you decided to take out your aggressions on—"

"Your bitchy ex-girlfriend who deserved every scratch and bruise I served up to her."

I stifle a smile. She sure is fierce.

All these women are—especially Penny. She's understated and subtle about it though. But faced with a challenge, I know she'd be able to throw down.

She learned her moves from the best—me.

But by no means do I want to be separated from her while she gallivants around town—and I lose hands in poker because I'm obsessing over her.

With this added stressor of transporting a bag of money, I need a clear head so I don't miss anyone following me or noticing anything out of place. I'll even need to get a rental vehicle just as a precaution.

"Let's table this discussion for now," Graham says, giving me the look. He knows I'm on a strict timeline to make my discreet deposit.

"Penny, I need to talk to you."

She looks over at me, her face marred with confusion. "It's time to go?"

I nod.

"We would give you a ride back," Graham explains, "but we need to swing by Dad's office first and drop off our donation check. Then Angie has an appointment soon afterward."

"Oh, for the charity event coming up?" she asks.

"Yes. Are you attending this year?"

I notice a sadness wash over Penny's face. She couldn't make it last year, but this year is different. She is stronger —stable.

"I'm going to try."

Her dad's ambitious efforts have continued to increase the overall donations every year to benefit the construction of community centers all over the state and the entire West Coast. It's honorable to help fund the production of buildings that benefit every age group and socioeconomic status for the patrons that choose to enter through their doors.

Graham gives her a look. "Please don't volunteer for the auction."

"Why?" Then she crosses her hands in front of her chest. "I wasn't planning on it."

"The last thing I need is to fake bid on my sister so no rich idiot thinks you're for sale."

Wait. What? There's a bachelorette auction? I better follow up on that later.

There's no way in hell I'll allow Penny to prance around on stage while some fuckers in the audience bid on her. I don't really need the details on any of it. Every scenario I can think of sounds equally horrible.

We finish up our goodbyes and walk out together to the front porch.

Penny turns to me. Her beautiful, crystal-blue eyes melt whatever hardness I'm feeling over the meeting with her brothers. "What's wrong?" she asks.

"What do you mean?" Am I really that obvious?

"You just look so tense."

"I need Chris to take you back to my place. Something's come up that I need to check on." It's a half-lie. I've been planning these steps for weeks now and agonizing over every little detail while biding my time.

"Does it have to do with Mark?"

I look away. I don't want to continue to lie to her, but I also don't want her to have a setback on her mental health. And that fucker has already created enough turmoil inside of this innocent girl. "I won't let him threaten you, Penny."

"So you're going to visit him in prison?"

I let out an exaggerated breath. "I don't want you worrying about anything. I have this under control."

"But that's why you are convinced I won't have to testify. It's because Mark is going to die beforehand?"

Warmth creeps up my neck, and suddenly I feel over-heated. "I'm not discussing this with you."

She takes a step forward. "No matter how much you try to shield me, I'm invested in the outcome for everyone involved. If you get caught, you'll go to prison. And I won't survive that!"

"I'll do whatever it takes to make sure he understands the message."

"What aren't you telling me?"

Silence.

"Seriously, Collins… This is my life."

"I just need you to go back to Sky View and allow Chris to get you there safely. I'll meet back up with you in two hours tops."

"Fine."

"Fine."

Sweat forms along my forehead as the weight of this mission rests on my shoulders.

I have a very short window of time to make this deposit, and the reluctance to leave Penny nearly made me blow up the entire timeline.

Opening up the back door of the rental car, I toss in a cardboard box with the description of "kitchen supplies" labeled along the side panel in black Sharpie. It's a decoy though. Actually inside the box is a black duffle bag that is full of cash.

It's a good faith deposit. The rest will be paid when the actual job gets completed.

Sliding into the driver's seat, I take a deep breath and secure my seat belt. I'm usually never nervous and yet this has me twitchy.

We are getting close to the execution of the endgame plan, and there's nothing that I'd like better than to see it all through.

Waste management costs a lot. Luckily the Hoffman brothers have the finances, and I have the intel to know just how to work around the system.

There's no way we could trust the legal system not to jack this up.

Now there will be no room for chance or loopholes or technicalities.

Putting the rental into reverse, I pull out of the parking spot and then onto the main road.

About three miles before I get to the meetup location, I pull over along the side of the road. I place my nondescript ball cap onto my head and then send a text from my burner phone.

So many things are running through my head as to how all of this might play out over the next couple of months. First, Mark Tanner needs to not be placed inside solitary for any reason. Then there's going to be a massive prison fight that will be sparked. And last, Tanner is going to need to take a trip to the hospital.

As soon as I get word that he's on the transport, I have to make my move.

No matter how many dangerous and seemingly impossible missions I've done in my lifetime, this one is crucial for the livelihood of the Hoffmans.

Mark Tanner being in prison is not enough to exorcise the lingering trauma from Penny's mind.

The only thing that could potentially do that is proof of a death certificate.

Rolling my shoulders, I shift the car back into drive and pull out onto the road.

When I get to the meetup location at an abandoned mechanic's shop, just three-quarters of a mile outside of the prison's southern perimeter, I wait for my contact to back in alongside me.

Lowering my window as he does the same, I hand over the moving box.

"Here's another phone," I say, handing over a new burner one just in case. "And inside the box is a little case with a tracking device inside. Place that on the transport vehicle, and I'll be able to know the exact location when it's go time."

"Then we're all set?"

"Yes. Just give the signal."

"You know they have him on suicide watch."

"He wants them to think that," I say with a sneer. "He has to know I'm gunning for him the first chance I get."

"Then it better be a brawl and not some hissy fit that derails this entire thing."

"Exactly."

Raising our windows, we leave the shop and go our separate ways. I turn on my phone that will be used to get the signal, just in case.

It's a waiting game now.

I drive in silence back to Sky View, with just the sound of the car and asphalt filling the space. My mind wanders to what Penny's doing. She's probably driving Chris nuts with a million questions.

29

COLLINS

"What in the actual hell is going on here?"

My eyes narrow in on Chris, who is supposed to be guarding Penny while I was tending to business.

Critically important business...

"What's up, Redeye?"

"What in the *hell* are you doing?" I ask again.

A few pieces of popcorn fall from his mouth. "Enjoying a snack with Penelope Hoffman."

A snack? *It looks like a meal.*

My eyes look at the movie playing. A freaking chick flick. Are they on a date?

"Did I interrupt?"

Penny has the nerve to look at me with her sassy smile, now deciding it's the right time to stop ignoring me. Then she places a finger to her lips and shushes me. She fucking shushes me. "It's the best part."

Shaking my head at her, I growl, "I'll deal with you later."

She pops another piece of popcorn into the air, completely missing her mouth. It gets stuck in her hair. "That sounds toxic."

I close the distance, standing right in front of the duo on the couch. "You had one job to do, man. One."

"And I'm doing it. The princess is safe—obvi."

"Don't call her that," I snap.

Penny looks at me with amusement. Why does she find joy in my torment?

I snatch the remote and pause the movie.

"Time to leave," I say to Chris.

I am three seconds away from relocating his body from that couch.

Chris gets up, a little too reluctantly. "Oh, c'mon. I need to see what happens."

"The boat sinks," I deadpan.

"Wow, way to ruin the entire movie!"

I look at him as if he's lost his mind. Clearly he has. "It's the *Titanic*."

Meanwhile, Penny can't stop from laughing and spilling popcorn all over my pristine living room. This place hasn't been free of crumbs since before she plowed her way into my life. And I still haven't adapted to the shock of someone so small making such a big mess.

But oddly, I'm not upset by it in the slightest.

She belongs here—crumbs and all.

But this fucker who is enjoying time with my princess? No. He needs to go.

My eyes catch Chris's feet as he walks past. "Dude, where are your socks?"

For fuck's sake…

"They are inside my shoes near the door."

"Why are your toenails painted?" I snap.

"It was pedicure day."

I must have entered some type of alternate universe.

"There's paint left if you want yours done too," Penny says with a smirk. "I'm sure your shade is Grumpy Grey."

"Yeah, Redeye, men should never neglect their cuticles."

I can't even with them right now. I help usher Chris out the door, smacking him on the back—probably a little too hard—as he leaves.

Then I stalk back toward Penny, who now has popcorn surrounding her on the couch and the floor. I wonder if she actually consumed any or missed her mouth entirely with each attempt? At least the piece in her hair is gone. That one was irking me.

"No sharing couches or Netflix or fucking popcorn with other men."

She hums.

"Did you even hear me?" I ask. I can tell my temper is rising exponentially with each passing second.

"Honestly, I've blurred out most of it. Why are you ranting again?"

She's being way too sassy today.

Stalking toward her, I grab her chin. Despite being furious with her, I keep my touch gentle and revel in how she just melts into my palm.

I pet her cheek. "I can see you want to be brave today. Is your mouth filter broken?"

Her eyes find me, and I want to get lost in their crystal-blue depths. "Maybe."

"You don't need to work for my attention, Princess. You already have all of it."

"But Chris is so—"

My touch turns more intentionally firm. "Do I need to fuck my memory back into you? Or wash your mouth out with my cum to remind you not to speak another man's name when we are together?"

"Yes," she says boldly.

Reaching into my pocket, I pull out her collar, rolling it around between my fingers. Undoing the clasp, I secure it around her neck.

"You look so pretty," I say with adoration.

I undo the button and zipper of my pants and slide them down along with my boxer briefs.

Wrapping my fingers around her neck just north of the collar, I embrace the energy circulating through my system of how it'll feel to slide right down her thin and delicate throat.

Rolling my neck, I feel the tension leaving me.

"Slide your ass to the edge of the couch."

I relish her compliance. Grasping my cock between my fingers, I rub it to attention, watching as Penny keeps her eyes trained on it.

"Open that sweet but defiant mouth of yours," I say, when I can't take any more of the torment. I give her collar a little tug. "Tongue out. Mouth wide."

I feed her only an inch, allowing her time to get accustomed to my size.

With her lips suctioned around my head, Penny uses my thighs for stability.

"Breathe through your nose, Princess. Relax that throat."

My thumb slips under the collar, feeling her pulse beneath the beat of my own.

I push in more.

"Look at you, swallowing cock like a good little girl."

She relaxes more.

Grasping both sides of her face, I thrust in deeper.

And deeper.

Penny coughs around me, and the sudden jerking sends ripples of pleasure through my entire body.

"Fuck, yes," I say breathily. "Choke on it."

And she does, gripping my thighs and sputtering out drool from around her pretty pink lips.

I slow my movements and allow her to readjust, pulling out and giving her a chance to get a breath.

"You're being such a good girl for me, Princess."

Sucking me in deep, she looks up at me with tears forming around the edges of her eyes. I tangle my fingers into her hair, savoring this feeling of her warm mouth massaging my cock.

"Just a little more," I coo. "You can take more, right?"

Penny relaxes her suction and forces herself forward, just another inch.

But it's her moan, coupled with the image of her in her collar, that is nearly my undoing. "Ahhh...I'm close."

Like the fucking good girl she is, Penny tightens her suction and wraps her tongue along the underside of me, causing me to plummet completely over the edge and spill all my seed down her throat in four strong bursts.

My spine sags as I slip out of her mouth, dribbling some cum on her lips and down her chin. Holding her face to my thigh, I massage her scalp.

"No flirting with other men," I remind.

With dazed eyes, she looks up at me, but it's her smile of satisfaction that stops my heart. "I missed you."

Her words are so sweet that it tugs at my heartstrings. "I missed you too, Princess. But I was gone two hours."

"And I wasn't flirting."

Pulling her up from the couch, more popcorn rains down onto our feet. My hands find her ass cheeks and give them a hard squeeze.

"When can we go back to Limit-X?"

What? "Never."

Her bottom lip pops out. "You lost the Labor Day bet."

"We can renegotiate."

Penny looks up at me and bats her eyelashes. Then she sticks that damn tongue out.

It doesn't make me see red. It makes me see green.

"Uh-oh," she says, backing out of my hold.

"I hope you run," I say smoothly.

And she does, taking off down the hall.

I kick my jeans and boxer briefs off and stalk after her with the thrill of the chase racing through my veins.

My cock comes to life.

What is this girl doing to me?

Looping my arm around Penny's stomach, I flatten her up against the wall, while my cock presses into her ass.

Breathing into her ear, I whisper, "There's not a place on

this planet you can hide where I wouldn't find you, Princess. *You are mine.*"

"Let me go, you brute."

"Tsk-tsk… That's no way to talk to your deliverer of pain and pleasure. At least be strategic."

It's this game we play, which walks on the fine line of going too far and not going far enough.

We both crave the excitement of being together.

Spinning Penny around, I grind my cock against her body, and then within seconds, I get all of our clothes off and puddling at our feet.

"There. Much better," I croon.

A hand traces up her leg from knee to hip.

"Don't touch me."

Lies.

It's all part of this dance we do, where Penny doesn't act like she wants me to have this control over her, and I help break through her perfectly erected walls.

And maybe, just maybe, over the course of the days we've spent together thus far, I became her safe way to psychologically flood out her demons. I've proven to her that she can have a fulfilling sex life with a man who will guide her passion and rein in her rebellious streak.

Effortlessly, I lift Penny into the air, while her legs wrap around my waist.

"Eek! Hey! Put me down!"

It's a valiant fight, but I'm just too strong.

"Do bad girls get fucked against hard walls in hallways, Princess?"

"Yes…" she hisses, her eyes glassy with desire.

"What do good girls get then?"

"They get their release."

"Yes, Princess, they do. So are you going to be good or bad?"

"Both."

Reaching between us, I tease her pussy, enjoying how responsive she is to my touch.

She wants my control. And no matter how reluctant I was in the past to give this to her, she *needs* it to heal.

Because it's more than just sex between us. It's therapy.

And if this level of trust restores a piece of Penny, then I'm lucky enough to be the deliverer of it.

"Are you ready for me? I'm going to slide my cock into that pussy of yours and stretch you out."

"Mm-hmm…"

"Lift your hips and relax your inner muscles."

Pushing off of me, she does, and then slides down onto me like the good fucking girl she is.

There is nothing bad about this feeling.

Penelope Hoffman is a fucking dream.

"Look at you being such a good fuck doll, getting railed against a hard wall by your bodyguard."

I bite at her neck, savoring the screams coming from her throat.

"You're going to keep this our little secret, right?"

"Mm-hmm…"

I push in farther, feeling the resistance increase as I go deeper.

"Fuck, yes…take all of me…"

"Ahhh…" she moans, creaming all over my damn cock.

"Fuck," I bellow and shoot my load deep into her pussy.

For several minutes, I hold Penny's limp body against mine as her breathing tries to return to normal.

Coming down from my own high, I kiss her forehead and then rest my head against the side of her neck.

Being with Penny restores me. She has given me a newfound purpose for wanting more out of this life other than being the best worker I can be.

Turning my lips to her neck, I give it a little bite. She squirms.

"Are you sore?"

"Yes," she pants.

"Good. Now you'll have a strong reminder not to cross me when it comes to other men."

"Next time don't leave me."

I swallow hard. "I never want to leave you, Princess."

30

PENNY

Collins is not a shouter. He commands a room with his quiet authority, and even when I think he'll lose his cool, his calm demeanor prevails.

But right now, he is shouting.

And I don't think I can keep my lips from curling up. Even I know that nothing good will come from a smile in this moment, and yet I can't keep it from happening.

He's been broody ever since he saw Chris enjoying time with me on the couch. I thought a good fuck—times two—would work out his aggressions over the situation and make him more pliable to agree to girls' night.

But apparently I was wrong.

Maybe he thought a good fuck fest would make me so tired that I would forget my ultimate goal.

Also wrong.

So here we are, standing in his living room, about to go head-to-head on the issue of him not wanting me to go out to the club with the girls.

"It's unfair not to allow me this girl time."

"You had girl time all afternoon."

"Well, I want girl night too."

"Then I'll take you back to Claire's house for a sleepover or you can have them over to your apartment. But you aren't going to some club," Collins forbids.

"Yes, I am."

"We have a contract in place."

"I know that," I say, propping my hands on my hips. "And the contract gives you the privilege to attend with me, but it does not give you the luxury to keep me locked up in your candy-coated prison."

"Candy-coated prison?"

I shrug. "Sugar-Daddy Shack was trademarked."

Collins's chiseled jaw tenses, as he takes half a step back. Sighing, he rubs at the back of his neck and casts his gaze away from me.

Oh shit. He's pissed off. Like really pissed off.

But this is what I do. I walk the line of pushing the boundaries, hoping I don't cross over to the side of no return. Based on the mean expression he is sporting, I know I'm approaching it soon.

But fuck it. I'm invested now. And he's being pigheaded over something as simple as girls' night.

"Can we at least discuss this?" I try.

"What's to discuss when the answer is a solid no?"

"Collins…"

"Penelope…"

"You are my bodyguard. You can protect me."

As if on cue, Collins's phone buzzes, and his sigh is

enough for me to know that I may be winning this battle after all.

"Here's my reinforcements," I say under my breath, knowing that Claire and Angie must have worked their magic with my brothers.

I really should take notes from them. It always amazes me when they get my brothers to give in to their wishes.

I know my brothers. They don't cave under pressure normally, which makes me wonder just what their women do to make them change their minds. But it's those details I really don't actually need to know.

Answering his phone, Collins keeps his eyes on me as he listens to who I assume is Graham or Nic on the other end.

"Seven o'clock?" he asks in a low, gravelly voice.

My face beams with the brightest victory smile.

"Yes, understood."

By the time Collins is off the phone, I am bouncing around him like a demented clown, pumping my fists into the air like I won the Olympics for some niche sport.

"You have forty-five minutes before the limo pulls up in front of the building to pick us up."

"Which dive bar are we hitting up?"

"Oh, no," he says smoothly, "we won't be going to any establishment where you need a tetanus shot first."

"Oh, c'mon. I heard epic stories from the girls."

"You think your brothers would ever allow their women to go to any club with security consisting of grainy surveillance cameras or plastic decoys?"

I fake pout. "No fun."

His eyes narrow. "Be glad you won this battle, because I'll always win the war."

"You seem certain."

"I am. And if you even think about flirting with other men while we are out, you won't like that side of me."

"I liked the side of you I just got from you thinking I was flirting with Chris. So..."

"Penelope..."

"Collins..."

"Keep your sass under control or accept the consequences that will certainly ensue."

And then an idea pops into my head. "So I was wondering if I can try getting your cock to go deeper down my throat. I have been practicing some tech—"

"What the actual fuck, Penelope?"

Well, that wasn't the reaction I was expecting. Now Collins looks frustrated, and he's rubbing at the back of his neck, which is a telltale sign that he's stressed.

"I was just thinking that it is fun to have my oxygen supply in the balance. I think I get off a bit on the panic... Who would have thought?"

"You can't ask questions like these when we have limited time to explore and then expect me not to be walking around with a hard-on all night."

"I can't help that when I'm around you, my brain turns to mush. I can just keep watching tutorials and practice with a—"

"Stop relying on the Internet to teach you things that I'll clearly provide education on."

"Fine. But just know that I'm currently horny."

"Noted. But you better not flirt with other men."

"No one is going to be flirting. We both know that men ignore me in social situations. Plus, I'm sure Claire and Angie aren't as wild as they were a few months ago. With one being pregnant and the other married, I doubt drama will follow them like it has in the past. But what do I know?"

"You know enough. And there never is a time when there isn't drama."

I have yet to see their true potential for a night out on the town. If the notorious stories about their shenanigans are true, I can see why Collins would be reluctant.

It's no surprise as to why my brothers have hired an entourage for their women when they want an adventure.

I think trouble just finds them. But that's not my fault.

"I will be on my best behavior."

Collins gives me a look. "Doubtful."

The limo picks us up right on time.

"Where are my brothers?" I ask.

"They are meeting us in an hour," Angie responds. "I'm pretty sure they just don't like to dance."

Claire gestures to Collins. "At least we'll only have one pair of judgy eyes to report back to them."

I stifle a giggle and stare out the window, watching the shops and restaurants pass by as we make our way to the southern part of the city.

It's a beautiful night, with crisp air and low humidity. I have on a tight, strapless minidress in a bright magenta color. The only way I was able to leave with it on was promising to Collins that he could rip it off me later.

I swear that man can be so feral at times.

If I didn't trust him, he would be scary.

"Where are we going?" I ask the girls quietly. It's not like Collins is even paying us much attention. He seems pretty focused on whatever is on his phone screen.

"You really don't know?" Claire asks, keeping her voice low. "I thought you'd figure it out by now."

Angie laughs into her fist.

"Okay, now I'm intrigued. We aren't going dancing?"

"Oh, there will be dancing," Angie says, nearly choking.

Claire leans into me. "But it's mainly watching and drooling."

"We are going to the Boom Boom Club?"

Both girls nod, and suddenly I'm the one giggling.

The limo driver pulls into the parking lot, finds a free spot in front of the building, and then helps us exit.

I glance at Collins. His forehead wrinkles, and he has his typical scowl.

"This better not be what I think it is."

I shrug. "If my brothers approved it, then why deny us our destiny?"

His mouth opens and then shuts. I can tell he wants to say more but resists, probably because we have an audience.

"Apparently, this place has really good security," Angie says, acting innocent. "Bouncers, guards, legit driver's license checks, and up-to-date surveillance. It's the only way Graham even for a second allowed me to ponder the idea of coming here."

Claire links arms with me and Angie. "It'll be fun." She

turns to glance behind her at Collins who is allowing us to lead the way. "What man doesn't love a good strip club?"

"Apparently that man," I grumble, loud enough for him to hear. "His frown is going to make this all awkward."

The girls and I get into line and flash our IDs when asked.

In true Collins form, he makes friends with the bouncer, slipping him something that I can only assume is a cash payout for being "extra."

When we are granted access through the metal door, the atmosphere comes alive.

"Is this how the Vegas one was?" I ask.

Claire clears her throat. "That one was more of a performance show. I can't wait to see what this one will be. Granted, we do have someone here that we actually know. Have you spotted Luke yet?"

I look around the space. "Not yet. I didn't even know we'd be here tonight, so I didn't give him a heads-up."

"Is that him?" Claire asks, pointing to a man who only has a bow tie on with a pair of booty shorts.

I shake my head. "No."

We meander around the space, until we find a vacant lounge area with comfy couches and a little coffee table for any food or drinks we purchase.

The girls and I plop down onto the sofa, with Claire in the middle. Collins takes the chair beside me, looking as uncomfortable as ever.

Leaning into me, he whispers, "Behave tonight."

And I mouth, "Always."

A waitress comes around and takes our order, and then

quickly scurries away when the lights start fading and brightening, signaling the start of the show.

"Wow, just in time," Claire says, relieved.

I know the girls have been to a strip club before, but this is my first one. I just hope I don't do anything stupid.

The crowd is lively tonight, but I have to say, this place is way more sophisticated than the image I created in my head based on how movies portray these places. I know the top-notch security at check-in was the only reason Collins let us proceed in the first place.

He gets off on all things security. So this place has something for every taste, I am sure.

An announcer walks up on stage, looking to be barely legal to be here himself. "Please help me welcome to the stage, the men who are all tens… It's time to get penis envy! Give it up for Max the Muscle, Lethal Luke, and Sergeant Sam."

"Please help me mourn the loss of my panties," Claire says with reverence. This is her love language—clearly.

The girls and I wave our hands and scream out in excitement. Collins looks like he doesn't know where to put his eyes, but manages to find a resting place for them…

On me.

"Stop making this weird," I whisper to him.

"I'm just plotting out how I'm going to punish you later for your straying eyes."

"He's my roommate," I remind him, low enough for only him to hear. "We basically bathe together."

It's a joke. Obviously. I'm barely at my own apartment, and he knows it. But that doesn't stop his look of disapproval and anger from shining through his normally blank expression.

Sheesh.

Lighten up, dude.

Then I see a flash of money as Claire waves wads of cash in front of my eyes.

"You brought the whole bank, didn't you?" Angie asks, giggling.

But when the men on stage catch sight of the money, all three make their way to our section and go to work.

Max sneaks behind Angie to give her a shoulder massage. Luke hops up on the table to do a gyration dance of some sort, in rhythm with the suggestive music blasting through the venue. I'm really trying hard not to look at him no matter how much eye contact he reserves for me.

And his smile...

Fuck, he's enjoying this way too much. And I doubt I'll be able to look at him again without seeing this image of him half-naked burning through my memory.

My eyes look for Sam as a distraction, finding him flying through the air and doing a flip. Then he somehow manages to lie across all three of our laps without hurting himself or us.

"Don't touch them," Collins warns, but I can't tell if he is talking to us or the men.

He basically looks like he's about to have an aneurysm.

Angie takes some money from Claire's hand and stuffs some into the skin-tight shorts the men have painted on. Then Claire and I follow suit.

When at a strip club...

31

COLLINS

I still can't believe I accompanied three wild women to a strip club and actually survived to talk about it.

I've concluded that there never will be a time in my life where I need to see that many men waving around their junk —for cash or not. Being deprived of that will be a sacrifice worth savoring.

And now I have to deal with putting back together Little Miss Humpty Drunkity.

At least I got her into the apartment complex, up to my floor, and inside the residence.

It wasn't an easy feat at all. Apparently, when Penny drinks, she also gets oddly ambitious, thinking she can walk on her own.

Nope. She can't.

Well, at least not until her body detoxes from all the fruity liquid she put in it.

"I, ah, feel like the floor is crawling…"

I see the color change on Penny's face, and I know if

I'm not quick, she'll be puking on the both of us. I scoop her up in my arms and carry her into the bathroom, leaning her over the toilet as the first wave hits, crashing against the clean white bowl.

"Arghh…"

I gather Penny's hair into one hand and rub at her back as another wave hits. And another. Her whimper pulls at my heart. Seeing her doubled over, looking small, takes me back in time to when I first saw her at Soulful Mind. She was a hollowed-out shell, coping with demons of the unknown then. While she got some answers when Mark Tanner was discovered, Penny is still trying to figure out how to move forward with her life while carrying around the burden of her old self.

Everyone has demons to fight. It's just that some people do a better job at hiding it.

When Penny seems to have finished, I help her stand, flush the toilet, and then guide her to the sink.

"You feeling better?"

She nods as she looks at her pale reflection in the mirror. "I think I may have overindulged."

I let out a hollow laugh. "You think?"

"Yup, I think… With my eyes and with my mouth."

I shake my head at her. "You had way too much fun watching naked men dance around on stage." Granted, some were definitely doing more, but I'm trying to block out those memories. "The beverages were just another bad decision."

"I'm not used to drinking like that. Why didn't you try to stop me?"

My jaw goes limp. "I did."

"Well, you suck at getting me to comply."

"Clearly."

"I just got carried away. Plus, there was plenty of pussy for you to savor. There's no need to be jealous."

I give her a smile and then cup hers. "This pussy is the only one I have eyes for."

"Good, because it feels sooo neglected."

I give her another squeeze and then resist taking things further. "I'm going to draw you a bath. It might make you feel better. Rinse your mouth, and I'll get you something to drink."

It takes just a few seconds for the water to heat up and the steam to fill the room. I add in some bubble bath and lay out some fresh towels for Penny. She probably feels gross.

"Thank you, Collins."

"You're welcome, Pen."

I exit the bathroom and walk into the closet to pick out a soft pair of pajamas to lay on the bed. Meandering into the kitchen, I grab a glass out of the cupboard and pour some cranberry juice into it.

Moving back into the bathroom, I sit along the side of the tub.

"Drink your juice, Princess. You need to stay hydrated."

"Collins?"

"Yeah?"

"Can you help me wash my hair? My brain can't get my hands to cooperate. I think they are extra drunk."

I smile, although she doesn't look. "Of course."

"Thank you."

"You're welcome, Princess."

Kneeling beside the tub, I use the rinse cup to dampen

her hair. Popping open the shampoo bottle, I revel in the smell of fresh strawberries.

She is covered in a sea of bubbles, and while my cock wishes they would dissolve, I'm glad that I can have this innocent moment with her when she needs tenderness.

"Ah, that feels good," she moans, as I run my soapy hands through her scalp. "More. Don't stop." Relaxing her body back against the side, she tilts her head up to the ceiling. "I could fall asleep."

"Soon," I promise, knowing that my own body needs the rest as well.

I rinse Penny's silky locks, getting all of the soap out of them.

She yawns. "I could get used to this."

So could I.

And that's what the underlying problem is to all of this. I'm stitching the threads between us with all these little moments, only making it harder for myself when it all ends.

When Penny's skin is all wrinkly and the water loses most of its heat, I grab a fluffy towel and wrap it around her.

Picking her up, I carry her into the bedroom and help her into her pajamas.

Pulling back the covers, I get her underneath and comfortable.

"I'm going to get some work done in my office, but I'll be back soon."

"Okay," she says with another yawn. "I'll wait up for you."

My lips curve up. "We'll see about that."

Bending forward, I give her a kiss to her forehead before

exiting her room to go make a few phone calls and check my email.

Seeing a voice message from Graham, I lock my door and return his call.

"Hey, what's up?"

"How's Penny?"

"She's okay." I deliberately try to be vague.

"I'm concerned she's going to get sick through the night after all the drinking she did tonight. And I imagine her roommate is working late?"

"Yeah, I thought the same thing." I swallow. I hate lying.

"Can you please check on her?"

"I actually have her with me in the guest room so I can keep an eye on her and make sure she doesn't throw up again. She's done it once already. I am overly cautious, so I thought this would be best."

I feel like such an asshole.

"Thanks, man. You'll make sure she replenishes and stays hydrated?"

"Yes, of course."

"Okay, good. I appreciate it."

When I get off the phone, I take a few long breaths. I have Penny here because I'm a possessive asshole who gets off on being in control. But it's not like I can tell Graham that there would be no way in hell I'd allow Penny to be anywhere but with me after all the overindulging she did with the girls at the strip club.

She needs a keeper.

And I'm all too content providing her those services.

Cracking open my email, I sift through all the junk that

somehow sneaks into my inbox, filtering out what I need to see right now and what can wait for a later time.

I stay absorbed in work, answering messages and setting up some future meetings.

When my eyes are glazing over from looking at the screen too long in the dimmed light of the room, I am startled by the sound of a high-pitched moan echoing down the hall.

Penny…

Rushing to get to her, I push open my master bedroom door, and in the shadowy darkness, I see a little ball in the center of the bed, wrapped haphazardly in the fluffy comforter. Her legs peek out from the bottom, and I imagine this is not very comfortable.

Moving closer, I see the goose bumps on her exposed flesh. Grabbing my phone, I open the thermostat app and change the settings to provide more heat. Then I grab a fleece blanket from the chair along the edge of the room and kneel on the bed to cascade it over Penny's chilled body.

Looking at the pillow, I see the dampened ring of water from where her hair has soaked into the fabric.

It's impossible not to find joy at the sight of her in my own space.

I'd be lying if I said she didn't belong here. Because every part of this vision of her lying sprawled out on my bed is exactly where she belongs.

Safe.

Happy.

Clean.

And soon to be warm.

I want to be her long-term provider. I want to take care

of her. And the thought of anyone else filling that role causes a murderous energy to run through me.

Mine.

Running a hand over the back of my neck, I watch as Penny stirs, her movements stiff.

And then she lets out a whimper in agony, as if she is reliving some nightmare in the depths of her soul.

"Penny?" I call out in worry. "You are having a bad dream."

Fuck.

Leaning in closer, I smell the scent of the strawberry shampoo, luring me closer.

"Collins…" My name comes out muffled, sending a dagger straight to my heart.

"Sweet girl, I am here."

Her eyes bolt open in horror and search for an anchor.

Let it be me.

"I'm here," I soothe, rubbing a hand over her back. "Everything will be okay."

Rolling over, Penny throws herself into my chest, her frail frame shaking against me. My arms encircle her petite body, as it molds itself to me. I fix the fleece blanket around her, providing her with the warmth her body needs.

Our entire journey into the one-hundred-day contract has been an exercise of blurring lines, and tonight is no different.

That's what Penny and I do. We continue to grow separate but also grow together, learning more about each other with every passing day.

When Penny's breathing slips back into that steady rhythm of gentle inhales and exhales, I realize that she is back asleep and likely won't remember the terror she just experienced.

And for that I am thankful.

I get her back under the covers and remove my clothes to provide her with my own warmth, snuggling up against her.

A soft moan escapes her lips, as I turn her to face away from me. Her soft curves fit against my muscular torso like a puzzle. But there's this nagging feeling of impending doom that I can't shake, like I'm one breath away from losing this girl that has wrapped herself around my entire heart.

Dammit.

I allow one hand to splay along her flat stomach and the other to cross over her chest and rest at her collarbone. Pressing my lips against the back of her head, I breathe in her sweetness.

And if this all ends tomorrow, at least I got to hold her for a second longer today.

32

PENNY

"How is the goal setting going for you?" Margo asks, leaning back in her chair and propping her feet up on her coffee table.

I think back over my list. I've done so many things from it that I almost forgot just how much. I've learned to drive. I've moved out. I've made some friends. I've kissed a boy and have been ravished.

"It's going pretty well."

She sits up straighter. "Yeah? Tell me more."

"I don't know what else to say. I made a list, and I checked things off."

Margo smiles. "Well, now it's time to keep adding to it. Maybe challenge yourself even more. Just don't be impulsive with your new goals. Make sure you think them through and keep them realistic."

I nod, as several ideas come to mind. I definitely need to have some soul-searching time to figure out how to tell Collins that I don't want our time to end.

I want to tell him that he's my forever person.

He's the one I want to be with in this life.

Grabbing my purse from the end table, I push myself up from the couch and give Margo a wave. "See you next time."

"See you next time. Oh, and Penny?"

"Hmm?"

"I'm really proud of you."

"Thank you," I say, getting choked up over the last word.

When I get out into the hall, I find Collins leaning up against the far wall.

"How did it go?"

"Pretty well."

"Yeah?"

My smile can't be contained. "Yeah."

"Then let's go celebrate."

Collins looks so eager that I don't want to convince him that a successful therapy session may not actually warrant a celebration. So I just go with the flow and follow him to his SUV, parked along the street.

He helps me into my side and straps me in.

"I am capable of doing this, you know?"

"I enjoy taking care of you, Princess."

It was just a few days ago when I wondered what he would call me after the contract ended. Would I go back to being Miss Hoffman? Would I be allowed to be called Penny?

But I can no longer visualize an end to us, despite that being part of the original plan, so I just don't ask.

I'm not ready to say goodbye, and I know Collins isn't

either. He has proven that to me in so many ways, so many times.

And I believe everything he has yet to say. I know deep down that he wants what I want, but neither of us is prepared to put it out there yet in word form.

When Collins shuts my door and makes it into the driver's side seat, I'm already crossing and uncrossing my ankles in anticipation of what will be happening next.

"Car sex?"

"Is that a question or an offer?"

"Umm, both?"

Collins chuckles. "Not today."

I pout. "Fine. But I feel like you enjoy rejecting all of my good ideas."

"I enjoy rejecting your bad ideas too," he says jokingly.

My lips curve up into a smirk. "Well, I rarely have those. So where are we going?"

"Patience…"

"I suck at that."

"The anticipation is part of the fun."

"Says the man who actually knows where we are going."

Collins starts the engine and maneuvers the vehicle onto the street. We sit in a peaceful silence. It feels good to be next to someone and not feel forced to talk.

I watch out my window as we make our way out of the city and onto a side road. When we pass through the patches of forest, I realize that we can only be going to one place.

Oh, yes…

And the excitement I feel bubbling inside is almost too much to take.

Collins glances over at me. "Are you okay? You seem squirmy."

"I am."

He looks back at the road but gives me the side-eye. "Why?"

"I'm not dressed for this soon-to-be memorable experience. You could have given me a heads-up, you know?"

"Then it wouldn't have been as fun."

I twist my hands in my lap, playing with my hem. I'm not even close to being dressed for the occasion, in a simple sundress and non-matching panties and bra. "I look like I'm going to visit an Amish farm rather than a sex club."

"You look beautiful, Penelope."

"I thought you said we'd never go here."

"Do you want to go ho—"

"No!" I practically shout. "I'm just curious about what changed your mind."

"A promise is a promise. I lost the vibrator bet at the Labor Day barbecue, and now I'm going to pay up and even out my debt."

I rub my hands together. "Oh, goody." Then I glance at the clock on the dashboard. "Wait. Is Limit-X even open at this time?"

Collins guides the SUV into the parking lot and finds a spot close to the entrance.

"It's a member's exclusive event," he explains.

"Fancy."

Collins glances over at me and smiles. Then he cuts the engine and gets out of the vehicle. Opening my door, he helps me out.

My eyes glance at the building, enjoying the contrast of

being here during daylight hours for once. It's as beautiful as ever, if not more so, with the sun casting a warm glow upon it.

"I'm going to be very clear about something…" Collins starts, verifying that my attention is back on him.

"Okay…"

"There will be rules, Penelope."

I tilt my head, as my eyes narrow. "I'd be surprised otherwise."

"Collins, I'm nervous."

"I know, Princess."

My eyes lock in on the walls surrounding us, quietly hoping that they hold up to the promised privacy of their description.

We are elevated above the dance floor but in a frosted glass cage. I've been here at the club a couple of times before but honestly never noticed this option—until now. Maybe it's a recently added feature.

"And you're sure no one can see us?" I ask. My question comes out slow and methodical.

"Members can witness what we are doing but we will be silhouettes. So you can have the thrill of having your fun but without the risk of me bashing in skulls of people seeing what's mine."

Collins grabs my ass cheeks through the fabric of my very conservative dress, as the thump-thump of the bass-heavy music from the DJ causes my pulse to quicken.

I feel intoxicated and completely in sensory overload.

But I want to do this. I want to experience Limit-X with this man—the man I seduced here what feels like a lifetime ago. We really have come a long way in such a short amount of time.

"I've never done this before," he whispers, placing his forehead against mine.

"Good. Then I'll be your first." But I really want to be his last.

He smiles knowingly and then starts to remove the innocent cotton dress from my body.

"Arms up."

I comply. "I should have worn something sexy."

"Every part of you is sexy, Princess. Even"—his thumbs play with my white panties with the little pink hearts over them—"these. *Especially* these."

The roar of the crowd outside of our caged booth erupts as the DJ switches rhythms and the music morphs into deeper, seductive tones.

It's easy to tune everyone out when Collins is massaging my breasts and removing my bra. He takes a step back in the cage, causing it to sway gently.

And then he is on me, biting my neck, sucking at my nipples, and possessing me with every part of him.

I help him get undressed, evening things out. Then I roam my hands all over his body, caressing the curves of his muscles and savoring the crackling energy being transmitted between us.

My movements are slow and intentional, as I try to commit this image of being locked in a glass cage with my possessive bodyguard into my permanent memory bank.

Looping an arm under my ass, Collins hoists me up into

the air and then hits a button along the side of the cage that lowers some type of leather contraption from the ceiling.

"What is this thing?" I ask, genuinely curious.

"It's a sex swing."

"Okay…"

"I'll show you," he says with a smile. "Reach behind you and grab the two leather ropes, one for each hand."

When I comply, Collins gently lowers my ass into a seat made of soft straps of leather. He then places each of my feet into stirrups.

I watch, suspended, as he watches me. It feels like I'm as exposed—if not more—than I am when I visit the gynecologist and keep getting told to scoot closer to the end of the table.

And seeing how open my pelvis is from this position, I can definitely see the appeal of this device.

"Ready for some fun?" Collins challenges.

"With you? Absolutely."

He stands between my spread legs and is directly lined up with my pussy.

Looping his thumbs along the sides of my panties, I think he's going to rip them completely off, but instead he gets down on his knees before me. Placing his mouth directly over the fabric covering my opening, he licks and sucks the cotton into his mouth. Then he uses his teeth to grip some of the material and bite a hole right where my entrance is located.

It's savage.

It's feral.

And it's causing me to leak out through the newly created hole.

VICTORIA DAWSON

Collins licks up my juices, making me squirm and thrash around in my swing.

"Easy, Princess. We don't want to rush things."

I moan out in pleasure and frustration that he's not giving me the pressure I need.

Using his thumbs, he pulls the fabric of my panties to make a larger hole that will support the penetration of his cock.

Getting up from the floor, Collins admires his handiwork. "Perfect," he says with a smirk. "You look like the most adorable little fuck doll that I've ever seen."

I throw my head back over his filthy words, enjoying the effect they have on my mind and my body.

Taking his hard cock in his hand, Collins moves to the side where he can have access to my mouth. "Slobber on it. Get it all nice and wet so I can work you hard."

I part my lips and am immediately stuffed full of Collins's hard length. "Mmmph…"

His fingers grip a handful of my hair, using it as leverage. "That's my girl. Take it deep. Yes, that's it. Now, fucking drool all over it."

"Uhgh…" I choke out, around his length. My eyes water but I don't care. I'm a prisoner to this man and am loving every second of it.

Collins pulls back to give me air but then pushes inside again. "I won't be gentle in this place, at least not when you decided to dress all innocent today." He toys with my ripped panties while still thrusting inside my throat. "You can fool the outside world that you are some sweet thing, but in this cage, you become my whore."

When his cock is lubricated with my spit, Collins pulls

out of my mouth and lines himself up between my spread thighs.

As he slides into me with ease, I throw my head back in surrender, not worrying about anything other than submitting to the pleasure Collins wants to extract from me.

"You might have shown up looking like a good girl, but I'm going to fuck you like a bad girl."

My pussy clenches as he thrusts in harder.

"Yessss..." I whimper, enjoying the fine line between pain and pleasure.

"Scream for me," he coaxes. "I want this entire club to be envious of us."

"Hmmm..." I moan quietly, but don't comply. It's a dangerous game I want to play.

A wicked grin forms on his lips. He knows he can get me to listen and that I'm just enjoying being a stubborn brat.

His hands grip my ass cheeks, applying pressure and squeezing me until I can't think straight. Then he places his thumb into my mouth. "Suck it." And when I don't, he forces it inside deeper. "Don't challenge me, Princess. You won't like how it ends."

Swirling his finger around, he gets the lubrication he's looking for before pressing it against my clit, inside the growing hole of my useless panties. He circles it.

"Collins!" I call out, as he hits the spot that sends ripples of electricity to every nerve in my body—against my free will.

Collins Stone owns me. And I doubt I'll ever be able to reclaim parts of me back again.

"That's it." He thrusts into me deeper. "You fucking take it."

"Yes!" I scream.

"You're doing great, Princess. Keep opening yourself to me. I'm taking everything you have. I just need a little more."

Collins thrusts hard into me, pulling on the straps that control the level of my hips.

And just like that, I come undone, screaming and panting into the charged air between us.

Until everything around me fades away...

33

PENNY

When my mind wakes up, I am surrounded by warmth and positive energy. I feel incredible and unlike anything I've ever felt before in my past.

The last thing I remember was having sex with Collins in the cage at...

Limit-X.

My eyes peel open, and it's then that I realize a huge chunk of time is unaccounted for—making me conclude that I passed out from the pleasure.

As much as I like to be coherent, I'd do the whole experience again in a heartbeat. It was that good.

"Collins..."

"I'm right here, Princess," he says, his voice super close.

Looking behind me, I see him and then I let out an awkward giggle. I'm literally curled up on his lap like a kitten.

Sheesh, this whole blackout episode is worse than those I've had from being under the influence of alcohol.

"You really did a number on my senses," I say, cuddling closer to him. He smells so good. I could breathe in his scent forever.

Glancing around the space, it doesn't even look like we are in the same building. This part of the venue definitely vibes more like a cocktail lounge than a sex club. The ambiance lighting and noise-blocking walls make it feel cozier than electrifying.

At least I am back to being dressed. Collins must have helped me put my cotton dress back on, but I doubt I was of any real assistance.

Feeling the draft of air between my legs, I press my knees closer together. "Where are my broken panties?"

Collins lets out a laugh. "Oh, those will forever be saved as a trophy. Maybe we can pin them to the fridge with a magnet."

I smack him in his chest, over his silly joke. "Seriously…"

"I used them to wipe up all of the cum leaking out of your greedy pussy. It sure was thirsty."

My lips form an O shape, while warmth creeps up my neck.

"Then I placed them into the pocket of my pants for safekeeping."

I wiggle my butt onto his crotch. "Hmm…okay."

I guess that's alright. At least they aren't hanging from the rafters for everyone to see that I sometimes wear white cotton panties with cute designs on them.

"You keep pressing that fine ass of yours into my cock, then you'll have the best access to find yourself impaled on it."

I suck my bottom lip into my mouth, caging it between my teeth.

"I'm glad you are back with us, little fawn."

I turn to Yuri's voice, recalling the obsession with woodland creatures some men seem to have here. He takes a seat on an adjacent chair to our couch, propping the ankle of one of his legs onto his opposite knee.

"Thank you," I say, not really knowing how to respond. There's something about him that makes me shy.

Leaning back into the cushions, Yuri examines me, which only causes me to stir. "Did you have a nice little nap?"

I nod but accompany the movement with a verbal response. "Yes. But what happened to me and why can't I remember any of it?"

"I think you just blacked out from the pleasure," Collins says, a bit smugly.

I press my face into his chest. "That's embarrassing."

"It's delightful," Yuri corrects, "isn't it? To completely submit to someone the desires of your soul?"

"Well, when you wrap it up like that"—I look up at Collins—"I guess it is pretty special."

Collins kisses me on my forehead, lazily massaging my back with his hand. It feels really good to be in a public setting and not have to hide all of our feelings for one another.

Daphne joins the group, along with Michael.

"Good seeing you, little dove," Michael says, while Daphne takes her place at his feet. "You can speak, pet."

"You look so pretty in your dress," she says, from the floor.

I smile, although she can't see when her eyes are cast downward. "Thanks."

Looking at Collins, I try to gauge his reaction if I were to ask some questions.

"Go on, Princess," he encourages. "Michael and Yuri are very open."

"I just wanted to understand the dynamics of the relationships you both seem to enjoy."

Yuri clears his throat but appears to be unfazed by my asking. "I find your curiosity absolutely enchanting, little fawn. You never need to feel shy about asking questions."

There has to be some deep respect Collins has for Yuri, because the jealousy I see with every other man who crosses my path isn't there between the two of them.

"The first step to understanding different dynamics is to detox the mind of how society and fictional entertainment often portray it. There are a wide variety of behaviors that could occur depending on where a couple falls on the dominance-submission spectrum. It also depends on whether or not they are looking for an open or closed arrangement, or if they are looking for a situation or twenty-four-seven power exchange."

"What do you prefer?" I ask, feeling a bit bold.

Yuri smiles. I bet he stops hearts with that smile too. It's all warm and yet holds so much power. "I much prefer closed partnerships with the twenty-four-seven power to be controlled entirely by me—in all ways."

"All ways?"

His demeanor is so gentle that I don't feel weird for my question. "I want to know where my submissive is at all times. I want her to ask for permission to use the bathroom.

I want her to only wear what I provide her to wear. I want to take care of her in all ways, including financially and by providing her nourishing foods."

"So she doesn't get any say?"

"It's at my discretion, but my goal as a dominant partner is to understand the submissive's heart and predict what would be best for her before she has a chance to decide for herself."

"Interesting…"

"But I have yet to find the perfect submissive who can handle my requirements," Yuri says softly. "And trust me, I've tried."

It makes me sad. Surely someone as attractive as he is can find someone who would relish in the feeling of being cared for and loved to the max.

Michael nods his head to the side, and Yuri motions with his hand to join the conversation we are openly having. "I prefer the opposite of what Yuri desires, but that's because I have fun dabbling in other kinks."

"Like what?" As soon as I ask, I feel suddenly shy. I cover my mouth with my hand.

I swear these men wash away some of my insecurities by their openness. They make me eager to learn, and that makes it easier for me to blurt out questions without any finesse.

Collins tucks me closer to his body, resting a hand on my ass in a possessive move. I can tell he doesn't feel threatened, and while it does take a mental adjustment for me to accept this public display of affection, I can't help but enjoy his touch.

And maybe I'm enjoying it too much, because I feel that

tingling feeling low in my belly that stretches out to my hands and feet.

"Public acts, group experiences, sharing my partner, video recording, role-playing, breath control, wax play, and if I'm feeling super in the mood—maybe even some degradation and humiliation." Then Michael smirks at me and wiggles his eyebrows. "That's just a condensed list of some of my faves."

"Yup, super basic," I say with an awkward laugh.

At least they all got my joke.

Collins's hand slides under my dress, and suddenly I'm no longer in a joking mood. What is he doing? My eyes look up at his, silently asking—*here*? Without acting like anything is happening, he works his hand between my inner thighs until he finds my bare pussy. My back goes rigid as I comprehend what's going to happen, all while casually chatting about sexual relationship topics with his sex club friends.

Dayum.

Yup, just a totally normal day in the neighborhood.

Yuri chuckles. "Michael basically likes everything Limit-X has to offer, but then also is begging me to agree to add in a few more *options* that are more at his hardcore speed."

He shrugs unapologetically, while playfully petting Daphne's head. "For convenience purposes."

I didn't even notice her collar and leash. No wonder she looks like she's in a state of euphoria. I think she gets off on the exchange of power.

"Right," Yuri says, expanding the syllables to be more than just the one.

"It's either that or I'll stray and find a better place to accommodate my particular tastes."

"Lies," Collins comments. "Everyone who knows anything about this place understands your loyalty, Michael."

I shift my position on Collins's lap, trying not to draw attention to the fact that his fingers are now stroking the inner lips of my pussy.

How can he be so casual about all of this?

And why does it feel so much better when I have this chance of being caught?

He kisses my neck, making me squirm.

"Are you okay, little fawn?" Yuri asks, probably sensing my sporadic changes in movements.

"Yup," I say quickly, jamming my elbow discreetly into Collins's ribs in hope he doesn't actually make me come again just from his touch. "I'm simply trying to absorb all of this information."

"Just don't get overwhelmed," Michael warns. "The Internet can be a very scary place if you ever decide to explore there. The best thing you can do is ask questions of someone who safely practices the lifestyle."

Like Collins...

But I don't quite understand the dynamic he's looking for other than the contracts he makes partners sign.

And what happens after the contract?

Part of me is afraid to accept that it was already made very clear once my signature hit the paper. When the one hundred days end, the idea of us also ends.

"Regardless, little fawn, I hope you find everything you are looking for in this life."

"I have the same sentiments for you. Thank you for accepting me and not making me feel weird for asking all of these questions."

"Never," Yuri says with a smile. "I welcome them."

While we continue to sit and chat, a waitress brings over drinks for us and some light snacks. I would probably enjoy them more, but I'm pretty occupied with Collins now sliding two fingers inside me and nonchalantly making small talk—something I rarely actually witness him doing.

I guess that's what it's like to have a network of people you trust and with whom you share similar overlapping interests.

When I first got out of Soulful Mind and made my goal list, I really yearned for a friend. And I found them. Angie and Claire are my friends, and while I once thought they were only accepting me because they were with my brothers, I now can see that I had what I always needed right there in front of me all along.

I'm glad Collins has Michael and Yuri too.

Oh fuck...

I mask a moan by coughing into my elbow, struggling to keep my composure while Collins is working me.

"You are very naughty," I whisper to him.

"And you are very much going to come all over my fingers soon, my little cum slut."

It's true.

I try to focus on what's happening to me, but Michael is distracting me by feeding grapes to Daphne from his fingertips. It's so sweet and yet so territorial.

I enjoy that contrast.

But that is how Collins is for me. He will help me

buckle my shoe if I need assistance but then will finger fuck me in front of his friends like it's just a normal hobby.

The feeling of a wave crashing to the shore hits me suddenly, as he changes angles and presses his fingers against my favorite spot.

And I do exactly what he promised I would...

I spasm and weep all over his hand...just like the good little fuck doll I am.

"Well, friends," Collins says, pulling his hand out from under my dress and helping me to stand up on my boneless legs, "it's time for us to head out of here. We have places to be."

"It was great getting to know you better, little fawn. Please come back whenever you desire—with or without Collins."

Collins fake scoffs. "Hey now."

"Thank you, Master Yuri," I say softly, out of respect and also because I'm not sure how to address him in general.

Collins pulls me away from that scene, tucking me close to his side. Before we get to the lockers, he stops me and then presents his two fingers at my lips for me to clean. "Taste us," he offers.

And I do.

"You are exquisite, Princess." He kisses me on the forehead. "I loved finger fucking you like a little puppet. You're always so responsive and such a good girl."

My pussy melts, leaking liquid down my inner thighs. I clench them together, but I know it's useless. It's the effect Collins's filthy mouth has on me. He adores me and defiles me at the same time, and the contrast in emotions is addictive.

We gather our things and make our way outside to the parked SUV.

"Where are we going?" I ask, sliding inside the passenger seat.

"Back home."

I gesture to the building. "You mentioned back there that we have 'places to be.'"

"Oh, we'll definitely be exploring a lot of *places* but for the sole purpose of being able to use your body again."

"Places like..."

"Hmmm..." Collins taps his finger along his jaw. "Perhaps on the countertop in the kitchen, against the wall of windows overlooking the view of the river, and maybe we can fuck in front of the vanity mirror."

A smile breaks out on my lips. "Sounds scenic. I love traveling."

34

PENNY

Mark's sinister laugh echoes in my ears, as he snakes a hand up my legs.

Beady eyes glisten with excitement.

It's as if he's morphed into someone else. Gone is the nice man trying to help me level up on my modeling career. Gone is the nice smile and the kind eyes.

Gone.

As his hand gets higher, my survival instincts kick in. I shake my leg to get him off.

No.

No.

"Please stop touching me there."

I don't like that.

I don't want to be touched like that.

It doesn't feel right. Nothing feels right. This all feels wrong.

"Get off me."

"You like it," he insists.

Do I? Am I sending mixed messages? No.

"No," I try again. My voice is raw. It burns to talk. Hurts. It's as if someone dumped acid into the back of my throat and a layer has peeled off.

He runs his hands over my body. "You'll like it more soon enough."

I try to wriggle away. "No."

"You crave the rough feel of my hands. Sluts love it rough."

I shake my head but it makes me dizzy. "No."

"You want to be a model, right?"

"Yes. Yes, I do."

"There's not an agency in the country that will take little whiny, pathetic girls who can't use their cunts, asses, or throats to get to the top. How do you think those models on the runway get there? Huh? Do you think they are actually talented? Use your brain, you idiot. This isn't a talent search. Walking in a straight line isn't a skill, darlin'. Anyone can wear clothes if they have a few curves in the right places, and those can be augmented anyway. This is the survival of the fittest."

"But I don't…"

"I will ask you again. Do you want to be a model?"

"Yes." I do. I *think* I do.

"Well, consider this my casting couch."

"Okay."

Mark laughs. It's so loud it hurts my ears.

"Prepare yourself to fuck your way there, you stupid girl. Stupid, stupid girl. So trusting. So innocent. So pathetic. You're probably thinking you have some type of talent. Stupid girl."

I was convinced in the past by this man that I have what it takes.

But he is a big liar.

Liar!

Stupid girl...

Stupid girl.

Stupid.

Stupid.

I shake my head.

"No."

"No?" Mark challenges.

"I'm not those things."

I'm not stupid.

I'm not stupid.

You're stupid.

You're stupid.

I'm...

"Well, you're stupid enough to think I have anything but ulterior motives. I have a little whore factory to run." He grabs me hard by the back of the neck, pulling me to him. "And you'd make the prettiest test victim. You know why?" Mark tilts back his head and laughs—like he might never stop. When he finally calms down, he looks me square in the eyes. "Because you are expendable. Because if something goes wrong...oh well."

I try to pull away.

I fight.

I kick.

I push and—

CRACK.

The sound hits my ears before the pain in my upper cheekbone registers.

He hit me.

Why did he hit me?

I'm being good.

I'm not being bad.

Why?

Tears burst from my eyes, blinding me. The only serenity I get is that they mask his evil smile.

"There. That should tame the fight out of you."

"You hurt me," I wail in confusion.

My stuttered inhales are coming at a faster pace than my exhales. It feels like my entire head is shoved into a bag with a limited supply of oxygen.

It's running out…

I double over, panting as the panic sets in.

"You better know your place. You are here as a test subject—nothing more."

"Model…" I whimper.

"You dumb fuck. You aren't pretty enough to model."

Loading up a syringe from a tiny vial, Mark grabs my arm.

"Stop!" I scream, but no words come out…

Silence.

"Time for a little dose of medicine." He twists my arm, making me wince. "It always makes poor little college students more compliant. As if a formal education will somehow make you less naive in thinking you actually have a chance of being a silly model. The best part is, if you die from an overdose, it will look like an accident."

My eyes laser in on the rubber band Mark is tying around my arm.

NO!

I wiggle to try to get it off, while my other hand attempts to pry the band from my skin.

"Get it off!"

"Dumb fuck."

With every ounce of energy I have, I go ballistic.

I thrash.

I claw.

I bite.

I knee.

"Fuck, you are delightful when you think you can fight me."

I kick.

I beg.

I plead.

I cry.

I...

I...

And then I feel the pinch of the needle, puncturing through my skin.

Heat rushes to the injection site, as the burn from whatever drug Mark injected into me floods my system.

"Oh, wow. You definitely look like a rabid bitch with that foam coming out of your mouth. I hope I didn't give you too much. I'm not into fucking the dead. I like a little life in my pussies."

No!

Noooo!

"Wake up, bitch."

He kicks me.

"You're drooling everywhere."

I open my mouth to scream, but nothing comes out.

Mark hovers over me, and I feel myself convulsing.

I'm going to die.

And part of me wishes I would.

I try to force the oxygen out of my lungs, hoping that my involuntary reflexes don't kick in. I just want to float away to another place and be at peace.

"Penny?"

I hear my name but it sounds like it's coming from a faraway place.

"Penny?"

It's Collins.

He's here.

It's so scary.

"Penny?"

Why is Collins here?

He's here in my nightmare.

Run, Collins!

Go away!

It's a trap!

Mark will kill you!

He's deranged!

Black fog fills my vision, and the only thing I see is Mark in the crowd of people watching me.

I'm in the water.

The river…

I'm taking pictures in the river…at the photoshoot.

My eyes focus on his black shirt, and on the pocket, I see the red rose logo for the little cafe.

My body convulses.

"He was there," I gasp, thrusting myself upward.

"Penny? Wake up. You're having a bad dream."

Gentle hands shake me.

"He was there."

"Penny. You're scaring me. Wake up, Princess."

"He was there."

"Who?"

My eyes flutter open, searching for an anchor to keep me from sinking back into the depths of my trauma.

"Mark Tanner was there."

Collins hugs me to him as I sob into his shoulder.

"You were having a bad dream," he explains. "I tried to wake you."

"It wasn't a nightmare. It was a memory."

Hugging me tighter, I let every tear that I ever held back consume me.

And I shatter—as all of the memories from the night I was drugged come flittering back like a boomerang.

"For nearly a year, I couldn't remember much from that night. But now I remember everything."

"Just let it all out. I got you. I'm never letting you go."

"I hate him."

"I know, Princess. I hate him too—more than you'll ever probably realize."

"He was at the river for my photoshoot. He was wearing a Rose City Cafe employee shirt. I saw him in the crowd. That's why I think I slipped back into that unresponsive state. He was there. I remember he was there."

Collins stiffens. "No, Penny."

"*Yes.* I saw him."

"No… I think you were just imagining him there."

"You don't believe me?" Why doesn't he believe me? "I saw him."

"I just know he wasn't there, Princess."

"How do you know? Tell me."

"Because when I was informed by Chris to come to the river to help you, I was paying Tanner a visit at the prison and was on my way back to the area."

"Oh." My mind races back through the nightmare. Was it truly a bad dream or was I remembering key information? "But…he was in the crowd. I saw him. He was watching me."

"It wasn't him," Collins insists. "He can't be in two places at once."

"Yeah…"

"We looked through all the pictures and security footage. We also questioned everyone we could that was present that day. Nothing seemed out of place."

"I'm going crazy. And I'm going to forever be plagued with the memory of that man."

Collins hugs me to him, cradling me in his arms.

"Don't you realize that you are so much bigger than that one moment from your past? I get that it has changed the course of your life, seemingly forever. But you have another life still to live." Collins fixes the stray pieces of hair behind my ears. "You have a second chance life where you can be strong and fierce and empowered with the knowledge that some people do suck. But finding the good ones will be easier for you now. Don't treat your tragedy as new lenses in your vision. Treat it like a turning point, where you now can start living your best life—letting go of what happened to you in the past. There will be many more moments. Better ones. But don't you want to be able to recognize them before they pass you by?"

"I do," I say softly. But I don't sound very convincing, even to my own ears. "What if I *can't* do it?"

Collins rubs a hand down the back of his neck. "You know how those dark thoughts—the ones that stay buried deep within your soul—can come out when you are at your lowest and not your best? That was where I was after I got discharged from the military. I thought my entire life was over. Then Graham hired me to work security and gave me a purpose again. I proved myself to be loyal and an asset to him. But then you were drugged, and your brothers needed extra protection and someone to help them discover what happened to you."

"So they shifted your responsibilities."

"Yes. And I accepted the new position because you were going to be my redemption. It was fate in a way, and I wanted to be the deliverer of the karma meant to take down the entire drug operation. I couldn't fight and win against those who drugged me and set me up in the military, but I could seek out justice for you. I will always want what is best for you, Princess. Always."

He kisses me on the forehead, as I snuggle deeper into his warmth.

"What is best for me is you, Collins."

"I'm starting to believe that as well."

35

COLLINS

"The contract ends in five days," Penny reminds me, as if I could somehow forget.

I've been dreading this day since the moment we signed the deal. I knew I'd catch feelings, and I hate myself for not being strong enough to resist this girl's charm.

But Penelope Josephine Hoffman has burrowed herself into my heart, and there's not a damn thing I can do about it other than embrace the love she has to give to me.

And with doing that, I need to talk to her brothers. I owe them an explanation, but it has to wait. First, I need to clear this earth of Tanner. Maybe when he's gone, they'll be in a more relaxed state to even consider the possibility of me being with their sister.

"I don't want you worrying about anything," I tell her. "Just focus on taking care of yourself and going to your meetings with Margo. I'll handle the rest."

Penny looks at me with trepidation, my words losing their calming effect.

I know her worry is real, as it mirrors my own, but I can't have her stressed and be able to concentrate on doing my job.

Hearing my phone go off, I rush to get it off the nightstand.

Every time it buzzes, I feel my heart flutter off rhythm, thinking it's go time.

"Everything okay?" Penny asks, trying to look over my shoulder.

Shielding her from the message, I read my screen.

"Your brothers need me."

Her hands snake around my waist. "I need you too."

I lift her hand and kiss each of her fingers one by one. "You have me."

"I don't want this to end," she whispers, and I can't tell if she's referring to our lazy time in bed or the future.

"I'll be back soon."

"I can stay here?"

"Of course." I much prefer it that way anyway. "Chris is living across the hall."

"So, I'll be safe."

"Yes."

It takes all my willpower to leave Penny in bed to get dressed and head to the boxing gym, a favorite meetup location for conducting our business. Being away from her makes me anxious, and it's hard to think clearly when I'm constantly wondering what she's doing.

Sure, I have trackers on her, but I much prefer having her within sight.

"I'll be back soon."

Her eyes connect with mine as I back out of the bedroom. "You better be back."

"There's no place I'd rather be than with you, Princess."

She sucks her bottom lip between her teeth and waves goodbye.

"Are you up for some sparring?" Graham asks, passing me some gloves.

"Sure," I say hesitantly. I wasn't expecting to get a full-on workout this morning, but some vigorous physical exercise always does my body good.

"Awesome." The eldest Hoffman cracks his knuckles, and I follow him into the ring. "Any word on the handwriting analysis for the mail going to Penny's apartment?"

"Inconclusive." I slide on my gloves and tighten them up.

Graham rakes a hand through his hair. "Isn't that odd?"

"Not when the sample is inadequate. There wasn't enough to analyze even by the most productive forensic software."

"Gotcha."

"Penny had a…" Fuck. I almost said nightmare but stop myself just in time. I don't need her brother suspecting me of knowing too many intimate details about Penny, her dreams and nightmares included. "Concern over Tanner getting to her at the waterfront during her photoshoot, but I was there that day at the prison."

"Yeah, and you get daily updates on what is happening behind bars?"

"Yes, and it's never anything to report. But something keeps bothering me about the whole thing. It's like I'm awaiting impending doom."

"You might be."

My left eye twitches. What's that supposed to mean?

Graham walks over to the side of the ring and grabs his own pair of gloves and places them onto his fists, readjusting them as needed.

"Where's Nic?" I ask when the conversation lulls.

"Something came up."

Okay...

Why is he being so secretive?

I stretch my arms above my head, grabbing my elbows with my gloved hands. Then I stretch out my calves, one at a time.

When we are both warmed up, we get into the ring and bounce around on our feet.

Bumping fists, Graham and I separate to opposite sides of the ring before meeting up in the middle to go head-to-head.

Evenly matched, we each get a few jabs in, moving about the space with quick feet.

The rhythm to boxing is what I enjoy the most. I love getting to know my opponents and striving to predict their reactions. Graham and I have sparred for a while now, so I always appreciate when he incorporates a fight sequence that forces me to think on my feet to counter.

He goes to kick, and I bounce back, causing him to miss.

Then out of my periphery, I see his fist barreling through the air to connect with my flesh in a stinging punch.

"Dammit," I groan, moving my glove up to see if he broke the skin.

Then he does it again.

This time, I'm caught completely off guard, something that rarely ever happens. Spit flies from my mouth, as my tongue grazes against my teeth. It's enough to cause the tissue to puncture and fill my mouth with the bitter taste of acid and rust.

"Hell, man," I say, with a biting edge to my tone.

Strengthening my form, I go back into fighting position, while still staying light on my feet.

And he charges forward again, shoving me against the ropes. My back ignites from the burn, and I use my momentum to stay upright, protecting my face before his fist comes coursing through the air in a full-on attack.

Hopping on my feet, I dodge him by mirroring his movements.

But when I duck a punch, his knee connects with my chin. My head flies back, followed by the rest of me.

Kicking my legs up, I bounce back to my feet. Blood splatters the mat. I can't even tell where it's coming from at this point. I just know I'm the source.

Then Graham throws his entire body at me. Tugging my thighs toward him, he sweeps my feet from underneath me. My back crashes to the mat followed by my head.

My vision goes black, and when it finally focuses again, it's Graham Hoffman's livid face that will haunt me forever.

His fist pounds into the side of my head, until I maneuver myself out of the hold and take control back.

I pin him to the mat but don't take out my aggressions on him, like he has me.

"What the fuck, man?"

He has the nerve to look unaffected. "What?"

I pant from the exertion, trying to get my breathing back to a normal aerobic state. "Are we sparring or brawling?" I snarl.

After several seemingly long seconds, Graham growls in what I can only assume is frustration—over what, I'm still trying to figure out for sure.

"I trusted you," he chokes out. "I fucking trusted you, and you went behind my back and did the one thing I never in a million years would ever expect you to do. You are a traitor."

His words feel like venom to my veins.

Dammit.

"Okay... Let's talk about it."

Anything has to be better than beating each other up over this.

"Talk about it?" he asks, as if the concept is the most laughable thing in the world.

"I'd like to have a real discussion, yes."

"You betrayed me. You betrayed Nic. And you have let the one person you swore to protect down. What's there to discuss?"

The blood drains from my face first and then from my arms, causing a tingling sensation in my fingertips.

Releasing my hold, I get up from on top of Graham. Then he rolls himself to his side and stands.

Running my fingers over the back of my neck, I feel the tension building. "I wanted to come to you first."

"For what? To get my blessing?" He scoffs. "Maybe

when hell freezes over. But I'll never accept that you found it in you to seduce my baby sister. *Never.*"

What else am I supposed to do now?

My fingers lace behind my head. "How did you find out?"

"Does it matter?"

I shrug. "It does to me."

"She's my baby sister!"

But she's my everything. "I love her, Graham."

But those words trigger him, and he punches me again. This time his force is stronger than the other times.

And again.

Again...

I let him beat the shit out of me. I don't even flinch.

Blood explodes from my lip, speckling the mat in even more dark spots. I wipe at my face, smearing the blood all over my white gloves. It drips down my neck, soaking into my workout shirt.

And I let it happen...

I let it be.

This isn't how I predicted this would end. I thought I had more time. And I definitely thought I could explain my way through how Penny and I came to be.

But my hope was stolen from me—too soon.

I fell for Penny.

And I fell hard.

Now all the time I've spent with her will be tainted by this memory of betrayal.

Fuck.

I should have come to Graham first. We were just days

On a Fault Line

away from the contract ending. Surely, anything would have been better than this catastrophe.

Deep down I thought if I rid the planet of Mark Tanner, I would somehow be granted immunity for any stupid shit I've done prior.

I'm an idiot.

And now I know with confidence that this man absolutely hates me.

"I'm sorry."

"That's all you have to say?"

He jerks me forward by my shirt just to slam me back against the ropes of the ring.

"It's not Penny's fault."

"Of course it's not her fault, you fucker! *You* knew better." He looks away as if the sight of my face alone disgusts him. "You preyed on my little sister when she was at her most vulnerable."

"It wasn't like that..."

But how do I explain that Penny tried for weeks to get me to cave to her desires? She's the one who pursued me, yet in reality I'll never actually blame her.

There's just no point... How would I even go about challenging the narrative Graham already has solidified in his own head?

I can't.

There's nothing I can say or do that will change the fact that I'm sixteen years older than the girl who has enraptured my entire heart.

When I think Graham's going to spit on me, he changes direction and walks off to the side of the ring.

"End it with her."

He makes it sound easy, as if I haven't already considered this scenario for the last three months.

I lean against the ropes for stability. My lip is already clotting, and the stickiness from the blood is making every motion of my mouth sore as I reopen the wound.

"I'm sorry," I try again.

But it's Graham's glare that makes me want to crumble. I broke more than just his trust. I broke his baby sister.

"When?"

My eyes twitch. "When what?"

"When did you think that double-crossing me was in the best interest of friendship?"

"Ninety-five days ago," I choke out.

But in reality, I betrayed him from the first moment I saw Penny at her twenty-second birthday party. It was that event that changed the entire course of my life and shattered the one I've spent years to rebuild.

Besides, it's not like I can even fight for her when she deserves better than to be estranged from her family, who mean everything to her.

Family comes first, and I'd never want her to choose between me or them.

They need her more than someone as fucked-up as I am does.

I've been destined to be alone.

Penny, on the other hand, needs someone who will nurture her—not destroy her.

No matter how many times I told myself I couldn't resist her charms, I did the one thing that completely shattered the trust from the two men who gave me another reason to live.

Now I don't even know how to go on with the knowledge that I'll never be back in their good graces.

Never.

Penny is the closest fucking thing I have to a home, and I am lighting my entire delusion on fire.

She's going to hate me.

But I hate me more.

36

PENNY

I am lying in Collins's bed when I hear rustling outside in the hallway.

"You're back soon," I call out, pulling myself upright and out of my protective cocoon. The blankets pool around me. "Which is good for me, because I'm super horny from you being gone."

The door to the room flies open, and I silently pray that I'm in the middle of another nightmare—which would be much better than this fucked-up version of reality.

"What the hell, Penny!?"

Oh, no.

This cannot be happening.

What is happening?

No...

No.

"Nic!"

I grab the sheets and pull them up to my neck. What the

fuck is happening? Why is he here standing in my bedroom?

Correction… *Collins's* bedroom.

I'm in Collins's bedroom.

And my brother just caught me in a smoking-gun scene.

Dammit.

"I can't believe this," he mutters.

"Me either." My words are barely audible even to my own ears.

Staring into the eyes of my brother, I think I'm hallucinating. What other explanation could there be as to why he's standing inside Collins's apartment, looking like he's seen a ghost.

Nic's hands slide to the back of his neck, as he pivots his body to avoid any more awkward eye contact.

"Get dressed, Penny," he snaps.

"What are you doing here?"

"Confirming that Graham and I hired a fucking traitor."

His words sting, and I quiver back into the pillows that have supported my addiction to Collins for months. I've spent a lot of time in this bed—my safe haven—and now my brother's presence here today has tainted my peace with being in this space.

"It wasn't Collins's fault."

"Not his fault?" he snaps. "How is this not his fault for fucking with my baby sister?"

"I consented." My words come out rushed—frantic— and when I don't think he believes me, I add, "I promise."

I did consent!

I consented to everything…

But why do I owe anyone an explanation or a play-by-play of those intimate details?

I don't.

"I consented, Nic," I reiterate. "Listen to me. *Please.*"

His body whips around, and it's now that I realize just how angry he is with all of this. He wasn't supposed to find out—at least not like this. We were almost done with the contract, and Collins promised he would handle the rest.

But how can things be made right when a trust so loyal has been broken?

"I didn't want to sneak around," I say, wiping the flow of tears streaming from my eyes. "I'm sorry for hiding it."

"You're sorry for *hiding* it?"

"Yes!"

Nic rubs at the back of his neck. "You've got to be fucking kidding me."

"Listen to me," I scream. I don't even recognize my own frantic voice. "I'm sorry for going behind your back, but I didn't know any other way."

"How about being sorry for ruining your life again?"

"Ruining my life? You're being heartless!"

"I'm being honest," he counters.

"Collins helped give me my zest for being in this life back. Don't you see it? I'm happy. I'm fucking happy again. The old me who was buried underneath trauma and the pain of my past has resurrected from the ash as someone who knows her worth. And it was Collins who helped me see it."

Every time I say Collins's name, he flinches as if I'm burning him with a hot iron.

Nic looks around the room, and for a second I think he's

going to go on a rampage, tearing apart the life I built here between these walls.

It's a life I'm not ready to let go. I won't let go...

His eyes scan over the four-poster bed. They land on the sheets and pillows. He looks at the nightstand and the charging cable plugged into my phone.

Nothing seems out of the norm, but Nic can't help but look at everything here with disgust and contempt. "I can't fucking be in this place without wanting to rip everything apart and burn it to the ground."

"What? Why do you care so much?"

"Because a man who should have known better used you for his sick fantasies."

"I love him," I blurt out. I'm not thinking straight but of that I am certain.

"Love?" Nic scoffs. "You're fucking joking."

"I love Collins Stone."

Just don't tell him yet. I want to make it special... I haven't officially expressed that sentiment to him.

"I'm going to fucking murder that man for taking advantage of you when you were most vulnerable. We hired him to *protect* you, not *abuse* you."

Why is he being so hateful? "He never abused me!"

"You don't know what you're saying right now, Penny. You are blinded by whatever false promises that man has conned you into believing. I don't blame you. This is all his fault."

"You are being so mean—so cruel. Please stop."

I cover my ears but I can still hear his rant.

"Go to your apartment and pack some things. I'm

bringing you to my house where I can keep a better eye on you."

I shake my head adamantly. I don't want to go anywhere. "No."

"Yes, dammit. You can stay in a guest room until Graham and I figure out what the fuck we're going to do about this."

"There's nothing to do, Nic." My words come out frantic, and I can't stop crying. "I'm not some petulant child. I can make my own choices."

"Well, you suck at them right now."

His words slap me right in the face. "All these months I had prioritized what Mark did to me—what I couldn't even remember—and then suddenly I switched and found someone else to focus on. Someone attentive and kind and understanding and loving... And you can't see past him crossing a line in order to comprehend just what Collins did for me. It's not fair! It's not fair that you are so blinded by the filter of betrayal that you can't see my progress."

"Go grab some things."

"Nic..."

"Now, Pen."

I shake my head at him. "Unbelievable."

It's like I'm looking at a man I don't even know anymore.

Rolling out of bed, I stomp into the closet to get dressed, while still wrapped in the bed sheet. There's no point fighting with my hardheaded brother when he's this mad. There's no point in reminding him that I'm a legal adult at the age of twenty-two and that he's not in charge of controlling who I date or not date—no matter if they are his employee or not.

Nic's already made up his mind that Collins is the villain, and I'm the victim. We both just need time to cool off and have a chance to calmly explain. And that realization is the only thing making me comply right now.

We just need time.

Maybe if he hears that Collins wants what I want, that we both are very much into each other, then he'll relax this choke hold on my freedom.

Maybe.

When I'm ready to leave, Nic escorts me back to my apartment, unlocking the door with his own key.

He's being unfair and deliberately making a point as to what level of control he has over my life.

It's my brothers who have funded my bank account for me to even get this apartment. It's my brothers who have advocated for me to get the best therapy center in Seattle when I needed it most. It's my brothers who introduced me to their top bodyguard and right-hand man, Collins, in the first place.

And it'll be my brothers who will serve as the instrumental force that will tear us apart.

But I won't let it happen. I'm willing to fight for us.

Pushing past Nic, I enter my apartment. I've spent exponentially more time at Collins's place than my own, so it's ironic that he brought me here to gather my things when I have more stored at the other location.

But I can already tell he is in no mood to listen to me disagree. So I just step into line, like the obedient little soldier.

"I'll be back in one hour. Do not leave."

"Where is Collins?"

"Don't worry about him," he spits out.

"But I am worried. Where is he?"

Nic shrugs nonchalantly and glances at his watch. "Oh, he's probably getting his face bashed in by Graham as we speak."

"That's messed up, even for you!" I snarl.

"He needs to be taught a lesson, Pen. It's as simple as that."

"With fists?"

"That is a way better punishment than he actually deserves."

Crying, I shove him out the door.

Why is he being so cold?

If it wasn't for the confidence in Collins's ability to handle his own, then I'd be busting out of here to go stop my eldest brother from doing something he'll ultimately regret.

But Collins doesn't need me to fight his battles right now, and a part of me is relieved I no longer have to hide our once-secret relationship. Now that everything is getting out in the open, we can start to push forward on being together long-term.

My brothers just need to calm down from the initial shock.

Fishing my phone out of my pants pocket, I find Collins's name in my list of contacts.

I hit the call button but get sent right to voicemail, so I leave one.

"Hey, where are you? Are you okay? Nic found me at

your place. He's livid. He just needs time to calm down. I hope you're okay. Graham probably knows too. At least that's what Nic implied. Be safe. I don't want them to hurt you. This is on me. I seduced you. I'm sorry. I won't let you carry all of the burden and all of the blame. I knew what I was doing. And I regret nothing."

My words come out as one big ramble, and when I disconnect the call, I fall to the floor in an emotional heap.

I love you.

I stay here in a curled-up ball until the doorbell sounds.

Nic…

He said he'd be back in an hour to collect me.

I don't want to go.

I just want to sleep away all of this pain pressing down on my heart.

The doorbell rings again, reminding me that I haven't answered it.

Pulling myself up from my own self-pity party, I make my way out of the bedroom and into the hallway. Moving to the door, I open it and discover a little box resting on the doormat.

Weird.

I glance down the hallway but don't see anyone around who could have delivered it.

Picking up the package, I pull off the lid to reveal a bracelet. Turning it over in my hand, I see that the underside is engraved.

"I'm an…" I read out loud.

Then all of the other mysterious gifts' messages come flooding back to me, reminding me that Mark Tanner still has a hold on me—just as he promised he would.

One.

Two.

Three.

I'm an...

What does this even mean?

One, two, three, I'm an....

Will I get another gift soon?

And who is delivering these to me?

Something seems off, and yet someone is taking their time delivering a cryptic message at his orders.

I walk the bracelet over to the kitchen counter and place it on its surface.

I'm over these haunting messages. Mark obviously has someone working for him on the outside who is able to deliver these strange packages.

He's getting to me, and I'm allowing every second of his torment to touch my life.

Suddenly the apartment feels claustrophobic and empty at the same time.

I don't want to be here alone. I'm fucking tired of being alone.

"Luke? Are you here?"

Maybe he came back home during my nap on the floor.

I meander into the living room, looking to see if there's any sign my roommate's here. Usually it's a drink left on a side table or the television being left on that indicates he's milling about the place.

But I see nothing.

Moving down the hall, I knock on his door, surprised it isn't in its typical locked state. Despite being very open about what he does at his job, he's a relatively private person. So when I find it left ajar, I'm shocked.

Pushing the door a little, I take a peek inside his room.

"Hey, Luke?"

No answer.

And then without thinking of the consequences, I walk in.

I blame it on the fish tank. It catches my attention.

Why didn't I know he had a fish tank?

Pinned to the side of the tank are little cutout name tags of goldfish. Blooper, Finneous, and Scaly-Gaster...

The fish are huge for being goldfish, clearly having months to grow.

Grabbing the food, I see the feeding schedule listed out on paper from a spiral notebook, dated back to the middle of summer.

Seriously, why didn't I even realize this?

Have I been so wrapped up in the world of Collins Stone that I don't even know what's happening in my own home?

The fish swim to the glass at what I assume is the sight of the food container coming into view, so I open up the top part of the tank and sprinkle in some of the shrimp flakes.

"There you go."

They swim toward the flakes, swallowing them up with each gulp.

I stare a little longer into the tank before closing the lid. I cross off the feeding cycle from the list and hope I didn't majorly overstep.

I just couldn't help myself.

But when I place the notebook back onto the dresser, a series of photos float out onto the floor.

Grabbing them, my heart stops.

These are of me...

And Collins.

What the hell?

We are standing in the hallway outside his place. One is of me at the coffee shop for the speed dating event. Another is of us making out in the alleyway afterward.

And there's a series of us outside in the parking lot at Limit-X.

No...

Why do these even exist?

"Penny?"

Whipping my body around, I come face-to-face with my slimy roommate.

"Who are you?" I demand.

"Why are you snooping in my room?"

I flash the photos in the air. "Why do you have pictures of me and Collins?"

"What?" he has the nerve to ask.

"Look!" I wave them in front of his face. "See them? Why?" I yell.

"I don't know what you're talking about." But then his eyes lock on to the photos, and instantly, I want to hide them from his view.

No one needs to be witness to these once private, intimate moments between me and the man I love.

"You don't need to keep lying."

Luke's forehead wrinkles. "I'm not."

I'll give it to him—he does sound convincing.

"My brothers hired you, didn't they?" Taking a step forward, I shove at his chest. "You've been lying to me this whole time?" He's not even denying it. "You moved in with me to keep an eye on me?"

"How can I keep an eye on you when you're barely here? That makes no sense." His words are barely a whisper, but they hit hard.

"That's not the point! Did you tamper with my speed-dating matches?" When he doesn't answer, I push him again. "I thought you were my friend. But you went to my brothers about the best thing that's ever happened to me and basically are ruining everything."

Tears flood my vision. I'm in truth overload. It literally feels like my life is crashing down around me, one sacred memory at a time.

Luke continues talking to me, but I block him out by covering my ears. I can't look at him. I can't listen to him. I can't be in his presence.

I need Collins. I need him to make this all better.

Rushing out of the room, I throw myself into mine and shut the door.

So much is happening all at once, and the only person who can keep me grounded is the one man my brothers are going to try and keep me away from.

They just aren't going to understand our connection, and I'm starting to doubt that they'll be able to calm down long enough to even try.

Flopping down onto the bed, I cry into my pillow.

This entire apartment now feels foreign to me.

If my brothers hand selected Luke to be their spy, along with Collins the hired bodyguard, then this entire operation was probably all orchestrated so I would find myself moving here.

It was too good to be true.

But I never expected it all to be one massive setup.

To find an apartment this perfect, with great security, and an opening where I didn't have to commit to a lengthy contract was way too easy.

My brothers made it easy. They were the puppet masters, and I simply played right into their hands.

Graham and Nic just never expected me to fall in love with Collins Stone.

Well, too damn bad.

Grabbing my phone, I text Collins.

Penny: Luke has been hired by my brothers. He tampered with my speed dating matches and probably told my brothers about us. They know. Nic found me in your bed.

Penny: I'm sorry.

And then a minute later.

Penny: I need you. I'm falling apart.

Penny: I can't breathe.

37

PENNY

I'm awakened from my fitful slumber with muffled arguing happening down the hall.

Sitting up in bed, I try to adjust my eyes to the darkness.

How long have I slept?

The memories of Nic finding me in Collins's bed and the discovery that Luke was hired by my brothers come flooding back to me.

Nothing seems to be going my way today, and I'm starting to doubt that things will fit back into place again.

Rolling out of bed, I try to get my wobbly legs to work. I feel like I'm constructed out of cooked noodles.

Stretching, I reach my hands above my head, recirculating the blood.

Moving over to the curtains, I pull them back and stare out into the city at night.

Great. I wasted an entire day away and nothing got accomplished.

The yelling coming from outside my bedroom gets

louder, and it's now that I can hear the distinct tone of Collins's voice. He's here.

Feeling a burst of energy, I make my way to the door and pull it open. Artificial light flitters in through the hallway, making me squint.

"I hear her door," Graham says.

"She can stay at my new house," Nic volunteers. "I have plenty of room and can keep a close watch on her."

"Okay," Graham agrees. "If you need me to send over anything while we figure out the next steps or switch off weeks to be at my place, just let me know."

"Sounds good."

They are discussing me—but without me. It's as if a divorce has happened and custody of a child needs to be arranged.

I'm the child.

Me.

Adult me is the child.

This has been the approach of my brothers for the last year, so why change things up now?

My feet carry me toward the voices, and suddenly all sets of eyes turn to me. Mine find Collins first, softening toward his appearance.

I wasn't expecting him to be here. And I definitely didn't expect his poor face to look as beat-up as it does.

Running, I throw myself at the man who has captured my heart. I wrap my legs around his waist and anchor myself to him like he's my lifeline. Deep down, I hope that my display of physical affection helps solidify my place in Collins's life for my brothers to witness. Maybe that will help them understand that Collins is my person.

"You are here," I say breathlessly, draping my arms around his neck.

Why is everyone being so quiet—so still?

"Get down, Penelope," Collins says, but just for my ears.

Then I realize that everything I'm experiencing right now is one-sided, and the coldness I never thought I would feel in this man's presence is now infiltrating the warmth we had toward one another for nearly one hundred days.

Collins's arms stay at his side. When I look into his eyes, I see that they lack the life and love I am convinced I once felt and saw reflected back at me. But it's vanished. It's like I'm hugging a cold statue at a museum.

It's like I'm hugging a stranger.

The fairy tale is over.

And I've been deluded enough to think it was all real.

My eyes look up into his, silently pleading. "Collins?"

He ignores me.

I give him a shake but am careful not to jostle him and cause him more pain.

His hands hover over me but don't actually make contact.

My brothers curse under their breath. But I don't care. They already know we're together and will be together. Once the shock wears off, they'll come around.

I'll make them see that Collins and I can be good together.

Looking closer at the details of his face, it fully registers to me that his cheeks are swollen. His lip is cut and there's bruising along his jawline. He needs some ice.

I slide down Collins's body, finding the strength to stand

on my own. With gentle hands, I cup both sides of his face and run my thumbs over all his wounds.

"What happened to you?" I choke out. I already know but I want to hear his words anyway. It guts me to see him like this, and deep down, I know it's because of me.

We may have crossed a line nearly one hundred days ago, but my brothers crossed one today.

"I'll be okay."

Turning my body, I glare at Graham. "You did this to him? You beat up Collins?"

"Yes."

"What the fuck is wrong with you? And why are you being so matter-of-fact about it?"

"It's over, Penny," he bites out. "Grab your things and let's go."

Crossing my arms, I hold my ground. "No."

"Yes!" Nic bellows.

And to think he's typically the calm one out of the two.

"No!" I challenge. "I'm not going anywhere without Collins."

"Let me have a chat with Penny," Collins says solemnly.

I hate seeing him this broken. I hate that our entire relationship is blowing up before our eyes.

Graham pushes hair off his forehead. "Fine."

"Gee, thanks," I mumble under my breath. "How generous."

My entryway clears out, leaving me standing face-to-face with the man I have fallen head over fucking heels for in less than one hundred days.

"Penny…"

"Can I get you some ice?"

I don't wait for an answer and walk into the kitchen to busy myself with making an ice pack out of a resealable bag and some cubes. I then take the bag and wrap it in a clean dish towel, to keep him from getting frostbite.

"I can't believe my brother beat you up."

I hand him the pack, but he just places it down onto the counter.

"We need to talk."

"I'm so sorry you are in this position."

"This isn't your fault."

"Both Graham and Nic just need to calm the fuck down and then they'll understand that we belong together."

His look of indifference is a vise around my heart, depriving my entire body of the air that once gave me life.

It's his silence that makes me squeeze my fingers inward, pressing tightly into my palms—so tight that I'd be surprised if I didn't leave marks.

I don't need him to talk, when I already know what's going to happen next.

I feel it.

It's like a cold front blowing through in a storm that is about to destroy all hopes for my future.

Collins moves into my living room and then to the wall of windows that overlook the city of Portland. I follow behind wordlessly, shuffling through memories that were made here in this building, and are now damaged with the realization that I no longer have a place in this man's life.

"Say it," I lash out.

"What do you want me to say, Pen? Huh?"

"Tell me that us making floor angels and you chasing me down to tickle me over taking pictures of you was just a misunderstanding. Tell me that you caring for me during the storm was just you doing your job. Tell me that us taking baths together at your place and fooling around on the terrace was just me forcing myself on you. Tell me... Tell me that I'm the"—I choke on my next word—"*crazy* one for believing in a figment of my imagination, conjured up in my own head from watching too many princess movies growing up." I smack at his chest. "Tell me!"

Our eyes meet and I no longer see the man I thought I loved. Instead, reflected back in his callous expression, I see all of my flaws, insecurities, and weaknesses with vivid clarity. I'm not his girl. I'm not his anything.

And when this is all said and done, I'll be a shell of who I was reinventing myself to be.

Tears cascade out of my eyes.

But Collins says nothing.

He does nothing.

He tries to save nothing.

The air between us is stifling, moving from slightly humid to borderline unbreathable.

We were created to break. This has always been the endgame, and I just refused to believe it.

It is in his seemingly uninterested gaze that my mind fractures, more now than when I was taken by Mark.

"I'm sorry," he says stiffly, but his words hold no emotion.

My nose flares. "I'm sorry too. I'm sorry that I thought you were a man who would do everything to fight for me. I was wrong."

"It's for the best."

"You are the worst kind of monster. You are the kind

that stands tall behind a code of honor you live by, only to shatter the lives of anyone who goes against your narrative."

I watch as he swallows and glances out at the river. But he says nothing.

"Look at me."

And when he doesn't, I jerk his shoulder to turn him.

"Look at me and remember this day. Because we will never come back from this."

My hand flies forward with so much force, it is as if my entire life has saved up this aggression inside with the intent to release it in this very moment. The sound hits my ears first, followed by the searing pain radiating through my entire arm, and then ends with the look of shock in his solemn eyes.

Collins doesn't even dodge the blow. Wiping at his cheek, he shifts his weight to his other foot. Blood spills from his reopened wound. "You hit me."

"You fucking deserve worse, you bastard!"

I shove at him. And I pound my fists into his chest. And I scream out a sound that is foreign even to my own ears.

Then I back away, trying to get as much distance between us as I can.

I can't look at him. So I keep walking.

But it's in that silence that the realization hits me like a brick.

I'm going to be alone.

A sharp, burning sensation scratches at the back of my throat, working its way up to my mouth.

I'm going to be alone.

Turning, I look back at Collins standing in the middle of

my living room. Tears continue falling like a waterfall from my eyes.

"Don't leave me."

Then I rush to him, falling at his feet.

"Please don't leave me."

My arms circle his ankles, tugging him. But he doesn't budge.

I'm lying in a heap of limbs at his feet, and he stands stoically still.

I am stupid.

Carelessly stupid.

My teeth chew at my inner cheek, puncturing the tissue from the force. This physical pain will never compete with the emotional breakdown I am having now—one-sidedly.

And in my humiliation, I vow to never give Collins an opportunity to break me again. That no matter how much of an asshole he is tonight, I'm the bigger one for ever thinking that a contractual relationship would end any other way than it is now.

Rolling to the fetal position, I look up at the man hovering above me.

"I hate you," I mouth. *You won.*

I know my message was received based on the flinch of his eyes, but he doesn't move to me or make me get up. Instead, he just stares—his hollowed-out eyes haunting my every twitch.

Crying to myself silently, I wonder if this was his endgame all along. Was this an inevitable act to a temporary situation?

Then Collins takes a step back away from my broken spirit and walks to the door to exit.

A guttural sob escapes the trap set with my lips, bursting through my mouth like a raging fire in search of oxygen.

I hate him.

My stomach works its way up to my throat, expelling bile and acidic juices right into my mouth, before lodging itself into place. Coughing, I sputter out the liquid burning my tastebuds, doubling over as I take in the influx of knowledge, hurting my brain.

It's over.

Collins and I are over.

38

COLLINS

"Is it done?" Graham asks, as I make my way into the hallway outside Penny's apartment.

"Yes." The single-syllable word comes out as a growl. And the entire experience gutted me.

I know the Hoffman brothers only want what they think is best for their sister, so I'm not holding a grudge, but dammit, that could have been handled differently.

"Good."

I'm more angry at myself for not going to Graham or Nic first before they had the chance to find out another way. I'd be having the same feelings of betrayal if the situation were reversed.

It's why I didn't fight back and accepted my punishment in the ring. Oh, and because my level of self-loathing is at my peak. I knew I deserved whatever I got.

"I've done more damage"—I point toward the door— "to your sister in there in this one instance than I ever have done since guarding her."

"She'll recover," Nic says, his tone lacking empathy.

"I broke her."

"In more ways than one," Graham responds.

I shake my head at him. "I love her."

Nic clears his throat. "Then that's why you have to walk away."

"I'm doing it because she needs to be away from me—she needs an alibi. I'm doing it because I know I need to repent first for what wrong I've done with your sister. But I'm not doing this because it's what's best for her long-term."

Graham takes a step closer, and I brace myself for another pounding. Maybe this time, I'll fight back.

But he doesn't make contact. Instead he hands me an envelope.

I glance down at it. "What's this?" But I already have an idea.

"Cash."

"No. I don't want your money." I turn to Nic. "I don't need money."

"Take it," Graham insists. "That way when we demand you move out of state, we'll feel less guilty about it."

"But not until Tanner is wiped from this planet," Nic adds.

"I guess I should thank you," I respond sarcastically.

Graham paces. "I don't care what you do." He looks like he hasn't slept in days.

I'm starting to wonder if the Hoffman brothers find me a bigger threat to Penny than the predator who drugged her and tried to rape her. But now's not the time for a logical conversation when both of them are spurred on by my betrayal of trust.

"I'll stay away from your sister, for now."

Graham's eyes narrow on mine. "Then take the money and have a fresh start without her."

"No, thanks."

This has never been about money, and it never will be about money.

I need to get out of here. "I'll let you know when I receive the signal."

"It should be soon," Nic adds.

It better be soon.

Focusing on something else will be a good way to get over the image I have burned into my memory of Penny lying on the floor, crying her eyes out—at my fucking feet. And I watched as she fell apart and did nothing to help put her back together. I let her pour her heart out, and I just stood there and said nothing of value.

She's never going to forgive me.

And I doubt I'll be able to forgive me either.

I glance at her door, and I swear I can hear her sobbing through the insulated walls.

I'm sorry, Princess.

I thought being discharged from the United States military was the hardest thing I've ever had to endure, but walking away from Penelope Hoffman right now has outranked anything I've experienced in my past.

Time doesn't fix anything. It just charges every cell in my body to a throbbing, constant ache. I'm running on a three-day migraine and just a handful of hours of sleep.

I didn't realize how easy it's been to sleep next to Penny such that now my body craves her mere presence.

I miss her.

I miss the giggles.

I miss her silly pranks.

I miss smelling strawberries and popcorn on every piece of fabric in my apartment.

I miss how she's destroyed all order in my life.

I miss it—all of it.

It's been days since I forced myself to break Penny's heart in order to help her move on from me. And in those days, I've only suffered the tragic loss of the girl I know I love.

When I left her, I crushed her false belief in me that I could be a good guy. And with each passing day, I know that I'm no longer the hero in this story, but without a doubt the villain.

Seeing Penny, beaten and broken from what I did to her, is the worst kind of punishment.

I'll never be able to move on from that. It's as if I'm stuck in purgatory, knowing that the end result will be hell. I deserve it too. Because no matter what words I can say as an apology, nothing will ever justify getting involved with her in the first place.

I crossed a line, and if I have to grovel to the entire Hoffman family after this nightmare is over, so be it.

Stepping into the shower, I allow the water to cascade over me.

My wounds from being ambushed by Graham in the boxing ring still burn, but I savor that physical pain and reminder of why I'm staying away from his sister in the first place.

But it still doesn't keep me from keeping tabs on her like a fucking creeper.

I can't help myself.

If I can't have her in my life, I sure as fuck am not going to sit back and allow some asshole to get to her either. As soon as the male population sniffs out that she's single, they'll be on the hunt.

I know I'm a ghost stalker.

I know it's messed up.

I just don't care.

Knowledge about Penny is my lifeline right now. I just have to be discreet about it and wait for my daily report.

Drying off, I slip into some lounge clothes and lie down in bed.

It feels empty and cold.

I feel empty and cold.

So much has happened over the last week, and yet nothing really at all.

It's the adrenaline coursing through me as I wait for the signal that Mark Tanner is being transported to the hospital that fuels my passion.

We've waited a very long time to rid this earth of his life. I'll be relieved when my hands are the ones that get to do the final job.

Resting my eyes, I allow my mind to drift off, thinking about what Penny is doing right now. I hope she is less of a mess over this than I am.

The only serenity is in the fact that I'm not a heavy drinker. I may otherwise be hospitalized right now if that was my vice.

My phone comes to life, followed by the sound of the doorbell, pulling me from my slumber.

Rolling out of bed, I make my way through the apartment and then glance out the peephole.

Unlocking the door, I allow Chris inside.

"Redeye, you have red eyes."

"I know," I say in exhaustion. I guess it's his first time really seeing me since the showdown at the boxing gym. Most of our exchanges in information have been digital.

He looks at me closely. "Are you okay, man?"

I shrug like it's nothing. "I deserved it."

He nods slowly. "No doubt."

"Do you have anything for me?" I probably sound like a junkie looking for his next fix.

"Yes. But just so you know, this goes against my morals."

My eyes narrow on his. "Righhhht."

"Sheesh, I thought I would at least get a smile out of you."

"Smiling hurts." And it does.

"Here," he says, passing me a folder. "Miss Hoffman has this event coming up. I figured you'd appreciate the direct delivery considering it's tonight."

"Thanks."

I look over the flyer. "Her father's architecture company sponsors it."

"It says there's going to be an auction."

"Okay." I vaguely remember hearing about this at Nic's new house. I just forgot to follow up on it at the time.

There's been too much on my mind.

"Like chicks selling themselves and shit. Can I come, please?"

I make a face, but it hurts too much so I stop. "No."

"Bummer."

"'This is a fundraiser, so stop making this sound pornographic. It's to raise money for the construction of community centers."

"So, you don't want me to kidnap Penny and assure that no one purchases her?"

"That does sound tempting."

"Okay, there's your sense of humor. I was worried it was lost forever."

"I'm not joking," I deadpan. "Penny might not even be participating as a contestant. There's nothing here that lists the auction participants' names."

"That's true."

I should be happy that I'm the only one moping around like my heart just got stabbed. I should be happy that attending a big social event is a good sign that Penny is doing okay.

I should be happy.

But I'm not.

The only way to restore my state of happiness is to get my princess back. But I have nothing to bargain with until I wipe out Tanner.

"Should I do anything?" my ex-military buddy asks. "I can shut down the whole thing. Just say the word."

"Nah," I say after a minute. "Penny's entire family will be there and they'll keep her safe."

"You really fell for her, didn't you?"

"I did."

It feels so weird admitting it out loud after all these months of keeping it a secret, but I owe it to our relationship. Being with Penny was the closest to happiness I've ever been.

I take a seat on the sofa and gesture for Chris to sit down too. I'm usually not this hospitable with the men I hire, but I could use a friend right now.

"Is it over-over?" he asks, genuinely interested.

"Not if I have any say about it. I thought I could move on knowing and believing I was doing the right thing, but I know I'll never get over her."

"It's different this time," Chris says thoughtfully.

"Everything about Penelope Hoffman is different. She changed parts of me irrevocably for the better."

"She chipped away at your hard exterior."

I think about his words for a moment. "Yeah. Yeah, I guess she did."

He gives me a lopsided smile. "She's good for you."

I nod. "I just need to make sure I'm good for her too."

Hacking into the security footage at Nic's previous apartment building, I'm able to catch a glimpse of Penny leaving for the charity event.

She's staying there, and I predict that was a boundary that she set.

A part of me wishes I had more self-restraint, but I can't resist having this access when it's all I have right now to feed my obsession.

My heart melts at the sight of her. She's all dolled up in a designer dress. Her hair is pulled up in an elegant style, secured with a clip.

She looks spectacular.

Enchanting.

And all alone.

My mind can't help but wonder what it would be like to have our relationship public.

Would Penny have allowed me to escort her to the fundraiser event? Would I have given her any other option?

There's no way I'd want her showing up alone like she'll be doing tonight.

Just seeing her in this gorgeous dress has my hands twitching from the strong desire to touch her, and that's just from witnessing these surveillance videos.

Pacing my living room, I think of all the scenarios that can happen where Penny and I can end up together.

And it's in my desperation that I vow to make that happen.

39

PENNY

The worst part of getting over a breakup is pretending that I'm not dying inside.

It's on days like these where I feel summarily inadequate. I stumble around, trying to keep the superficial smile plastered to my face, while forcing myself to inhale and exhale at the appropriate time to at least appear human in public.

I've been just surviving for days—and doing it barely.

But it's when I allow the thought of *what if* to creep in through the cracks that I trigger the unabridged panic to rise and the abyss of rejection to deepen.

Collins Stone wants nothing to do with me.

His look of pathetic indifference sealed that conclusion for me.

It's when I'm confronted head-on with the reality that my heart may survive, but it will be forever fractured, that I try to envision my new life—a life without the man I love in it—and the silent wish that the darkness lurking from the sidelines will fade with time.

I feel like a fraud.

I'm faking my motivation to get dressed up and to pretend to enjoy small talk with people who will see my outward smile and genuinely think I'm happy.

Spoiler alert, I'm not fine.

And I'm questioning if I'll ever be able to find contentment again.

I'm falling apart at my core, and there isn't a single person on this planet who understands that I've fallen in love and am devastated from the loss of that love.

My family doesn't even believe me.

How could I possibly fall for my hired bodyguard?

How does someone sixteen years older than I am have anything in common with me?

I know that's what my brothers are thinking, at least.

Collins has been an invisible string woven into my past and my present, tying my life together in ways I can only now see once that string got cut.

And despite being over, my heart still yearns for the kind of love I disillusioned myself into believing I deserve.

But why strive to be whole when the person who holds the glue walked out at the first sign of trouble?

Instead, I'll aim for being just a shell.

I just need to go through the motions and hope no one really notices anything is off so I don't get more privileges stripped from me with the overarching explanation being, "I'm doing this for your protection."

If moving forward means putting one foot in front of the other, then that's what I'm trying to do. Besides, I promised my dad I would participate in his annual charity auction. I owe him my presence here tonight and a tad bit more.

So here I am—participating—with my fraudulent smile in place.

This will be the first social event I'll be attending since Collins walked out of my apartment, leaving me covered in my own tears and vomit.

I don't take pride in being the one who was hurt the most out of the two of us. I'd much rather take the physical pain he received at the hands of Graham than the emotional torture he put me through when he acted like what we had was just a business transaction.

But it's that fresh reminder of pain that keeps my heart guarded from anyone who might want to do it more harm.

Grabbing my name card and the seating number, I weave between the beautifully decorated tables until I find the correct one.

In agreeing to stay away from Collins, I made my brothers promise to give me some space. I'm shocked that they seem to be complying.

Ever since that horrible day where I threw myself at Collins's feet and begged him to stay, I haven't talked with my brothers. I am angry but don't even know who to channel my frustration to the most.

The fact of the matter is, my brothers found out about my secret relationship with their right-hand man, and Collins didn't do a damn thing to fight for what I thought we were building.

Then there's Luke…

I thought he was my friend. But I can't be mad at him

for taking the exuberant amount my brothers probably paid him. Anyone in his position would have done the same.

He's tried to reach out to me multiple times in the last week, still sticking to his story of not knowing anything about being paid to spy on me.

I just wish he would fess up so we can move forward. I don't want a beef with him.

Portland is too small of a city to have enemies.

I take my seat at the huge circular table and wait quietly for more guests to arrive. I hate being first.

My fingers trail along the golden fabric of the table-cloth. Hurricane vases of beautiful white flowers make up the centerpiece. Every table is unique, yet sticking with the central core theme.

I'd be shocked if Momma had nothing to do with the artistic touches I'm now noticing in the details. It looks like I'm attending a wedding, and a glance at the menu that is resting on my dinner plate lets me know that there's no way my stomach is going to fit all of the food.

Regardless, this will be more than I've eaten this week combined.

"I'm glad you are here," Momma says, arriving next.

At least now I have company.

She gives me a hug. Wearing a floor-length, sheer red dress, she looks as stunning as ever.

I've been avoiding her and Dad since everything went down. They are the safety net that I couldn't utilize in my life without them being upset with my brothers for how they handled things.

In a way, I'm protecting them from choosing sides. I'm

not sure why. It's just another example of how messed-up I truly am.

I don't want to talk to anyone, and I sure as hell don't need someone to rub in that this whole experience is for the best.

It's not.

I don't need the luxury of hindsight to understand that my life will never be whole again. I'm broken beyond repair, teetering on the edge of a major setback.

I'm going through the motions like a hollowed-out shell, doing what is expected of me, but not doing anything actually for me.

Collins was for me.

But he tossed me away just as he promised at one time he would.

That's what happens when you build an entire relationship on a fault line. Things are destined to get shaken up eventually.

Leaning into me, Momma squeezes my hand. "I'm not going to ask you questions or suggest I have some wisdom to offer. But I just want you to know that I'm a call-all-hours-of-the-night mother. And that when you are hurting, so am I."

I squeeze her hand back, fighting back the tears that want to escape. "There's something wrong with me."

"Oh, Penny," she whispers, "there's something wrong with all of us then."

"I'm not sure what Nic and Graham have shared with you…"

"Nothing. They tell me nothing. I'm just going off my own intuition that never lets me down."

I nod, biting at my bottom lip. "I've gone behind their backs and pursued someone who they don't approve of, and now I am heartbroken and lonely and unlovable."

Reaching into her handbag, Momma pulls out a handkerchief. "Have I ever told you about the time your father and I broke up?"

I shake my head and wipe the tears from my eyes with the fabric. "No. I didn't know you two ever broke up."

Glancing off to the side of the room, her eyes catch Dad's as he helps someone elderly to their seat. "We were separated for a few months before we got back together."

"Why though?"

"Because both sides of our families interfered."

I don't have much memory of any of my grandparents and just assumed nothing rocky ever happened in my parents' relationship.

I guess I was wrong.

"What changed?"

"We both realized that it's our lives we are living. It is simple and yet so much interference can cause such tension in partnerships—especially new ones that are trying to form."

"Hmm... I had no idea."

"My sweet Penny, I'm sharing this so you can see that sometimes the storm brings the most beautiful of rainbows. That separation bonded us tighter together. It made us an unstoppable force and really helped us understand what we wanted out of our relationship." Taking my hands into hers, she gives them a squeeze. "Listen. I'm not saying things will work out. I'm simply saying that you need to do what you think is best for you."

"Thank you," I mouth. I'm so caught up in the emotions of it all that I can't even form the syllables and make a sound.

The sad part is…I am so mixed up that I no longer know what is best for me.

More people enter the room, including Graham who makes his way toward us.

I haven't seen him in days.

He gives me a side hug. "It's good seeing you, Pen." Then he hugs Momma.

I've been staying at Nic's old apartment. That was our compromise. I'd move out of Sky View if I could have space to myself to heal.

But I'm not sure the separation has done anything to help me feel better.

I don't leave. I just lie in bed and mope around.

I eat just enough to not land myself in the hospital on IVs and can't even find enjoyment in the numerous channels that Nic has subscribed to on the television.

I'm pretty sure the person living across the hall is a spy, but it's not like I even care anymore.

I live a boring existence. And I trust no one.

I take a deep breath, channeling all my inner strength to get through tonight. But it's not until I see the faces of Angie and Claire that I can no longer stand it.

"Let's go to the restroom," Claire says, wrapping a hand around my back.

"It's going to be okay," Angie promises.

"It's not. It's never going to be okay again."

My parents may have worked their differences out, but

that was because they both wanted to put in the effort. Collins wants nothing to do with me.

"It will," Claire insists. "Just give it some time and let things smooth over."

"He doesn't want me anymore," I sob, not needing to fill in the blank that I'm talking about the one man who holds the power to start and stop my heart.

Angie frowns. "I can't imagine how he could not want you, Penny."

"Even if he did, he won't do anything about it, not when my brothers are ready to castrate him for even going near me. It's not his fault. It's mine. It's all mine. They don't realize that I was the one who was making the moves on him. I'm not the innocent one in all of this. I'm literally the catalyst who set this whole thing into motion."

"Just breathe," Angie says, pushing me down onto the sofa in the lounge that's an offshoot from the main restroom area.

I'm thankful there's a comfortable place to rest. The only thing I've wanted to do since the breakup is rest.

Oh, the joy of sleeping away this nagging sorrow, grieving for a man who is back to not even realizing I exist.

Sure, he is loyal to my brothers and probably feels that sense of urgency to make things right, but to act like what we had was nothing hurts the most.

He hasn't called.

He hasn't texted.

He hasn't even spied—and I would know.

If it wasn't for the physical ache my heart is going through, I'd start to wonder if I made the entire thing up. It definitely feels like I'm the only one suffering.

"I'm never going to get through this," I say, panting out my exhales.

The air feels thick. It's like I'm trying to breathe through a narrow straw.

My hands smooth out my pink tulle dress. If I wasn't walking around with the look of utter devastation on my face, I imagine I would appear to be pretty.

Why did I even choose this color when black would have been a more fitting shade?

Like a funeral... To mourn the loss of my happiness.

I fix a stray piece of hair behind my ear, instantly regretting not leaving it down. If I left it loose, then I could at least hide behind it.

Claire levels her eyes with mine. "I'm working on a solution. I just need you to trust me."

My eyes move to her stomach. She's just a couple of months away from welcoming her first child into this world. The last thing she needs is to worry about my pathetic existence right now.

"You have enough on your plate already."

"Penny, we are friends. But more importantly, we are family. And I never really had a family network until I fell head over fucking heels for your sometimes oblivious brother, so I have zero intention of sitting back and watching it all break apart over this tragic misunderstanding."

Angie rubs a hand on my back as my shoulders shake, while keeping another hand on Claire's who is also now crying.

I hate crying. Yet when I'm with these women who always seem to provide compassion and empathy, I can't help but let out the emotional release I seem to need at the time.

"Thank you," I say between sniffles, "but there's no fixing this."

"That's not true," Angie says softly.

Oh great, now she's crying too.

"I'm sorry for making you cry," I say softly.

Angie wipes at her nose. "It's the hormones." Then she covers her mouth as a sob breaks out. "I didn't want to make this about me."

"Please tell us what's happening," I encourage. "We love you."

"We're struggling to conceive," she blurts out, as tears drip down her face.

Claire grabs some tissues and tries to wipe them up as fast as she can before they speckle the fabric of her dress.

"How can we help?" I ask, trying not to become too emotional.

"You already are," she responds. "I simply need a distraction while I wait to see if this round of hormones I'm on has done the trick. I just never thought something as natural as making a baby could be this hard."

"I am really sorry. I read that it's rather common," I point out. "Something like one in eight women struggle to conceive."

Angie nods, looking relieved that she isn't bottling all of this up inside. I wish she would have mentioned it to us sooner. We could have been more supportive.

"Do you have a backup plan?" Claire asks hesitantly.

"We'll probably move forward with IUI or IVF then."

I clear my throat, fighting back my tears. "We are here for you."

"Always," Claire chimes in.

I imagine Claire feels weird as we get closer and closer to her due date. It would be hard being pregnant while your best friend is struggling with her own fertility battles.

"See?" Angie asks. "This is what I do... I make things about myself."

"Nonsense," Claire says, giving Angie a hug as I join in. "We are in this life together and all the struggles that it brings to us."

"Things will work out with you, Penny," Angie says confidently, "just like they will work out for me. It might not be the path we choose but it will be the path that chooses us."

I allow her words to linger. "I'm not going to beg someone to choose me." I mean, I basically did already and it didn't work. "We have been playing this game all this time on uneven fields. And I was just naively stupid for thinking that anyone would want someone broken like me."

Claire snaps her fingers. "Listen. My rules for getting a man's attention still apply. It's—"

"Please don't say foolproof," Angie interrupts.

She shrugs. "It's basically foolproof."

"Except it's not"—Angie gives her a serious stare—"and never is."

Claire glares at her bestie. "I'm going to choose to ignore your pessimism today and grant you some grace." Then she turns to me. "The trick to luring a guy in is to act like they are the ones who don't exist. Men are hunters, and not one of them enjoy easy prey."

Leaning over, Angie grabs a tissue box from the little decorative side table, and I instantly wonder just how many women have sat on this sofa and poured out their soul with friends. Every ladies' room needs a comfort couch.

And I'm glad I found mine.

I clear my throat. "And how do I do that?"

"You go out there"—she points to the exit—"and live your best life. We are here to make some money for your dad's charity. We are not here to soak in the sadness that surrounds us when our overbearing men think they have the upper hand, which they don't. They have a penis, but we hold the power in the pussy."

"That's actually a solid speech," Angie says in disbelief, making me laugh-cry.

"And I can be your emotional support animal for the night," Claire says to me.

"Thank you," I say, wiping my nose.

"And I have zero qualms about kicking that stubborn and pigheaded brother of yours in the nuts. Well, maybe shins." She taps her finger along her jawline. "Yeah, let's go with shins since I want more babies with him."

What was I thinking getting involved in a sexual relationship with my hired bodyguard?

And how did I not fully prepare myself for this all to blow up massively in my face?

But I am here.

And I can do this…even with a shattered heart.

40

PENNY

I'm going to throw up.

Yup. I am.

Not even the thick curtains can shield me from the crowd that is buzzing with excitement, as I stand waiting my turn from the sidelines.

This isn't me.

Sure, I enjoy a little male attention just like most girls, but doing it this way seems so unnatural.

The announcer hypes up the crowd with his voice inflections, getting the girl being showcased now to be "sold" for three times more than the starting bid—and all in the name of charity.

I'm up next.

The stagehand guides me through the curtain's opening and gestures to where I should go stand.

"Stepping out onto the stage is the daughter of our main man and the soon-to-be *officially* retired, Germain Hoffman." The announcer takes a step back to give me more space to pass by. "Give a round of applause to the beautiful, the radiant, and the single, Penny Hoffman."

I wave my hand and try to perfect my best fake smile, especially after the words "the single" hit me like a slap to the face.

The overhead lights are blinding, preventing me from seeing anything past a couple of yards in front of me, and for that, I am thankful. I drown out the crowd and just anchor myself to the stage, so I don't pass out.

My entire family is in the audience, and none of them truly understand how torturous this is for me to be up here, selling my soul off for the night, when I'm falling apart inside.

But that's what life is like now. I still feel indebted to my family, and coming here is my reparation for all that they have done for me.

I'll always owe them.

And that is a sucky feeling, knowing that no matter how hard I try, I'll still feel like they've done more for me than I have for them.

It's probably the reason I can't be too mad at my brothers. They're doing what they think is best, even if they are preventing me from being with the one person who makes me feel alive.

Collins should be the one fighting for me, not anyone else. And the fact he isn't speaks volumes to my belief that he means more to me than I ever did to him.

"Let's start the bidding at one thousand," the announcer says, using his hand to try to energize the crowd.

When several people in the room call out, he whistles.

I'm on display, but at least someone is raising the minimum. It volleys back and forth between about three men—none of whom I can actually see from this distance with the glare from the overhead lights.

If it wasn't for a worthy charity, I'd feel like a bigger loser than I already am. Instead, I just try to take deep breaths and calm my mind.

My family is here.

I'm doing this for my dad.

Everything is fine.

"Okay," he says in awe, "anyone want five thousand?"

There's a buzz circulating in the crowd—an energy—and I'd be naive to think it's not over me. I'm sure a few men here would love to take out the boss's daughter if just to say they did.

I just hope he's not gross. Oh, and that the food is good at the restaurant that gets selected.

There's more back-and-forth between the men, as the amount to go on a date with me increases gradually.

This really should be a confidence booster, but it's not.

Deep down, I wish Collins would bust through the back doors and wave his paddle into the air, blurting out some obscene amount of money to shut this whole operation down for good.

But that doesn't happen.

And I blame every chick flick that has ever existed for falsely portraying men doing these over-the-top grand gestures to win their ladies back.

It's not reality.

"You're quite the popular one, Miss Penny."

Yup, this is cringe. I might as well hold up a sign that

has an arrow pointing down at my head that broadcasts the words S-I-N-G-L-E and A-L-O-N-E.

That's how funny life can be sometimes. One second you think you are on top of the world, and the next you feel buried alive by the disappointment of things not going your way.

"Anyone want to go higher than seven thousand?" He pauses.

"Eight thousand!"

Oh, fuck.

"Nine," a voice calls out confidently.

"I'll do ten grand!"

"Eleven."

The voices quiet down, while hushed whispers flood the venue. I have people talking. I can't see anyone, but I know that they are talking.

"Going once..." The announcer pauses, scanning the crowd for any more takers. "Going twice..." He places a hand along my shoulder, giving me a squeeze. "And sold!"

To whom though? Who bought me for a date for eleven thousand dollars? It seems like a waste of cash for it to be spent on me.

I'm boring and worth way less.

But it all goes to this charity, so I guess it's okay.

Now that Collins is done with me, the only thing I have to offer is even more emotional baggage than I had a few months ago.

Damn him.

I get ushered off stage by a teenage volunteer, probably earning service hours for school or something.

I resist offering unsolicited advice to her to never fall in

456

love, but I don't. There's nothing good that would come from me being jaded toward anyone else who has an easier time coping with life's disappointments. And it surely wouldn't convince her that men sometimes suck and often provide truth to every emotional stereotype they get labeled.

Collins did.

He proved to me that men want women for sex, and that anytime real feelings get involved, it's best just to run away.

"Hey, Penny."

I turn to the familiar voice coming from nearby. "Oh, hey, Ivan."

"I'm so glad no one contested my bid."

My jaw loses muscle function. "You bought me?"

He shrugs, almost sheepishly. "It will be worth every *penny* to get you away for an evening."

I hope he keeps his expectations low…

"Yeah…"

"You look beautiful tonight," he says, coughing into his arm. "I meant to say, you look beautiful always." He rocks on his feet. "But especially tonight."

"Thank you."

He really is a sweet guy.

"Can I help you to your seat?" Ivan says, offering his bent arm.

I link mine with his and allow him to escort me back to the table, where my entire family is beaming with excitement over me being selected for a date. Even my brothers look decently happy…

This is weird.

They are all acting weird.

Momma gives my hand a squeeze, and Dad is looking at

VICTORIA DAWSON

me like I hung the moon just by showing up today. It's too over-the-top in the gratitude department.

I'm not at prom or a sweet sixteen party, yet it sort of feels like it.

It's a little-Penny-is-growing-up moment I don't want to experience right now.

"That's really special that Ivan chose you," Momma whispers.

"Yup," I lie.

Does she think our conversation earlier was about him?

Momma has to realize how biased she is toward her friend's son. Of course she would lean toward a man who she already knows belongs to a good family. Dad has to be excited too since Ivan is now part of the business that he'll soon be leaving.

But I don't want Ivan.

I want Collins Stone.

And no matter what smile I plaster on my face, it's hard to feel special when the man who I actually want has been MIA for days.

I glance around the room looking for him, yet not expecting to actually see him. But when my eyes scan the perimeter, I don't find Collins...

I find Mark Tanner.

"He's here," I whimper, but my words get stuck in my throat.

He's here.

"Who's here?" Angie asks, looking around.

Claire leans in. "Yeah, who? Anyone I know?"

Turning, I look back to where Mark was standing. He's gone.

458

Getting up from the table, I stumble but catch myself, shooing off anyone who wants to offer me help.

"I'm just going to take a breather. Maybe I'll get some fresh air."

But what I really need is help.

No one can fix me when I'm this messed up.

I just keep walking through the room, weaving myself between tables. I allow my legs to carry my body down the hallway and out the back door. When I'm on the balcony, I step toward the railing that overlooks the Willamette River. Leaning over, I stare down at the sidewalk where people are coming and going from the charity event.

Taking a seat into the chair in the corner near the potted, fuchsia flowers, I sink down into the cushions, thankful for a break away from my well-intentioned family.

I feel electric, but not in the positive kind of way.

I'm stressed, and when I feel this overwhelmed, I start to see things that aren't there.

And it freaks me the fuck out. It happened before at the waterfront, and I'm still trying to recover from that trauma.

Playing with my hair, I twist strands around my finger. It needs dye and a bit more love than I've given it this week. I've been just fully embracing the survival mode. I do the bare minimum to live and nothing more.

Pulling out my phone, I am entranced by the local headline that pops up right after I unlock my device, but before I can fully comprehend the words on my screen, the door opens and out walks a man.

Taking a seat on the other side of the balcony, he bends his knee and props it up on his opposite leg.

And when my eyes meet his, I realize that I know him.

Well…sort of.

"You?"

He was who I saw in the room today.

"Me."

My eyes glaze over, as I struggle to see past the fog filling my vision.

"I thought you were someone else," I say breathily, my words coming out mumbled.

"I get that a lot."

"You just look like someone I know." Someone I hate…

My eyes scan over the man who has a striking resemblance to Mark Tanner but isn't actually him.

And that should make sense. Mark is in prison. I saw him there myself, and Collins confirmed he was there recently.

"Did you hear about the big news?" the man asks, pointing at his phone.

I look down at mine and skim read. "There was a fight…"

"Yeah, a huge fight. That criminal Mark Tanner is being transported to the hospital right now. I saw the live footage that is being broadcast on every news channel. Isn't that crazy?"

I flinch at that last word. "Yeah… *Crazy.*"

"Apparently he fucked up some stupid, pathetic girl."

A shiver runs up my spine.

Standing up from his chair, he stops in front of me. His laugh is sinister.

Evil.

And then I see the little rose emblem at the pocket of his

black shirt that has the words Rose City Cafe embroidered into the fabric.

But why?

What's the connection?

"Who are you?" I choke out.

"I'm your worst nightmare."

"You were at the waterfront?"

"I'm everywhere your fear takes you."

Placing my face into my palms, I rock back and forth.

Go away, go away, go away...

My heart rate picks up, and I feel like I'm going to hyperventilate.

So much is happening at once, and my emotions are getting the best of me.

When I pick my head up to look at the man...

He's not there.

Where did he go?

I walk over to the rail and look over. He's gone.

It's like he vanished into thin air.

Stupid, pathetic girl...

I'm a stupid, pathetic girl.

Walking back into the main building, I see a security guard standing at the end of the hallway.

"Did you see someone walk out onto this balcony"—I point behind me—"in the last five minutes?"

"I haven't seen anyone else, ma'am. I was going to come out and join you, but you looked like you needed some time alone."

"I am going crazy." My words are barely a whisper.

"Come again?"

I shake my head. "Never mind."

My eyes scan the area for a way to get out of here.

"Elevators are down the hall to the right," the guard offers, predicting my dilemma.

"Thanks."

My phone vibrates in my handbag, which I ignore.

I just need to get out of here, before my own fears suffocate me.

Hitting the button for the elevator, I enter the car when it arrives and then smack the button for the first floor.

My legs feel like they are made of sand, barely strong enough to transport me outside and onto the streets of Portland.

I hail a cab and shove my body into the back seat.

"Where to, miss?"

41

COLLINS

My phone comes to life with the signal, alerting me that Mark Tanner has been in a fight and is en route to Portland General Hospital for medical intervention.

Finally…

Racing to the bedroom, I throw on some of my preselected clothes, strap my holsters to my torso and leg, and unlock my guns from the hidden lockbox.

It's go time.

And there isn't a cell in my body that won't rejoice in seeing Tanner take his last breath as I steal the life out of him.

Grabbing my keys, I race out the door and into the elevator.

Hopping into the rental car that I've had sitting idle and ready to go for weeks, I shift it into drive and pull out onto the street.

I use the GPS tracker on my phone to see the exact location of the transport vehicle that has Mark Tanner inside.

He's just a few miles out from the prison, following the pre-discussed route and taking his time to allow me a chance to bypass his path.

Everything is coming together like clockwork.

Using the call feature on my dash, I give Graham a ring. We haven't talked in days, and we definitely haven't reconciled over Penny, but my loyalty still lies with the Hoffmans no matter how much they see me as the one who betrayed them.

"It's time," I say into the speaker.

"Penny's missing."

My stomach twists. "What do you mean *missing*? Isn't she at the charity event?"

"She must have left."

"How long do you think she's been possibly missing?"

"I don't know…"

"I need a ballpark," I say frantically.

"Hmm, maybe about forty-five minutes. I'm not sure."

"Did you track her?"

"Nic and I never found the need to be that intrusive since we hired you," Graham bites out. "And she made us promise to give her some space while she recovered."

Recovered?

He's making her sound like an addict, when it's me who is addicted to her.

"Did she actually leave the event?"

"We're not sure."

I feel sweat beading on my forehead, and my fingers are sticking to the steering wheel as I maneuver the rental onto the streets. "Maybe she's on a different floor or got side-tracked? Did you look in the restrooms?"

My mind races with all the possibilities. If I was there, I wouldn't have let Penny out of my sight.

I know she would have felt obligated to help out at her dad's charity—especially right before he retires—so it doesn't make sense why she would leave early.

"We looked everywhere here," Graham says. "Hold on."

I hear chatting on the other end of the phone and Nic's voice.

"Graham," I say into the speaker, "don't leave me hanging here."

"Okay, so Nic just informed me that two security guards confirmed they remember her exiting the building in a very distraught state."

"When?" I snap.

I hear a muffled discussion happening in the background, and it's only causing my blood pressure to rise.

"At least an hour ago."

Fuck.

How did no one notice she was gone for that long?

And how am I going to do my job when I'm so worried over Penny?

We might not be together, but she will always consume my thoughts.

"Why didn't you inform me the moment you noticed she went missing?"

"Because you've hurt her enough."

I let out an angry sigh. This has gone on too long. I fucking miss her. I've only ever wanted Penny to soar. And now I broke her heart by not fighting for us. The truth is, I also hurt myself in the process by not fighting for us.

Flipping through my phone, I pull up the trackers I have

on her shoes, hidden in her phone, and on numerous pieces of jewelry. I sift through the list of potential ones, hoping to see movement on at least one of them. I also check the ones I have on her new car.

"Her car is still parked in the garage."

"That wouldn't stop her from hitching another ride."

I'm all too familiar with that scenario. Hell, I sure hope she is using some self-preservation skills at the very least.

I should have had eyes on her despite being apart. I wanted to give everyone space from me so they could calm down and hopefully come to terms with what transpired between us. Time can heal a lot of things, but maybe that's not what was needed at all. Maybe I should have verbally professed my desire to be Penny's man, regardless of those who opposed it.

Looking at the screen while still driving the car toward where Tanner should be, I discover Penny's current location.

"She's on her way north. The tracker keeps moving."

"Toward Seattle?" Graham asks in disbelief.

"Yes, probably. Her phone must not be working or is out of battery."

"Do you think she'll admit herself back to the facility?"

"I would assume so."

And as soon as Tanner takes his last breath, I'll be going to get Penny and make her see that I've always chosen her even when I was going through the motions to make her brothers happy. They just need time to see that Penny belongs with me, and that I'll fight until everyone accepts that we are together.

I'm done doing what others want.

I have my own life to live, just as Penny made it her life's mission to do the same.

Now she's possibly going back to the very facility she fought so hard to leave. And she'll be there alone.

This is a major slip in her forward progress.

"She's probably at least one hour away."

I hear Graham talk to someone, telling them to try her phone.

"Nic keeps trying her phone and it goes right to voice-mail. How close are you to your destination?"

"Five minutes."

"I'm going to grab Nic and head up to Seattle."

"You need to stay at the charity event where there's news crews and digital proof of your alibi. You are in the perfect location to have witnesses to verify your hands are clean from this mission."

"Fine. But as soon as this is over, I'm going to go get my sister. This ends tonight."

"I'll say it again. I want what is best for your sister, no matter how much you still view me as the villain."

"You are sixteen years older than she is," Graham chokes out.

"And I have the experience and the restraint to give Penny what she needs, even if it's not easy for you to come to terms with what that is. Would you rather have her pissing around with some asshole who has a statistically higher chance of hurting her or have her be with someone who can give her everything she needs physically, in addition to financially and emotionally?"

"I'm not doing this over the phone."

I steer the car, gripping the wheel with white knuckles.

"Well, you haven't been up for having a man-to-man conversation with me about it either. You just wanted to pound my face in and hope I move on without a fight."

"I know what's best for my sister, Collins. So you better get that straight."

"I've only ever done what is best for your family. Falling for your sister was a byproduct of getting to know her. I couldn't help myself."

"You stay the fuck away from her. Do your job and take the payout. I'll triple it."

"This has never been about the money, and you know it."

"We had a contract in place," he snarls.

"And I honored the terms of said contract. I've always kept Penny safe and went above and beyond doing so."

"She's not safe from *you*!"

His words sting. I'd much rather him beat the shit out of me than listen to him anymore. I might have fallen head over fucking heels for the girl who stole my heart like a thief, but I've only ever wanted to make sure she was happy and cared for—that's it. My entire purpose for joining forces with the Hoffmans was to figure out who drugged Penny.

I put her first then, and while she doesn't see it this way, I'm also putting her first now.

It's just that now I need to tie up this one last part of the whole operation and eradicate Penny's mind of the evilness that still lurks there by eliminating Mark Tanner.

It's always been about Penny.

It was Penny who was first drugged, and it is Penny who we all want to see well.

Killing Mark Tanner will ensure she stays well.

"I know you think I've been disloyal, and I guess in a superficial look at the situation, that would appear to be true. But I love your sister, Graham. I've only ever wanted what's best for her."

I turn off the highway and exit onto the off-ramp, trying my best to maintain a clear head for the mission I'm about to do. But I can't.

I want things to go back to how they were but with Penny as my girl. I don't want to hide, and I don't want to feel guilty for loving who I love.

If I have to grovel to the two men who gave me my life back, so be it—just as long as they don't snatch it away again.

I am prepared to beg.

"I know about the sex contract."

Well, damn. "What? How?"

My mind goes through all of the scenarios on how this could even be possible. Did Penny tell them about it? Very few people know about the dynamics of my lifestyle and how I conduct relationships like business transactions. I just never thought I would be having this conversation with Graham of all people, and especially not now.

"I had a copy arrive at my residence a few days ago."

"Something's not right…"

"That's the understatement of the fucking century," he snaps. "Of course, something's not right."

"Did you read it?"

"No. Well, not any details." He grinds his teeth together. "But I saw enough."

No wonder he's so adamant about getting me away from Penny.

"It was consensual," I say, but my words fall flat even to me.

"She was coerced."

"I assure you, she wasn't."

"How could you put in writing what your intentions were with my sister? One hundred days? Are you fucking kidding me? She's my baby sister!"

"She's a woman, Graham."

"Stay away from her."

"I will for now. At least until this mission is over…"

"Penny's roommate is acting super suspicious too."

Luke? "How so? I had him checked out multiple times and there were no red flags."

"He is convinced that Penny thinks Nic or I have hired him to spy on her."

I allow that perspective to roll around in my head. "Well, that would make sense."

"Except we didn't."

"She was supposed to have a female roommate, and then Luke showed up."

I can hear Graham's exaggerated sigh. "But we didn't hire him. Nic and I both agreed to be less intrusive than we have been in the past. That's why we hired you to be the source of her safety without providing us the unnecessary details. And we both know that was a bad decision."

"Whatever, man. At some point you're going to need to see things from my perspective and acknowledge that I've kept your sister safe when she was under my care."

"So Luke's not on anyone from your side's payroll?"

"No."

"I can't think straight."

I glance at the GPS, feeling very uneasy. My instincts never lie, and everything about this entire mission feels like it's about to blow up in my face.

It feels like I'm about to be set up.

Going to prison would be one way to keep me away from Penny—permanently.

No.

It doesn't matter how mad Graham and Nic are at me, there's no way they would try to put me behind bars.

"And at some point, you're going to have to come to the realization that Penny is no longer a kid."

"I'm done talking about this."

"And at some point you're going to have to quit avoiding the conversation."

"Let me know when Nic and I can get on a plane to get to Penny."

After several long seconds of silence, I sigh. "Okay." Then I end the call.

Gripping the steering wheel tightly, I take a sharp right onto a side road. I've run through this entire route and scenario every day in my head since the plan was set.

But something seems off.

I can't tell if I'm about to be the hero in this story or suffer as the victim.

I'm just hoping that I'll be alive to share my side regardless of what goes down here tonight.

I cut the engine to the rental, glancing at the GPS on my burner phone just to make sure the transport vehicle is stopped in the exact location that was previously agreed upon during the initial discussions.

Grabbing my mask, I pull it over my head, concealing my hair and any distinguishable facial features.

I roll on my leather gloves and wiggle my fingers to increase dexterity in their movements.

I'm sweaty and my nerves are getting to me.

With my gun loaded and ready to go, I get out of the car and take off running in the direction of Mark Tanner.

I arrive in three minutes. Nestled between tall trees is a little dirt road where the transport vehicle idles. This particular path is used for service vehicles coming and going from a landfill.

But there will be no one showing up at this hour of the evening.

I make my way closer to the van, seeing the driver leaning against the window with his head turned from me.

I knock on the glass to get his attention, but he doesn't budge.

"Hey, you hear me?"

Pulling on the handle, I watch in shock as his body falls to my feet.

Turning him, I see the knife sticking out of his chest and fresh blood soaking into the fabric of his shirt.

Fuck.

What the hell happened?

Extending my gun out in front of me, I carefully move around to the back of the vehicle where Mark Tanner's body should be bleeding and in need of medical attention.

Pulling open the heavy doors, I choke on the heavy pungent smell first. Then my eyes search for the body of Mark Tanner, who is sprawled out on the metal floor face-down, covered in bodily fluids.

Hopping into the van, I flip him over.

But it isn't Mark Tanner that I find without a pulse.

It's a fucking imposter.

42

PENNY

The benefit of having two wealthy brothers is that spending a thousand dollars to get driven three hours away from Portland is easily manageable—albeit impractical. I can think of so many other ways I could have used this money, but I'm in that anxious level of desperation.

I just don't trust myself.

I'm either being haunted or I'm going crazy—and both sound plausible and equally horrible.

I need help. Plain and simple…

Except nothing is easy.

Nothing.

The con of coming back here is that it gives me the newfound fear that I may never be able to leave. Maybe my short-term living mindset is best viewed as a long-term arrangement, and it's that possibility that freaks me the fuck out.

What if my mind is too damaged to be saved?

All these months I've tried to assimilate back into society, and where has it gotten me? I'm heartbroken and lonely, and my brothers are tainted with a warped impression that being with Collins is what hurt me.

The truth is, being with Collins healed me.

He was my lifeline.

But with him gone, I fear that I'll forever be in a state of mental unrest, and the glimpse of happiness I had at my fingertips is just a ghostly reminder of losing a once-in-a-lifetime love.

Collins is my once in a lifetime.

"Hi, how can I help you?" the worker asks from the call button's speaker.

"I'm a previous patient," I say as clearly as I can into the built-in microphone.

"It's long past admission time."

"Please, I'm desperate. I need to be here."

After several seconds, the door cracks open a few inches. When the worker catches sight of me, she grants me complete access.

"This is against protocol."

I sigh. "I know."

"What brings you back?" she asks, giving me the once-over.

I follow her inside the building, where she moves behind the front desk and resumes her position.

"I am going crazy," I blurt out.

"Oh, dear. This isn't an outpatient facility."

"I know that." I angrily wipe at tears dripping down my cheeks. "I just paid someone one thousand dollars to drive me here. I'm in the system and spent many months here recovering. I'm not a new patient. I'm a returning one."

"I see. Your name?"

She must be new. She must not realize that my brothers made a hefty donation to this facility when I got discharged months ago. She must not realize that I would never come back here if I wasn't desperate and sick—really sick.

"Penelope Josephine Hoffman." Opening up my handbag, I pull out an insurance card and some credit cards.

"What are your symptoms?"

"Do you really need to know all of this?" I'm not at some shop getting my hair done. "Doesn't this violate HIPAA?"

Her eyes follow mine as I look behind her and pray there is someone else here to check me in. It shouldn't be this hard. If I have the money to pay for the hefty facility and medical fees, then why bother with the interrogation?

"Please let me stay. I need to be here."

She types onto her keyboard, looking at her screen. Then she hums.

I decide to throw her a bone. "I'm hallucinating."

And as if there's a major aha moment when she pulls up my file, she smiles endearingly at me. "Yes, okay, sure. You can stay."

There must be something starred on my file for her to suddenly be accommodating.

"Good."

"I'm going to page Dr. Radinsky though so she is aware. She's our on-call doctor."

"Fine," I say hurriedly. "I know her well."

I honestly don't care who they inform. I just need to clear out my sick mind. It's being infiltrated with a looming evil that I doubt I'll ever be able to exorcize from my system—at least not completely.

"I'll see if there's an available room in the main wing. Otherwise, you can stay in the overflow space."

I nod. I don't really have a preference. I just need help.

"As you are aware, all of your personal belongings need to be placed inside a locker. Here's a bin."

I place my handbag into the plastic tray. Then I place my connection to the outside world—my phone—into the bin. It's useless anyway without a charge. I have a habit of forgetting to plug it in at night when I cry myself to sleep, and I drained the battery at the charity fundraiser.

Grabbing a bag down from a shelf, she hands it to me. "This is a set of clean garments for your comfort. There are more items in your room for you to use until your family can drop off some personal items."

"Thank you," I say, clutching my new supplies to my chest.

Doubt seeps through my conscious thought.

Am I doing the right thing coming here?

Should I be here without any tangible connection to my family who will probably worry about me?

"Follow me," the worker says.

She uses the keycard around her neck to access several locked hallways.

It's now late into the night and everything is calm and relaxed here, just as I remember it to be during my long-term placement.

But something is different this time around.

For one, I don't remember ever checking in the first time. I definitely don't have any recollection of handing over my personal items, although it makes complete sense. It's just that there are huge chunks of time that have dissolved in the recesses of my mind. They are grayed-out memories I may never get back.

But it's in my nightmares that I gained back the memories from the night Mark drugged me. I remember those vivid details now.

I don't even know how long I'll stay this round. I just know that I can't keep going through life thinking that every man standing in the shadows is Mark Tanner. I refuse to be haunted by him forever.

Maybe a doctor here can hypnotize me or offer some kind of reprogramming.

I actually feel like I'm going insane, as if Mark is lurking around a corner just waiting to pounce when I least expect it.

"Here we are," she says, glancing at her watch. "Lights-out is in fifteen minutes, but I'll send Dr. Radinsky down to visit when she gets here. She's on her way now."

"Okay, sounds good. Thanks."

I wait until the door closes and locks before I start undressing out of my charity event gown. Just kicking off my heels causes me to groan in satisfaction. I definitely didn't anticipate needing a getaway outfit.

That's what I get for being impulsive.

There's something about being back in this space that I find oddly comforting. I didn't expect to actively choose to come back, but here I am—just as fucked up as ever and arguably worse.

I glance around my room. It's nothing to write home about. Everything is functional, but some effort has been made to make it a bit cozy. At least my bed linens are tinted in color and not the bleach-white ones that remind me of a hospital.

Folding my dress in half, I place it over the armchair near the window. I haven't missed the cold, starched clothes that are a staple here, but appreciate not having to sleep in pantyhose and layers of tulle. Anything is better than that. I'd rather sleep naked than be itchy.

Moving into the connecting bathroom, I unwrap a fresh bar of soap and scrub my hands and face, before rinsing off all of the suds. I brush my teeth with a new brush and travel-sized paste.

When I'm all freshened up, I walk to the bed and pull back the covers. Lying down, I roll to my side and tuck my knees up into my chest.

Then I cry.

I let out the roar of breath that it seems like I've been holding in ever since Collins walked out of my life. Lying still, I try to flood out the pain that I've been forced to bury.

There's no pretending anymore. There's no wishful thinking or going through the motions.

And in this moment, I can't tell which is worse—having a broken heart or having a broken mind. But right now, I definitely have both, and the combination of it all is debilitating.

Outside the room, I hear some clicking sounds, followed by the creak of the heavy metal door. Rolling onto my back, I see the fluorescent hallway lights flicker through the little window in the door.

Getting up from the bed, I move to the outside window

VICTORIA DAWSON

and pull back the blackout curtains just to discover it's raining out—pouring, actually.

I guess I arrived just in time before the storm moved into the area.

The sky lights up with streaks of lightning, allowing me to see the puddles forming along the parking lot and sidewalk.

There isn't a car in sight though, and all of the parking lot lights are out.

Weird.

Thunder sounds, causing me to jump.

Something seems off, but I can't put my finger on it. It's just a feeling though, and feelings aren't facts.

My eyes move to the tree path lining the border of the facility's property, and when the sky lights up the earth with the flash of lightning, I see a creepy man in a trench coat and rain hat staring at me.

Fuck.

My feet are frozen in my stance, but when I'm given another glimpse a few seconds later, he is gone.

I feel pieces of my mind crumbling to dust one by one.

I'm seeing things. That's why I'm here—to hopefully get better.

I am safe.

I am fierce.

*I am...*loved?

Flopping backward onto the bed, I stare up at the ceiling.

I'm going to be okay.

Taking a deep breath, I roll to my side, facing toward the door.

Through the glass window, I see the lights from the hallway shut off, realizing that we've officially hit the lights-out target time. It's either that or the power source got compromised with the storm and the backup generator is taking some time to kick on.

I try my nightstand lamp, but it doesn't work.

I need to sleep. My mind is playing tricks on me, and maybe rest will fix this feeling of being in a limbo state.

Placing my hand under my pillow, I feel the rustle of a piece of paper underneath it. Lifting it up, I discover a note with what appears to be a handwritten word on it, but I can't make it out in the darkness of the room.

The lights in the hallway flicker like a strobe light.

Getting up from the bed, I move toward the door and my only real light source at the moment. It's locked as expected for this facility, but Dr. Radinsky should be here soon. She'll know how to help me.

Placing the paper near the window, I allow the flickering light to illuminate the message.

No.

In black marker, as clear as can be, I see the one-word message.

ESCAPEE.

Why is this here?

Then I think back to all of the other cryptic notes that have been sent to me.

One.

Two.

Three.

I'm an...

And putting them all together, I have that epiphany and

finally realize they spell out one big, premeditated message: One, two, three, I'm an escapee.

Fuck.

Mark Tanner is free. He is on the loose.

Dammit.

And I'm sure he is coming for me. Feeling the blood drain out of my face, I crumble up the piece of paper and throw it over to where the wastebasket is, missing the toss and watching the ball roll onto the cold tiled floor in the shadowy flicker of the lights.

Something is wrong...

Instinctively reaching for my phone, I realize that I dropped it off at the front desk, as per protocol. It's in the little plastic bin stored away for safekeeping.

The battery is drained anyway so it wouldn't be any use, even if I had it in my possession.

Moving back to the window leading to the outside, I spot the trench-coated man now on the sidewalk.

He's real.

I can feel it.

He's not a figment of my imagination.

And he's coming for me.

I am no longer in a facility that can help me. I'm in a place where I'm going to die.

The sound of the door opening causes me to scream.

"Penny, calm down. It's okay. Everything's going to be okay."

My body whips around to see Dr. Radinsky standing in the doorway, wearing her signature dress pants, camisole, and cardigan. "You startled me."

"I'm really sorry about that. The power is acting finicky but other than that, you are safe here."

I shake my head. "I'm not safe at all. We need to get out of here."

"What? Why?"

"I see him."

"See who?"

I point to the window. "He's outside."

But when I turn to look, I see nothing but the ghost of my memory. I grab my head. It's throbbing. "He was just there." My words come out as a whisper.

"Shh…don't cry. Let's get you tucked back into bed."

I try to push past the doctor, only to have two male workers wearing white scrubs and surgical caps join her, one on each side.

Then I remember the note. "He's sending me threatening messages," I say, pointing over to where the crumpled paper is resting on the floor. My eyes blink. *Was.* "The paper was right there."

My throat closes up. I'm going to be sick.

"I'm going…" Crazy. I'm going crazy.

I look at the male worker on the left, pleading with my eyes for some sign of comfort. But when my focus locks in on the man on the right, I am struck with familiarity.

"What the hell…"

He grunts in response, morphing before my eyes from someone safe to someone determined to bring me harm.

I see the evil behind the twinkle in his eyes.

"Rex?" I choke out. My throat feels dry, and suddenly I'm overcome with a nagging thirst.

It can't be. I'm seeing things.

Blinking hard, I feel the start of a migraine forming at the center of my head.

Nothing is making sense.

Like blocks falling from an unstable tower, I feel the pieces of my mind plummeting down into a pit of uncertainty and despair. I'm not putting a puzzle together. I'm tearing a constructed one apart.

Then I see Dr. Radinsky take a little vial out of her pants pocket, followed by a clear plastic syringe. She's convinced I'm a danger to myself, and maybe I am.

Except everything about this feels wrong, and Rex's sneer is indication that's so.

"No, no, no," I say slowly, backing up until I'm pressed firmly against the wall. "No drugs. *Please.*"

It was drugs that landed me in Soulful Mind to begin with last year, and here I am full circle and just as helpless as I was then.

Nothing has changed. I'm still just as broken but for a completely different reason.

I can blame it on Mark all I want, but it's my inability to stay afloat when I feel like I'm drowning that is causing all my turmoil.

I put myself here.

So it's me who will have to get me out.

My fists lash out when the three move in on me.

"You need something mild to help you relax," Dr. Radinsky says, her voice soothing, as she dodges my flailing arms. "Don't you want to sleep and have an opportunity to wake up refreshed?"

"No!"

I dart to the side of the room, only to be flanked and restrained by the two men. Rex holds me tight—*too* tight.

"Why are you doing this to me?" I ask, truly dumbfounded as to why the man I met outside the coffee shop in town almost four months ago is the one who is holding me hostage now.

"I'm just following orders."

I swallow hard. It's not the doctor's orders he's following though. Dr. Radinsky is just doing what she thinks is best for me. It has to be Mark's plan that he is executing instead.

"Let me go!"

"Hold her steady," the other man calls out.

And without warning, I feel the prick of the needle as it punctures through the skin of my arm, then the warmth radiating through the surface at the site of the injection.

I'm fucked.

And I'm going to die at the very place I came to get saved.

43

COLLINS

"It was a setup!" I yell into the phone, as I frantically rush back to my rental car.

I peel off my mask, hoping that I can see better in the fog.

The air is burning my lungs, I'm breathing that hard.

"What does that mean?" Graham asks, his voice going up an octave. He sounds like he's out of breath too. "Do you need backup? I can go to you now."

"No. He's gone."

"Who? Tanner?"

"Yes. He escaped and put someone who resembles him in the back of the transport vehicle. Both the fake and the driver are dead and I'd assume by his hands."

"For fuck's sake!"

I hop into my rental and start the engine. Ripping off my gloves, I toss them into the back seat.

Staying on the line, I send a text to Chris.

Collins: Use GPS to get exact location of transport vehicle. Tell police two dead. Real suspect missing and on loose.

Chris: On it

Collins: Stay in town and start trying to track Tanner.

"I'm going to take the helicopter to Seattle."

"Why there? Don't you think he'll be trying to leave the country?"

"I think he's going for Penny."

"Fuck. Really?"

"Yes." I think it over, as I pull out onto the main road. "He's going to use her as either a hostage or to fulfill some revenge plot."

"Do you think murder-suicide?"

"I wouldn't put it past him."

"I'm grabbing Nic. We'll take the private jet and be in the air within an hour."

Then we disconnect the call.

Racing down the highway, I turn left and head east just long enough to arrive at the private airport where we have the helicopter stored.

I just never thought I'd have to resort to our backup plan.

At least I had one in place.

"Dammit!" Graham snarls into his cell phone, slamming his device down onto the cushioned seat in his private jet.

My eyes lock in on my own screen, as I witness his reaction through video chat. On the off chance that one of us got delayed or something happened en route, we decided to use different transportation methods.

And considering the numerous hurdles we've already had to jump over, I'm glad we did.

"What's wrong?" Nic asks, pacing in front of the row of seats on the private jet. He's going to hear this news first-hand with me apparently.

The elder Hoffman gets up, and based on his stance, I know it's bad—very bad.

My hand grips the armrest, while my other adjusts my headset. I can't take any more bad news.

Graham looks at me through the screen. "Basically there are several huge power outages in and around the city of Seattle from the storm and several crises happening that are pulling all available units in the entire region, not to mention several road closures due to fallen trees."

"Well, then it's good that we are in the air and can avoid some of those potential delays," I say with confidence.

Nic tilts his head to the side, his brow furrowing. "True. But that's assuming we'll be able to land if the storms are still raging and actually get our vehicle to the facility."

"Where are you landing?" Graham asks me, making eye contact through the screen.

"Hopefully on the roof. There's a pad there. But if not there, I'm rappelling down."

"Do you have any eyes out there at all?" Graham asks.

"Not anymore. There's been a bunch of new hires, but other than that I haven't kept tabs."

Graham nods. "I still can't believe Tanner tricked us. How did he know we'd stage a fight that would get him free from prison long enough to make a switch?"

"A guy on our payroll there decided to change teams."

"Fucker."

"Well, it cost him. He didn't even have time to enjoy it before our loyal men took care of him."

I glance out the fogged-up window of the helicopter. Luckily, we had one on standby just for emergency purposes, but I never dreamed of actually having to utilize it.

Granted, nothing about tonight has gone to our plan, and I'm mentally kicking myself for not having more safeguards in place.

We've been served up the shittiest slice of shit pie.

So many little things have worked in Mark Tanner's favor tonight, and while we are making huge assumptions, I know he's going for Penny and he won't stop until he destroys every part of her. We don't need actual trackers on him to know that he's heading her way.

Tanner might assume he's a dead man, so why not leave this world with a bang?

Rain pelts against the window, streaking and splattering. My eyes follow the little vertical rivers while they make their way north from the wind beating against the glass.

The pilot steers the helicopter through the night sky. I can't help but have flashbacks to the numerous times I've been in the air on night missions with the military, and I can't help but draw symbolism to what I plan to do when I get to the facility.

My mind races with so many worst-case scenarios that can still happen before this all ends.

It will end.

I'm done living in limbo where Tanner's concerned.

"Who's watching the girls?" I ask.

"My guy, Tyler," Nic responds.

I nod.

Graham takes a seat. "And another three of my men."

It's best that none of us take anyone's safety for granted. Who knows who's ready to pounce at the first sign of a weak entry point.

"I can't believe this is happening," I mutter. I really can't.

Out of all the work I've done for the Hoffmans, this will be the most important yet and a life I'll never take for granted.

And when I get my girl back, I'm never letting her go.

Glancing at the weather app on my phone, I see that the West Coast storms have let up enough for the flight to hopefully continue as expected, cutting down the trip's time by two-thirds. But every minute I'm in the air and not at Soulful Mind is terrifying enough. I can't help but wonder what is happening to Penny, and the thoughts of her suffering in any way because of that madman are causing soul-crushing anxiety to hit me hard.

"Our baby sister is potentially trapped in a mental institute with a psychopath, and authorities don't think it's worth checking out?" Nic asks, appearing to be at the end of his rope. "Not to mention that a prisoner has escaped and is on the loose."

"They fucking want to run a DNA test on the corpse they found resembling Tanner," Graham scoffs. "We gave them the exact address for the transport van, and they are all over the news gloating about how amazing their department is."

"I'm not surprised," I mutter.

"And just as a very small precaution, since I obviously pushed back on their lack of urgency, they promised to send out some local search teams in a three-mile radius from the crash site. You know, in case they are wrong."

I sigh. "It's asinine. The guy obviously wasn't Tanner. It can't be that hard to confirm."

"Right. Yet they think if Tanner isn't dead, then he'd be moseying around on foot," Nic adds sarcastically.

Graham sighs, while rolling his shoulders. "And then they'll wonder why we decided to take matters into our own hands."

"I'm going to murder Mark Tanner," I say with certainty. "And I'm going to enjoy every second of it."

Graham runs his hand along the back of his neck, glancing at his screen. "Not if Nic or I get to him first. For the record, I don't want any time wasted on ending things. We can't ever leave this up to the authorities again."

"Understood." And I wholeheartedly agree.

"Nic and I may have been bitches to the system in the past, but I don't give a fuck about the justice department right now. Penny's probably terrified. We need to stick to our mission and not deviate from the end goal."

I nod and then glance at my watch. "I'm twenty minutes away from the landing pad."

"We're about thirty from the airport," Nic volunteers.

"We'll need time to get into the car and race to the facility," Graham adds. Then his eyes lock on mine through the screen. "If you arrive before us, which it appears that you will...please protect our sister."

I swallow hard. "I'll protect her with my life."

And I will without hesitation.

Despite what they think about Penny and me entering into a sexual relationship, I've always tried to do what was best for her. Maybe tonight will prove that I'll always put her life above my own.

There's a silence that transpires between us, but so much is said without words that a part of me finds hope that we will work things out after this is all over.

We have to work this out.

The connection goes staticky, and I end the call.

Looking out the helicopter window, I only see dark clouds and no sign of the city or neighboring towns yet.

C'mon.

Time is ticking and the longer I'm away from Penny, the higher the chance there is that I won't find her alive.

And it's that realization that has my heart in a choke hold.

The helicopter lands after a rocky descent on the roof of Soulful Mind.

I gather my bag of supplies, just in case I need to do some breaking and entering.

The entire aura around this place feels eerie, and I've never felt this way before now. Any other time I've visited here, I've felt at peace.

Not tonight.

I disconnect my seat belt and bump fists with the pilot.

"I appreciate you getting us here safely," I say with pride. "You're one hell of a pilot."

He dips his head forward, accepting my praise. "I'll be here in case anyone needs another lift."

"Sounds good."

I take off running toward the staircase entrance. The perk of being in the air for an hour was that it gave me the chance to map out my plan. I already had physical copies of the layout for the building when the Hoffmans first brought Penny here. The security protocol has always been top-notch.

I just hope that those measures don't come back to bite me today.

Because right now, I need to go and find Penny and eradicate this world of any monsters set out to do her harm.

Trying the door handle, it's locked.

Swinging my bag to the side, I unzip a compartment and pull out some lockpicks I like to keep on me for times like this.

Then I go to work trying to manually unlock the door.

Turning the pick, I feel the click, but when I try the door handle, it doesn't budge.

Fuck.

My eyes search the premises, looking for another entrance point.

I can't help Penny if I can't get inside.

With the rain beating down around me, I wipe at my brow. I have a rain jacket on but the droplets are still finding my face and impairing my vision.

Moving to the edge of the roof, I look down, seeing a steel service ladder attached onto the side along the back part of the building.

Grabbing ahold of the side, I make my descent.

When I get to the base, I try every door I encounter, until one finally gives.

"Hold on, Princess," I whisper. "I'm coming for you."

44

PENNY

Through determination and willpower, I force my eyes to open, but no matter where I look, I see my room through a blurry film. It's like my eyes have been smeared with petroleum jelly.

The backup lights have kicked on from the emergency generator, casting a reddish glow onto the space from the illuminated EXIT lights around the building, I assume.

I blink.

And blink again.

But nothing seems to clear the cloudiness from my eyes.

Staying alert is a priority and yet I can't quite get my brain to cooperate.

Rolling to my side, I—

"Omph," I huff, feeling a pain in my shoulder as I hit the ground.

Seeing the floor now at my eye level, I allow the coldness from the tiles to penetrate through the thin linen fabric of my garments. Maybe this will wake me up from this drowsy state.

Pulling myself along the floor, I army crawl toward the bathroom in the dim lighting. I need to get my legs working again. I feel boneless—made of jelly.

And I damn well need to get my ass out of this place.

It's not safe.

My memory burns with the realization that Rex is a bad guy, and that everything I know about him is one big lie. Our random meeting outside of the coffee shop where he introduced me to the speed dating event was probably all part of one big master plan...

To what?

To make me trust him?

To make me feel unworthy of anyone liking me?

Someone tampered with my scorecard, and looking back, Rex would have had the access to do just that.

And for the last week, I've only blamed Luke.

No matter how many attempts he made at explaining himself after the initial confrontation, I just kept ignoring him.

Dammit.

Moving to my knees, I press my palms down and will myself to push forward.

One inch at a time...

I can do this.

Pulling the shower door to the side, I maneuver myself inside and use the tiled wall for stability as I try to get up on my knees.

Reaching for the knob, I turn the water on cold and

allow it to soak into my hair and clothes, causing an energy to move through me with each shiver.

Relaxing my mind, I allow it to wander as my thoughts begin to clear.

Limit-X.

I got invited to a sex club randomly by someone who handed me a postcard at the coffee shop event. I don't even remember who handed it to me, but at the end of the night, I was enticed by the mysterious invitation.

Rex.

He probably wanted to send me there. But why?

I don't remember him handing it to me. I would have remembered that—right? Someone else handed it to me, although some of my once-solid memories of the night have since faded.

Thinking back on that first visit, I discovered that Collins had a kink for pain and pleasure.

Rex must have known about it too then. He wanted me to see.

This wasn't kismet. This was calculated evil, orchestrated by men determined to do me harm.

Well, it backfired. Collins became my lover, rather than me being so appalled after the shock wore off that I would request another bodyguard.

This was probably some master plan to get him away from me and make my brothers distrust their most powerful weapon.

Because if I didn't have someone like Collins watching over me, then I would have been easier to manipulate.

But in the end, Mark Tanner won.

Whether he orchestrated it or not, I came here on my

own and in my most vulnerable state. Getting me isolated hours away from my family and my bodyguard was an ideal situation for Mark Tanner to end me for good. His minion, Rex, is just following orders.

Fuck.

And Collins is not here.

These evil men got what they wanted. They wedged themselves between my brothers and their most trusted employee, because now I'm alone.

And the irony is that it's of my own free will.

I brought me here.

Stretching out, I wiggle my toes and fingers, fighting life back into all my movable parts.

I take a few deep breaths and give myself my mental pep talk.

I may have brought myself here, but I *refuse* to die here.

I am safe *for now*.

I am fierce *in theory*.

And maybe with time, I will be loved again. I just can't think about any endgame right now.

Rex might have made it easier for my brothers to find out about Collins and my secret relationship, but my brothers would never have approved of it regardless of the revelation surrounding it.

But I can't focus on that.

In this moment, my top priority is getting myself better to be whole again. That was the purpose of coming here anyway.

Rex didn't cause my mental turmoil. He just made it easier to use it against me.

And I played right into his hands.

I rub at my sore arm where I was…injected.

Dr. Radinsky. She was here. She came to see me. She'll help. She doesn't know Rex is playing for the wrong team.

Feeling electrified, I shut off the water and manage to pull myself up to standing. Reaching for a towel, I dry off and dig through the cabinets to see if there are more clothes.

None.

Trying to stay upright, I use the wall for balance but fall into it instead, blinking to adjust my vision to the red light. It's making me dizzy.

Water drips from my still soaked clothes onto the tiled floor.

I'm barefoot.

Huh.

I guess I took my shoes off? I look around. I'm not even sure where they would be.

I just need to get out in the hallway and find Dr. Radinsky. She needs to know that…

Oh yeah, she drugged me.

I rub at my arm.

She's not evil. She probably had no choice.

Wait, I just had that thought already—right?

It's like my brain is some old record player I see in older movies, skipping when the vinyl gets scratched.

My brain is skipping.

I am a mess.

My mind jumps from idea to idea, unable to form a complete thought.

Why am I here?

How did I get here?

Rubbing at my temples, I feel the pounding as my

migraine continues to develop. I need to hydrate. Maybe my blood sugar is just low.

I brought me here.

Maybe someone has juice.

I could go for fresh pineapple mango.

I'm so thirsty.

Collins would have juice.

He's not here.

He left me.

I brought me here.

Toddling to the door of my room, I try the handle and am surprised when it opens.

Leaning forward, I look down both sides of the hall, but I can only see a few yards in front of me with the red fog. I find no one.

I find the exit sign at the end of the wing. It's my beacon in the darkness. The black box outlines the red letters, although they are blurry from this distance.

I stare at each illuminated dot, focusing my energy on getting closer to that sign and hopefully out of this mental prison.

I brought me here.

My feet carry me zigzag down the hall. I'm like a baby deer learning to take its first steps. Whoever is watching me on the security footage must be laughing.

Cameras.

There's cameras here—all over. There's twenty-four-hour surveillance. The workers take shifts around the clock. My brothers would never have chosen a place for me that didn't host the best security features. That I know.

Waving my hands into the air as a call for help, I

look to see where the black eyes are, presumably on the ceiling. I've never really noticed before. I just assumed they were watching me when I stepped out of my room.

Someone's always watching me…

I mouth "help!" just in case anyone in the control room can read lips. I'm wishful thinking someone can read my mind instead. Maybe then they can let me know what I'm thinking.

Everything seems so fuzzy.

I brought me here.

When I get halfway to the neon exit light, a door opens, followed by a sack of something falling out—right at my bare feet.

Looking down at the source of my shock, I gasp.

My hands fly to my face as I cry out, "Dr. Radinsky!"

Oh, no.

No!

And then I wail. A guttural, deep in my soul, weeping sound…

Dr. Radinsky is covered with blood and it's appearing to come from her head. Tar-like streams pour into her closed eyes, pooling until she blinks, sending them plummeting south. Her hair soaks up the mess.

Her beautiful hair…

I'm going to throw up.

"Ahhh!" I yell, watching her eyes look at me pleadingly for help. It startles me.

I'm not even sure how she can see through the blood.

She's alive.

Thank goodness she's alive.

Her eyes just stare at me, as her hands try to cover over the wound gushing with the dark, thick syrup.

"I'm sorry," I groan. "I'm *so* sorry."

She has kids.

Three kids.

We would often sit in the courtyard together and enjoy feeding the koi fish in the little pond. She helped me get set up with horseback riding lessons as part of my ongoing therapy regimen. She was my advocate when it came to group sessions.

Dr. Radinsky never forced me to talk. She waited until I was ready, and it took me a very long time to be ready.

She made me feel safe.

She treated me like a human and not some vegetable that needed to be fixed.

I try to tug her up, but she's all deadweight. She came here tonight because I was admitted. She was the on-call doctor at the time. And now she could die.

There may be blood on her head, but there is more on my hands.

I'm at fault for her getting hurt.

It's my fault.

And I can't help her. I can't even help myself.

Glancing down the hall, I look for a lifeline—anyone who can help—and I am struck with the distinct and startling vision of the trench-coated man.

Oh, hell no!

I can't do anymore scary shit today!

"I'm so sorry," I murmur to her. "I'm just so sorry."

But I can't stay here and die without a fight.

A wheezing sound hisses from her lungs, as she tries to clear her throat enough to talk.

"Rrr…"

With no time to think or to wait for Trench Coat to catch me, I pivot and throw my body forward and away from Dr. Radinsky.

Stumbling into the door she fell out of, I feel the piercing pain in my elbow from the sudden movement.

The man takes a step toward me, as I stay cemented in my place. But I can't stay still for long. The floor he continues to walk on looks like rolling waves. He's floating.

Or surfing…

He removes his rain hat, tossing it to the side, and it is then that I confirm that he is who I think he is and my vision isn't blurry anymore.

"Hello, Penny," his deep, ugly voice booms from his throat.

The blinders are off.

The air has cleared.

And…

Mark Tanner is here to get me, and he won't stop until I'm destroyed.

So I run.

And I run.

It's not pretty, but I do my best with the lingering effect of the drugs still coursing through my system.

I slip and slide on the floor from my dripping wet clothes, tumbling forward as the searing pain hits my elbows first and then my chin as they hit the ground.

Blood dribbles from my fresh wound, contaminating the sterile tiled floor. I focus on the black specks in the glow of the emergency lights. Rolling to my side and using my knee to prop myself up, I look back down the hallway.

Fuck!

Now there are two.

It's like I'm seeing double.

I'm hallucinating. I have to be.

Two men.

Two trench coats.

Two rain hats. One is hanging from Mark's fingertips. The other one is worn by the other man.

I'm doomed.

The two stalking men stride toward me.

They are strikingly similar—yet different.

I struggle to get up and get my legs to hold my weight.

They are closing in on me.

My head whips around again.

Now there's three.

Mark takes up the center of the pointing V, leading the march down the hallway toward me.

My eyes squeeze tightly shut, praying that this is all one bad hallucinogenic dream. I pray that I wake up in my own bed and can be thankful that my imagination is what was playing tricks on me, and not this evil lurking at the periphery of my life.

Grabbing my damp hair, I pull. Clumps of strands pluck out, making me cry loudly in agony.

They are getting closer.

Closer.

I can hear their breaths exhaling from their lungs, they are that close.

"Ahhhh!" I scream into the charged air.

I recoil as a hand touches me, and I twist out.

And I run. And I don't stop until I crash right into a white coat.

Looking up, and through the filter of my pooling tears, I plead. "Help me. I need help. He's coming for me. Look!"

I punctuate my urgency by grabbing hold of the collar of the coat of the man and shaking.

"There, there, Miss Penny," White Coat coos. "There, there."

But when my eyes focus between the layers of tears, I see that it's Rex.

"Rex."

"Yes, sweet Penny. I will keep you safe."

Lies.

He's been deceptive from the first moment we met.

"You set me up?"

"Yes," he confirms.

All the memories of him weaving himself seamlessly into my life come rushing back like flipping through a picture book on high speed.

"Nothing was random?"

"No. The first meeting, tampering with your dating matches, and paying someone twenty dollars to hand you a postcard."

"You made it look like Luke was the untrustworthy one."

"That was just for fun."

"Fun?"

He shrugs. "I was bored." Then he smirks. "I especially loved sending you the mystery message mail. Scaring you is my kink."

"I hate you."

"No, you don't. You hate yourself."

"Shut up."

"You should have seen your oldest brother's face when he saw the contract. It was amazingly twisted."

Oh, hell.

Rex pets my hair. "You're such a beautiful, easy victim. But you shouldn't have left a copy in your bottom nightstand drawer. Tsk-tsk." He places his hand in front of my mouth. "Kiss the hand that fed you the lies and the deceit."

"Listen to me!" I scream, trying to move away from his hand. "Mark Tanner is going to kill and—"

"Shh…"

"And dispose of you!" I bellow. "He's using you to destroy my family. You're expendable."

"Take a deep breath," Rex says, waiting for me to comply. His voice is hypnotic as if he's the one under some spell. "Hold it for the count of five, and then release slowly. One, two, three, four, five. And deep inhale through the mouth, and release through the—"

"Listen. To. Me!" I clap my hands together with each spoken word, making my own head throb. Gripping his shirt for balance, I try not to fall over.

Placing his hands over mine, he helps to release my fingers from the fabric of his uniform. "There's a side effect to the medication you were given." His finger touches my nose to bop it, as if I'm some petulant child who has a history of overreacting. "Everything's going to be okay."

Why does he not sound stressed? I glance behind me to draw attention to the three men following me.

In just a slow blink, tears trail down my cheeks, soaking into my already soggy clothes.

But the trench-coated men are gone.

Vanished.

Poof.

And my sanity is now in the balance.

It's as if the atmosphere has swallowed them up into some cosmic black hole and the only thing left are the haunting images of them once being there.

I blink and hope it helps me think clearer. Then I remember my trauma.

"Dr. Radinsky is hurt," I say in a rush. "She's bleeding."

I don't know why I'm trying to convince him. Maybe if this man who is now just a stranger to me has some sympathy, I can turn him to be on my side.

Holding up his finger to his lips to shush me, I see dark stains around his fingernails. And on the sleeve of his coat, I see the specks of maroon.

"She suffered a teensy, bitsy head wound," he says in a singsong voice.

I take a step back. "No." And then placing my hands up in front of me in defense, I take another step back.

I have to remind myself that the person I thought was a friend is not a safe haven.

My mind shifts between a calm and a fragile state. I feel so confused. It's as if my mind is snapping the threads that bind it together—one by one.

This stranger is part of the problem.

When Rex closes the distance between us in two short strides, I shove him away, causing myself to stumble onto my ass.

Scrambling to my feet, I dart past him, only for him to grab my arm and jerk me toward him. His bloody fingernails dig into my skin. I wince, tugging with all my might to get free.

Then I remember the lesson Collins taught me so many months ago in the gym on the cushioned mats.

"The first step to defending yourself is trusting your instincts."

I take a deep breath.

And I take my free hand and grip his fingers, and then pull up toward his thumb. "Back off!"

Then I knee him in the groin, while hitting him between the eyes in one sudden blunt move with the palm of my hand. He falls backward, hitting his head on the tiles.

Turning, I race down the hall, until I collide with the heavy metal door. Pushing against it, I realize that I need the keycard.

Looking back toward Rex's lifeless form, I see his badge attached with a clip to his chest pocket.

"Fuuu-ck," I moan, extending the syllables to be two. "Like *really* fuck."

Bouncing on the heels of my feet, I tiptoe down the hall toward the incapacitated man who I knocked out, keeping my eyes trained on his closed ones.

I can do this.

I just need to get the keycard—that's it.

I'll just get it and go out the door and then get to safety while I wait for the police to arrive. Surely by now my brothers know I'm missing. I left abruptly from the charity event, and knowing them, they are already out searching for me.

Stay focused, Penny.

Then I see it—the crumpled-up ball of paper.

Escapee.

Mark Tanner is an escapee.

I'm not going crazy.

Everything I've been experiencing has been reality. I was just being made to think I'm not in my right mind.

When I'm within reach, I bend forward to snatch the plastic card for the taking, just as Rex's eyes open in a bloodshot stare.

His hand gets my ankle first, tugging me down to the floor.

Then the entire place goes…

Pitch.

Black.

45

PENNY

My arms and legs flail in the darkness, as I try to wrestle my way from Rex's hold. But he has me gripped.

I wiggle and kick and punch anything I can connect with.

"Let me go!" I bellow.

But it's useless.

The ogre presses my back onto the tiled floor, and my hair slides along the surface, soaking up his blood from where his head hit the ground.

Adrenaline rushes through me, sobering me up enough to recall Collins and my self-defense lessons. I think of the blindfold and the whole purpose of those practice activities. I think of the words he shared on how to get out of the hold if someone was lying on top of me.

And then I apply them all.

Rex grunts as I maneuver my way in the darkness and roll out of his grip. Taking his head, I slam it against the tiles, hoping he blacks out long enough for me to get the hell out of here.

As he lies there unconscious, I rip the keycard from his body and dash down the hall in the direction I think makes the most sense.

I've spent nearly a year here.

I know this place well.

I just need to trust the instincts that I'm already in tune with and stop overthinking things.

When I get to the end of the hall, in the pitch blackness, I slam my body into the door. Taking the keycard, I swipe it against the box.

Nothing.

Dammit!

Of course it wouldn't work. The electricity to the generator was probably cut.

I'm an idiot.

A stupid, pathetic girl.

But I can't stay here waiting for Rex to get up and look for me. And I can't take the chance that the three Mark Tanners are real and not some figment of my imagination. I refuse to be a sitting duck. So I sneak my back along the perimeter, staying alert with my fighting fists level with my face.

When I find a door handle to a patient room, I open it softly and sneak inside. Then using only the light from the stars and moon seeping in through the windows, I go about barricading the room with furniture and anything that I can get my hands on.

It's not much, but at least I have the illusion of being safe.

When I push the last piece into place, I see a shadow move from the attached bathroom.

My breath gets stolen from my lungs, with the thief being fear.

But then I don't see it again.

My mind is just playing tricks on me. It was my own movement reflected back to me in the mirror. Leave it to me to be afraid of my own shadow.

I am safe.

It's a lie, but I think it anyway.

Moving to the window, where I can at least see better, I hop up on the windowsill and dangle my feet. Then I think of the most calming Grace and Jace slow song and allow that to be the words in my head while I wait and pray that someone rescues me from this hellhole.

With winter's end,
Spring blooms,
Cascading emotions,
Romance looms

Out of the darkness,
I can see the light,
Good things are coming,
Just hold on tight

My breathing returns to normal, and the tension that was once in my shoulders releases.

Someone will find me here.

I just have to wait.

Then I hear it. Screaming. Bloodcurdling bellows.

Gunshots sound, and I tug my knees up, wrapping my arms around them. Rocking back and forth, I try to block out everything happening around me.

But it's the sound of footsteps I hear from outside the door that pulls me from my tranquil state, followed by the buzz of an alarm blaring throughout the building.

In the darkness, I hear the screeching of the legs of the furniture scraping against the ground inside the room and see the movement of the door opening.

Fuck.

The scratching sound returns and the once darkness becomes a sea of moving shadows.

Then the lights flick on, and…

I am face-to-face with the devil himself.

"Hello, Penelope," Mark greets, pulling off his rain hat and tossing it on the bed that is now barricading the door.

My back goes rigid. My throat tightens.

I hop off the ledge and glance around the room for anything that I could possibly use as a weapon.

"What do you want from me?" I cry out.

"My life back," he says nonchalantly. "And I'll get it back."

"How?"

"At the expense of yours."

"That still doesn't answer my question," I snap.

Mark snickers. "Because the entire world now thinks I'm dead in the back of a police transport vehicle. It's amazing how life can be so ironic. One second, I'm in prison. The next"—he makes his fingers go poof—"I'm free."

"Who was back there then?"

"Oh, just some poor guy who looked like me. Sadly, he had to die, but at least he did it in a sacrificial way. And just think, if I hadn't had help arriving here in time, I'd miss all the fun that's about to go down. And that would have been the most tragic thing of all."

"They'll do a DNA test and know that's not you."

"How can you do a test when the bodies are burned beyond repair? Oops, I forgot to tell you that little detail."

I look at his face in confusion, trying to keep my mind from shutting down.

He smiles a wicked grin, while tilting his head to the side. "Remember when I paid you a little visit at the waterfront during the photoshoot?"

I don't confirm or deny. I just stay still.

"Well, that was courtesy of my lookalike. Granted, I have several. The world just needed more of me, I guess."

"Lookalike?"

Mark shrugs. "Well, the genes are strong from my dad's side of the family."

"You are related?"

He nods. "Yup. It's just me and my twin brothers left on this planet. But that's the thing about family—the bond of blood is thicker than water. And when I introduced the plan to them, they nearly salivated and decided to come out of hiding and fly across the world just for this special occasion."

"You are sick!"

"It's kind of amazing the resemblance, yeah? Striking?" Mark makes a weird face. "I think I'm much more handsome than they are, but I'd be interested in hearing your thoughts. Oh, and if you're wondering, we don't mind sharing our women."

I want to throw up.

All this time he's been putting the pieces together for his ultimate plan and working somehow through the prison system to still conduct business.

"And my brother who met you out on the balcony at the charity fundraiser? He nearly fooled you too." Mark makes a face. "I think you missed me and thus started seeing me in your fantasies."

"Try nightmare," I mumble, my voice sounding so meek.

"It's so fun to play head games with your fragile mind."

"I hate you," I snarl.

"Me? Nah. You should thank me for giving your weak brain something to focus on while you stupidly thought you could leave this place and magically be healed. Stupid, pathetic girl."

"Why Rex?"

Mark frowns. "Aww, you thought he was your friend. Now, that's cute."

"But why him?"

"My psychotic nephew isn't fit for society." He winks. "And that's saying something coming from a monster like me. I was simply giving him some purpose in his lonely life."

"You all are going to die here." I don't know why I say it, but as soon as I do, I regret it.

Fire blazes behind Mark's cold eyes, swollen from the prison fight. He looks like he's been to war and I guess he has. He leans forward and grips my jaw between his rough fingers. Then he spits on me.

I try to turn away but he's just too fast, and the whole shock over him doing something so vile has me spiraling down.

I wipe away his nastiness, using my formless cotton outfit. The fabric is still damp from the shower and is sticking to all of my curves.

"You won't get away with this."

"I already have."

"No!" I snap.

"You made it too easy for us. Once my brother saw you leaving the charity event, he followed your taxi and alerted his twin of your predictable intentions. Said twin came to my rescue by intercepting the transport van and voila, I got here just in time. Fun fact, my brothers have been living in the little abandoned apartment above the Rose City Cafe and working there for cash so their transactions didn't have a paper trail."

"But how did you get inside here?"

"Paying off the receptionist so Rex could enter with his dad without a fuss was impulsive." He scratches at the back of his neck. "Sometimes you just have to go with the flow."

"You are evil!"

"I am an opportunist," Mark counters. "And just think, I'm the normal one in my family. My brother who went to the waterfront to watch you slutting it up in the water wanted to take you right then. But he's such a sicko that he makes me look docile." He leans forward, lowering his voice. "And he's a hoarder of lifeless women. But, shhh, that's our little secret."

"You'll never get away with this."

"I already am. Except it's not officially over until I wipe out every person you love before we say our goodbyes. The good news is your brothers decided to show up for you."

"No."

"No? Aren't you relieved to end this once and for all? May the best team win."

"Where are your brothers now?" I ask in panic. They were in the hall the last time I saw them before they vanished with Mark.

"Wiping yours off the face of the planet."

I feel my face contorting with confusion.

He laughs at me. "Apparently that doctor bitch was faking her injuries a little too much and crawled to the end of the hall where the door was locked when I was distracted. Good for her. Bad for you. Now my two psychotic brothers are hunting for yours. Oh, fun fact. Did I tell you they love the sight of blood?"

"Shut up!" I snap, not believing what he's saying.

"Show some respect," Mark spits at me, accompanying it with a slap with the back of his hand on my cheek.

I rub at the sting. "I hate you!"

"Quit flirting with me."

Mark may have tried to knock me off guard with the threat to my brothers, but they are survivors.

And I am too.

So I decide to fight.

Charging forward, I push Mark and send us both plummeting onto the twin bed.

"Now we're talking," he says seductively, making me want to claw his eyes out.

VICTORIA DAWSON

I get up and start pushing items from the door in a panic, but Mark loops his arms around my waist and pulls my back to his front.

Rubbing his nose into my hair, he breathes in my scent. "My only regret is not fucking the life out of you when I had the chance. We could have been good together."

I twist and try to dislodge him from my body.

His mouth licks at my ear. "But we can remedy that now. It's not fun going through life with unfinished business. Yeah?"

"Get off me!"

"I bet whatever family that survives your loss will have a memorial for you here in the courtyard where they pay remembrance to your name. Won't that be so sweet? What kind of flowers should they plant?"

I thrash and dig my nails into his skin, finding my efforts futile.

"It's a lovely place, here. You should thank me for facilitating your reason for being here. It's fate really. And a wonderful place to die."

I allow Collins's voice to replace my own inner monologue of self-doubt. And it's my mental version of him who walks me through my next steps.

I can do this.

Even in the darkness of my own mind's breakdown, I can still do this.

I am strong.

I stomp my foot onto Mark's, and then immediately follow it up with a backward punch to his groin. While he's distracted, I push all the furniture from the door and race into the hallway, distancing myself from the key player in this horrible game.

But when I get into the fluorescent light, all chaos breaks out.

"Penny, get down!" a familiar voice screams.

Collins.

And I do.

Throwing myself to the floor, I cover my head and ears.

"Mark's in the room!" I yell, hoping he doesn't have a chance to escape through a window or something. "Get him! And his twin brothers and Rex! His family!"

Gunshots fire around my head, whizzing past me and making chills run up my spine.

Feet stomp around me, and then suddenly I'm covered by Collins.

He wraps his arms around my body and rolls us toward the other side of the hall, so I'm facing the painted bricks and he is—

"Ugh," he chokes out. "Who gave him a fucking gun?"

Turning my head, I see the blood at his neck.

"You've been shot," I cry out. "You've been shot!"

His hand goes to the site. "I'll be okay. It grazed me."

But I don't believe it.

Collins's blood gushes from his wound, and when I look up, I see Mark Tanner and the smoking gun that did it.

46

COLLINS

I've been shot before—but never like this.

There's something about the nerves in the neck that hurts more than anywhere else.

"Leave us alone!" Penny screams at Tanner's body that stands over us like a dark cloud.

His pistol is aimed in the air between us. One of his brainwashed goons must have gotten one and left it in the hallway. I doubt he had it during his prison time.

But then I remember Penny's declaration.

Brothers.

They are twin brothers.

Well, that explains their motives for helping a demented, psychopathic criminal.

Mark looks down the barrel of his pistol. "But I only have one bullet left."

"Liar," I call out, making him smirk. I need to keep him distracted.

He alternates the weapon between both Penny and me. "Choices, choices."

But when he points it back at me, I sweep forward and knock him on his back.

His gun goes sliding across the waxed floor.

With no time to waste, I reach for the weapon, but Penny has it first. So I pull out my own from my holster and aim it at Tanner's head.

"Well, this was a fun ride," Tanner snickers, getting up from the floor.

I track him with my weapon. "Hope the temperature is perfect for you in hell."

Tanner laughs deeply. "Only time will tell."

"Give me your gun, Penny."

She shakes her head no. "I want to end this once and for all."

"If you end me, my brothers will avenge my death."

"You're not that special," I say.

"To them I am."

"Too bad they're already all dead," I say with a smile. I got a text earlier confirming their fates, as I rushed to find Penny stranded here with a madman. "You can thank the Hoffmans for their dedication to waste management. You will soon be a forgotten name. No legacy. No lasting impression."

"My brothers are safe then?" Penny asks, her voice quivering and full of hope.

"Yes."

Mark snarls. "It's not over. My nephew will retaliate."

"If you're referring to that fucker, Rex, well, he'll have

to come back as a ghost if he chooses to haunt us from his grave. Killing him was my pleasure."

Tanner's eyes twitch. He has no way out of this now. "I just wish I would have seen your face when you opened up the back of the prison transport van and found that poor guy dead instead of me alive. Did you at least take a selfie of your reaction?"

"I'm done with your little games," I respond. He's deflecting.

"I hope you stayed for the fire that followed the big reveal. No?"

"I'm tired of you messing with my head," Penny says with an exasperated voice, pulling his attention from me to her. "And killing you will be my cure. I *need* to be the one."

I move behind Penny. Lining up our weapons beside one another, I allow my breathing and heartbeat to match her rhythm. Then I take the gun from her hand and into mine.

"Rip off some of my shirt and make a blindfold for your eyes. You don't need this image inside your head, Princess."

Penny listens and once the fabric is secure and cutting off her vision, I hand her back her gun.

"Isn't this romantic?" Tanner taunts.

Leaning into Penny's ear, I whisper, "On the silent count of three."

Taking a deep breath, I line up my aim and then use my free hand to line up hers, placing my trigger finger over hers.

One in the heart…

One between the eyes…

"Are you ready?" I ask her.

"Yes."

Inhale.

One.

Exhale.

Two.

Inhale.

Tanner charges toward us in one last-ditch effort to survive, as Penny and I press down in unison on our triggers.

BANG-BANG.

Sirens echo in the distance, followed by the sound of police forces infiltrating the building.

"You're going to be okay," I say, trying to soothe Penny. I hug her to me, drawing circles on her back. Untying the strip of fabric, I release it from her eyes for her to see.

We are covered in sweat, blood, and tears.

Staring down at her, I turn her so she's shielded from the horror scene in the hallway of bodily fluids and gunshot wounds.

"You're hurt," she says frantically, while craning her neck to see my wound.

"I'll be okay." I can already feel the stickiness from where the blood is trying to clot. "I'm way more concerned over you."

She must be in shock. I know I've experienced a lot of gruesome things in my life, but I've never been this scared to lose someone I love.

"We need to get you a doctor."

I smile down at her. "I'm fine, Princess. Promise. It was all worth it to end this once and for all."

"It's over? It's really over?"

I kiss her forehead and then her lips. I just can't help myself. For the last few hours, I've been running on adrenaline and hope, silently praying I would find her alive—that it wouldn't be too late.

"It's over," I say with certainty.

"What about Dr. Radinsky? She needs help."

"We'll find her. It was her who helped open the locked doors at the end of the hall that let me in."

Penny's shoulders relax, as the revelations move through her mind. "That's what Mark said too, but I didn't know what to believe. He's been fucking with my mind this whole time."

"Shhh…it's over now. I got you."

"Police!" a group of officers call out.

"We're over here!" I yell, drawing attention to our location. "Just two hours late."

Yeah, I'm bitter.

But they all can be thankful this ended the way it did. We all did society a favor. I have no clue how Tanner kept his family hidden from us, but it probably had everything to do with fake passports and name changes.

Dammit, this could have all ended disastrously.

But it didn't. We survived it.

Now my focus is getting Penny out of this place. The faster the authorities can locate the dead bodies, the faster we can be free.

"I never want to come back here," she says, with her lip quivering.

"You'll never be back," I assure.

Leaning forward, I scoop Penny into my arms, feeling the strain of my muscles pull against my neck wound.

"You are hurt," she whimpers.

"So are you."

I refuse to allow Penny to look at the scene. She's already endured enough trauma to last a lifetime. Why create even more vivid memories?

Before finding her, I took out Rex—that fucker—and shoved his body into a room to be sorted out later.

I'm just glad I found her. I couldn't live with myself if something happened to her.

"Please help Dr. Radinsky," she sobs.

"Let's go look for her," I try to soothe. "I bet she is outside by now and getting tended to."

I tuck her closer to my body, and back us up away from Mark Tanner's corpse.

"How did you find me?" She stares up at me, as I keep her cradled. "Trackers?"

"Yes," I confirm.

Penny is silent for a few seconds. "I honestly forgot they are on me."

I nod. "I could see that you were heading north when you left the fundraiser event."

"I…" She takes a deep breath as a shiver rocks through her. "Needed help. I thought I was hallucinating. Mark and Rex were making me go…" She struggles to say the last word, but then lets out a choked sob. "Crazy."

"You are not crazy, Princess. It was all a part of the big plan to break you down."

Penny nods, burrowing her face into my chest.

I tuck a stray strand of hair behind her ear. "You were right about him still being a danger to us. I had staged a big fight at the prison that was going to get him sent to the hospital. The whole goal was to end things before they ever went to trial."

"And then he tricked you?"

"Yes."

"He had his minion," I add and then correct myself, "his *brother* intercept the transport van before I could get there, kill the driver, and put some guy in the back who was probably in the wrong place at the wrong time."

"His other brother followed me from the charity event so they all knew I was heading to Seattle."

"Exactly," I confirm.

"He had one at the waterfront for the photoshoot. I had that nightmare, and I remember seeing the Rose City Cafe shirt on Mark. It's because his twin brothers were living above the cafe and working there."

"Fuck. I knew I hated that place but couldn't ever find anything out of the norm when I would have my men check it out.

"And Mark's nephew…" A sob breaks out. "Rex… He led me to Limit-X. It was all part of his plan to pull us apart. And it worked."

"Shh…" I try to soothe Penny, but she is an emotional ball of energy right now.

She grabs her head, giving it a shake. "You're sure everyone is dead."

"Yes." I want to resurrect them all just to kill them again, I am that mad. "Your brothers confirmed they got the twins. And Rex is definitely dead. I took care of him before I got to you."

"He planted pictures in Luke's room at our apartment. I found them and I thought my brothers hired him to spy on me. I thought Luke was the one who caused us to break up." She can't stop crying. "I yelled at him."

"None of this is your fault, Princess. None of it. It's over now. Mark, his demonic brothers, Rex...they are all rotting in hell. No one will ever hurt you again."

Several more police officers enter the scene. I shake my head at a group of them, annoyed that it has taken this long to even make it to this wing of the facility.

"This is a bloodbath," one says, glancing around. He looks barely out of high school. "It's a real horror movie."

He's so in awe of the scene, I'm shocked he doesn't pose with Tanner's body for his social media page.

"I'm getting her out of here," I say to him.

"Oh, we need to record your names."

I tip my chin to Penny. "She needs to be seen by a medical professional."

"We have questions to ask," a different officer says. He looks like he is dressed for a routine call for domestic abuse or something.

Did the state send their rookies here to add to their resumés?

Unbelievable.

"Well, you can ask them at another time or trust that I took care of the job you all were called in hours ago to serve."

I continue walking, not even sticking around to be granted permission.

I shift Penny in my arms, trying to calm down her shakes. She's in shock. Her chin looks to be bruising around the dried blood that is clumped together in patches.

"Where are my brothers?" she asks, stuttering out the syllables.

Every time she talks, more of the cut on her lip opens.

"They are probably outside."

And as if on cue, as soon as we get into the misty night air, both Hoffmans come charging toward us in a full-on run. They look like they didn't have it easy either. Cuts and scrapes blemish their arms. The fabric of their outfits are frayed. And the worry lines on their foreheads more pronounced.

"Oh my, Penny," Graham says, when he's just a few feet away. "I'm so sorry."

I set her down on her feet, allowing her brothers to hug her.

"I was so scared," she whimpers. "I didn't want anyone to get hurt."

"We know," Nic says, rubbing circles on her back.

Then the attention of the Hoffmans is on me. And so much is transferred between us with that one look. "It's over," I confirm. "Rex and Tanner were taken care of."

"And we got the two lookalikes," Nic replies.

"Tanner's twin brothers, you mean?" I add with a snarl.

"Dammit." Graham rubs his hand along the back of his neck, looking to come to terms with that revelation. Then he sighs, looking at his sister. "It's over."

Picking up Penny, I place her onto a gurney and then wrap a wool blanket around her.

Two EMTs start to examine her injuries, making me

exhale slowly in relief that she is staying coherent and in the present. I can't have her slipping away inside her head like she has in the past.

"You are bleeding, sir," a paramedic says to me. "Were you shot?"

"Yes," I answer, not feeling the need to have anyone fuss over me. But I accept the help anyway because it keeps me close to Penny.

She places a damp piece of gauze over the wound, causing me to hiss at the sudden pain. "Sorry. I need to clean this so you don't get infected. It doesn't look like you need stitches."

"Good," I mutter, making Penny look over at me. "How are you doing, Princess?"

Her sad smile makes her look even younger. "I'm okay."

Then looking at the doors of the facility, we see a gurney being rolled out with Dr. Radinsky being worked on.

"Is she going to be okay?" Penny asks frantically, as they load her into the back of the ambulance.

"Yes," a worker confirms. "She's going to be just fine."

As I get finished with the bandages on my neck, I see Graham and Nic motioning for me to join them.

"I'll be right back, Princess."

"Okay."

Sliding off the gurney, I make my way over to the Hoffman brothers.

"How did the bastard die?" Nic asks, far enough away so his sister can't hear.

"Penny shot Tanner near his heart, and I got him right between the eyes."

"She shot him?" Graham asks in shock.

"Yes. And now she can move on without this weighing her down ever again."

He looks back at Penny. "And she's okay from that?"

I nod. "She didn't witness anything other than what occurred before I could rescue her. He had her trapped in a fucking room. He made this personal so his death became personal as well."

I can tell Graham is thinking over what I just revealed. He may not have done things my way, but I did what I thought was best given the circumstances and Penny's mental state.

"Thank you," he says softly after several long seconds.

My eyes glance to my feet and then up to Nic whose clothes are saturated with blood.

He looks behind me at the building that is only visible in the muted outside lights, causing me to turn in that direction as well.

Five body bags get carried out. "Five?"

Graham clears his throat. "The receptionist got caught in the crossfire and caught a bullet from one of the looka-likes'"—he stops and shakes his head in disgust—"I mean, twins' guns."

I nod.

"She had a wad of cash on her," Nic explains, "and probably was paid off."

"Makes sense. They had easy access to the entire wing where I discovered Penny."

"I have to give it to Tanner," Graham says with a half laugh. "He sure was able to keep his brothers and nephew a secret. I had no clue he had any living family members."

Penny makes a high-pitched squeal, causing us all to look.

The EMT at least looks apologetic as she goes to work on cleaning up Penny's wounds.

I make my way back over to her, hopping up on the gurney with her and tucking her to my side. It feels oddly natural to be this close to her in public, and I dare anyone to ask me to move.

Both Graham and Nic can't help but stare at me holding their baby sister. I refuse to let her go. I'm never going to let her go.

I don't give a fuck if anyone thinks it's wrong.

I love this girl.

And I'll spend this next part of forever trying to prove to her that I'm worthy of her heart.

47

COLLINS

When I arrive at the Hoffmans' residence in Hillsboro, I start to feel the nerves creep up my throat. I'm not used to being here under such tense circumstances, but I won't let my fear of rejection squash the hope I have for my future.

In a short amount of time, Penny has burrowed herself under the icy layer in my heart and melted it with her grace, her witty humor, and her sensitive nature. She has stolen it and has kept it hostage from the moment she smiled at me during her birthday party just a few months ago, and it has been a defining moment in my life.

It was during that time spent with Penny that I saw her less as a broken girl who needed saving and more as the spirited girl who could save me.

Everyone deserves someone like her in their life, and I'm damn lucky she decided to even put her energy into pursuing me.

And she relentlessly sought me out.

Why? I'll never know.

Now she's the only thing I could ever want, and I'll be absolutely miserable if I don't fight for her now like she has fought for us in the past.

I just need to get her family on board so I don't have to stumble through life anymore with crippling guilt weighing me down.

Cutting my engine, I slide out of the driver's side and step onto what I hope is neutral soil.

The last visit at this residence was for Labor Day, and just thinking about that time I spent with Penny seems like a lifetime ago.

Walking up to the front door, I'm surprised when it opens before I even have an opportunity to knock.

Donna Hoffman greets me in a warm hug.

I wrap my arms around her and savor the comfort.

Hugs are weird. You don't realize you need one as badly as you do, until someone offers you one. I'm thankful for Donna to see me when I'm struggling to see myself.

"I am glad you are here, Collins."

I fight back tears that have come out of nowhere. "I am glad I am here too…"

This woman really knows how to make someone feel welcome. It's no wonder Penny is the person she is today. She had the ideal role model to help guide her along her path into adulthood.

"Thank you for protecting Penny from those criminals."

"I will always protect her." It's a promise rather than just a statement.

She smiles. "I know it's your job and all, but you risked your life to protect those I love, who consume my life and are the source of my personal happiness. And for that I'm forever indebted to you."

"I will always be loyal to your family, ma'am."

She glares over my show of respect. I know the matriarch has a beef with me unintentionally aging her with my labels, but she deserves all of the honor.

"You always have been, Collins."

I glance down at my feet, feeling overcome with emotions. I know I have a lot of penance to do. "Thank you."

"What brings you here today? You didn't exactly provide much detail when you texted us about coming over. I hope it's nothing too serious. I'm not sure my heart can handle anything bad."

I tip my head. "I wasn't trying to be intentionally vague. I just wanted to make sure that what I say is done face-to-face."

Donna takes a step back, extending her hand. "Well, come on in."

"I appreciate you opening your home again to me."

"You are always welcome here."

"Thank you."

"I made some snacks, so I hope you are hungry."

I smile. I'm not the least bit surprised. "I am." It's a semi-lie, but I refuse to cause this woman unnecessary sadness by not accepting what she has to offer. Donna always goes all out for even the simplest of gatherings. I just think she really enjoys all aspects of entertaining.

She looks at me suspiciously. "Something's wrong. I can feel it. You aren't going to break up with us, right? What did my sons do? They can be such hardheads sometimes. You aren't retiring, are you? Just for the record, neither of my sons tell me anything of importance going on in their lives. Like, nothing. I know nothing."

An awkward laugh bubbles out from my diaphragm. "I'll try my best to explain what has happened."

"Please tell me this isn't going to end like one of those Wiley Quinn books that my damn book club keeps selecting. They are a bunch of rich bitches who think their reading material makes them somehow more sophisticated. I wish they would just pick something smutty. It sure would bring some actual joy into their lives." She leans into me. "And heaven knows, we could all use a little more joy."

"Umm..." I have no clue what she's talking about, which is kind of on par when Donna starts going with her offshoots from the main conversations.

"Spoiler alert, the main character gets cancer, or dies overseas during combat, or becomes a religious person sworn to be celibate."

Germain steps into the dining room, where we end up settling. "Oh, is my wife ranting about the Wiley Quinn books?"

I nod.

"If you call an intellectual discussion ranting," Donna chides, "then that means you've been watching too much of those lawyer shows." Then she looks at me and mouths, "Boring."

"Take a seat, Collins. I'm glad you came to visit." Germain clears his throat.

I pull out a chair and watch as Donna and Germain do the same. Resting my back against the wood, I take a deep breath.

"I know your sons deliberately refrain from providing you details about their lives. And while I don't want to over-step any of those safeguards they instill for your protection, I want to share with you why I came into the picture in the first place."

"Okay..." Donna says, placing her hands in front of her on top of the table's surface.

"Years ago, I was drugged as a revenge plot and forced to discharge from my duty to the United States military. After that abrupt departure, I slipped into a state of depression and lost my purpose in life."

"I'm so sorry," Donna says, patting me on the back to encourage me to continue.

"Then I crossed paths with your son Graham and started working security for him. But it wasn't until I was under his employment and Penny got drugged that I realized just how bonded we are through our tragedies."

"And you felt like avenging Penny was your way to find meaning to the senseless act that was done to you years prior?" Germain asks.

"Absolutely. And despite thinking that having Tanner behind bars was the end of it, Graham and Nic were shocked when Penny decided to visit her abuser in prison."

"So they hired you to become her personal bodyguard and keep her out of trouble?" Donna asks.

"Yes," I confirm. "My duties were shifted primarily to Penny."

Donna nods, probably mentally piecing together all of the information of what she already suspected to what I'm currently revealing.

"During this time, Penny was using what I concluded

was a psychological flooding technique to try to get over the hurdle she thought she was faced with when it came to relationships with men."

"Oh dear," Donna gasps. "She became a wild child, didn't she?"

Careful not to reveal too much, I think over how I'm going to say my next words. "I think she thought that if she confronted her fears with men head-on, that she would magically get better. So, as I guarded her, I was bombarded with the realization that Penny was constantly putting herself in danger."

"But she had you to watch out for her."

"Yes. But I was trying to balance protecting Penny and giving her space to blossom and grow."

Donna reaches for my hand and gives it a squeeze. "I imagine she didn't make it easy."

"No," I say with a chuckle. "Not at all."

Germain clears his throat. "As a father of a daughter who is very much an adult, I had to weigh whether to give advice or give support. And I'm not sure I even did a good job at either of those things, looking back."

I frown. "Penny loves you both. And as an outsider to the family, I value and admire your dedication to your children."

"Thank you," Donna mouths, overcome with emotion. She takes the tissue box her husband passes to her.

"During my time with your daughter, I tried my very best to keep things professional and provide Penny with the boundaries I thought she needed while she tried to cope with assimilating back into the real world. The problem was…it was me who didn't respect the boundaries."

"Okay…" Germain says, leaning forward as if to not miss a word.

"The more I was around Penny, the easier it was for me to see how amazing she is. And I fell for her." I pause, expecting them to gasp or stand up from the table. But instead, Donna and Germain just look at me, silently encouraging me to continue. "I crossed the professional line in spite of both Graham and Nic, the men who trusted me to watch out for Penny, and I went behind their backs to pursue an intimate life with her instead."

"Oh, Collins," Donna says, "I can clearly see you feel bad about this."

I nod eagerly. "I do. But I'm not sorry I fell in love with your daughter, ma'am. I'm just sorry that I didn't give anyone in your family a chance to support the idea of us and instead kept it all a secret. I know I am older than Penny. I know that I don't have my own family structure to bring into the relationship for balance. And I know that both Graham and Nic see me as a traitor who betrayed them rather than as a man worthy enough to provide for their sister. And for all of that"—I choke on the tears I've been holding back—"I am deeply and regretfully sorry. Truly, I am really sorry."

Getting up from the table, Germain leaves the room quietly.

And I break down…for the first time in my life.

Scooting her chair closer, Donna places her arm around my shoulder. "I never once questioned your loyalty to our family. Never once. And I still don't."

The sound of the chair sliding against the floor causes me to look up. Germain Hoffman is back at the head of the table, looking thoughtfully at me. Then he places a folder onto the table.

"Open it," he says.

And I do, revealing pictures taken last year when Penny entered Soulful Mind Therapy Center. Sitting in a wheelchair, unresponsive, is my princess.

Her head is slumped to the side. Unfocused and glassy, her eyes just stare at the floor.

It looks like Penny is doing nothing but just breathing and existing. She isn't thriving and living.

The digital proof of Penny's struggles spans over months, and with each glance at the evidence, it's plain to see that she has come a long way to get to where she is currently.

"It pains me to see these pictures," I admit. "Some I haven't seen until today."

"It guts us as well," Donna agrees. "But it does help to look back if just to keep everything in perspective."

Leaning forward, Germain reaches for my hand to shake, and I accept. "You have given our Penny life again. When she was released from the facility, we were all terrified she would slip back into her catatonic state. Seeing someone you love suffer so much does something to the brain. It causes real fear and worry. But all these months, Penny has had you."

"Thank you for not hating me."

"Hating you?" Donna asks, her shock portrayed by her gaping mouth. "Never."

"We could never hate you, Collins," Germain echoes.

"I went about this all wrong…"

Germain places his hand on my shoulder. "Well, if you

are solely here to ask for our blessing, then you wasted a trip. Because how can we deny either of you what has been clearly set as your destiny?"

Wiping at another tear that forms at the corner of my eye, I nod. "Thank you. Truly, thank you."

"Now, as for my stubborn and overbearing boys," Donna says with conviction, "I'll handle them."

I laugh through all the emotion. "Good luck."

48

COLLINS

"Collins, I wasn't expecting you," Claire greets at the doorway of her new home. She takes a step back to grant me access. "Nic is at Graham's place."

"I know. That's why I decided to stop over."

"Okay…"

I follow her into her living room and take a seat on the chair, as she sits down on the couch. She is less than two months away from giving birth and looks like the aches and pains have set in full force.

Guilt stabs at me for even considering involving her in my personal dilemmas, but I'm past the stage of being desperate.

"I need your help."

Claire makes the gimme-gimme hands. "Please. Keep going…"

"I need you to lure Penny to me so—"

"It looks less like a kidnapping."

"Exactly," I say with a laugh.

VICTORIA DAWSON

"Count me in."

"You haven't even thought about it or heard the details."

Claire shrugs. "I don't need to. I'm all about the ride or die…"

"No one is going to die," I clarify.

"It's an expression."

It's one I'll never really understand apparently. "Okay… I appreciate your help."

"You and Penny belong together."

"Not according to Nic and Graham."

She shakes her hands in front of me as if to magically erase the words I just spoke out loud. "They'll come around. Don't let their overprotectiveness sway your efforts. Penny was the happiest when she was with you. I have no doubts that you are her person."

"Are you sure you're up for the challenge?"

Claire taps her finger along her jaw. "If this means going against my fiancé and pissing him off, count me in. I have been in such the mood for makeup sex."

I narrow my eyes at her. She is something else. And no matter how many times I think I'm prepared for what will come out of her mouth, she changes direction and surprises me.

"I do appreciate you."

"This is going to be epic."

"So here's what I had in mind…"

It's been exactly a week since I rescued Penny from Soulful Mind.

And it's been exactly a week since I declared to her that I'd be pursuing her.

I've said sorry. I've sent flowers every day. And I've given her the space she seems to need.

But I'm done with doing things her way. She's had ample time to come to terms with things going back to it being "us," so she can't be all too surprised that I'm currently waiting for her to arrive at a restaurant.

I know she'll be here. And when she realizes that I know she'll be here, she's going to lose her shit.

I can't wait.

There's an excitement moving through me at seeing her face and her reaction.

I know she won't disappoint.

Penny's been staying at Nic's old apartment since we broke up, and I'd do anything for her to be back under my roof so I can keep a better eye on her. But knowing her, she's going to fight tooth and nail.

That's my girl.

She is stubborn.

She is independent.

And she is brave.

I'm just tired of seeing her go about all of this alone. Relying on stalker updates from Chris and my own security footage access, I can't tell if Penny is sleeping enough and eating enough. I want to take care of her but can't do it as well from afar.

It's time I take my girl back and claim what's mine.

"Can I get you anything, sir?" the waitress asks politely.

"Sparkling water, please."

"Any flavor?"

I tap a finger along my jawline. "Strawberry."

"Very well. I'll be right back."

Scanning over the menu, I distract myself with the various options, hoping that Penny doesn't become so angry with me that she refuses to eat. I need her strong and feisty today for what I have planned, not weak and under-nourished.

I sense Penny's presence before I can locate her in the room. Scanning around the restaurant, I finally spot her talking with the hostess at the entrance.

She looks spectacular. But then again, she always does.

I watch intently as she weaves herself through the room, settling at a two-person table that is within sight range.

My beverage arrives over ice. Taking a sip, I lean back against the chair, admiring my perfect view of Penelope Hoffman.

Whipping her body around, she catches me staring, and my boldness makes me refuse to look away.

Looking at Penny is like staring into the sun. It gives you life, but if you're not careful, it can burn you.

Uh-oh…

Here she comes…

I quickly cross my ankles at my feet, bracing myself for whatever she chooses to dish out in anger.

"You are making this weird," Penny snaps.

"Are you really stomping your foot?"

She props her hands on her hips and exaggerates her foot movement. "Yes."

"You keep ignoring me."

"And I'll continue ignoring you."

I can't help but smile. She clearly isn't ignoring me now.

When she catches on, she bares her teeth, and it's a beautiful sight. "Leave."

"No. I was here first."

It's true. Now, granted, I was ninety-nine point nine percent sure she would be here as well. But that's irrelevant.

"What are you doing here?"

I look around the Mediterranean restaurant. "I'm not doing anything other than enjoying this fine establishment." It really is beautifully designed. I'm thankful Penny's stubbornness has led me here. At least I'll eat well while I stalk her.

"You followed me."

"Maybe you followed me," I tease. "Remember"—I tap my jawline and then prop my chin on my hand—"I was here *first*."

Penny glances around the place, while rocking on her heels. Is she looking for someone? Actually, I know that answer already. She most definitely is. And that's the reason I am really here.

"Please leave."

"No. It's a free country."

"Nothing is ever random with you."

"Oh, my feelings for you are very intentional."

"You had your chance." She makes a too-bad-so-sad face.

"Have you been enjoying your flowers I've been sending?"

"No, but my trash has been."

I resist smirking. Penny's a horrible liar. "You'd best stow away all your sass if you don't want to add kidnapping to my list of faults." I wiggle my brows. "I've been on a roll lately of doing things that piss you off. What's one more?"

She shakes her head at me. "Why are you doing this?"

"Because I love you."

"Shut up."

"I do."

"Shut up."

"I love you, Penny."

She blocks her ears. "Shut. Up. Shut up. Shut up!"

"And I'll spend the next forever-many years proving just how much."

"It's over."

"It's not, Princess," I say with confidence.

She moves her hands back to her hips. "Yes, Collins, it is. And stop calling me that!"

"I got your parents' approval."

"I ne—" Her words cut off, and her mouth closes shut. Then after a long pause, she lets out an exasperated exhale. "You are un-be-liev-able."

I shrug, leaning back in my chair. "I've been called worse."

"I'm not going to be with a man who walked away when he had a chance."

"I never walked away from you, Penny."

"Oh, that's right… My bad. You actually *ran* away."

"I didn't do that either. I walked silently beside you the entire time."

"I wish you would choose silence now."

Ignoring her, I continue. "And if it takes longer for you to accept the reality of this whole situation, so be it." I lean back in my chair and bend my arms behind my head. "I have all the time in the world."

"My brothers will never approve."

"I'm not living for your brothers' approval when it's yours I need most."

"I'm on a date," she blurts out.

I look behind her. "That's cute. Is he invisible?"

She scoffs. "No."

Well, at least they didn't share a ride together.

I use my leg to kick out a chair at my table. "By all means, please sit down."

She doesn't.

The waitress drops off a bread basket and a dish of olive oil with herbs, and I can't help but chuckle over Penny's growling stomach.

"Please, join me while the bread is fresh."

"No."

I rip off a chunk that is still hot and dip it into the olive oil bath. Popping it into my mouth, I savor the flavor combination and moan.

"This is so good." I gesture toward the basket. "Are you sure?"

"Stop it."

Despite refusing, Penny doesn't move. She just stands here watching me devour a chunk of bread like I want to devour a chunk of her.

"Aren't you hungry?"

"No."

"Then why are you here?" I make a knowing face. "You are stalking me."

"What?"

"Don't worry, I am flattered."

"Ew, no."

"Well, who comes to a restaurant if not to eat? And you claim you aren't hungry, so that must mean…"

Then I see Ivan Moreno in my periphery. My eyes catch his, and I track him.

The kid is dressed like he's about to attend his own wedding—or funeral. At least his over-the-top suit is versatile.

"What are you doing, Penelope?" I say slowly.

Penny must see that my attention has shifted to something behind her, but she doesn't look. "Learning to live without you."

"By being reckless?"

"It's not reckless when we aren't together anymore."

Before Moreno has gotten over to us, I lock eyes back with my princess. "Just because you don't want to acknowledge that we most definitely are together, doesn't make it any less true."

"Do *not* make a scene." Smacking her hand on the table, she tries to punctuate her demand.

I put my finger up to my lips. "Shhh…" This is way too much fun. "It looks like you are the scene-causer right now."

"You are so annoying."

Yup, she's getting angrier. And I'm going to savor every bit of emotion she's giving to me.

She's delicious.

"Enjoy your pretend date, but just know that if the kid touches you"—I rotate my dinner knife between my fingers

—"I'll have ample supply of kitchen tools to torture him with and exact my revenge."

"You are crazy."

"Crazy in love, yes."

"Stop saying that," she hisses.

"Love, love, *love...*" Then I do something really cheesy by cupping my hands to make a heart at my chest.

"You're a clown."

"And you are beautiful." I blow her a kiss. "And all mine."

"You made me close a chapter in my life that I wasn't willing or wanting to close! You did that. You are no longer entitled to be sulky and jealous when I move on to another book."

"You are my plot twist, Princess."

"Quit being"—she struggles for her next word—"awkward."

"I settled for being the villain in the past. But the future has me striving to be the hero."

"Penny, it's good to see you," Moreno says, looking my girl over.

She most definitely looks good, but I don't need his nasty eyes roaming over her and tainting her with his grossness.

The kid better be careful if he doesn't want to be watching her through two forks sticking out of his pupils.

This outing is about the charity fundraiser, and I guess tonight he's decided to cash in on his prize.

"Good to see you too," Penny says, leaning forward and giving him a hug.

My eyes narrow as she embraces him a tad bit too long for my liking.

I'm keeping score, Princess...

It's not often that I impress myself with my own patience, but enduring this supposed date that Penny and Ivan are on is testing every limit of mine.

If it wasn't for the fact that going to prison would severely put a wrench in my plan to win Penny back, then I'd have carried Moreno's body out to the dumpsters in back and poured hot grease all over him.

He has to be loving the fact that I'm here dining alone, and he has my girl.

But I'm being the good Boy Scout that I've been labeled to be.

The fact is, Penny isn't going home with him when she belongs to me.

Leaning back in my chair, I angle it so I can look directly at her while she tries her damnedest to avoid eye contact with me.

And the more she tries to ignore me, the more I enjoy the experience.

"Can I get you anything?" the waitress asks, doing her rounds at her assigned tables.

I'm sure asking her to add poison to Ivan's drink is frowned upon, so I settle for something more subtle. "Can you bring me a piece of paper and a pen?"

She doesn't even act like my request is unusual. "Of course."

When she returns with my supplies, I go to work making my goal list.

Goals for the Next 24 Hours:
1. Shut down the stupid date with "the kid"
2. Kiss the fuck out of my princess
3. Help said princess to be reasonable

If All Else Fails: Kidnap my girl

Then I fold the paper into an airplane, recalling how at Penny's birthday one of the family games was landing the plane. I can only hope to have a lifetime of making memories with Penny during family game time.

She just needs to see reason.

When Ivan gets up to use the restroom, I carefully fly my paper airplane and manage to land it right on Penny's plate.

Damn, I'm good.

Well, that got her attention.

"Calm down," I mouth, just making her fidget even more in her seat.

I can tell she doesn't want to open it, but I know she's too curious not to allow herself.

"Open it," I whisper-yell, using my hands to mime out what she should do.

"Quit being stupid."

"Quit being cute," I counter.

Then I watch with bated breath as she unfolds the panels and discovers my short-term goal list. Masking her feelings behind a cold expression, Penny crumbles the paper into a ball and then hovers the side of it over the scented candle that is serving as a centerpiece. And it catches the flame. Quickly, she tosses the semi-charred ball into her glass of ice water.

Then she looks over at me and smiles her wicked grin, and I can't help but burst into laughter.

Except now I can't stop.

Ivan returns and busies himself by showing Penny photos of his dog, probably hoping a pet sparks some romance between them, because he's clearly not doing it on his own.

The kid's probably thinking—*women love puppies and babies, right?*

Meanwhile, my princess would much rather look at popcorn flavor options and homemade prank videos. I know her love languages.

Probably bored out of her mind, Penny excuses herself from the table to use the restroom or hide from the man with the personality of a ten-year-old. I wait outside the ladies' room door for her. But growing impatient, I decide just to nonchalantly walk inside.

What could go wrong?

I find Penny in front of the row of sinks, staring blankly at her reflection. And in this lighting, where I expect peace on her face from knowing she's alone, I find only sadness.

"My apartment feels hollow without you."

Her body whips around to find me. "Collins…"

"I'm done with you pretending."

"Pretending what?"

"That we don't exist. I'm done with it. If it means getting my face bashed in by your brothers again until they feel less angry about the whole situation, then so be it."

"You can't waltz in here and start throwing statements at me and hope one is enough for me to change my mind."

"Seamlessly, you filled the cracks in my life that I told myself I didn't need filled. I miss you there. I miss your hair ties on all my doorknobs. I miss you completely ignoring my cabinets' organizational methods and improvising. I miss the fun you've brought to my life."

"We both know I stress you out. You pretty much described me as *uncooperative* on the daily when we were sharing space."

"Well, I miss that too."

A knot rises in my throat, restricting the air flow, as I watch tears threaten to pour out of her eyes. Why is she depriving herself of happiness now that I've paved a path for us to be together?

"It's over. I can't put myself through this again. The last breakup put me back in the"—she chokes on her words—"you know."

"You aren't crazy, Penny. You are heartbroken."

She rotates her body to look at me. "That's presumptuous."

"It's accurate. Well, guess what? I am heartbroken too. And I am sorry."

"Sometimes sorry isn't enough."

"You are the chaos my orderly life needs, Penny. You've wrecked me, but in the best ways possible." My eyes hold her gaze. "You are the air I breathe. Without you, I'll suffocate in my own rigidness. Come back."

"When you left, it was like you didn't even see me. I

wasn't even a blip on your radar. Then you just went silent. And that silence was deafening. You made yourself loud and clear. You don't want me. And you never will long-term. So whatever you're doing now is just fucking with my head. I just wish you'd give me the clean break that I obviously want."

"I see you, Penny. I see everything about you. I see the way your eyes soften when you think about those you love. I see the way your nose scrunches up when you laugh. It is cute as hell. I see how you smile when something really makes you happy or how you wiggle your fingers when you are stressed. I see you—every part of you. And the only thing my life is missing is your acknowledgement that you are mine."

"I don't know if I can get back to what we once had..."

"Then start focusing on progress and not perfection," I challenge.

She shakes her head. "I can't make big life decisions right now."

I nod and take a step closer. "Then let me take the choice away."

"Collins..."

"In about ten seconds, I'm going to place my hands on your ass and lift you so your legs can wrap around me. Then I'm going to grind you until you get so needy that your only choice is to beg me. If that isn't something you want, then here is your one chance to walk away from me. But if you choose to stay, know that it will be forever."

"You can't—"

"Ten."

"Barge in—"

"Nine."

"Here and—"

"Eight."

"Take what—"

"Seven."

"You want—"

"Six."

"Without asking—"

"Five."

Penny pushes on my chest. "Collins!"

"Four."

"I mean…"

"Three."

"It."

"Two."

She takes a step back but I match her move.

"One."

"Uh-oh…"

49

PENNY

Collins's hands are on my ass cheeks, just as he promised. My dress rides up to accommodate the movement, and my legs wrap habitually around his waist—betraying my trust in my own self-control.

His kiss claims the breath from my lungs, commanding it and matching it to his own rhythm. Pulling away, I pant for air.

I hate that we fit together like this, like we were made for each other, because it confuses the fuck out of me.

Chills run up my spine, as pleasure surges just from his mere touch.

I miss him. I miss his taste. I miss how he feels. I miss everything about this man.

Falling asleep without him has been torture. And waking up alone is yet another reminder of everything I've lost.

But I can't be that masochist who allows her heart to be stomped on again.

I can't.

Besides, I'm the one who seduced him in the beginning. Everything about us was a fabrication of my own desperation and delusion.

"I think my princess likes when I take charge," he growls.

My neck arches back as he grinds his cock against my core, and it takes everything in me not to rub myself all over him until I'm too far gone to think straight.

"Don't tease me with your attention, just to pull away in the end." There's a warning edge to my voice.

"There's no end, Penny. There will never be an end."

My eyes search his for lies—some inclination that he is feeding me what I want to hear—but the only thing reflected back is truth.

And it fucking terrifies me.

As I try to slide down his body, Collins pulls mine closer to his. Resting my back against the wall, he presses his weight onto me and into the tiles, causing me to scream out his name.

I do love when he takes charge, but I'll be damned if I admit it to him now.

"Tell me you don't want this, Princess."

And when I'm silent, he maneuvers me so that he can undo the button and zipper of his pants.

Lowering his hips, Collins thrusts up and dry humps me.

That's the thing with us. The foreplay is just as good as the real thing.

But I'm not supposed to be enjoying myself. I'm furious with him for even putting me in this predicament.

"Fuck," I bite out, between closed teeth.

"Yes, Princess. Tell me to move your soaked panties

to the side. Tell me to slide my hard cock along your length and into the depths of your sweet pussy. *Tell me*."

"No," I whine. The single-syllable word is unbelievable even to my own ears and surely to his.

His hands roam over me, grabbing and squeezing, causing a surge of goose bumps to multiply over every surface he touches.

"Tell me you don't want me to thrust inside your depths and hit your favorite spot."

I shake my head no adamantly.

Then leaning down, his warm breath right at ear level, he whispers, "Tell me you don't want to drown my cock in your cum as you detonate around me."

My teeth dig into my bottom lip, nearly breaking through the sensitive flesh.

Fuck.

With featherlight touches, Collins trails his hands along the path of my hips, against my stomach, and up to my breasts. He gives them a territorial squeeze, forcing me to moan out in ecstasy.

He's playing dirty, hitting all my favorite erogenous zones.

"Do it," I half beg.

He groans but doesn't comply. "I'm going to need a little better than that."

"Put your hard cock in my pussy, dammit, before I change my mind."

Releasing my breasts, Collins grips my panties with one hand, while the other hand hoists me up. He pulls the cotton panel to the side to grant him the access he's been laser focused on probably since he followed me into this restroom.

But even knowing his ultimate plan, it doesn't stop me from wanting to submit to this man—one last time—and then say my final goodbye.

"Ahhh…" I call out, thrashing my head back and bumping it against the wall.

"Don't knock yourself out," he warns. "I need you coherent and awake for this."

Then with amazing precision and dexterity, he slides his cock into my entrance—just an inch. And he stays there.

"More," I groan.

I rock my hips.

"Patience. I want to savor this."

"Now you want to go slow?" I ask, but more as a rhetorical question.

And he laughs.

He fucking laughs!

"My princess is always so full of jokes."

Then, without warning, Collins pushes forward, plummeting his cock deep into my pussy, stuffing me full.

"F-u-ck," I whimper, closing my eyes shut.

The pleasure is almost too much to endure while staying coherent, and he's not even really doing anything.

That's how good we are when we're together. And the realization that this will be our last time together makes me sad that it's done in a place that isn't that romantic.

Why do I even care?

Thrusting inside of me, Collins picks up speed. His once calculated, small movements become uninhibited and wild.

My back presses into the wall and my legs become limp

as he takes from me what my body has no choice but to give.

It is dirty and animalistic the way we fuck. Our mouths crash against one another's, as our bodies rut with the only goal being to get off.

Collins enraptures me.

Claims me.

He reaches between us to play with my clit, pressing into it aggressively and circling his fingers like an expert.

I am the puppet, and he is the master.

After a few seconds, I can't take any more and skyrocket into oblivion.

"Yes, Princess," he hisses, joining me in paradise.

He marks me with his seed, spilling some out of me and down my ass crack, as he lazily pushes inside a few more thrusts.

I stay clutched to him like a bear cub, as I come down from my high. But then Collins kisses behind my ear and plays with my hair, and it reminds me how badly I just sent him mixed messages.

"We can't do this again."

He pulls back his upper body to get a better look at me. Then his eyes narrow with realization of what I'm about to do. "We'll be doing it as often as we can."

"This wasn't makeup sex, Collins."

"No?"

"It was goodbye sex."

A laugh flutters out from deep in his chest, as his eyes flash back to mine. "Believe what you want"—he kisses a path from my ear to the sensitive skin at the base of my neck—"but I know the truth."

I push against his chest. I can't keep breaking my heart over and over again. "Stop."

My one word makes Collins halt. Then he helps me to my feet, making sure I'm on stable ground before letting go.

What am I doing? I'm supposed to be having a date with one man, not fucking around with a different one.

"Penny…"

I fix my dress, smoothing down the fabric. I fluff my hair so I don't look like I've been doing anything in here other than using the facility.

"I need to go."

"Then go with me."

"No," I snap. "I need space to think."

"You can think with me. We can sleep in separate bedrooms. We can talk if you want to talk. And I won't pressure you if you don't. I just want you to be in close proximity."

"You just don't get it."

"Then explain it to me over dessert."

Feeling suffocated, I push open the restroom door just to find a man in a restaurant logo shirt waiting outside in the hallway.

Collins's arm stretches out, and several one-hundred-dollar bills are placed into the palm of the worker, who then quickly retreats through another door labeled Employees Only.

Of course, he'd get someone here on his side to stand guard while he made his move.

I glare at Collins over my shoulder. "You are so…"

"Resourceful?"

"Barbaric."

He shrugs. "I love it when you talk dirty to me."

I roll my eyes. "Shut up."

"No, thanks. I much prefer getting under your skin."

It's working, but I don't share that. Collins doesn't need any more ammo to use against me. "I'm going to go back to Ivan. He's probably wondering where I am."

"Just explain that you were getting railed against the tiled wall in the restroom by the man who owns your greedy pussy." He shrugs and has the nerve to feign innocence. "I'm sure he'll understand." He taps his jawline. "Now, that there is what I'd call barbaric."

I shake my head at him. "You really can be so smug."

"Confident," he counters.

"You need to stop."

"You know what, Princess?"

I look at him expectantly. I really wish he'd stop using my nickname, the one I once loved but no longer can stand hearing. "What?" I snap.

"I bet you don't have to say a word to your date." He spits out the last word like it tastes like poison.

"And why not?"

"Because he'll probably be able to smell the scent of our cum mixed together that is now leaking out of your pussy from a mile away."

"Go home, Collins."

"Only with you."

"No. You took from me enough tonight. So leave me alone."

"Maybe I didn't make myself clear, so let me reexplain. There's no scenario where I walk out of here without you beside me."

"Beside you or behind you? Because let's face it, now that you suddenly want to be honest, you have never put me first." As soon as the words fly out of my mouth, I instantly realize that they aren't true. But I'm too committed in this fight to back down now.

"I'll always put you first, Princess."

Ignoring him, I walk back to my table with Ivan who is nearly done with his meal.

Was I gone that long?

"I'm sorry," I mumble.

My lemon pepper fish and tomato cucumber salad rest untouched at my place setting.

He gestures to my dish. "Please eat."

So I do, but only because I'm too nervous to hold a real conversation.

"I would love another date."

I shovel in another forkful of fish and pretend to chew it way more than it actually needs. But if I'm chewing, I'm not talking, and that's the best alternative to letting him down with a rejection.

I'm just not that into him.

Of course, I feel bad about him paying so much for this date, just for it to be super lame, thanks to my crazy stalker ex-bodyguard boyfriend staring at our table as if he's about to drag me from it by my hair and spank my ass until I see reason.

But I refuse to look at him.

He can sulk all he wants.

I'm not his.

I'm not anyone's.

My phone buzzing in my handbag pulls my attention to

it. Looking at the caller ID, I see that it's Claire. "I need to take this. I'm sorry."

"Of course," Ivan says softly. "Go ahead."

"Hey, Claire," I answer. "What's up?"

"I'm watching hospital commercials with the sick children and eating a key lime pie straight from the tin."

It sounds like she's having a better night than I am.

"Okay..."

"I need an intervention or my hormones are going to ignite, and I'm going to drive your brother to leave me for someone easier to deal with."

"He'd never leave you, Claire," I comfort.

"Angie's on her way. I need girl time. Come now, please."

I glance at the phone. It's after seven in the evening. "Where is my brother?"

"He's with Graham handling some business thing they refuse to give me details about."

"Ha, sounds like my brothers."

"Exactly. And I'm stuck here without a car. I mean, it's not like I can fit between the steering wheel and the seat anymore anyway, even with it pushed entirely back. This baby has doubled in size, I think, in just the last week."

"Okay, I'll be there in probably twenty minutes. I'm going to schedule a ride now."

I disconnect the call and am confronted with Ivan's sad expression.

"You don't have to explain," he says gently. "I'm glad I found closure on forever wondering if we could be a thing."

"I'm sorry..."

He offers a sympathetic smile. "I'll settle for just being friends."

"Of course. I can refund you the money you spent."

Ivan holds his hands up. "It was for a good cause. I appreciate your dad taking me under his wing and teaching me the business before he steps away entirely."

Sliding my chair back, I grab my handbag and rush out of the restaurant, not even bothering to acknowledge Collins.

Claire needs me.

And it feels damn good to have this friendship network in my life.

50

PENNY

I pay my taxi driver money for the ride, and then hop out of the back seat at Claire's new home. It's such a new address that I had to rely on memory when the GPS failed to deliver us here.

Glancing around at the wooded area, it's easy for me to see that Claire has peace and privacy here on their multi-acre lot. The landscaping alone must have cost a small fortune. It's crazy how such a new home looks so good already.

Claire really has an eye for beauty like my momma does. She deserves happiness and will surely make this house a home. It's just a shame that her family in Virginia is missing out on seeing her shine like this.

Their loss is our gain.

Breathing in the fresh smells of the vegetation around me, I glance up at Claire and Nic's coveted forever home. While I'm not jealous of them, I definitely am sad that my opportunity for this level of companionship has been given and taken from me in the matter of one hundred days.

Collins may think he wants me back, but I'm not reentering a relationship just for the shoe to drop back onto me when times get tough. My heart has been broken enough in this lifetime.

And right now, it needs a chance to heal.

I make my way up to the front door, admiring the classy decorations Claire has out for fall. The entire aura around this house is that of a positive energy, and being here is exactly what I need in order to push Collins out of my mind —if just for a few hours. Then I can go back to Claire and Nic's old apartment and cry myself to sleep at night like I have since I fell at his feet, begging him not to leave me.

Claire opens the door before I have a chance to knock and envelops me into a huge hug. It's the kind of hug where the person doesn't let go.

Wrapping my own arms around her, I relax into her hold.

And just breathe.

Inhale through my nose.

Exhale through my mouth.

And I do it deeply again, melting into Claire.

It feels good to be wanted, to be loved.

Claire Nettles lives and breathes acceptance and warmth. It's no wonder my brother is so smitten with her. She brings excitement and vibrance into his life.

And I am so delusional to think that I did that for Collins.

If anything, I brought to him anxiety and clutter.

What started out as a spark soon fizzled from the weight

of the outside world. If only I was strong enough to move past what that man did to me. Sadly, I fear I'll forever be living in the past and comparing every new relationship to the man who was the epitome of a gentleman on the streets and dominant master in the sheets.

And on the countertop…

And in the front seat of the car…

And against the wall…

And on top of the bathroom vanity at my parents' house…

And inside the suspended cage at Limit-X…

Collins Stone officially ruined me for every other man I may encounter after him. They will never measure up. And I doubt my body will ever respond to anyone who isn't him. He owns me, and the only way to detox my body from him is to avoid being in his presence.

I need to quit Collins cold turkey. He's a bad habit that I no longer need right now.

My mind flutters to the restaurant and the moment he followed me into the restroom. Clearly, I can't trust myself around him when his presence alone dissolves my willpower to resist him. That man had to have left that place rather smug.

He knew he won.

Claire finally releases me from her hold. Her eyes scan over me. "Hi."

I snap out of my daydream, looking into the eyes of my soon-to-be sister-in-law. "Hi."

"I can't even put into words how terrified I was when you went missing from the charity event. It took everything in me not to follow you up to Seattle and find you myself."

"Punk would have lost his mind," I say with certainty.

"That he would have, but I didn't want to sit back and wait for those I love to not return back to me. I'm," she says with a pause, "just glad you came back to us."

Tears start to pool in my eyes, but I keep them at bay.

"Thanks for the hug," I say, trying to get the topic back to less emotional territory. "I needed that more than you know."

Claire's eyes turn serious. "Are you okay?"

I stand like a statue for what feels like a long time, then I give a shrug. "I honestly don't know."

Claire nods in understanding, and then she steps back to grant me entrance into her home. "Angie's in the kitchen making us some snacks. After I consumed three-fourths of a key lime pie, she got nervous."

I let out a laugh. "I'm just glad there's some left. You have the best cravings while pregnant, which we all benefit from when we hang out."

Tilting her head back, she giggles, then quickly straightens her spine. Her hands move to the side of her rib cage. "Ouch," she whimpers.

"Claire, what's wrong?" I ask in an octave higher than my normal tone. My gaze follows her hand movements, as she rubs circles against the side of her round belly.

I try to guide her to the couch, but she stops me before we get there.

"I'm fine." She shoos away my overprotective gestures. "Let's just go and find Angie. I'll grab some water."

My eyes narrow. "Are you sure?"

"Positive. This baby is an attention seeker like its momma."

I allow Claire to lead the way into her kitchen. When we arrive, we find Angie pulling out a tray of bacon-wrapped jalapeno poppers from the oven.

"Oh, Penny, I'm so glad you are here." She tosses her oven mitts onto the counter and races over to me. "Thank heavens you are okay. Graham made me promise to give you space and not overwhelm you with my"—she makes a face—"aggressive affection."

I roll my eyes. "Please tell me my brother didn't state it that way. Surely, he values his life more than to do that."

She laughs. "He didn't use those exact words per se. But that's how I took it. Anyway, I'm so sorry you were terrorized by…"

She doesn't want to say his name, and I'll be perfectly fine if I never hear it spoken again for the rest of my life.

"He was going to live inside my mind forever unless I did something to evict him. I'm just glad that Col—" I cut off the second syllable of his name.

And just like that, my tears start to flow.

"Oh, Penny," Claire says, giving me a warm squeeze.

Angie sniffles and wipes at her eyes. "And I only cry when someone else cries."

I take a deep breath but it's shaky. "I'm sorry."

"No need to apologize," Angie says softly.

"Seriously, though, you both don't need to coddle me. I'm fine." I think about my last statement. "Well, I'm not really fine, but I'm also not fragile either."

"I'm just glad you came over," Claire says quietly. "I need both of you in my life."

"I feel the same way."

I pour her a glass of water. She's not usually this muted.

Trepidation seeps into the otherwise comfortable state I usually have around these women. Something's off...

"So, you weren't going to have a sugar binge fest?"

"Oh, I basically already did when I called you. I just said all of that for dramatic effect to ensure that you would take me seriously and come right over."

I shake my head at her. Yup. Punk surely does have his hands full with her. I almost feel bad for him.

Almost.

My stomach growls which is plain weird because I did eat something at the restaurant. I guess getting out of the angsty scene between Ivan and Collins has relaxed me enough to realize I could consume more, now that I'm not so tense that I could throw up.

And the sight and smell of the poppers isn't helping my self-control.

"Let's eat," Angie says, getting down some plates from the cabinet. She uses a spatula to serve up some of the crispy appetizers onto each plate, along with marinara and ranch dipping sauces.

Claire rubs her hands together. "I sure have been loving the spicy things in life lately." When she leans over the island to grab the plate from Angie, I hear her groan.

"Umm, what's wrong?" Angie asks, stealing the words that I was about to say.

"Nothing," Claire promises, but when we both make a face that we aren't buying what she's trying to sell us, she holds her hands up in defense. "Listen... I've already talked to the doctor."

"And...?" Angie pries.

"It's just Braxton-Hicks contractions."

"You're sure?" I follow up.

She waves us both off, sinking her teeth into a popper. "Yesh," she says, her mouth full. "It's all normal and apparently just something pregnant people have to endure." Her words come out muffled, and her relaxed response helps me to calm down as well. "It's really nothing to worry about."

"And you would tell us if you weren't okay?" Angie asks.

Claire sighs. "Yes. My goodness, you both need to chill. You both are morphing into Nic and it's starting to stress me out." She moves over to the fridge. "You overreactors should be glad I saved some key lime pie during my binge fest." She pulls it from the shelf and holds it up like it's Simba from *The Lion King*. "Sharing my beloved pie is love. Do either of you want some?"

I nod eagerly. "That sounds wonderful."

"Be warned. It looks like a child cut it."

I glance at the butchered pie through the clear plastic wrap and can't stop laughing. It still has a knife sticking out of the pile of slop that is now smeared all over the covering. Well, she wasn't lying. "I'm sure it still tastes great."

"Dish me up some too," Angie says finally, after probably accepting that Claire is just experiencing some practice contractions.

The last thing she needs is to be stressed out by one of us.

"I am just glad you both are here," Claire says casually while she spoons out the sloppy key lime pie from the tin. "I'm pretty sure I was on the path to needing an intervention, and it all started with this pie."

I take my first bite. "I believe it."

"I almost ordered a fake boob feeding system from some shady website all because I'm predicting how tired this baby is going to make me when he or she is out of the womb. Nic can grow a pair and feed it then."

"I'm pretty sure it's his *other* pair that got you in this situation in the first place," Angie says with a laugh, nearly choking on a mouthful of pie.

"This is really good," I admit. "Thanks for sharing it."

Out of the corner of my eye, I see Claire grimace. "What's wrong?"

She lets out a whimper and rubs a hand along the side of her rib cage.

Angie looks at her with concern evident in her eyes. "Are you okay?"

"Yeah, I think the baby just kicked or something."

Angie and I help her walk to the living room.

"You need to rest," I insist.

"What I need is for you to see the love that is right in front of your face, Penny," Claire says in a rush. It takes her several breaths to complete the sentence.

"I know you both love me," I say softly, helping her sit down without just flopping down into the cushions. "And I love you both too."

For someone so petite, she is doing a great job growing this baby. Her stomach is so round, and the pregnancy glow has kissed her skin.

"Not us," Claire exclaims. "Well, of course, us. But I was thinking of someone else." Her breaths come out as pants. "Ever since our bathroom couch session at the charity event, I've been thinking about how the two of you can get back together."

I shake my head. "It's complicated, and I'm done being an option."

"I think you should keep the door open and not closed."

"Umm, I'm not an expert, Claire," Angie chimes in, "but you are struggling to breathe."

"How about you lie down more?" I suggest.

"Just on the couch," she says breathlessly, kicking up her feet and reclining her back on a pillow. "I do want to spend time with both of you."

Angie and I help her get settled.

"Are you thirsty?" I ask, trying to do something to ease her discomfort.

"I hate complaining," she says, turning to Angie, "when I know you would do anything to be in my position."

Angie gives her a hug and helps her elevate her feet up on a stack of pillows. "There's not a single second in my life when I'm not happy for you, Claire. I love you and love this baby more than my own words can explain. I never want my struggle to conceive to impact your reason for having joy."

The doorbell rings, causing us all to stop our conversation.

"Can you go get that, Penny?" Claire asks, melting into the cushions of the couch. At least she looks comfortable.

"Yeah, sure." But why would my brother ring the door-bell to his own house?

Walking to the door, I look out the side window and see Collins standing on the welcome mat and a car driving away.

I flick the lock and allow him access. "What are you

doing here? And why did you not drive yourself?" Actually, Angie didn't come with a vehicle either.

"So you could hear me out and see reason," he explains, causing me to growl. "And there's no cars for you to steal and run away from the words I want to say."

He helps himself inside and locks the door back into place.

"I love you, Penny. And I'm done giving you space."

"You can't keep doing this."

"Yes, I can. And I will."

I feel sabotaged. "Was this whole operation planned?"

He doesn't answer, which confirms my prediction.

"Just keep in mind, I one hundred percent will take you away from all of this noise until you accept that I'm not going anywhere. I know you think I rejected you before, but it was what I thought you needed until I figured out things with your brothers."

"You should have stayed, but instead you made the easy choice to desert me and make me beg for you not to break my heart. But you did it anyway."

"I know, Princess, and I'm really sorry. I was wrong."

"You should have fought for us."

"I'm fighting now."

I rock on my feet, thinking over his words in my head. And then, Claire's echoing scream causes us both to run toward the sound.

51

PENNY

My heart races as I rush to Claire, who is standing near her coffee table, doubled over.

"Claire, what's wrong? You're supposed to be resting."

"I had to use the bathroom for the one hundredth time today."

"Are you sick? Hurt? Is the baby okay?" I ask at a frantic pace.

"I think it's just my body's way of preparing for the baby to come in six weeks."

Another wave moves through her, and she calls out until it passes.

"Are these contractions the practice ones?" Collins asks.

Standing up taller, she shrugs. "I'm not sure. I thought they were."

Angie looks at her watch. "I'm going to time them."

"Why?" I ask, quickly forgetting everything I've ever learned about pregnancy and childbirth from the high school classes I took years ago.

"Because if the contractions start coming in a rhythm and closer together, then that means Claire is going into active labor and the baby is coming soon."

"The baby can't come," Claire says boldly. "It'll be too early. It needs more time to bake."

My eyes move to Collins's as he stares at Claire and her belly. Then I tug his arm to step away from the scene and out of earshot of her. "What?" I ask him. "Tell me what you're thinking."

Pausing for a few seconds, he finally responds. "I'm going to get Nic and Graham here."

"Why?" I snap, my nerves getting the best of me.

"Just as a precaution."

I shake my head at him. "I'm scared. Is Claire going to be alright?"

"This is not happening," Claire calls over to me, just as another one hits. "This is about you and Collins." She gulps in air between each spoken word, twisting her face as she endures what her body is forcing on her. Then when she's able to focus, her eyes connect with mine. "I had the perfect plan to hold you hostage until you listened to him."

I should have known that Collins would do a stunt like this one, involving the two people I can't say no to...

"You can play matchmaker another time," Angie tells her. "Are you feeling any pain?"

"Hell yeah, I'm in agony but not all the time. Like, right now? I'm fine."

My eyes move to her pristine white area rug to see the pinkish stain forming as she holds her stomach.

"Oh, my goodness, Claire," I squeal. "You're bleeding."

"Her water must have broken," Angie explains. "Oh, my…"

"This happened suddenly," I comment, trying to figure out what to do next.

"Well, I think I was in denial about how hard it was to talk and breathe earlier," Claire clarifies. "I was just so determined to get you here and get Collins here to fix this giant mess you both created."

Collins grabs his phone and taps his fingers on the screen. "Claire's water just broke. She's at home. We have no way to get to the hospital without calling for a ride. Call 9-1-1 and get here fast." He pauses for a second. "I'm not sure." He looks at Claire, who has her hair lying limp around her face and sweat beading on her forehead. "She says she's contracting. Get here now."

"Noooo!" she screams out as another contraction ripples through her. "It feels like a tidal wave."

"Here, lean on me," Angie says, trying to offer support.

Amniotic fluid pours down Claire's legs like a river. "The baby is coming."

I stand in shock—basically as useless as a decorative statue—while Collins jumps into action.

"And Nic isn't here!"

Collins curses under his breath and then wraps an arm around Claire to keep her from falling or passing out—I don't know which. "Angie, run and get some clean bedsheets and blankets. There's probably some in a linen closet upstairs. Maybe get a couple of pillows if you can find any. Just make sure they are clean."

"Okay," she says frantically, rushing upstairs to go search.

"Penny, go get a clean bowl and fill it with warm water. Then find me some fresh dish towels or ones for the bath. And clean your hands. We're about to deliver this baby if the ambulance doesn't get out here in time."

"What? We can't deliver this baby," I snap.

"We don't have a choice. Now go," he demands. "Claire needs us."

I run off to the kitchen to get the supplies, thankful to have something to focus on.

When Angie comes back to the living room, she prepares a makeshift bed on the floor and Collins helps lay Claire gently onto it.

"I need Nic here," she cries out, her face twisting in pain. "He can't miss the birth of our first child. This isn't how the plan was supposed to go." Her words break apart midsyllable as she struggles to get them out.

I dampen a cloth and wipe her forehead. "Just breathe," I try to soothe. "Sometimes the most unexpected things are the best things."

As she bends her legs, Claire's maternity dress shifts to a more natural position. Angie runs to get her some ice chips from the freezer to suck on. And we all just wait to see if help will arrive in time.

"The ambulance is ten to fifteen minutes away," Collins informs, placing his phone back into his pocket.

I'm not surprised by this, as the house's location is so far out from the main part of the city.

Collins leaves the room and comes back, drying his hands on a paper towel.

"Ahhh," Claire bellows, arching her back and squeezing

her fingers into tight fists of bedsheets that have pooled around her. "There's so much pressure."

"What does that mean? Are you cramping? Do you need to change positions?" Angie asks, looking at both Collins and me for support.

We are all terrified—and in shock.

"I think I need to push."

Another contraction hits and Claire screams out, just as Graham and Nic make it to the scene.

"Fuck," Graham growls under his breath, but then snaps into action.

"I'm here, Baby Girl," Nic calls out, rushing to her side. "I'm going to carry you to the back seat of the SUV and get you to the hospital."

"No," she says. "The baby is coming *now*."

"You're sure?"

"Yes. *Now*," she clarifies.

Nic looks at Graham, then at Collins.

"It's probably safer to do this here and wait for help to arrive," Collins suggests, "than to be stranded on the side of the road on the way there."

His focused but calm demeanor helps me not to completely freak out, which would normally be my default reaction.

Nic runs into the bathroom to wash his hands and returns with a look of apprehension. I know he's scared that the baby is too small and will possibly need more medical intervention than we are equipped to handle, but he doesn't express his fears verbally in front of Claire.

"You guys got here fast," I comment. I'm relieved they

are here, and that Nic won't miss out on the birth that very well could go down in his living room.

"We were already en route to my place," Graham explains. "So, we just made a detour here."

Claire does a series of exaggerated breaths. "I was trying to help Collins kidnap Penny and make you men see that they belong together and to get your heads out of your asses."

"Is that so?" Nic growls.

"Yes," she cries out. "I am done with this tension and feud. It ends right now."

"Let's discuss this later."

Claire looks at each of us one by one. "You all are the family I never had. I'm not allowing anyone to leave me."

Nic helps put a few pillows under her hips. Then he leans over to kiss her on her lips. "No one is going to leave you, Baby Girl."

"It's always an adventure with you, isn't it?" Claire chokes out.

Nic lets out a nervous laugh. "I'm up for the challenge."

Graham helps prop Claire's body up to give her more back support.

"Angie and Penny, grab a knee," Collins instructs. "Nic, remove anything Claire has on from the waist down."

"How do you know so much?" I ask him. He's basically a pro.

"I watched a lot of medical dramas."

We all laugh, while Claire screams about how badly she wants this baby out and that it's all Nic's fault for putting one inside her in the first place.

"I'm going to put another one inside you as soon as it's

safe to do it again. I have never seen you more beautiful than when you've been carrying our child."

"You are such a caveman!"

"You're doing great, Claire," Nic soothes, ignoring her anxiety-induced rage.

"This baby is coming too early. I can't lose it."

"You won't," I promise blindly, helping to hold her knee back and give her the angle needed to push this baby out.

Another contraction hits, and Nic moves between her legs, holding a towel.

"Push now," he demands. "Push, Claire—like you mean it."

"You're doing great," Collins says with confidence, not seeming the least bit scared over all the blood and fluids surrounding us.

And with a bellowing wail from Claire, the baby comes out.

"It's a girl!" Nic announces, full of pride and love.

"It's a girl," Claire whispers, as tears flood her eyes.

I am overcome with every emotion as I stand back and look at the scene before me.

This room encompasses my entire heart, with each person holding a special place inside.

Claire is propped up against pillows, holding her precious baby girl—Scarlett Ann—while Nic and the medical staff tend to both of their immediate needs. I couldn't be more proud of my brother and the love of his life for bringing this child into this world safely, despite being early. And the little miss is such a little squish, looking healthy and content being close to her momma.

Graham and Angie embrace in a hug, and the worry wrinkles that once lined their foreheads have since vanished. I know witnessing her best friend deliver her baby on the rug in her dream home, while she is unsure if she can conceive one of her own, has to feel bittersweet. But I wouldn't know it by the beaming smiles on everyone's faces.

Momma and Dad are fluttering about, making sure everyone is comfortable, and a gazillion pictures are taken to capture this moment. They were destined to be the best grandparents ever, and I can already tell they would gladly welcome more children into their hearts if the circumstances allowed for it.

Then there is Collins standing on the sidelines, like he has for the last year and a half of my life, like an invisible but constant thread, woven into my support system. I feel him looking at me, while I look at all of them. And it's in his quiet, calm nature that I see his true heart.

I am his, as he is mine.

He accepts me at my best. But embraces me at my worst.

Looking up at him, I see the worry broadcasted back at me, probably wondering what I'm thinking and what my next move will be.

But I'm tired of pretending...

I'm tired of acting like I'd be better off without him, when he's never really left me.

He's been with me the whole time.

Collins shows up in my life when it matters most, and he'll keep showing up.

Then without thinking, I slide my arm around the back of him and settle my head on his heart. He tucks me into his side and gives me the gentlest squeeze. His lips press against my hairline and it's the sweetest thing.

This is love.

And we do it through the good times and the bad times, through the hard times and the easy times, and in sickness and in health.

It's about showing up and fighting for who we want to spend our short time on this earth with...

And I choose him.

"Collins?"

He pulls back a tad, just so he can see my eyes. "Yeah?"

"I'm willing to try."

He smiles down at me and then presses a gentle kiss on my lips. "All I need is a chance."

52

COLLINS

I escort Penny inside the corner coffee shop where just months ago I almost committed murder on the streets in her name and where I came face-to-face with my true feelings for her.

So much has happened since then. While I wish some things didn't have to occur, I have to find gratitude that every moment since then has led to us being able to be together—out in public and as a couple.

Linking fingers with mine, Penny snuggles in closer to me. She has snuck her way into all aspects of my life, and I'm forever thankful she pursued me when I was so scared to reciprocate.

She is the sunshine my dark life needed.

And I'll forever be trying to be the man I know she deserves.

I may say I own this girl in the bedroom, but in reality, I've been hers way longer than I care to admit.

I'd do anything for her.

I want to take care of her financially, make sure she is fed properly, and assure she attends her therapy sessions regularly.

Penny Hoffman has softened my hard, protective shell and has helped me to see my full potential.

Moving our linked fingers up to my mouth, I kiss each one of hers.

Her skin smells of strawberries. And I'm obsessed.

"Who would have thought Collins Stone could be so romantic?"

I smile down at her. "Shhh...don't share our secret."

Penny huffs out a laugh. "I'm pretty sure the entire world knows by now. You are pretty famous."

She is referring to the World News reporting on the Soulful Mind takedown. Apparently Tanner's twin brothers have been wanted for years and by many countries for their terrorist behaviors.

Clearly, Graham, Nic, and I did the world a big favor to rid the planet of their lives.

Walking hand in hand toward the back of the shop, I take note of all of our surroundings and the people present, just like I'll always be conditioned to do.

Penny's eyes scan the area. Her bottom lip pouts out in the most adorable way. "I don't see him."

"He's over there." I point with my free hand.

Realization hits her face and then she detaches from me and breaks off into a semi-run. Within seconds, she finds herself scooped up into an embrace by her former roommate, Luke.

Chuckling at their over-the-top reaction, I stalk toward the duo.

"I am so sorry, Luke," Penny says, her voice muffled as she cries into his shoulder.

I pay close attention to the roommate's hand placement on my princess's back and allow for them to enjoy this reunion without me ripping her from his clutches like my initial instinct suggests.

It's hard to relax in a setting where my girl is in someone else's arms. But I try.

And not beating the shit out of him is progress toward being "less of a caveman"—which are Penny's exact words from the pep talk she gave me prior to arriving.

Even an old dog can learn new tricks. Again...her words.

"I was set up by that fucker who used me to get closer to you. I don't blame you for distrusting me," Luke says calmly.

Oddly enough, his personality has grown on me. But not enough for me to allow Penny to watch him shake his junk for cash. Nope. That will never happen again. She had her one and done fun.

"I'm still sorry. I was so mad at life and used you as a scapegoat without even trying to hear you out."

"I'm not upset," he promises.

Penny sniffles, and I pass her a tissue from a box at a little book table in the corner. "I'm just glad we all lived to tell about it."

Luke's eyes catch mine, and then they move back to Penny's. "Does this mean you are moving back in?"

I let out a half laugh, not because his statement is funny, but because hell will have to freeze over first before I let this girl out of my sight.

Luke then looks pointedly at me. "I'm being serious."

"No."

"Give it some thought," he says, appearing to fight back a smile.

"No."

Penny looks at me with puppy dog eyes. "But…"

"No, Princess."

"He does have a queen…"

Leaning down, I kiss her ear. "But this princess is owned by a king."

"This isn't taking it slow," Penny says, with a teasing smirk playing on her lips.

"I actually am taking it slow." I click my tongue. "You should have seen my alternative plan if you decided to continue to be unreasonable."

"Now that may have been fun."

It's been a week since Claire and Nic welcomed sweet Scarlett into the world, and I finally got Penny to move back into my place with me. It's where she belongs. I'm just glad she came to her senses and decided to submit to my wishes.

Luckily, with my quick thinking skills, I was able to prove just how serious I was about the whole thing by sending over a moving truck to Nic's old place to make sure she followed through on her verbal agreement.

There's no way I would take a chance she would change her mind.

"You are a naughty girl."

"You bring that side out of me."

"It's like you wanted me to kidnap you…"

She shrugs. "Maybe I still do."

I carry Penny into the bedroom with my hard-on pressing against her backside and toss her onto the center of the bed. I flip her around so she's on her belly. Despite her struggling, I get her wrists secured into the leather straps.

"Clearly you have more sass to work out of your system."

She kicks her foot out backward, and I catch it.

Massaging her ankle, I secure the cuff around it and then repeat the process with her other one, rendering her motionless.

"There. Now you can relax and be a good girl without having to think too much about defying me." It really is her default to be difficult.

Penny struggles against her bindings. "Quit looking so smug."

"Oops, I almost forgot one thing. Thank you for reminding me."

I bend down and kiss her along her spine, working my way up to the side of her face and then her nose, which only pisses her off more.

Penny can be so adorable when she is trying to be angry.

Leaning over, I reach into the drawer in my nightstand and grab a few fun items from my freshly stocked supply. I've upgraded since our breakup, utilizing what Angie and

Claire often refer to as "retail therapy" to cope with life's troubles.

It worked.

I had way too much fun finding "torture" devices to use on Penny the first chance she was back in my possession.

Resting my hand on her ass cheek, I massage it in circles. "I feel like this was a long time coming and well overdue."

Then wielding it in the air, I allow my palm to connect with her fleshy globe. I savor the sting, as well as Penny's high-pitched squeal.

She's delightful when she's at my mercy.

I repeat the process with her other cheek.

Penny bucks off the bed, with whatever slack I allow in her chains.

"That's payback."

I spank her a few more times, evening out the redness all over her sensitive skin.

"Your turn," she says jokingly.

I smile down at her. "You look so sexy wearing my mark. You'll look even sexier with some more jewelry."

Kneeling beside her, I place the red ball gag at her lips, reveling in the euphoric feeling of Penny's shock.

"No," she says, shaking her head.

"It's your mouth that always gets you into trouble first," I say, tracing her lips with my thumb. "And it's your"—I jerk my finger away—"ouch."

She fucking bit me.

Straddling Penny, I suck my thumb between my lips, making a point of licking the blood from where she extracted. "Little vampire."

I secure the ball gag into her mouth, tightening the straps around the back of her head.

"Hmph…"

"Perfect."

Then I detach Penny from her chains, just long enough to put her on her back and reattach them with a simple click to the corresponding posts.

I want to see her eyes better. I want her to know just who is going to be claiming her—for keeps.

Bending over her, I kiss around her lips with controlled gentleness and then move down to her perfect nipples to reciprocate the treatment she did to my finger.

What's fair is fair.

Reveling at how the restraints allow for Penny to thrash around but just with a few inches, I sit back on my heels and admire my view.

But she is missing something.

Leaning back over the bed, I reach into the drawer and then dangle the collar on my finger.

Penny's eyes watch my every move while I latch it around her neck.

"I hope you know just how exquisite you look right now wearing my collar."

Her eyes soften their once hard stare at me. I think she's a bit salty her attitude got exactly what it deserved. She should know what I'm capable of and what I'm not willing to put up with in regard to her sass.

"If this becomes too much for you or you want me to stop, all you need to do is close your eyes. Nod if you can understand me."

And she does.

"I want you to free your brain of any thought other than the one where I own your entire body. You have one purpose right now and that's to be my little fuck doll. Don't think about talking. Don't think about moving. Just relax and enjoy the ride. I am making up for lost time."

Spreading her pussy lips, I examine Penny up close, making her squirm under my scrutiny. I love when she's vulnerable to my wishes. It's in these moments where she submits to me just a little bit more that I feel the closest to her.

We are peeling back each other's layers, baring our hearts, and attaching strings that will be impossible to break ever again.

Settling my face between her legs, I flatten my tongue and go to work at tasting every inch of her pussy and enjoying the guttural moans breaking through the ball gag pressed into her defiant mouth.

I keep my movements lazy, like I have all the time in the world to please her.

And I do.

Because I no longer want a one-hundred-day commitment. I want forever with this girl. And even then, it won't be long enough.

"Mmmph…"

When I think she's going to explode over my tongue, I pull away and crawl up her body, chuckling at her growl of disapproval.

Staring into her eyes, I push just the tip of my cock into her, and hover there at the end of my insanity. I want her. But I want to send a message to her loud and clear that there will never be anyone else for me but her.

Bending forward, I kiss around her ball gag, feeling the softness of her lips.

Then I slide my cock all the way in without much preparation. She is that slick.

Using just one hand, I remove her gag and savor her sweet sounds of surrender as I fuck her into ecstasy.

53

COLLINS

"You made us late."

"It's not my fault you were all tied up with things to do." I resist laughing.

Penny sighs. "It was most definitely your fault, Collins."

"Next time, come a little faster."

"We aren't going to find a parking spot. And the popcorn concessions will probably have run out by now, at least of the good flavors. I'll probably have to run to make up for lost time and then get blisters again that will fill up with pus by the time the night is over and be squirting out all over the sidewalk for everyone to step in. Someone will slip and fall, sue me for all I'm worth, and then I'll forever feel guilty for them spending the rest of their life in a wheelchair."

I look over at Penny who can't stop fidgeting in the passenger seat. "That is quite the visual. Anything else to add?" I laugh. "I feel like you're on a roll now."

She turns in her seat glaring. "And I'm sure we missed the opening act."

"Why must you have so little faith in me?"

"Because you chose giving me orgasms over prioritizing this epic concert I waited like half a year for."

"Why limit yourself when you can enjoy orgasms and the concert?" I challenge, feeling extra logical.

"It would have been best just to give me those orgasms at the concert and save a whole hell of a lot of time."

"You do like public intimacy," I point out. My sweet princess has a dirty side for sure.

"Don't sweeten what I want with flowery words. I want to be railed and taken advantage of by you in *any* setting— public or private. I'm not picky."

I smile brightly as I turn on the road for the Japanese Garden. It feels like we are coming full circle, and maybe in a way we are. Penny has that effect on me of making me see the sentiment behind normal everyday things. She's turned me into a sap who now might consider himself partially romantic.

Maybe.

"I can do that too."

"Only if my hands aren't tied, and I can eat popcorn while you do your *thang*."

I shrug. "The options really are endless when you are content picking kernels out of your teeth."

"Okay, now you're killing the romance... Like stabbing it to death."

Well, that didn't last long.

This evening's concert performance is being given to

just five hundred people, so I find a parking spot easily, despite Penny's initial trepidation.

The weather is comfortable for late fall, with low humidity and clear skies. Penny has on a pair of perfect-fitting jeans that have subtle sparkles all over them and an eyelet pink blouse. She looks amazing and definitely outshines me, in a pair of jeans and white button-down with the sleeves rolled up.

"Wait here," I say, a warning tone to my voice, as I exit the vehicle and make my way to her side.

"Ready to *Fall in Love*?" I ask, utilizing the name of Grace and Jace's tour title as a play on words.

Taking my offered hand, she allows me to assist her. "I already have."

I bend down to capture her lips with mine. "Maybe we should skip the concert and have car sex."

"No," she snaps. "Grace and Jace..."

Now she changes her tune?

I close the door and lace the fingers of my hand with hers. "Oh, the irony. I do recall many times of you propositioning me for car sex."

"Wowza, you're dating a slut."

I pull her closer, tickling her sides. "And I love every second of it."

Escorting Penny to the check-in area, I provide the worker with the tickets that I got for Penny for her birthday. It feels so good that we can do this together. So much has happened in the last few months that it almost seems like we are living in a dream.

Once we get through the gates, I turn to the girl who has captured my entire heart. "I love you, Penny."

She stands on her tiptoes and places a kiss on my lips. "A lot?"

"More than a lot."

"Me too, Collins. I love you more than a lot. Somewhere between your brooding silence and your chivalrous nature, I fell for you. And I fell fucking hard. I never want to let you go."

"Penny, I fell in love with you long before I even realized it was happening. You make me want for things I thought I couldn't have. You are imprinted on my heart, ruining me for anyone else. It's been you, Princess. It's *always* been you. Even when having a romantic relationship was far from my mind, you consumed my life. You beguile me."

Tears fill her eyes, and I use my thumbs to hijack any that escape to make their journey south.

We keep walking along the paved and lit path, until we reach the beautifully decorated concert space. It's enchanting with white and pink roses adorning the stage and elegant seats for all the guests in attendance. Little tables are speckled about for resting any food and drinks.

The crowd buzzes about while drinking specialty cocktails and snacking on appetizers.

"I don't see popcorn," Penny says, scanning the options.

"There," I say, pointing to the little cart set up with a worker dishing out cotton candy-flavored popcorn into little pink snack boats.

"Oh, my goodness, my two favorite things as a single treat."

We walk over to the cart and I order her popcorn and a

strawberry daiquiri that is served in a heart-shaped flute. I settle for some cider.

If I'm going to deal with Penny's impending crash in roughly thirty-four minutes, I shouldn't also be dealing with one of my own.

Placing a hand on the small of her back, I trail my fingers along her spine. "Ready to go to our seats?"

She nods, as her mouth is entirely full of pink popcorn. I'm pretty sure that's the only thing I'm in competition with for her heart. Me versus popcorn…

Her mouth gapes. "We are in the front row?"

I shrug. "I thought you would like to see better."

Penny practically squeals. "Umm, yeah!"

Getting settled at the table, she places down her snacks and then leans over to give me a hug. She didn't realize that I'd upgraded the tickets from the original pair that I got her for her birthday. Seeing her this happy makes any extra cost worth it.

Penny is worth it.

The opening act is a solo artist who just needs a piano and a microphone. The music spreads throughout the garden, making the entire space feel alive.

Penny offers me a sip of her drink and laughs at me when I make a face over the sweetness. Yup, she is most definitely going to have a sugar crash.

"Good, yeah?"

I kiss her. "Hmm, I think it tastes better off your lips."

She playfully smacks my arm. I fake wince, pretending to look offended.

Penny makes it easy to get lost in the moment.

Once the opening act finishes up, Grace and Jace make it to the stage and the crowd goes wild, standing and chanting for them.

"Wow, I can already tell that this," Grace says, looking out into the crowd, "is going to be an amazing night."

"It's a true blessing to be here tonight," Jace continues, "and I hope that you take those pictures, sing those songs, and make those memories."

"And fall in love," Grace says, looking up at Jace, "all over again."

He wraps her in his arms and kisses her, while we all cheer.

"Because tonight is going to be unforgettable!" Jace yells into his microphone.

Grace smiles at the audience, blowing kisses to a few members and waving. "How about we kick off the show with our first single from our new album titled, 'Forever With You.'"

Sitting back in my chair, I listen to the two of them sing, enjoying the slow rhythm and the delivery of the message.

Once I realized you exist,
I had no willpower to resist,
And am thankful beyond measure,
Forever mine to treasure

Lacing my fingers in Penny's, I kiss each of her bent knuckles.

Even from a long distance I see
It's so logical to me
It has always been true
I want to spend forever with you

The concert extends beyond the normal set, taking in requests and doing some covers of other popular songs that allow for duets.

Hours pass, and by the third boat of popcorn, I think Penny is on an all-time high.

Luckily, she switched over to sparkling water after the first daiquiri to stay sober.

I most definitely need her to be coherent tonight.

"I'll be right back," I say, getting up from my seat. "I need to use the restroom."

Penny looks over at me. "Okay." She tosses some popcorn up into the air and catches it on her tongue like a pro. "I'll be here."

I nod and exit to the side where the restrooms are located.

Sneaking behind them, I move my way over to the side of the stage and wait for the worker to give me the signal to approach.

Taking two steps at a time, I walk across to where Jace is standing. He pats me on the back, while Grace gives me a half hug.

Passing off the microphone to me, Grace and Jace move to the side, allowing me to be front and center.

Looking out into the crowd, I find Penny who is wide-eyed and scooted all the way to the edge of her seat. She must have given up on her popcorn, because the boat is flipped partially over on my seat, with kernels scattered about where I once sat.

She is my beautiful, chaotic mess of a girl.

"Hi, everyone. I'm Collins."

"Hi, Collins," the crowd says back.

"I hope you all don't mind if I call the beautiful Penelope Hoffman to the stage to join me for something a little off script tonight."

Penny hesitates for a few seconds, but when several people nudge her forward, she stands up and makes her way to the side where the stairs are located. The crowd erupts in cheers as she finally joins me on stage, creating an energy circulating among us.

Rocking on her feet, she twists her fingers together in front of her.

I take one of her hands and give it a squeeze. "Don't be nervous. Everything is going to be alright."

"What are you doing?" she mouths, unable to produce sound.

Speaking into the microphone, I make my declaration to this girl who has enraptured my heart.

"Penny, I love you."

"I love you too," she says with a raspy voice.

"My whole life, I thought I wasn't good enough or easy enough to love. Then I looked into your eyes and saw the reflection of myself in them. It's you, Penny. It's always been you, and it will forever stay you. You are my endgame. You are everything that I'm willing to fight for and won't ever stop fighting for... When I look at you, I see more than just today—or even tomorrow. Princess, I see the next one hundred years of my life with you in it. And there isn't a measure of time long enough when it comes to you. But I will settle with forever."

"Oh, Collins…" she whispers. Then she grabs the microphone. Keeping her eyes on me, she smiles. "I love you, and I will keep loving you, for all the days of my life."

Bending forward, my mouth captures hers, and I quietly —and with intention—surrender my life to her.

"Penny, I lived a tortured life before you." I place my hand over where my script tattoo of the word *Litost* is located. "But it was you who helped me out of my own misery and made me believe in the possibility that someone could love a man like me."

"And I do," she chokes out, probably overcome with the implications of the next steps.

Then, reaching into the back of my jeans pocket, I pull out a little box. "Penelope Josephine Hoffman…" I get down on one knee and reveal the heart-shaped diamond to her and those now standing in the audience in anticipation. "Would you do me the great honor of becoming my forever partner, my wife?"

"Yes!" she screams, flopping down onto the stage floor to join me in a hug that knocks us both off-balance.

The crowd goes wild with excitement.

"Thank heavens," Donna says, her voice cutting through above anyone else's. She snaps a few pictures of us on stage, while she's down below.

"This is awesome," Angie calls out.

Claire echoes the sentiments. She chants and waves her

fist into the air, careful not to jostle Scarlett, who is resting against her chest sleeping.

"Congrats," Graham and Nic say in unison.

Beaming with pride, Germain speaks next. "I couldn't be happier."

"My family is here," Penny says between sniffles.

"Yes, of course."

I could never do something this profound without the people who have loved and supported Penny along the way being here. It felt right to invite them.

"So, they knew about this?"

"Yes. And everyone has accepted what I've known to be true for a while now. I want to spend forever with you, Penelope Josephine Hoffman."

"And I'd be honored to be your wife."

I stand up from the stage. Then I lean forward and scoop up an emotional Penny into my arms. I carry her down and off the platform, then set her back on her feet. Grace and Jace play one last song, while Penny's family hugs us. Champagne is served, and the love surrounding us expands to complete strangers, wishing us well on our future together.

Taking Penny into my arms, we start to slow dance to the softer ballad.

"Thank you," she says softly.

My brow furrows. "You are welcome. But for what?"

"For loving me at times when I wasn't sure I could love myself."

I kiss Penny on her forehead, feeling the most at peace I ever have in my entire life. Around us those invisible strings are tied a little tighter, binding us by the promise of forever. And the boundaries I thought my heart wouldn't be able to stretch expand enough to make room for all the future has to offer us.

But I know for certain just one thing…

Forever won't be long enough.

ACKNOWLEDGMENTS

I thank you with my whole heart for picking up one of my books and deciding to give it a chance. I can only hope that my words have made a positive impact on your life and provided an escape from the real world.

-Victoria Dawson

ABOUT THE AUTHOR

Victoria Dawson is the creator of books with fiery heroines and possessive heroes. She thrives on writing stories that transcend the minds of readers, allowing them to get lost in the journey to love—and all the drama that entails. Prior to delving heart first into the romance writing world, she taught middle and high school students mathematics for ten years.

Victoria is a unique combination of hopeful realist and hopeless romantic. She is an iced coffee connoisseur, a reality TV enthusiast, and a habitual wearer of stretchy pants. If she is not chasing after her three active children, she is often found scouring social media for her next book boyfriend.

Having grown up in an itty-bitty town in Pennsylvania, Victoria is a little bit country. She currently resides in Maryland with her family.

www.ingramcontent.com/pod-product-compliance
Lightning Source LLC
Chambersburg PA
CBHW022232020726
47496CB00004B/860